Praise for *A Sea Change*

'Brilliant use of a momentous journey to tell the story of a Jewish boy's rite of passage into adulthood. A gripping and adroit fusion of history with personal drama.'
Rose Tremain

'A moving and heartening story in which spirit triumphs over political barbarity.'
Edna O'Brien

'Michael Arditti has got into the head of a young boy who is both facing an uncertain, and possibly terrifying, future, and finding his first love. This tale of the ill-fated *St Louis* carrying a thousand German Jewish refugees to Havana, with its determined, fair-minded German captain, is moving, understated, and beautifully and sensitively described.'
Rabbi Dame Julia Neuberger

'Using fictional characters, Arditti sensitively recreates the historical incidents that took place on board ship. By grafting a coming-of-age drama on to a gripping episode in international history, Arditti succeeds in creating fiction that is morally serious, moving and intense.'
Sarah Davison, *Times Literary Supplement*

'This is a famous story, retold by Arditti with warmth, vividness and gentle wisdom.'
Kate Saunders, *The Times*

'This moving rites-of-passage tale is as readable as it is profound.'
Neil Richards, *Daily Express*

'As in his last novel, *Unity*, Arditti brings historical events and private emotions seamlessly together, his instrument here his storyteller's steady yet flexible voice. Karl is a superbly realised fifteen-year-old. Less formally experimental than Arditti's previous fiction, *A Sea Change* is an advance in sheer intellectual authority and breadth of sympathy.'
Paul Binding, *Independent on Sunday*

MICHAEL ARDITTI

A Sea Change

ALSO BY MICHAEL ARDITTI

The Celibate

Pagan and her Parents

Easter

Good Clean Fun

Unity

MICHAEL ARDITTI

A Sea Change

Published in 2006 by
The Maia Press Limited
82 Forest Road
London E8 3BH
www.maiapress.com

ISBN 10: 1 904559 21 2
ISBN 13: 978 1 904559 21 4

A CIP catalogue record for this book is available
from the British Library

Printed and bound in Great Britain by Cromwell Press
on paper from sustainable managed forests
9 8 7 6 5 4 3 2

The Maia Press is indebted to Arts Council England
for financial support

For Caroline and Samantha

This is the story of how I became a man. Millions of people died and I became a man. Which, as I would be the first to admit, is a gross imbalance. I have no ambition, however, to elegise a nation. To quote that other great twentieth-century monster, the Georgian peasant not the Austrian corporal: 'A single death is a tragedy, a million a statistic.' I know how profoundly statistics bore you, so I shall stick to the singular: my family – your family – and some of the people we encountered as we fled from Germany: our fellow exiles; our oppressors; and the girl who was torn between the two, Johanna Paulsen. Just writing her name brings back all the promise of first love, along with all the torment of its loss. But I anticipate myself. You will meet her in due course, off the coast of France. We were in the same boat: a phrase that in English has a double meaning but in German, like so much else, was extremely precise. The boat was the ill-starred *St Louis* and it was taking us from Hamburg to Havana to begin a new life.

I am writing the story for my grandchildren: for you, Marcus, and for you, Leila, and for you, my little Susan, who, unless I am to defy fate a second time, will be unable to read it until long after my death, and especially for you, Edward, who appear to have inherited a streak of your great-great grandfather's entrepreneurial spirit. I remember your parents' horror at the first hint of it – when you sold the conkers you had gathered from my garden to your friends at nursery school – and your own dejection when the expected approval was withheld. On the surface, it seemed that such mercenary schemes offended their milky socialism, but I wonder whether there were a deeper reason, one that they might not have realised and certainly could not have acknowledged: a fear that there was some truth in the old anti-Semitic slurs and that you were reverting to type.

I harbour no illusions that any of you children will rush to read this. None of you has so far shown the least curiosity about your heritage. The present is so vast and fast-moving that the past appears to be doubly obsolete. You search for stories in other galaxies rather than other ages. You create your myths in the infinite expansion of space. Nevertheless, had you studied the basic facts, Marcus, you would never have admired a rock band called Stormtroopers or failed to appreciate the distinction between shock and offence. Nor would any of you have turned *wicked* into a term of commendation. Your mother sees it as the sign of a living language; I see it as an abuse. I have witnessed how easily language can be distorted and a whole group of people objectified. I am aware that to insist on purity of any sort makes me seem like a relic. Yet, when I am dead and these notebooks have attained a sentimental value to outweigh their literary flaws, one or other of you may flick through the pages and a word or an image catch your eye. You may even look back in sympathy at your grandfather's guttural accent and his emphatic refusal to contemplate buying a German car.

This is also the story of how I became a Jew. I was born to Jewish parents in 1924, but I became a Jew nine years later when Adolf Hitler seized power. It was not the ultimate perversity, let alone a protest on the lines of the Danish king's threat to wear the Yellow Star when the Nazis occupied his country. It was rather that race became my sole definition. I collected stamps; I supported Hertha BSC; I was a champion swimmer and an avid bird-watcher, but the only thing that counted was that I was a Jew. I suspect that this will seem utterly alien to children whose mother sets school essays such as *Religion is the opium of the people: discuss,* when what she means is *Religion is the opium of the people: approve.* It made little enough sense to me, whose religion had until then been a fact rather than a factor in life. It wasn't that I had attempted to hide it. After all, I was born into one of the most distinguished Jewish families in Germany. Frankel-Hirsch is a name for you all to be proud of – or it would be if it hadn't been chopped to Frank when we settled here. It was balanced by Karl, as neutral as a name could be – and far too neutral for the Nazis, who decreed that any Jew with a first name outside a narrowly Semitic list had to take Israel for a second. In our tradition, whenever a person is in mortal danger, he is given a new name in order to deceive the Angel of Death. Which may be how I survived.

My family was not observant. My mother and grandfather were what was known somewhat derisively as 'three-day Jews', which meant that they attended synagogue on Yom Kippur and the two days of Rosh Hashanah. The rest of the year they expressed their faith by serving the community. My grandfather was on the board of numerous charities and even my mother, who baulked at assuming anything resembling a traditional female role, organised galas and concerts on behalf of those less fortunate than ourselves, which, in material terms, meant virtually the entire population of Germany. My grandfather, whose constant concern was to show himself a German first and a Jew second, was meticulously even-handed. If he gave to a Jewish organisation, he was careful to make an equal, if not larger, donation to its gentile equivalent. He adopted the same principle in politics, his belief in the middle way informing his decision to give to both Left and Right. It was rumoured that, in the early days, he had even helped to finance the Nazis. But, by the time I was old enough to put the question to him, it would have been too cruel.

I went to a regular, rather than a religious, school, which was called a gymnasium. I see your eyes light up, Edward, but that didn't mean that our lessons consisted of climbing ropes and jumping through hoops (or, if they did, the hoops were metaphorical). Gymnasium was the name for a secondary school and its emphasis lay less on athleticism than on Latin and Greek. I was one of a handful of Jewish boys in a school that, until the terms were redefined, catered to what was known as the elite. But, in spite of certain physical distinctions most apparent in the changing room (I trust I have no need to elaborate), I did not stand out.

My grandfather encouraged me to bring my friends home and, at first, they were keen to accept my invitations. I fear that you wouldn't have found it to your taste, Leila – you who dislike houses that you 'have to go around with a guidebook', but I'm sure that, had you grown up there, you would have appreciated its charms. It was one of the finest houses in Berlin and filled with furniture that required you to be on your best behaviour even when there were no grown-ups present (so no motor races across Biedermeier sofas or crayons on Persian carpets – I name no names, not even ones that begin with an E!). The walls were hung with Old Master paintings that generations of my ancestors had lovingly collected. The subjects were largely religious although, with the same even-handedness that informed my grandfather's philanthropy, there were as many Christian saints as Jewish patriarchs – a range that drew increasing scorn as the country grew more sharply divided. We even had our own synagogue, with a roof that could be winched open at Sukkot, our harvest festival, and replaced by a canopy of branches and fruit although, no matter how hard I begged, it remained closed. The room itself was only put to its designated use on the anniversaries of my grandmother's and uncle's deaths. At other times it hosted chamber concerts and recitals. And before any of you asks – yes, even you Leila – whether you can go to see it, I should point out that it was destroyed in an Allied air-raid during the War. In the 1950s, they built high-rise flats on the site. You may as well visit a tower block in Bethnal Green.

I presume that I have now caught your attention since no child can resist a peep into Aladdin's cave, but it is not my intention to seduce you with a story of lost wealth. Besides, our treasures were looted by the Nazis long before the house was bombed. Yet, when the opportunity arose, I made no claim for reparations. This was not on account of asceticism or self-sacrifice for, as your grandmother could tell you and your mother no doubt has, I am a creature of comfort. I have, however, seen where such claims have led in the past: the resentment stoked, followed by the search for scapegoats. I was too afraid of provoking it again – especially when the beneficiaries and scapegoats would be one and the same.

The foundation of our family's fortunes was the Frankel department store, which would have been both a household name and a civic landmark to any Berliner in the fifty years before 1939. It occupied an entire city block and was so well-known that it didn't identify itself anywhere on the facade. In its heyday, it employed fourteen thousand people and such is the lingering effect of Nazi propaganda that, even now, I feel obliged to state that they enjoyed exemplary conditions, including a holiday complex in the Black Forest, to which my grandfather himself made frequent visits – although, much to my relief, my mother drew the line at our accompanying him. The store's proud boast was that it sold everything. My grandfather used to sit my sister and me beside him and challenge us to find exceptions. To my frustration, Luise only ever asked about toys and dolls, but I thought up ever more ingenious items until one day I demanded an armoured tank, and he had to admit defeat. But by then more than the game was over. Aside from the range of its stock, the store's most celebrated feature was its lobby, from which a series of intricate staircases connected with the upper floors. It was dominated by a life-size portrait, originally of President Hindenberg and then of Hitler. It seemed to me that the entire decline of Germany was embodied in the switch from the Great War hero's luxuriant whiskers to the Führer's mean moustache. At the entrance, liveried footmen greeted customers, offering adults a glass of punch and children a sweet, or several if they made particularly shameless use of the revolving door. You might suppose such munificence to be a ploy, but you never knew your great-great-grandfather. He regarded the store as an extension of his home and everyone who stepped inside as his guest. So he laid down strict guidelines for the treatment of customers. The assistants should never put pressure on them: their job was to serve, not to harass. Needless to say, when positions were reversed, no one extended the same courtesy to him.

By the time of the Nazi ascendancy my grandfather was an old man, although I realise as I write that he must have been at least ten years younger than I am now. His appearance was a measure of his distinction. He was of medium height and slight build with a full head of white hair and a trim beard that was tinged with yellow. He sported a pince-nez on the bridge of his nose, a balancing act which, try as I might, I was no more able to master than a walk on the high wire. His invariable dress of a dark grey suit and tie, and a shirt with a wing collar, gave him the air of a professional mourner – and it suddenly strikes me that that may have been deliberate. The austerity was relieved only by the gold chain of his pocket watch which hung across his waistcoat. It had belonged to his grandfather and he, in turn, had promised it to me, although, as you shall see, it was sold on the *St Louis*. How Luise loved that watch! At an age when other girls were dressing up or playing hopscotch, she would sit on my grandfather's lap and twist it to and fro. Then she would put it to her ear and listen to the tick, chuckling as if it spoke a language only she could understand.

My grandfather left for his office at seven thirty every morning except Sunday. His timekeeping was such that I could have set my watch by him, although mine was a mere wristwatch and as wounding to my pride as short trousers. My mother used to fret about his health, urging him to step aside for a younger man. But she knew, and he knew that she knew, and she knew that he knew that she knew (and I know from listening to Leila that this sentence could go on forever), that he had no choice. For, although he had sold a share in the store to an American consortium, whose annual visit was the occasion for great excitement (and a frenzy of present-giving), he ran it alone. Frankel, as the name suggests, was a family concern and I was his designated successor. I had, in fact, made a solemn vow to decline the honour, partly from a determination to become an ornithologist and partly from an aversion to early rising (I conveniently discounted the dawn chorus), but, since I was still at school, the matter wasn't pressing. My grandfather's original heir was my Uncle Karl, after whom I was named, who had been killed in Lithuania in 1917. My grandmother died of grief six months later, leaving my mother and grandfather doubly bereft. My mother sometimes spoke of her brother, usually to express the disappointment he would have felt in his nephew; my grandfather rarely uttered his name. My mother urged me to respect his reticence, warning that any mention of my uncle would plunge him into misery. There could have been no stricter injunction on a boy who dreaded the prospect of other peoples' anguish more than his own. I would examine my friends and relations for signs of grief like a medieval officer searching for symptoms of plague.

For a few years my grandfather had a successor in my father. For a few years I had a father. He had also fought in the War but escaped without a scratch: a blessing which my mother at times articulated as a reproach. Having discovered a talent for poetry at the Front, he went to university to study literature. Shortly afterwards, the country was hit by a slump and people – even relatively rich ones – found themselves short of food. My father, with uncharacteristic altruism, abandoned his studies to help his parents. The best way, or so he later asserted, was to marry my mother. Here I must digress for a moment. Hard as it may be to credit in an age in which personal choice has been raised to a moral imperative, marriage at the end of the First World War was not the private matter that it became at the end of the Second. My grandfather was looking for a husband for his daughter and a director for his firm, my mother's consent having been assured by her brother's death. My father was their distant cousin and therefore eligible. Introductions were effected, a contract drawn up, and the ceremony took place. By all accounts it was a glittering occasion, although for me it became a mystery since, after my father's defection, the photographs were taken down from display and I was made to understand that asking my mother about her wedding was as taboo as asking my grandfather about the War. What I do know is that my father moved into our house and into an office alongside my grandfather. Eighteen months later I was born, supposedly the cause of great jubilation although, by the time of my earliest memories, little joy remained. The reason for the change was my father, who had disgraced himself by, as I was to learn much later, falsifying accounts at the store. Why, as my mother asked, he should have needed the money, when he had been given everything that he could ever want, was a puzzle. From then on, *Thou shalt not steal* became my obsession, especially since *Honour thy father and thy mother* had lost half its force.

My father, meanwhile, had taken to drink. This was not the measured tots enjoyed by my grandfather and his friends but great gulps of whisky, sometimes straight from the bottle, that transformed his kisses into *bierkeller* blasts. So I squirmed to escape and he accused my mother of turning me against him. He was quietly dismissed from the store but he could not be so easily removed from our lives. Aunt Annette (don't worry, I'll catch up with myself soon), in a rare criticism of my grandfather, charged him with doing too little to promote a reconciliation. But, in an equally rare criticism of Aunt Annette, I charge her with being too harsh. It was surely enough that he tolerated my father's presence: that he sat down with him at the end of each working day (that is for my grandfather) and swallowed his disgust; that he didn't put a padlock on the cellar door but left my father to struggle with his conscience, which was never the most daunting opponent. My father and mother started to lead separate lives, meeting only at mealtimes, when the length of the table militated against intimacy even as my grandfather's presence precluded confrontation. My father drank more and more until one night, when the drink had, in that serviceable English phrase, got the better of him, he forced himself on my mother. Nine months later Luise was born, and my father's impact on our family was complete. He had stamped his image on her innermost being, poisoning her cells and befuddling her brain. She was steeped in father's whisky long before her first taste of mother's milk.

The day after Luise was conceived, my father left us. He leant over my bed, and for once I did not recoil since his breath was as fresh as my mother's. He whispered, even though it was morning, that we might not see each other for some time but I must always remember that he loved me. Then he clasped me as hard as if he were squeezing out the last drop of toothpaste, laid me back on the pillows, and disappeared. He was right, at least in one thing, since, in the eight years before we quit Germany, I never set eyes on him again – although I was to do so soon after-wards, as you will discover. I made as determined an effort to forget him as I did Johannes von Hirte, my former blood brother, whom I had seen waving a banner in the Hitler Youth. Some-times my guard slipped, such as when I was driving through Berlin with Aunt Annette and we passed a line of vagrants, them-selves soon to be expunged from the Third Reich. 'There's Daddy!' I screamed, taken in by a fleeting resemblance and refusing to be silenced until Aunt Annette ordered the chauffeur to stop and let me out. My mistake acknowledged – and my embarrassment assuaged by the gift of a handful of marks – she informed me that my father was living comfortably in Breslau on an allowance provided by my grandfather. She did not, however, offer any explanation as to why my parents were flouting every precept in my schoolbooks. She simply declared that my father needed time to work through his problems. But, as time wore on with no sign of his return, I grew increasingly certain that the chief problem was me.

Dear Aunt Annette. . . . I promised to flesh out my reference to her and I do so with more pleasure than almost anything else in this account. She had been my grandmother's best friend although, with the strict demarcations of my schoolboy mind, I was surprised to find that she was nearer in age to my mother. She told me that, when my grandmother lay dying, she had made her a solemn vow to take care of her husband and daughter – yes, and her grandchildren too, she added quickly to quieten my clamour. She had acted not as a house-keeper but as a house-preserver – assuming that such a title exists. She had a sitting room, which she imbued with her own warmth and to which she would retreat at times of tension with my mother. She found such tension particularly painful since, as I pointed out to my mother, her entire existence was dedicated to smoothing everyone's path. 'Starting with her own,' my mother replied, with disturbing disloyalty to the adult cause. I hated to see them quarrel, but Grandfather assured me that it was inevitable when two women shared a house. Which was odd because, when I was fretting about him and my father, Aunt Annette had used the very same phrase of men. It filled me with apprehension. If two women or two men could not live together in harmony, what did that bode for the Christians and the Jews?

While Mother was so thin that Grandfather was always tempting her with titbits, Aunt Annette was so plump that he shook his head whenever she reached for a cake. Mother once banished me from the dinner-table for suggesting that they should have an operation so that some of Aunt Annette's fat could be transferred to her. Yet, when I crept upstairs to apologise, Aunt Annette was so far from taking offence that we shared a tray of truffles. The one meal at which she could eat as much as she liked was breakfast, which she had in bed – a privilege that was never extended to me, even on my birthday. I had only to conceal a biscuit beneath the covers for my mother to detect a telltale crumb. To her, lying in bed was a form of malingering – a charge that carried added weight when I discovered its usage during the War. She herself rose early, hurrying to her studio and spending as much time as possible at her easel before she was beset by distractions – for which read 'me'. She accused me of lacking respect for her art and yet, try as I might, I was unable to repress my innate reverence for realism. My efforts to praise her paintings always fell flat. Once, when Grandfather described Aunt Annette as looking 'as pretty as a picture', I asked if he meant one of Mother's. The words were no sooner off my lips than I regretted them. But, instead of issuing the expected reprimand, my mother tore into my grandfather, itself an extraordinary occurrence. 'Congratulations, Father,' she said, 'you've bred yet another Frankel with no feeling for art.'

By then, of course, my mother had come to hate me. It was quite understandable. In addition to my own failings, I offered her a daily reminder of my father's. Our physical resemblance, regularly remarked upon by scores of malevolent well-wishers ('He'll grow into such a handsome man, the spitting image of his father'), was a pointer to the moral. It was small wonder that I longed to remain a boy.

Aunt Annette did her best to reassure me, insisting that, far from hating me, my mother loved me so much that she would sometimes grow impatient with my imperfections.

'But she's not impatient with Luise,' I replied, 'and she has far more imperfections.'

'It's not the same and you're intelligent enough to know that,' Aunt Annette said, as ever cushioning the rebuke. 'Which is another reason not to take everything your mother says to heart. She's constantly worried about what will happen to Luise.'

'In which case,' I said, 'she should treat me better since, when she and you and Grandfather are dead, I'm the one who'll have to take care of her.'

'I don't suppose she's looking that far ahead,' Aunt Annette said.

With hindsight, I think it was that casual remark that gave me my first intimation of Luise's mortality. I saw then what everyone else had seen since the day she was born: in the eyelids that constantly fluttered and the eyes that failed to focus; in the arms and legs that gripped her in a permanent tug of war; in the massy forehead and lumpen chin; in the slurred speech that didn't emerge at all until she was five years old and then only in burst-pipe spurts of inarticulacy; in the wild, self-destructive furies that would flare up for no apparent reason. I saw the fear, not of what would happen to Luise when she grew old, but of whether she would grow old at all. And yet, in spite – or perhaps because – of that, my mother insisted on preserving the illusion that Luise was simply slow and that, in true fairytale fashion, she would grow up and amaze us all. I don't know if she felt that, by articulating the wish, she would make it happen, as she did with everything else in her life, or rather that, by stressing my sister's normality, she could justify ignoring her. Either way, the pretence became harder and harder to maintain.

Luise was born with Foetal Alcohol Syndrome. Although we didn't have a name for it then, we had the diagnosis of a visionary doctor: one, moreover, who was willing to look beyond an abstemious mother to a drunken father. I can't remember how I came to learn of my father's guilt. No one put it to me directly, not even my grandfather, who used to twist his mouth whenever he spoke of him as though he were trying to dislodge a piece of gristle from his teeth. I expect that even he realised that it might not be wise to inform a growing boy of a parental rape. In your case, Marcus and Edward, I am trusting to the passage of time, not to mention the ubiquity of sexual imagery, to mute the effect. In my case, the facts of even loving procreation had never been explained. As a Jew, I had been banned from biology lessons. I was far too overawed to ask my grandfather and I lived in horror of any such discussion with my mother, whose grasp of anatomy – at least to judge from her paintings – was even hazier than my own. I scavenged for information in the school playground and in the pages of *Der Stürmer*, an anti-Semitic scandal-sheet full of predatory Jews preying on Aryan maidens, which, paradoxically, became my primary source of both sexual knowledge and erotic stimulus. The dual burden of shame made me determined never to marry but, rather, to devote myself to Luise the way that Aunt Annette had to Grandfather. Yet, when I told her of my resolve, Aunt Annette merely tousled my hair and suggested that I wait until I was older: one of the few occasions on which her placid wisdom afforded me no relief.

Even before my friends' defection, I spent as much time as possible with Luise. I brushed aside my grandfather's warnings that she would hold me back, since I knew that I could make her smile more broadly than anyone else. My only rival for her affections was Sophie, her governess and my honorary sister. Sophie had come to us at the age of twenty-three in flight from some unexplained heartbreak. I was aware that this was another sorrow that it would be dangerous to probe and yet it made no sense, for how could any man break the heart of someone as loving and warm as Sophie? Her arrival had been the only good to come out of Luise's condition. Until then I had had an English nanny, Miss Snape, who had instilled in me such a rosy view of her homeland that, when I finally arrived in London, I was half-expecting to be welcomed by both Christopher Robin and the King and Queen. Luise's problems had overwhelmed her and my mother had engaged Sophie, a Bavarian beauty, whose blonde hair and blue eyes were an even greater reproach to Nazi propaganda than my own. At first she wore a traditional white blouse that laced up the front, and I would sit at her side and toy with the laces, but she soon became a buttoned-up Berliner. Besides, I grew too old and lost my place of privilege. How I longed to turn back the clock... but I wanted it both ways: a ten year old's licence with a fifteen year old's hands. If adolescence were the threshold between childhood and maturity, then I was stuck in a permanently revolving door.

Sophie entered my life in the same year that Adolf Hitler entered my consciousness. He and his National Socialist party gained power – legally it has to be said, which should be remembered if you wonder why we stayed put for so long. A government that had been voted in could just as easily be voted out, or so people thought. This government, however, behaved like no other. A matter of days after taking office, it waged war on a group of its own citizens, declaring a boycott of all Jewish businesses. The tactic backfired, at least in our case. Far from shunning the store, Berliners made a point of braving the Brownshirts at the entrances. The day's sales actually rose, which filled my grandfather with a misplaced confidence in the goodwill of ordinary Germans. His belief that their show of support had wounded the government was confirmed by the lack of any action to follow the boycott. Anti-Semitic threats peppered the speeches of the Führer and his Minister of Propaganda, Joseph Goebbels, but, for the most part, they remained veiled. My grandfather's conviction that the government must acknowledge our indispensability was boosted when, three weeks after the boycott, the army placed a large order for new uniforms. Meanwhile, he welcomed high-ranking SS officers to the store as warmly as his father had done members of the Imperial family.

If I had a pound for every time that I've been asked over the years why we didn't leave Germany in 1933, I'd be a rich man . . . although I should know better than to use an idiom which contains what many of my questioners (I might almost say my *accusers* since their tone makes us as much to blame as our enemies) already regard as the reason: that we were more concerned with our comfort than our lives. In other words, nothing so validates Jesus' warnings on the danger of riches than the fate of the German Jews. But, while it's true that my grandfather was devoted to his business, he viewed it less as a source of wealth than as a sacred trust. He was justifiably proud that, in little over a century, a peddler's cart had grown into the most prestigious store in Berlin. Even so – and although I was too young for him to take into his confidence – I know that he contemplated leaving. Many of his friends had bought tickets and their brandy-and-cigar conversations assumed a new urgency, yet, just as he had drawn comfort from the Nazis' electoral mandate, so he did from his friends' departure. Their freedom to travel meant, paradoxically, that he saw no need to rush. Besides, as an acknowledged leader of the community, he felt a twofold obligation, first, not to abandon his less privileged coreligionists and, second, to prove to their Christian persecutors that the boy David was not the only Jew ready to stand his ground. The final cause of our apparent complacency was that, even when the government had begun to legislate against us, the process was not clear-cut. The restrictions came in dribs and drabs and, initially at least, were accompanied by a host of exemptions. It was even possible if you tried hard enough – and, believe me, people did – to see the Nuremberg laws in a positive light. After all, they gave the Jews a measure of recognition: to be second-class citizens was preferable to being no citizens at all. As my grandfather said: 'They've done their worst. What more are they going to do? Murder us?'

I've taken pains to defend my grandfather against any charges that you or your contemporaries might bring, because there is no court more unjust than that of hindsight. At the time, however, I was less tolerant of his inaction. When the Nazis came to power, I was eight and took little notice of the world outside my windows; four years later, I was carrying its entire weight on my shoulders. The country's political turmoil was echoed inside our home. I defined the difference between my grandfather and myself as that between Job and Joshua. He believed that history was destiny. Having suffered – and survived – persecutions in the past, the Jews would do so again. I, on the other hand, demanded that we fight back. Please don't misunderstand me, I was not so naïve as to suggest a running battle with the SS, who had taken to marching through Berlin as though it were their private parade ground. I held, rather, that we should secure the land that was ours by right: Palestine. At first, without my grandfather's knowledge, and then, in express defiance of his will, I began to attend meetings of the Young Pioneers. I came home flushed with Zionist fervour, soliciting contributions from my grandfather, who refused as brusquely as if I'd asked for a non-birthday present. Unlike my mother, who dismissed the Pioneers as harmless idealists, he viewed them as dangerous fanatics. 'Are you too young to see?' he asked, offending every ounce of my twelve-year-old dignity, 'that the moment they provide us with a home elsewhere, they'll be justified in throwing us out of our homes here?' And, though the move from a bleak and banner-ridden Berlin to the holy city of Jerusalem struck me as highly desirable, it was my grandfather's greatest nightmare. No matter what the Nazis did to him, he remained a dedicated patriot. He maintained that to categorise people by their religion was medieval. 'We're living in the twentieth century and should define ourselves by nationhood. Never forget, Karl, whatever they may tell you, that you're a Jewish German, not a German Jew.'

This simple distinction eluded the majority of our fellow countrymen. Their confusion was most apparent where it was least appropriate: at school. The government imposed a series of restraints on Jewish pupils. From the start, only a handful of us were permitted to attend any state institution. I, as my grandfather never ceased to point out, was 'one of the lucky ones', but then he had said the same of a man who had returned from the Front without legs. Friends, who had enjoyed my family's hospitality – no, that is to think like them . . . friends, who had enjoyed my company, now shunned me. They made an elaborate show of not speaking to me, channelling their guilt into a game. They chalked caricatures of my face on the blackboard, the crudity of their drawings making up for the modesty of my nose. They held me down and punched me until I agreed to read out anti-Semitic passages from *Mein Kampf*. Then, when I demanded satisfaction, they refused to fight on the grounds that, as a Jew, I had no honour to lose.

The teachers were equally craven, condemning acts of violence while rewarding the perpetrators, shielding them from pollution by shunting me into a corner like a dunce. I gained my revenge by excelling in every subject. But, the better my work, the lower my grades, since even the cleverest Jew was by definition inferior to the stupidest German. By 1937, even my token presence at the school was regarded as a threat and I was sent instead to an all-Jewish establishment where, to my horror, I felt even more alien. Most of my new classmates were immigrants from Eastern Europe, the very people whom my grandfather and his friends blamed for provoking Hitler. Not only did they look different from me (it isn't just your father whom you have to thank for your blonde hair and blue eyes) but, whether from diet or inadequate sanitation, they also smelt different. This time I would have been grateful for a desk apart, but the class was so overcrowded that we were virtually in one another's laps. To these boys, my name was a symbol of luxury, and they lashed out at that which they couldn't hope to attain. Night after night I returned home covered in bruises which, on the rare occasions that she took note, my mother attributed to street brawls. I suffered her rebukes in silence. At the time I felt humiliated that, although I was almost a man – a fact impressed upon me by the number of my classmates who were preparing to be bar mitzvah – I had failed to protect myself. Looking back, I wonder if I were not also trying to spare her the humiliation of her failure to protect me.

My classmates' bar mitzvah ceremonies were a reminder that I would soon have to go through one myself. Every Sunday morning, a rabbinical scholar came to the house to prepare me for my portion. As he guided me through the intricacies of the

Torah, I yearned for that earlier era when the focus of the service had been on the father rather than the son. Instead of a wretched thirteen year-old whose strained nerves and pounding heart made a mockery of his newfound manhood, it was his father who had stood in front of the congregation and relinquished responsibility for his son's religious conduct. Having reached the age of maturity, the boy – the man – now had to take charge of himself. In my case the thought was even more fantastical, since my father had assumed no responsibility for any aspect of my conduct, religious or otherwise, since I was six years old. That role had been taken by my grandfather, who showed no sign of wishing to give it up, even symbolically. Our rows about my resolve to emigrate to Palestine had moved beyond even Aunt Annette's powers of mediation. Nevertheless, his adjectival Judaism found room for the bar mitzvah ceremony, which he regarded as less of a religious ritual than an election to a gentleman's club. Besides, he relished the prospect of a party to cheer us up at such a miserable time. It would be the biggest he had thrown since my parents' marriage – which was not the most auspicious precedent. Yet, although I was flattered and excited and even comforted by the plans that were being made on my behalf, I was increasingly convinced that I could not allow them to be put into effect.

My mother and grandfather were incensed. They accused me of disrespect and disobedience. They bribed me with gifts and privileges and then threatened to take them away. They used every weapon in the parental and loco-parental armoury, but to no avail. The irony was that, at the same time as I was losing faith in my coreligionists, they had warmed to them. Whereas, in the past, my grandfather had condemned the skullcaps and side-locks of the East Europeans as an affront to modern Germany, he now wondered whether his own attempts to assimilate might not have offended a traditionalist God. Like the soldier who dies with 'mother' on his lips or the sceptic who requests the last rites, he had reverted to his childhood credo. He and my mother saw my refusal to become bar mitzvah not as a principled stand against Jewish pusillanimity but as a petty attempt to punish them. Of all their charges, the most serious was that I had taken the Nazis' ideology to heart and was ashamed of being Jewish. I assured them that, on the contrary, I was proud of being Jewish but ashamed of my fellow Jews. I congratulated myself on the wit of my reply until my grandfather made me repeat it, first to the student who had taught me, and then to the Rabbi whose synagogue he endowed, although rarely deigned to attend. They attacked me with a ferocity that would have defeated Daniel.

'You claim that your decision isn't personal,' the Rabbi said. 'So who are these Jews you feel ashamed of?'

'The Jews who allow themselves to be banned from cinemas and sports clubs. The Jews who allow themselves to be spat on in the streets. The Jews who allow their jobs and their homes to be taken away from them. The Jews who allow their sons and daughters to be expelled from schools. The Jews whose greatest act of protest is to throw a party.' I aimed this last charge at my grandfather, who was seething at the Rabbi's tolerance of my tirade. 'The Jews who prefer to suffer any amount of insults in this country rather than endure the least hardship in the land that was given to them by God. Since those are the Jewish men I see all around, why should I want to be one myself?'

'What right have you, a mere boy,' the Rabbi asked, 'to sit in judgement on your elders?'

'Very well,' I replied, 'if I'm a mere boy, then I've no need to go through the farce of pretending to be a man.'

I'm telling you this, not to encourage you to defy your elders – particularly not Marcus, whose talent for disputation is already Talmudic – but to show you how I won my case. Victory, however, felt hollow. Luise was the only member of the household who still smiled at me. Even the servants sniffed their disapproval. But my own problems paled when, on 9th November 1938, a date forever etched on my brain, the Nazis launched a devastating attack on our community. Windows were smashed throughout the country, which is why it became known as *Kristallnacht*. But the damage was far more extensive than that name might suggest: houses, shops and synagogues were set ablaze; hundreds of people were killed and thousands of men were arrested. One of them was my grandfather.

There were drawbacks to our isolation. We had heard the clamour in the streets and seen the flames in the sky but, without any neighbours to warn us, we had no notion of what they might portend: whether it were another attack on the Reichstag or purge of the literary canon, or simply a Party celebration. For once I was grateful that, following the government's cruellest edict, Winnetou and Shatterhand, my two red setters, had been spared the spate of explosions that would have terrified them. My reflections were punctured by a pounding on the door and the invasion of a Gestapo gang.

With no pretence of courtesy, they rushed through the house, trampling anything in their path. Their quarry was my grandfather, whom they found, bolstered by Beethoven, alone in his smoking room. The uproar roused the entire household, who appeared in various states of distress and disarray. Sophie struggled to control Luise, who ran up and down the nursery landing, moaning and banging her head against the banisters. My mother, along with Aunt Annette and Felix, Grandfather's valet, demanded an explanation from the officer in charge, but his curt reply that the Jew Frankel was being arrested on suspicion of arson merely intensified the shock. Felix placed a conciliatory hand on the officer's arm, only to be knocked to the ground by his gun. While Aunt Annette stemmed the blood streaming from the old man's nose, my mother remonstrated with his attacker, who appeared to be torn between childhood training and adult ideology. Fearing that the latter would triumph, I pulled my mother away. Her surprise at my intervention was matched by my own that she accepted my restraint. I trembled at my daring but, when the guards bundled my grandfather through the hall, I was petrified that they would arrest her too. She screamed that her father would catch pneumonia if he went outside in his slippers, but she might have been the lone dissenter at a Nuremberg Rally for all the effect that it had. A surer approach was made by Thomas, our butler, who, with his innate blend of deference and authority, carried my grandfather's coat up to his captors. 'If you please,' he said and, without waiting for a reply, deftly released each of my grandfather's arms in turn and slid them into the sleeves. Then, either from force of habit or in a gesture of defiance, he flicked a speck of dust from the collar, before the men thrust him aside and hustled my grandfather through the door.

For a moment we stood in silence. Then, prompted by Luise's wails, everyone sprang into action. The servants set about clearing the mess, as if grateful that their role was so clear-cut. Sophie carried a now limp Luise to bed. Aunt Annette led a babbling Felix to have his face washed. I was left alone with my mother, my arms still encircling her waist. She gently disengaged herself and turned to face me. I braced myself for a furious attack on my presumption or, at the very least, a bitter rebuke for my failure to persuade the guards to take me in place of the father she loved so much. Instead, she kissed me softly on the forehead and walked into the study. In retrospect, it strikes me as a turning point: her first recognition that I was growing up. At the time, it just made me shiver.

'What are we going to do?' I asked. 'We must make a plan.'

'Not now darling,' she replied. 'There are a lot of people I have to telephone.' At a stroke, my new-found status vanished, and I was back to being a boy.

The next day we came to terms with our vulnerability. For all our wealth, we were still Jews. We could no more escape the orgy of destruction than my classmates in their slums behind the Alexanderplatz . . . and *orgy of destruction*, like so many well-worn phrases, conceals a deep truth. Looking back, I am convinced that there was a link between the new sense of power – of physical possibility – that surged through my body at the most inopportune moments and the men, adolescent in impulse if not in years, who rampaged through Germany that night. Meanwhile my mother confirmed my suspicions that her unworldliness was a pose, when she systematically contacted everyone who might raise a voice on my grandfather's behalf, starting with his American associates. Their partnership, which had produced the anomaly whereby my grandfather retained charge of his business after all his fellows had been forced out, may have lulled him into a false sense of security, but there can be no doubt that it facilitated his release after barely five weeks, just in time for Christmas: that festival which, to my growing disgust, he had always so loved. But there were to be no festivities for him in 1938: no dressing up as Santa Claus to distribute presents to his employees' children; not even a family dinner. The veneer of assimilation had been stripped away. Christmas was no longer a holiday which people of good faith – of all faiths – could celebrate together, but a day on which our enemies could celebrate their ascendancy over us.

For as long as I could remember, my grandfather had remained unchanged. Indeed, his consistency in appearance, habit and attitude had made him my model for that other immutable patriarch, God. But, during his five-week absence, he had undergone a total transformation: he had visibly shrunk; his eyes were sunken; his skin was pallid and his hands shook. It was as though he had been starved of something even more precious than food. He had been imprisoned in Sachsenhausen, a place yet to acquire its murderous associations. I pestered him for details of his treatment and, to my surprise, my mother made no protest: a clear sign that she was afraid to put the questions herself. Grandfather was too pained – or proud – to say anything, except that for the first time he could truly comprehend what Uncle Karl had suffered at the Front. I thought that excessive since Uncle Karl had slept in a trench and washed in a ditch, until I overheard Felix telling one of the maids that the master had come home riddled with lice.

Our joy at my grandfather's release was muted since, far from having the charge against him dropped, he was now accused of trying to burn down his own store in an insurance fraud. His sole recourse was the payment of a fine so vast that it required him to sell half his stock. This he did with barely a sigh, his arrest having succeeded where my arguments had failed in persuading him of the need to emigrate. Through a business associate, he obtained visas for England, only to reject them on the grounds that the country was too close to Germany both geographically and politically, its toadying to Hitler having strengthened the dictator's hand. He settled instead on America, where his extensive assets would offset the government's meagre allowance of ten Reichsmarks per emigrant. Deferring my dreams of Palestine (I was not to abandon them for another five decades), I found myself sketching the Statue of Liberty on every available scrap of paper; but the poem in its pedestal was belied by the President's strict limit on the number of the 'tired' and the 'poor' and the 'huddled masses yearning to breathe free' who were allowed in. Even my grandfather's influential friends failed to sway the State Department. Our one hope was to obtain a US visa and wait in a third country, perhaps for years, for our quota number to come up, but even temporary refuge proved to be out of reach, until my grandfather discovered that the Cuban consul in Cologne was willing to provide entry permits – at a price. Having paid it, he booked berths on the *St Louis*, a cruise ship that was sailing from Hamburg to Havana in May 1939.

We were forbidden to apply for passports until a month before our departure, knowing full well that the authorities might turn us down, for no other reason than to delight in their own caprice. So, in early April, the six of us – my disengaged mother and broken grandfather, my grief-stricken aunt and unpredictable sister, her governess and myself – faced the final obstacle to our escape: the maze of the Reich's emigration office. It had been set up in a Jewish community centre which, my grandfather informed us with a wealth of irony, he had helped to fund. The jostling crowds displayed little sense of community as they vied for a place in the queue. The officials mocked their desperation, sending them running from desk to desk like clowns gathering water in a sieve. I raged at the Nazis' brutality and a part of me – I dared not calculate its extent – longed to punch at least one of them in the face. I knew better, however, not least because, in the realignment of the family, I had assumed certain responsibilities. My most pressing concern was Luise, and I worked with Sophie to ensure that she should not be unnerved by the crowd or the uniforms; that no brusque order drove her darting forward to dash her head against a desk from which she could only be prised by a party of guards. So I greeted every taunt about my habits and hygiene with a sporting smile. I heaped thanks on each official, as we collected forms from one and had them stamped by another and then climbed the stairs to obtain our passports from a third, before making a symbolic descent to the basement where, in the final indignity and ultimate sign of our lack of status, they were stamped with a single J.

We had three weeks to prepare for departure although, to judge by my mother, it might have been three years. Faced with the need to squeeze each of our lives into the allotted ten suitcases, she threw up her hands and retreated into her studio. When my grandfather gently remonstrated, she accused him of trying to destroy her creativity, which stifled any argument as effectively as a rabbi's citing of the Torah. Sneaking into the studio, in itself a serious violation, I saw that she was doing on canvas what she refused to do in life. There were Grandfather, Luise, herself and me – identifiable more by general characteristics than by individual features – squashed inside packing cases beside a ship. With Mother occupied at her easel, it was left to Aunt Annette and Sophie to see to the arrangements. Ten cases appeared to be a meagre allowance even for a fifteen year old, so I persuaded them that, since I was still growing out of my clothes, it made sense to buy new ones in America (in my head, I already shared a tailor with Jimmy Cagney), thereby leaving more room for my treasures: the photographs, books, stamp albums, phonograph records, binoculars and, above all, collection of birds' eggs, each one painstakingly wrapped in felt.

I was fortunate that none of these attracted the attention of the assessors who ransacked the house for valuables. Their concern was for the paintings and furniture, gold and silver, ornaments and jewellery, all of which had to be surrendered to the authorities. But the much-vaunted Nazi efficiency proved to be flawed and my mother, finally goaded into action, kept back several diamond necklaces and rings, which Sophie concealed in the linings of coats and heels of shoes. My criminal aspirations, already boosted by the discovery of Jewish gangsters in America, received a further fillip when I literally became Diamond-Soled Karl. Meanwhile, my mother relaxed her definition of essentials to include her own paintings, filling three cases with work which, to her fury, the assessor had dismissed as worthless, and my grandfather, driven to defy the law at the age of seventy-six, cut his favourite picture, Poussin's *Flight into Egypt*, out of its frame and hid it beneath the false bottom of a trunk. It now hangs in pride of place in my dining room. You may remember, Leila, how baffling you found it as a child. The minuscule figures lost in the landscape, although perfect for a lunchtime game of I-spy, made a nonsense of the title. It was a study of mountains and trees not people. But if – God forbid – you'd been forced into exile, whether by Herod or by Hitler, then I think you would have understood.

We all dreaded saying our goodbyes, apart from Luise for whom the word was an excuse for a frenzy of waving. My own were largely domestic, to the men and women I had known since birth: Wilfrid, my grandfather's driver, who had taken me fishing and deftly swapped my tiddler for his two-pounder, a deception with which I was happy to comply; Frau Herzen, who had cooked it for our dinner but whom I primarily associated with jams and cakes, an expression of her own sweet nature; Felix and Thomas, to whom you've already been introduced; Charlotte and Gunhild, our maids, whose age allowed them to remain in our service when their younger companions had been forced to quit. Aunt Annette asked if I wanted to take my leave of my classmates, but I declined. I knew that they would see my escape as yet another mark of privilege, especially when several of their fathers had been arrested on the same night as Grandfather but had yet to – and would never – return. My thoughts were far more focused on my former school. I dreamt of walking through the gates to find the last few years sliding away like stage scenery as my friends jumped out of their hiding places. 'You fell for it,' they would shout with a single voice, 'you dupe!' All the treachery, all the cruelty, all the violence would be revealed as a huge, if tasteless, practical joke, and I would once again be one of them. But God, in whom my trust had been severely shaken, although my faith remained firm, allowed me a moment of truth when, walking down the Kürfurstendamm, I bumped into some of my old gang in their new uniforms. Their only sign of recognition was a globule of spit which landed a few centimetres from my feet. I tried to tell myself that the distance was deliberate, but his fellows' jeers confirmed my own recollection that Joachim Tressel had always been a hopeless shot.

I wondered if I should say goodbye to my father – or, more accurately, if I should want to say goodbye to him. The silence of the last eight years was about to become permanent. Since he hadn't deigned to make the journey from Breslau to Berlin, he was hardly likely to travel to Havana. Sometimes I worried that the reason for his absence was that he had been arrested and, instead of the weeks endured by my grandfather, he had spent years in prison. Then, with the same ambivalence I had felt at my classics master's recovery from a stroke, I reflected on his talent for disappearing. At other times, I imagined that he was leading an underground cell and preparing to fire a bullet into the Führer's flinty heart. On the eve of his execution (his own death being a key part of the picture), he would write a long letter to his family, begging us to forgive him, explaining that he had sacrificed our happiness for the sake of our fellow Jews. Then, with tears welling in my eyes, I dismissed the thought in favour of the probability that he himself had left the country some years earlier, along with the children he had fathered in a bid to forget us.

I warned myself not to waste my goodbyes. Yet my deep sense of loss demanded a focus. I decided therefore to take my leave of places and, on successive afternoons, my colouring the perfect camouflage, strolled unmolested through Berlin: to the Brandenburg Gate and the Tiergarten; to the Universum cinema,

where in recent years the posters had been my closest contact
with the films; to the Deutsches Theater where, as a small boy, I
had been enchanted by the spectacles of Max Reinhardt, and the
Kunstlertheater where, only slightly older, I had sat through
Winterreise with that same sense of smugness and discomfort as
when puffing on one of Grandfather's cigars. I took the tram to
the Hertha BSC stadium, where I had spent long afternoons with
my friends at a time when our only enemies had been on the
opposing team. I walked about the city which had become less of
a landscape than a second skin, and wondered if I would ever
return. Finally, I reached my favourite street, Unter den Linden,
only to find that it belied its name, since all the trees had been
chopped down to make room for the endless parades. I knew
then that I could leave without regrets.

There was one goodbye that I could not shirk and, the day
before our departure, Wilfrid drove me, along with my mother,
grandfather and Luise, to the cemetery at Weisensee. While synagogues and shops had been desecrated and destroyed, it had
survived intact: an anomaly which, even at fifteen, I attributed
less to the Nazis' sense of respect than to their belief that a
necropolis constituted a perfect home for the Jews. Nevertheless,
I was grateful that my mother and grandfather were spared the
sight of further graffiti as they took a final farewell of their
mother and brother and wife and son. Both were interred in the
family mausoleum: a black marble replica of the Parthenon,
which had terrified me on my first visit and to which I had never
become reconciled. The sole virtue of our enforced emigration
was that I would not have to take my place among the bones of
my ancestors. Yet, as I clutched Luise's hand and watched
Grandfather painfully bending to place two stones at the side of
the tomb, I was filled with rage at the thought that we would be
unable to bury him among his family. He looked so frail that I
feared that his own death might be imminent, and I swore to

myself that, no matter the cost, I would bring his body back from America like Joseph bringing Jacob back from Egypt.

I was roused from my reverie by my mother who, having left her own stones, nudged me to lead Luise up to leave ours. I set mine down, pausing to note that they were the roundest and smoothest in the line, and tried in vain to feel a connection to the two dead people whom I had never met and yet who had exerted such an influence on my life. Luise, however, refused to give hers up, banging them together like cymbals, which prompted my mother to stride up and prise them off her. While she was dragged screaming down the path, Grandfather directed my gaze towards the countless rows of white stone markers that commemorated the soldiers killed in the War. I expected another lecture on the valiant Jews who had died for Germany but, instead, he dismissed them in a single word: 'Fools!' Then, looking back towards his son, he added 'And he knew.'

Wilfrid drove us home and took his final leave, since it was Ernst Sengler, Thomas's son, who was to drive us to Hamburg. Ernst had joined the SS, a fact that caused his father the same mild embarrassment as if he'd shopped at a rival store. Ernst was himself embarrassed by his loyalty to my grandfather, who had paid to put him through university, where, ironically, he had first been exposed to Nazi ideas. With the same sophistry that would later permit the government to class as 'honorary Aryans' the Japanese, a nation of far more exotic appearance than the most Semitic-looking Jew, Ernst exempted our family from Hitler's strongest charges. He warned his father that we might face trouble on our journey to Hamburg – a so-called 'spontaneous' protest against rich Jews who were spiriting their money away from the Reich. He therefore offered both his services and his insignia, and, with a heavy heart, Grandfather accepted. In part because the car was so cramped but, in the main, I think, to distance himself from Ernst, he sat in the back with Mother,

Aunt Annette and Luise, while I squeezed into the front with
Sophie. Our hopes of tranquillity were dashed by Ernst, who
kept up a constant stream of chat or, rather, propaganda. After
describing our voyage as a pleasure cruise, he explained why, as
aliens, we were unable to feel genuine sadness on leaving
Germany. He even tried to reason with us, giving us a final
chance to acknowledge the genius of the Führer, like an
Inquisitor thrusting a cross at a burning heretic.

Then, realising that there would be no last-minute conver-
sion, he assured us that we would be happier in America since it
was populated largely by Jews.

'That's not true,' I protested.

'Apart from Negroes. In any case, America's a vast country
. . . a continent. There's room for different races. Germany's
small. We're all muddled up. Why did the Roman Empire fall?'

'Barbarian attacks,' I replied, looking round for support.

'Interbreeding,' he insisted. 'The Romans coupled with their
slaves and diluted their blood. National Socialism will protect
the Fatherland from a similar fate. Never again will Germany be
a mongrel nation.'

'Mongrels are stronger than pedigree dogs,' Sophie interjected. 'They live longer too.'

'Do you want us to have an accident?' he asked crossly.
'You're taking my mind off the road.'

I envied the passengers in the back who had no distraction
but Luise's whimpering, although I was afraid that her constant
demands for food, drink and lavatories would confirm Ernst in
his view of Jewish inferiority, especially when our reluctance to
risk an inn obliged her to relieve herself in a field. I roundly
rejected my mother's suggestion that I should do likewise, until
the pressure of a bursting bladder combined with Ernst's own
lack of inhibition to change my mind. The rest of the journey
passed without incident, apart from Ernst's paean of praise to

the newly opened autobahn and his insistence that we echo the picture-book Aryan family on the billboard who, glazed with appreciation, declared that 'Our beloved Führer gave us this.'

We reached Hamburg shortly before nightfall to find the streets decked in bunting. For an instant we feared that the beloved Führer was preparing to pay a visit but, to our relief, found that the city was celebrating seven hundred and fifty years of its foundation. 'Surely, there must be some mistake?' Sophie said. 'Do you mean that Hamburg had a history before the Nazis?' Ernst took such offence at her tone that he refused to say another word, driving us straight to the hotel where, with a curt salute, he left us. We entered the lobby, of which Grandfather had many happy memories, but it was clear that circumstances had changed. No sooner had we proffered our names than the desk clerk drew our attention to a notice stating that 'Guests of the Jewish persuasion should not eat in the dining room but in the first floor lounge.' His suggestion that they were catering to our dietary needs rather than their own prejudice fooled no one. Further humiliation followed when it was revealed that our booking requests had been ignored and I had to sleep in a child's cot in a room with Luise and Sophie, the prospect of which gave me an unexpected, inexplicable thrill.

'I promise I don't mind,' I said, hoping to impress my mother with my cooperation.

'I don't care whether you mind or not,' she said. 'I'm thinking of Sophie.' I was searching for a suitably damning reply when my grandfather, who from the moment of our arrival had kept his eyes fixed on the revolving door (which Luise had finally been dissuaded from using as a roundabout), shot me a look of warning. Then, turning to the clerk, he accepted the room keys with a humiliating profusion of thanks.

I anticipated a thrilling night in which Sophie and I would lie awake, confiding all our most intimate hopes and fears, but, in a mortifying repeat of New Year's Eve, I fell asleep the moment that my head hit the pillow. I woke to find Sophie, fully dressed, attempting to rouse a resistant Luise. A chambermaid brought breakfast to our room – a snub that was actually a blessing – but, the moment that she handed me my tray, my mother strode in and, dismissing all talk of special occasions, insisted that I ate it at the desk. I was surprised at how smart she looked. Her hair was wound in an elaborate bun and, in defiance of the law, she wore a diamond ring and a string of pearls. Setting aside our travelling clothes, she insisted that Luise and I made a similar effort, determined that we should leave the country like people of distinction, not vagabonds. Her words galvanised Sophie, who hurried to her suitcase for a change of blouse (I felt honour-bound to concentrate on my herring). When we assembled downstairs an hour later, it was clear that Grandfather and Aunt Annette had been inspired to a similar elegance, so much so that we might have been the Krupps setting off for their yacht.

At the docks we were ushered into a huge shed that was even more chaotic than the emigration office. I was seized by a sudden panic and longed to go home and lie low until the country wearied of Hitler. Then I remembered Ernst's warning that, in the forthcoming war, the German people would ensure that the Jews had no chance to profit from the blood of its heroes, and I knew that there was no turning back. I tried to shut out the terror by focusing on my family. My grandfather and mother ignored their own instructions for us all to stick together, the one seeking out porters to fetch our advance baggage and the other finding suitable candidates for her patronage in an elderly couple cowed by the crowd. Luise started to whine and Sophie promptly proposed a game of Spot the Colour, although their usual reds and blues and greens were subsumed in the swirl of greys and browns. Only Aunt Annette paid attention to me, and I took her hand, doubly grateful for the pretence that I was the one protecting her. After an enforced wait, we trudged through the embarkation channel where an inspector with an alarmingly familiar moustache insisted on examining every one of our cases. When a porter bent to put the first on the table, he ordered him to leave it to my grandfather, who could barely lift it from the floor. Leaping to his aid, I grabbed the case and flung it in front of the Inspector, who punished my defiance by the thoroughness of his search. I winced as he pawed my mother's most intimate clothing and raged as he tore the spines off her sketch books. Then, as he rummaged through the coats, all other emotions gave way to the dread that he would discover the jewels. But, after years of silence, God answered my prayers, and the Inspector passed the case. My relief, however, was short-lived for the next one that he opened contained my stamps. He leafed through the albums with unwonted care, no doubt picturing such gaps in his son's collection as the Bavaria Number One and Red Mercury, before declaring them forfeit as items of value to the Reich. My vehement protests drew no response, other than the horrified glances of people nearby who were submitting to a similar outrage.

'Karl please,' my grandfather said. 'We'll buy you more albums – bigger ones.'

'How?' the official asked. 'With your ten Reichsmarks? Or are you trying to smuggle funds out of the country?' He gestured to his confederates to frisk us.

'No, sir,' my grandfather said quickly. 'Not a pfennig. I meant that, in America, I'll find work. I'll earn money to buy more albums.'

'Oh yes,' the man spat. 'You Jews make money everywhere. Well go and cheat the Americans instead of us.' He smiled triumphantly and slipped the albums into a crate. He then proceeded to do the same with my binoculars, veterans of five years of field trips, dashing my hopes of spotting any rare birds on the voyage. Finally, he came to my collection of eggs, lifting out the trays with a sinister smile. He scoffed at my claim that their sole value was sentimental, refusing to believe 'that a Jew would collect anything he couldn't sell,' and then slowly, very slowly, smashed each one in turn. I watched dumbstruck as he gave way to a wanton violence that would have shamed any woodland predator. He stopped only when Luise started to clap, delighted that a grown-up was playing the game that she played every morning with her boiled egg: her boiled hen's egg; her common or garden, one-million-eaten-every-breakfast egg: not a brambling's egg; a nuthatch's egg; a dunnock's egg; a chaffinch's egg; a hawfinch's egg; two linnets' eggs; a siskin's egg; a pere- grine's egg; a goldcrest's egg; a goshawk's egg; and a cuckoo's egg that I'd mistaken for a meadow-pipit's, until Herr Weisel, my Nature Studies teacher, set me straight. My mother struggled to silence Luise, terrified that the brute might suppose she was laughing at him and smash her head with equal insouciance. He, however, drew back, conscious of having held his night-time self up to the light. 'You're correct,' he said, 'they have no value. There's nothing concealed inside.' Then, with a wave of his hand, he dismissed us, bored of the game or perhaps of the players, anxious to pit his strength against the fresh contingent waiting in line.

Aunt Annette led me swiftly through the shed. I was shaking so much that I could scarcely maintain my balance: I was as speechless as if he had crushed my tongue along with the shells: I felt as though *Kristallnacht* had been replayed in my own suit- case. Escape, however, was at hand for, after a final check of our passports, we were ejected unceremoniously on to the quay. All my feelings of despair disappeared at my first sighting of the *St Louis*. As I craned my neck to take it in – from the vast

expanse of hull, through the panoply of decks and lifeboats, to
the glow of the red and white chimneys – I told myself that this
was the shape of salvation. My musings were interrupted by my
grandfather, who whisked us towards the ship, as though terrified of a last-minute hitch. At the accommodation ladder we
were greeted by a group of young officers while, to one side, a
line of sailors, as spruce as an operetta chorus, stood with their
hands behind their backs. Then, in a final taste of the life we
were leaving behind, and a timely reminder of why we were right
to leave it, the porters dumped our cases at our feet. An officer
immediately instructed a trio of sailors to carry them aboard.
My mother, mistrusting their motives, grabbed the first one by
the arm.

'Where are you taking them?' she cried.

'To your cabin, madam,' he replied, perplexed. She backed
away, her face a heartbreaking mixture of gratitude and shame.
Meanwhile, further down the quay, the company band began to
play as if we were regular passengers. My grandfather stopped to
listen. A young officer, misconstruing, offered him his arm,
which sent him into a paroxysm of weeping. The officer looked
bewildered, but Aunt Annette moved to reassure him. Then,
wiping his eyes, my grandfather turned to me.

'The *Count of Luxembourg* waltz,' he said. 'It was your
grandmother's favourite. Franz Lehár often came to play for us
before the War. Do you suppose they realise that he was a J too?'

I could place neither the name nor the reference, but I knew
that it wasn't an appropriate moment to ask for clues. So I
smiled brightly, which seemed to set my grandfather's mind at
rest, and followed him on to the ship. Yet, far from racing up the
accommodation ladder like the heroes whose flights I had
cheered on the screen, I staggered forward as though my shoes
were filled with lead. Once on deck, my euphoria was replaced
by apprehension. Although we had escaped from German soil,

we were still on German territory, as was shown by the swastika flag flying from the mast. At any moment, a party of officials might march on board and confiscate our papers. My fears were evidently shared by my fellow passengers. Of the nine hundred or so due to travel, only a handful dared to stroll about in the open, the rest preferring to lock themselves in their cabins until we were safely at sea. But, when I saw the sailors sagging under the weight of our cases, I wondered whether I were being overly gloomy and the absentees were simply eager to unpack.

The sailors were so solicitous that we suspected them of mockery. 'He called me sir,' my grandfather kept repeating, shocked by the return to his former self. It was a reversal of everything that, for six long years, we had been taught was the natural order. Now we were the ones who risked rudeness with our guarded replies to their genial chat. The courtesy with which they led us down the labyrinth of corridors, pointing out the various public rooms, was itself such a surprise that I failed to take note of the names.

Further confusion awaited me when they showed us to our cabins and I found that I was to share one with my grandfather. While prepared to concede that, under the circumstances, no other arrangement was practical, I dreaded the enforced intimacy. Grandfather was a person who commanded respect, in the main because of his age and manner, but in part because of his clothes. Even at the height of summer, he never appeared without a collar and tie. Now I risked seeing him in his underwear – or worse. An adolescent revulsion to his ageing flesh mingled with a fear of acknowledging his frailty. I had a further cause for unease, one that I'm loath to admit to you, who, I suspect, view my body with the same disgust that I did his (I am starting to draw a wry consolation from the prospect that this chronicle may go unread). Ever since my abortive bar mitzvah, my mother had persisted in describing – and treating – me as a boy, and in regarding my principled refusal to compromise as a wilful refusal to grow up. The allocation of the cabins was the first indication that she considered me to be a man. I was convinced that this new status was a response not to a practical need but to a change in me, yet I was at a loss to determine what it was. The only visible change had been to my genitals and I kept that well hidden – from my mother most of all. I was scared that, now we were sharing a cabin, my grandfather would chance on me undressed and, with an unfailing instinct, see not only that I had hit puberty but that I was actively exploring its effects.

The one redeeming feature was that the cabin was spacious and the beds set against opposite walls. I was half-expecting bunks or even hammocks and made the mistake of saying so to my mother, who scoffed at my overactive imagination (which you might have thought that, as an artist, she would have admired). 'Just remember who you are,' she said with an assurance that she had regained far more quickly than the rest of us. It was hard to equate the woman who proclaimed that we were bona fide passengers, not beggars, with the one who had prodded me in the car to prevent my antagonising Ernst. Given her more combative mood, I wondered how she would bear to share a cabin with Aunt Annette, especially since, as an acknowledged adult, I was no longer obliged to pretend that they liked each other – at least not to myself. Even if their bathroom were as big as ours, it would be too small for all the pots and potions that Aunt Annette, in an unusually martial flourish, described as her 'war-paint'. I imagined their drawing an imaginary line across the room, or even a real one like Clark Gable and Claudette Colbert. But they went off together in apparent amity, followed by Sophie and Luise, whom I had consoled with a promise to tap messages on the dividing wall. I was left alone with Grandfather but, far from treating me to a few wise words which would sum up the entire journey, he sat on his bed in a daze. I offered to help him unpack, although my mother's reluctance to earmark cases for shipboard use made the prospect daunting. He didn't reply, but simply sat trembling, his eyelids aflutter, rubbing the crown of his head. My search for some way to revive him was checked by the entrance of a steward, who announced that tea would be served at four o'clock and dinner at eight. After Hamburg and the furtive eating arrangements, not to mention Berlin where the only restaurants open to us were Chinese, there could have been no clearer sign of our return to grace.

My grandfather's lethargy unnerved me and I told myself that it would be kinder to leave him to rest while I set out to explore. With painstaking precision, I determined to work from the promenade deck down and climbed the single flight of stairs from our cabin. Heaving open the door, I was hit by a pungent blast and the squall of seagulls, which, unique for birdsong, failed to move me. With the taste of salt on my tongue, I began to feel the excitement of the adventurer rather than the misery of the exile. Turning my back on Hamburg, I mapped out the territory from the quoits rings to the swimming pool. One glimpse of its grimy emptiness, however, dashed all my hopes of practising my favourite sport. I headed back inside, only to be warned by a passing sailor that the walkway was reserved for first-class passengers. Suppressing my annoyance, I assured him that I was eligible and entered a glass-covered area which, with its air of a convalescent home, struck me as perfect for Grandfather and Aunt Annette. I tried out one of the lounging chairs and, with a newfound deference, the sailor offered to fetch me a blanket. I declined but, to put him at his ease, asked a routine question about the tourist passengers.

'They have their own deck,' he explained. 'Like this, only not covered.'

'But in storms they must get wet.'

'Not half as wet as us.'

Sensing a slight reproach, I left him and continued my tour. I passed a cinema which was closed, although its programme promised hours of excitement. I immediately set about scheming to win round my mother, who distrusted any activity that took place in the dark. I entered the games room which, from its air of well-upholstered luxury, seemed set up for nothing more strenuous than dice. From there, I went into the smoking room, which was dark and plush with panelling as mellow as its patrons' cigars, and the social hall, which resembled a cross between a Tiergarten tea-room and a lecture theatre. Whether from a new spirit of freedom or an innate sense of anarchy, I felt a strong urge to bang the solitary drum sitting on stage, but – Edward, please note – I suppressed it. Finally, I wandered into the first class lounge, an airy room on two floors, which, with its sweeping central staircase, black-and-white marble tiles and elegant flower-festooned balconies, put me in mind of the ballroom at home.

Delicacy deterred me from visiting the rooms reserved for tourist passengers. I decided instead to sneak a glance at the nightclub, which I knew would be out of bounds to a fifteen-year-old whatever his ticket – not for the first time I wished that my new growth of hair had been on my upper lip where it might have served some purpose. From outside the door I heard a piano, but, as soon as I ventured in, the notes coalesced into one of the Nazi songs that had been stuffed into my mouth at school. My attempt to creep away was checked by a sharp voice from the dais. 'Young sir,' it announced in a tone suggesting that the two words stood in contradiction, 'a moment!' I turned to confront the speaker: a tall man with blond hair so fine that he might have been bald, a handsome, if flushed, face, and a rumpled steward's uniform. He slammed his beer mug carelessly on the piano. His six companions, whose unfamiliar uniforms were in similar disarray, watched while he lurched towards me as unsteadily as if we were already at sea.

'What are you doing in here?'

'Just taking my bearings. I'm sorry, I didn't realise it was private.'

'Are you spying on me?' He thrust his face in mine, sickening me with the sourness of his breath.

'How can I be?' I asked, determined to stand my ground, 'when I've no idea who you are.'

'Otto Schiendick,' he said proudly. 'Now you have me at a disadvantage. You are . . .?'

'Karl Frankel-Hirsch,' I replied, regretting yet again the compromise of my parents' marriage.

'Is one name not enough for you? Must you Jews have two of everything?' He affected the same wit as the classics master who had referred to me as hyphenated Hirsch, until the joke wore too thin for even my classmates' amusement. I remembered my mother's claim that we were bona fide passengers and went on to the attack.

'Shouldn't you be at work?' I asked. 'There are people who may require assistance.'

'I am Party representative on board,' he replied, taken in by the tone that I had shamelessly purloined from my mother. 'I have my own work.'

'And your friends?' I asked, intent on pressing my advantage.

'They are firemen.' He gazed at them wryly.

I failed to see why the ship needed so many firemen when it was surrounded by water. Schiendick, however, declared that a boatload of Jews brought its own danger. The voyage required particular vigilance against saboteurs. 'But never fear,' he said in a voice as curdled as his lip was curled, 'we're here to protect you.'

From the sneers on the firemen's faces, I feared that their

pumps might be filled with oil. My dignified exit was halted by Schiendick's cry of 'Heil Hitler!' Turning back, I saw seven arms poised like javelins in the air.

I ran up two flights on to the open deck. I started to retch but willed myself to recover for fear that a passer-by should suspect me of a prematurely weak stomach. My attention was diverted by a strong tremor in the bowels of the ship, which I soon identified as the weighing of the anchor. A glance at my watch showed that it was seven forty-five: in a quarter of an hour we would be free. I rushed to the side to take a final leave of my homeland, with the same sense of security as when I had stared at the snakes in the zoo. My elation was echoed by my fellow passengers, crowds of whom now left their cabins to line the rail. I smiled at the instinct that made them congregate in a single spot while a solitary man occupied the prow. Then I noticed the man's shaven head and shabby clothing and realised that there was another instinct at work. Defying the general cravenness, I wandered up to stand beside him but, far from expressing gratitude, he declined to acknowledge my presence. The stench emanating from his coat made me gag; nevertheless I was determined to conquer my disgust and attempt to strike up a conversation. I introduced myself and he finally turned towards me, revealing a far younger face than I had expected, apart from the eyes, which (and I swear to you that this isn't hindsight) betrayed a pain that predated it by hundreds of years. It was almost with relief that I shifted my gaze to the visible mark of suffering on his forehead. Lost for words, I thought of my mother and asked if he were travelling with his family.

'My family are dead.'

'All of them?' I asked, as if such misfortune must be relieved at least by a distant cousin.

'All of them,' he repeated, more in irritation than in grief. To keep from dwelling on such desolation, I asked if he were travelling with friends. His scornful laugh rendered his reply obsolete. 'I have no friends.'

'None?' I asked, appalled that such a fate could befall an adult.

'I had a travelling companion for whom I made the mistake of feeling compassion.'

'Where is he?'

'To the best of my knowledge, in Hanover.'

'Was he imprisoned?'

'No, by God.' His need to vent his anger outweighing his relish of my confusion, he told the story. 'You know what day it is?' he asked, by way of preamble.

'Of course. 13th May 1939.'

'No. What day of the week?'

'Saturday.'

'Right. Tali was a Hasid who refused to travel on the Sabbath. We should have arrived yesterday morning, but we were pulled off the train by the Gestapo. We were questioned – not just verbally – for the rest of the day. We begged to be set free. We showed them our tickets. But it was a quiet afternoon and they wanted their fun. When they finally spat us out – and I mean *spat* – it was dusk. Tali sat outside the building. I told him that God would forgive him for breaking the Sabbath. I reminded him that the Rabbis had allowed soldiers to eat pork in the trenches. I promised him that he could atone by studying Torah for the rest of his life. But he wouldn't budge.'

'It's dusk now.'

'So?'

'He might still come.'

'How?' he asked with stinging scorn. 'Do you think God will send a chariot of fire to fetch him like Elijah?'

'I'm sorry,' I said. 'But you mustn't assume the worst. Perhaps they'll let him transfer his ticket to another ship.'

'It's not him I'm concerned about, it's me! How could I ever have lumbered myself with such a credulous fool?'

He peered at the shore, where the gathering darkness seemed to muffle the pain of departure. Unlike the other passengers, however, his eyes were fixed not on the lights of the city but on the docks.

'Have you been to Havana before?' I asked, with first-class politeness.

'Oh sure. I was there in '22 with Leni and Fritzi. We yachted over from Miami. . . . What do you think?'

'I'm just trying to be friendly. You're worse than the firemen.'

'What firemen?' For the first time I had captured his interest.

'The ones who were singing Nazi songs in the nightclub.'

'You boy,' he said, as if it were the greatest insult. 'They're Gestapo agents.'

'But we're leaving Germany.'

'We'll never leave Germany.'

'You mean they won't let us sail?'

'No. There's no need to look so worried. Now I must go back to my cabin.'

'To bathe before dinner?' I asked over-eagerly.

He gazed at me and burst out laughing. 'You've made me laugh. Thank you.' Then he moved away, leaving me afraid both that I had betrayed my ignorance and that I might never have a chance to speak to him again. He was so alien from the world of my childhood that I felt sure we had met for a purpose. If I were to start a new life in America, then it would have to encompass, or at the very least acknowledge, men like him.

'I don't know your name,' I said. He turned back and, without speaking, pointed to the scar on his forehead. As he disappeared down the deck, I was left to reflect on the gesture. Was he telling me that a blow to the head had left him with amnesia and he no longer remembered his name? Or was it a riddle whose clue was the scar? If so, my first answer, born of my love for gangster films, was Scarface. On reflection, however, I realised that it was far simpler: not a scar but a Mark. And, with renewed faith in my powers of perception after my failure with the firemen, I turned to watch as, following a mournful blast on the whistle, the *St Louis* slid sedately out to sea.

The departing ship was accompanied by a flotilla of small craft that clung limpet-like to the hull. A loud cheer rang out, so harmonious that it sounded rehearsed. I felt a surge of goodwill towards my fellow passengers: I may not have known their names but I knew what was in their hearts. The years of ignominy were over. Never again would I hurry down a street on which a Jewish boy was being beaten, or hide from a crowd that was forcing an elderly rabbi to dance. No sooner had I framed my resolve, however, than it was threatened by the man heading towards me. It must be hard for you children, blessed with parents who are, if anything, over-protective, to appreciate my hatred of the father who had abandoned me. To see him stroll down the deck so casually was my worst nightmare. Stifling a shout, I darted into the shadows and, steadying myself on a lifebelt, watched him walk by, as oblivious of my presence as he had been for the past eight years. I willed myself not to panic. Logic dictated that it must be a delusion, a repeat of my error with the vagrant. Although the likeness was uncanny, a moment's reflection on the full head of hair and boyish face was enough to reassure me, since no one – least of all someone so gnawed by conscience – was immune to the passage of time. My treacherous mind was playing tricks, teasing me with a final image of home.

My stomach rumbled in confirmation. It came as no surprise that, having eaten nothing all day, I should begin to hallucinate.

Help, however, was at hand. A glance at my watch showed that I was missing dinner. I raced back to the cabin to find my grand-father, in evening clothes, balancing a tray of soup on his knees. He assured me that he felt fine but added that the effort of dressing had drained him and he was not yet ready to brave the dining room. He demanded a full report, warning me to hurry as the others had long since left. Ashamed of having neglected him, I offered to stay but, whether he detected a note of reluctance or simply relished his solitude, he refused to hear of it. So following a quick change of shirt, I made straight for the dining room, where I was met by a maître d' so schoolmasterly that I half-expected to be banished to the corridor for the duration of the meal. With a slight bow of the head, he led me to our table. 'This is my son, Karl,' my mother announced to the assembled company. A swift assessment of their ages convinced me that nothing would charm them more than a display of perfect manners combined with concern for their own generation. So I apologised profusely for arriving late, explaining that I had stayed to help my grandfather. Sophie shot me an ironic smile which I affected to take at face value. I sat between her and Aunt Annette, while my mother introduced me to our fellow diners: a retired professor of linguistics and his wife from Bremen and a banker and his wife from Cologne. It turned out that Mrs Banker (I trust you'll forgive the nursery epithet since I cannot remember her name and, in view of all that occurred on the voyage, I'm loath to bury her in a fiction) had served in the Cologne branch of the Jewish Winter Aid Fund that my mother had chaired in Berlin. But any hopes she might have entertained that this would foster a shipboard intimacy were doomed to disappointment, since Mother regarded the work, however valu-able, as a distraction and her colleagues as a bore.

My reflections were interrupted by the presentation of the menu. I could not believe its scope and, as I gazed at the wealth of dishes, it struck me that the greatest of all freedoms was choice. Mine, however, was cruelly curtailed when my order of asparagus followed by rack of lamb (largely for the picnic pleasure of eating with my hands) was countermanded by my mother on the grounds that I risked being sea-sick.

'I've never been sea-sick in my life.'

'You've never been to sea in your life.'

'Exactly. So how can you know?'

She heaved a sigh which, to my exasperation, suggested that she was the one who was suffering. 'He's at a difficult age,' she declared to her new allies. Over the years, I had gleaned that this was equally true of middle-aged women (although, to my mind, it involved them in nothing more arduous than restorative trips to the hairdresser and beautician) and was preparing to say as much when Aunt Annette gave me a restraining tap on the thigh. We struck a compromise whereby I would sacrifice the lamb but keep the asparagus, which I took particular pleasure in jiggling in the sauce.

Leading us out at the end of the meal, Mother pronounced it to have been an ordeal, which was unkind because I could tell that Aunt Annette had been about to say how much she enjoyed it. One point, however, on which they did agree was that, after such a gruelling day, they needed to go straight to bed. Sophie, declaring that she had found her second wind, proposed to take coffee in the lounge. I offered to accompany her.

'You don't drink coffee,' my mother said.

'You're always telling me I should change.'

'Not one of your few good habits.'

'So Sophie has bad habits?'

'Sophie is old enough to decide what's good and bad for herself. You should listen to people who've been on this earth a little longer than you.'

'By that reckoning, I should listen to Hitler and Goebbels.'

'There's no arguing with you,' my mother said. 'Just don't come running to me when you lie awake all night.'

As she walked away, I turned to the others. 'It's not fair. She says that there's no arguing with me when what she should say is that there's no winning an argument.' Aunt Annette, as emollient as ever, claimed that Mother was under a great deal of strain, worrying about Grandfather.

'But you're worried about him too,' I said.

'Thank you, my dear,' she replied, and, to my embarrassment, tears welled in her eyes as she kissed my cheek.

As soon as she left, I turned to Sophie and offered her my arm. 'Don't be ridiculous,' she said and strode off so fast that I had difficulty keeping pace. Her mood softened as we entered the lounge, which was already quite crowded. The gentle motion of the ship appeared to have heartened the passengers, who greeted us with smiles and nods. Once we had found a table, Sophie asked if I ever thought about anyone but myself, a question that was not only cruel but stupid since she, of all people, knew how often I thought about Luise.

'We're like a couple,' I said.

'A couple of what?'

'Friends,' I replied, feeling very small.

'Karl, I'm twenty-eight years old,' she said, a statement as pointless as her question, since her age was as familiar to me as my own. I could name each of the five birthday presents I had given her and, with a pang, I realised that my memory of them was probably sharper than hers. 'I don't suppose it occurred to you that I might want to be alone?'

'You mean to meet a man?'

'What?'

'Who'll kiss you in the moonlight, even though he's married. Then we'll all have the right to stone you. As it says in the Torah, "the adulteress shall surely be put to death".'

'And where are you going to find stones on the ship?', she asked, staring at me in amazement.

'We can throw lifebelts.' She burst out laughing. 'Don't laugh at me!' I shouted. 'You laugh, and Mother laughs, and no one takes me seriously.'

At that moment, the waiter brought the coffee. I gritted my teeth and asked for mine black, which I knew to be the grown-up way. Sophie looked surprised but said nothing.

'I'm sorry if I've been sharp with you,' she said, as the waiter moved off. 'I must be on edge about leaving.'

'Aren't you excited about Havana?'

'What'll there be for me to do there?'

'Look after Luise, the same as always.'

'I love Luise with all my heart. I love you all. But I want something more out of life.'

'You could be a film star.'

'Oh Karl . . .'

'I mean it. You're pretty enough. You could go to Hollywood and be in magazines like Lilian Harvey.'

'You're very sweet . . . and that's just it. One day I want a child of my own.'

'I am not a child!' And, to prove it, I gulped my coffee, which tasted so bitter that it burnt.

'Don't forget I'm leaving behind more than you are.'

'Just more years.'

'And my family.'

'We're your family.'

'Maybe now. But there's also the one I was born to.'

'I thought they were dead.'

'Only to me. Or rather, I am to them.' She went on to explain that, although declaring them dead eased the pain of their disaffection, her parents, two brothers and three sisters were all alive and living in Füssen. She added that, as a Berliner born and bred,

I could have no conception of small-town mentality, before admitting that, now that it had taken over the entire country, perhaps I had. She herself had escaped to university at the age of twenty, only to learn, on returning home, that her father had joined the Nazis. I expressed astonishment that a Jew could ever be a member of the Party. After a momentary confusion, she declared that anything was possible in a world gone mad. Her disputes with her father had turned so violent that he had thrown her out of the house, forcing her to abandon her studies and find work. She insisted that she had no regrets about her decision, except for the people that it meant she would never see again. I tried to imagine never seeing Mother or Grandfather or Aunt Annette or Luise and, while a part of me felt a disconcerting rush of relief, the rest filled with horror. Then I thought of my father and the figure I had glimpsed on deck. I confided in Sophie, explaining that, while I knew it to be an illusion, it was preying on my mind.

'There's one simple way to settle it,' she said, as, with enviable authority, she summoned a waiter and asked him to fetch a passenger list.

'He may be travelling incognito,' I said, sure that everything about my father must be underhand.

'It's hard enough to obtain a passport in a real name,' she said, 'let alone a false one.'

The waiter returned with the list. A quick flick through the names confirmed that my sighting had been correct. There he was: Hirsch, Georg, Passenger Tourist Class.

I was suddenly, sickeningly, aware of the ship's motion. I dug my fingers into the arms of the chair but failed to regain my balance. Never had the scale of Hitler's policies struck me more forcibly than that a family so at war with itself should be fleeing from the same fate. I felt as though a stowaway had hidden in my cabin and held me captive. I had to think fast. My prime concern was to protect my mother from a meeting that would, in all probability, kill her. I voiced my fears to Sophie, who insisted that my mother was stronger than I supposed before adding – inexplicably – that protecting others was often a way of protecting oneself. Eliciting her promise to do nothing until I had consulted Grandfather, I left her in the lounge and returned to the cabin where I found that, although the light was on and his eyes were open, Grandfather appeared to be fast asleep. His head rested darkly on the pillow and the only sign of life was in his hands, which flitted over the sheets. My entrance must have disturbed him, for he called out my name. 'I'm here, Grandfather,' I answered, adding that I had been downstairs drinking coffee, in the hope that he might be reassured by this new sign of maturity. 'Is there something you want?'

'Karl,' he said. 'I want Karl.'

'But I'm here,' I declared, doubly disturbed by his confusion. I leant over to meet his gaze when, with unexpected force, his hands sprang up and grabbed me by the throat.

'No, you're an impostor! My Karl: what have you done with him?'

I realised with a jolt that he was referring to my uncle, in whose shadow I was once again lost. Loosening his hold, I tried to comfort him. 'He's well, Grandfather,' I said. 'Uncle Karl is well. We've received a letter from the Front. I'll read it to you in the morning.'

'Thank God!' my grandfather said, slumping back.

'Amen,' I replied mechanically. While giving thanks for the simple ploy that had relieved his mind, I saw no other reason for gratitude. It was clear that, however else I was to solve the problem of my father, I could no longer look to my grandfather for help.

Sleep was fitful, punctuated by my grandfather's moans and mutterings. When I finally dozed off, I was gripped by a nightmare in which my father fell overboard, although I have to admit that it was not the prospect of his drowning that scared me so much as an uneasy feeling that I was the one who had pushed him. Prompted by passengers who had heard his cries, I dived in to save him (the elegance of the dive should itself have alerted me to its being a dream). As I raised his head above the waves, his teeth turned into a shark's and he tore a chunk out of my chest. No sooner had he swallowed it than he underwent a further transformation and I found myself in the belly of a whale, confronting an elderly, rubicund man with a short temper. He accused me of trespass, insisting that the stomach was too small for both of us. When I protested that I had as much right to be there as he had, he hurled insults at the Jews who stole other people's living space. I replied that he was a Jew himself, called Jonah, and his story was in the Bible, at which he raged even louder and showed me his Party membership badge. Then, just as he started to strangle me, I woke up. A dull grey light filtered into the room. I crept to the window and peered out on the misty seascape. I was weighing up whether to return to bed for another hour's sleep when two terns swept majestically into view. Their grace and zest shamed my sluggishness and I resolved to join them. Justifying my reluctance to wash as a fear of waking my grandfather, I pulled on my clothes and, grabbing the binoculars that Aunt Annette had bought me from the ship's shop the night before, I ran up on deck.

A soul-stirring sight awaited me as a flock of tern soared through the sky, sublimely indifferent to the human travellers below. I watched rapt and, although able to hear nothing, I seemed to be seeing in sounds as they formed into notes from a

Chopin étude. I was grateful that they were so familiar for, while I would never have admitted it to Aunt Annette, the replacement binoculars were barely powerful enough to make out the basic markings, and I feared that she had wasted her meagre allowance of shipboard marks. I was so lost in my fantasy of flight that I failed to notice that I had company, until I found myself face to face with a sailor, no taller than myself though a good forty years older, with sparkling eyes and a speckled beard and a drop at the end of his nose that, had we met indoors, would have disgusted me but that, out here, felt at one with the elements. He made up for his lack of height by the dignity of his bearing. I had never seen such a ramrod back, which put me in mind of a wooden figure beating the hour on a town hall clock.

To my alarm, he introduced himself as the Captain and asked what I was doing out here so early. I was terrified that I had broken a rule and, in my babbling apology, swore that I had not been spying but rather looking at birds. He was clearly perturbed by my agitation, assuring me that I had done nothing wrong and that, on the contrary, we shared an interest, since he had been a fervent birdwatcher from the age of five. Growing up on the land, he had known the names of the different species the way that city boys knew cars. He had never supposed them worthy of study, however, until, one Sunday, the Pastor had taken as his text Jesus' injunction to observe the fowls of the air who did not sow or reap but were fed by God. That single line had served to legitimise his love. He dug fields and chopped wood for neighbours until he had saved up enough to buy a pair of binoculars. He made himself a hide in the woods and his interest had remained undimmed ever since. Then a shadow crossed his face and he apologised for mentioning Christ.

I assured him that there was no need, worried that he might suppose me either ignorant or blinkered. 'Sometimes I think there is,' he said, fixing me with his most powerful gaze. Then, with a smile, he added that he suspected he had only gone to sea to savour something of a bird's freedom.

'You could have piloted a plane.'

'It wasn't so easy back then. Besides, I had no money. Some paths aren't open to everyone.'

'I know,' I said, feeling both sad and wise.

'Yes, I suppose you do.'

Encouraged by his friendliness, I explained how, when I was young (a phrase that made him smile, but sympathetically), I had a recurrent dream of flying. I once delighted a group of my mother's friends, although not my mother herself, by informing them that, in my true life, I was a bird and my human body was a mere disguise. My father bought me a book by Leonardo da Vinci, whose name alone fed my boyhood fantasies, with drawings of a flying machine that had been invented over four hundred years before. I think he believed that, by steering my mind in a practical direction, he would save me from future disappointment (in relating the story, I felt an unexpected surge of filial affection), but no sooner had he handed me the book than my mother confiscated it, fearful that it would shift my dreams of flight from the safety of my bed to the danger of the balcony. A compromise was found when my aunt gave me a pair of binoculars and a guide to native German birds. My imagination was fired. I set up a bird table in our garden in Berlin and went on field trips in the country. I enlisted two of my friends and, when they defected, carried on alone.

'The birds were there for me,' I said, 'when people proved false. However low I might be, I felt better just for looking out of the window and seeing them. There might be nothing more than a pair of sparrows. On the other hand, there might be something really special. One holiday in Saxony, I saw a white-tailed eagle.' I searched for a sign of scepticism that a mere boy should have seen a bird that had eluded seasoned ornithologists, but he simply nodded. 'What's odd is that I'm not naturally patient. I can go mad when a train arrives late or I'm waiting for a meal to begin. But, out birding, I lose all sense of time. I'm happy to spend hours watching for a bullfinch or a brambling to return to its nest.'

To stress my credentials, I explained that I'd built up an extensive library, as well as a set of research notes and a collection of eggs. . . . I shuddered as my tongue outstripped my memory, but I felt that it would be discourteous to elaborate. Instead, I expressed my determination not to leave Cuba without seeing the bee hummingbird which, as well as being the world's smallest bird, had a heartbeat over ten times faster than ours. Fired by my enthusiasm, he quizzed me on the world's largest bird, which, as you all know, is the ostrich . . . although I had to admit that it interested me as little as an unseaworthy ship. He then told me about an even larger bird that had lived 150 years ago in New Zealand, the Dinornis Maximus, a giant moa, that grew to twice the size of a man. I feared that he was able to read my mind for, just as I was wondering whether that was twice the size of a normal man or simply twice the size of someone as small as him, he specified 'almost four metres tall', adding that it became extinct under human pressure.

'It's hateful to think of something as beautiful as a bird being destroyed by something as cruel as a man,' I said.

'Often it's not just the birds that are victims.'

His implication emboldened me. 'Some people think that Hitler won't rest until he's made all the Jews extinct,' I replied.

'That's nonsense,' he said sharply. 'Hitler is just one man. Besides, the Dinornis Maximus couldn't fly. It was stuck on the island. You can migrate like the terns.'

'But they come back again every spring,' I said, gazing skywards. 'It won't be so easy for us.' My words alerted me to a sorrow that I hadn't realised I felt.

'I must go inside,' the Captain said. 'I'm neglecting my duties. . . . No, don't worry, this has been a most agreeable encounter. But I'm in the middle of an inspection.' He pointed to my binoculars. 'Keep up the good work. Should you see something remarkable, be sure to let me know.' His confidence increased my frustration and, without thinking, I told him what had happened at the docks, adding that I doubted I would make any discoveries since the lenses in the new binoculars were too weak. He replied, with perceptible bitterness, that orders had come down from Hapag head office that the shop was not to carry its usual range of merchandise but to buy in inferior stock. 'I'm sorry, but my jurisdiction only stretches so far.' As he turned to go, I was struck by an image that I was eager to share.

'You're like Moses leading the Children of Israel out of Egypt.'

'I'm an Egyptian, Karl. Whether I like it or not.'

At breakfast, the excitement of my meeting with the Captain was eclipsed by the appearance of my grandfather. As the ladies of our party fussed over him and the others at the table cooed their pleasure at an introduction to the owner of the legendary store, I consoled myself with the thought of the supposed madman who declared that he talked to himself in order to enjoy intelligent conversation. My poor grandfather must have wished that he had stayed in the cabin as Mother and Aunt Annette bickered over how best to build on his recovery, their respective suggestions of a brisk walk and a rest being almost too neat a reflection of their characters. With Grandfather's morning mapped out like a school timetable, I mused on the comparison between children and the sick in a way that was flattering to neither. My reverie was interrupted when the Professor's wife berated the waiter about the state of her egg, claiming that her request for it to be boiled for three and a half minutes, which (and, here, she appealed to the rest of us for support) she trusted that she had enunciated clearly, had been wilfully ignored. 'Three and a half minutes means three and a half minutes, not three and certainly not four.' Having subjected the hapless waiter to a humiliating rebuke, she then demanded that he return with a second egg, correctly cooked.

'How soon some people forget,' my grandfather murmured.

'I beg your pardon?' the woman asked, proving that her ear was as sharp as her tongue. Grandfather, assuming a diplomatic deafness, simply asked her to pass the jam. Meanwhile, the Banker's wife regaled my mother with an interminable story of how her husband had sold her Persian carpets for the price of coconut matting. Watching him slice his cheese, I suspected that, after two weeks of such close confinement, it would not be the Nazis that my fellow passengers would want to flee so much as their husbands and wives. Then I gazed at the one wife who had no idea that her husband was aboard and all my anxiety returned.

A gentle-looking woman, all cardigan and curls, came up and introduced herself to Mother as the shipboard guardian of two young girls who, having spotted Luise at the table, hoped that she would play with them. She pointed across the room to where the girls, in identical dress despite their age-gap, smiled and waved. I alone opposed the plan, although I was aware of undermining my case when, provoked by a sceptical glance from Sophie, I concluded a list of hazards with 'falling overboard and being eaten by sharks'. Mother chose to let Luise decide for herself, which she only ever did when she could be sure of obtaining the desired response. Luise, who could barely tear her gaze from her would-be companions, startled the woman by thumping the table and roaring 'She wants!' Mother blithely explained Luise's verbal idiosyncrasies. 'She always speaks in the third person and the present tense. There's no I, you, he or they in my daughter's vocabulary, just a blanket she. It's as if, in her innocence, she's removed all distinctions between past and present and herself and the rest of the world.' The woman's uneasy smile betrayed her doubts. I felt my usual contempt for my mother's disingenuousness in attributing Luise's defects either to innocence, which implied that the rest of us were guilty, or slowness, which implied that she might one day catch up.

Luise's lumbering gait and dragging foot looked more pronounced than ever as Sophie steered her through the maze of tables and trolleys. I was appalled that my fears for her safety had not been shared, and reproached my mother for entrusting her to strangers when I had promised to take her exploring myself. Her no doubt withering reply was pre-empted by the Professor's wife's interjection that, last night on deck, she had met two charming boys of about my age – I winced – who were planning a game of shuffleboard. She was sure that they would welcome a third. 'Oh that won't suit Karl,' my mother said. 'He's always been a loner.' I stared at her in amazement and wondered whether she knew anything about me at all. In her words, I saw the origins of a myth: Karl's a loner so we'll buy him a book for his birthday; Karl's a loner so he prefers birds to people; Karl's a loner so he won't be interested in girls. Were she to give it a moment's thought, she would see that Karl was a loner because his friends had betrayed him; Karl was a loner because a class of twenty-two pupils had become twenty-one in all but name; Karl was a loner because his faithless blood brother, Johannes von Hirte, had sworn that, if he ever told a soul about their thumb prick, if he ever breathed a word about the mingling of Jewish and Aryan blood, then he would denounce him to the SS.

I spent the morning on deck, confirming my mother's view of my disposition by standing alone among hordes of happy people who were relaxing, taking photographs and making friends. I replied politely to the occasional remark but refused to join in the general chatter. The problem of my father preoccupied me and I decided to seek him out, making it clear, lest he should harbour any illusions, that he would never be able to claw his way back into our hearts. I reminded myself of the effect that he had had, not just on Luise, his most blatant victim, but on Grandfather, who had been forced to assume a new set of responsibilities, and on Mother, who had withdrawn into her art. I looked back with longing to the time before he left home – not to my father himself, on whose image I placed as many prohibitions as the Orthodox did on food, but to my mother, who had since become a different person. It was like comparing pictures of before and after a fire. She had not only turned against my father but me. No longer did she come upstairs at tea-time to question me on my day and plan how we would spend the evening; no longer did she rub every bruise and soothe every slight. Instead, she shut herself up in her studio where she must only ever be disturbed in an emergency; instead, she raged against every interruption to her 'flow', whether it be a visit from a friend, a meeting of a committee, or a request from her son.

The only time that she chose to spend with me was when she was painting my portrait – which she did with alarming frequency. To make matters worse, the results were hung in an annual exhibition in the central hall of my grandfather's store, in full view of all my classmates. For one interminable term at the age of ten, Blueface became my universal nickname. The following year, however, even the most inveterate mockers were silenced by the giant canvas in which I appeared to be attacked by a swarm of butterflies. They no doubt regarded its public display as humiliation enough. I was relieved to be beyond their reach when, during her final show in the summer of 1938, my fourteen year-old face looked as creviced and cracked as an ancient mosaic. I had no redress. Any attempt to elicit a meaning would precipitate a lecture on my place in her iconography, while a refusal to sit unleashed a tirade on my efforts to sabotage her work. I blamed her behaviour entirely on my father. Without him, she would have been content to play Scarlatti and embroider napkins like other boys' mothers, rather than holding up her pictures as though they were the Scrolls of the Law.

Desperate to prevent my father's return from reopening the wounds of his defection, I resolved to seek him out and give him the chance to hide honourably in his cabin until we reached Cuba, when he could head straight for some remote part of the island. I scoured the ship without success and was contemplating whether to knock on his door when I caught sight of Mark, gazing out to sea. I hurried up to the rail, as eager to talk to him as I was to avoid the rest of the passengers.

'You look sad,' I said, 'is there anything I can do?'

'Such consideration,' he said. 'You first-class Jews are so kind.'

'My grandfather built holiday homes for his employees.'

'Then he's assured of his place among the righteous.'

'I don't think you should say that.'

'I don't think you should stand here harassing me.'

'I'm a loner. We're two of a kind.'

'You must have heard the expression: "the half is often better than the whole"?'

'Of course.'

'Well, it applies to us.'

Although I was hurt by his tone, I was grateful to be talking to someone whose horizons weren't limited to carpets. I braced myself to ask the question that had been haunting me from the first moment I saw him: had he been sent to one of the camps? He congratulated me on my perception, but his irony was exposed when, having established that he had been released for almost a month, I asked why he had not grown back his hair. Receiving no answer, I supplied my own: that he wanted to make the rest of us feel guilty. It was for the same reason that, in spite of the ready supply of hot water, he had still not bathed.

'I've obviously met my match in you,' he said, before adding with flagrant perversity: 'So why do you seek me out? Have you been so brainwashed by all the talk of dirty Jews that you'll only be happy when you are one? Am I what you want to become?'

Refusing to stoop to a reply, I told him that my grandfather had been imprisoned for six weeks last November. He had suffered no ill-effects apart from fatigue (loyalty drew a veil over the lice) and, as ever, smelt of eau-de-cologne. I offered to bring a bottle for Mark and, when he asked why, explained that it might encourage the other passengers to talk to him. 'Or do you think you have nothing in common?'

'I have everything in common but nothing to say.'

Baffled, I focused on his accent and asked where he was from. 'Somewhere East of Eden,' he replied and, failing to provoke a reaction, added 'a town in the Ukraine'. He stared at me intently and then, as though deciding that to tell his story would cause me more distress than to withhold it, described how he had been settled in Germany for nearly twenty years. At first he had made a living as a pedlar, selling ribbons and cloth, but he had been driven out by the competition. 'You know my greatest complaint against the Nazis?' he asked with a sly smile. 'That they took the decency out of peddling. It used to be an honest profession until all the riffraff – the doctors and lawyers, no longer able to fleece their clients – packed their suitcases and went on the road.'

Eager to establish a bond, I told him that my family had started out as pedlars and felt that, for the first time, I had caught him by surprise. Quoting from the history that my grandfather had commissioned in the 1920s, only to see it suppressed in the following decade, I told him how the source of our prosperity could be dated to 1812, when Napoleon's army was retreating from Moscow. The soldiers had abandoned their weapons in order to carry back as much booty as they could. By the time that they reached Prussia, however, they were demoralised and famished, and ready to trade the most precious treasures for a handful of potatoes, beans or peas, or even, according to family legend, for a kiss from a pretty girl. So my canny ancestor bought up all his neighbours' provisions and loaded them on his sledge (along with his ruby-lipped daughter), returning home three days later, laden with gold and silver and jewels. Although aspects of the story made me uneasy, I took heart from the thought of Jacob, whose deception of the ravenous Esau was the model for all such transactions. It was his house that God had favoured just as, four thousand years later, he had ours.

'So now you intend to begin again: to become good Americans as you were once good Germans, saluting the Flag and celebrating Thanksgiving. Until they throw us out in their turn.'

'They'll never do that. Haven't you heard of the Statue of Liberty? In any case, we must stand up and show the world that we'll thrive, no matter how cruelly we're treated.'

'You think that the world will thank us for it? Such naivety in one so young!'

'And if we don't – if we stay in the dirt where they kick us – who'll be the ones to suffer? Ourselves.'

'Oh no, we'll be hurting someone much greater and more powerful than ourselves.'

While I was working out whether he meant Hitler or some other leader, he looked me up and down and, with a curt 'You bore me!', walked away. Though initially stung, I soon shrugged off the charge. That I was callous (my mother), parasitical (the Nazis) and ugly (myself) had struck home, but I utterly denied being boring. For a start, I could recite the name of every species of bird in Germany, along with an account of its natural habitat, breeding habits and approximate population. The accusation was especially unfair, since I had only approached him out of charity. I took comfort from an image of myself in some conversational soup kitchen, doling out platefuls of nourishing words. But the image faded and the sting returned and, in an attempt to forestall further harm, I retreated to my cabin, where I was shocked to find Grandfather lying in bed, tended by Mother, Aunt Annette and the Ship's Doctor. I realised that his condition must be grave when I fired off a battery of questions and, rather than silencing me, Mother hung attentively on the Doctor's replies. He explained that Grandfather's heart was failing. Having used up all his strength in preparing for the voyage, he had collapsed from a mixture of strain and relief. The most that anyone could do for him now was to make him comfortable.

'That's not true,' I protested, 'the most we can do is make him well.'

'You can always pray,' he said, breaking off in embarrassment as though our prayers were by definition defective. Neither my mother nor my aunt spoke. I studied their faces which, for the first time, were fixed in identical expressions, and that scared me most of all. The Doctor packed his bag and Mother saw him out of the cabin, establishing that she was the one to whom he should report. Meanwhile, I looked to Aunt Annette for reassurance. I failed to see how strain and relief could do such damage to a person's body . . . but then I was fifteen, the age when, to escape the frustrations of puberty, my body was at its most detached from my emotions. She insisted that the hurt had been inflicted in the camps.

'He told us that he had been well treated.'

'Do you think that he told us the truth?'

'Perhaps not to me, but surely to you?'

'I saw the truth; I didn't hear it.'

I was stunned by her disloyalty, not just to my grandfather but to the adult cause. I had presumed that grown-ups reserved their lies for children; here was evidence that they practised them on each other.

'It was the same with your Uncle Karl. He wrote letters from the Front that gave no inkling of the horror of the trenches. Right to the end, your grandmother believed that, every night after a hard day's fighting, he went back to a well-heated hut.'

My mother's return put paid to further revelations. I joined her and Aunt Annette in their vigil, envying their unfeigned concentration on the comatose figure in bed. My own patience soon gave out and I dropped heavy hints about lunch. My mother refused to quit the cabin and, when even Aunt Annette claimed to have lost her appetite, I knew that I must be totally uncaring. The realisation increased my desire to escape but, on reaching the dining room, I found that Sophie had taken Luise to sit with her playmates, leaving me totally at the mercy of the Professor's wife. She began by relating, with relish, the 'tragedy' of the two little girls who were travelling alone to Havana to meet their father, since their mother, a Catholic, had chosen to stay behind with her boyfriend. She pronounced the woman's religion with such contempt, as if it explained both her adultery and her desertion, that I wondered whether we were not as guilty of intolerance as our enemies. Then, shamelessly sliding across two empty seats, she filled the gap between courses by quizzing me on my grandfather's financial arrangements in selling the store. Convinced that my confusion was a ploy, she pressed for answers until her husband finally told her to 'leave the boy alone'. She snapped that she was only showing an interest and, besides, she had a right to ask since she had yet to be reimbursed for a chipped teapot. Deciding that no chocolate cake in the world was worth such torture, I fled, postponing a return to the cabin in favour of a visit to the tourist deck, where I was more determined than ever to confront my father, whose reappearance in our lives would now be a disaster.

I was deflected by the sight of a girl my own age, standing at the rail, throwing bread to the terns. She was so beautiful and poised that, in normal circumstances, I would have slunk away, but her solicitude emboldened me to approach her.

'They're wonderful, aren't they?'

'They're all right.'

'I hope you don't mind me butting in, but it's my hobby.'

'Accosting strangers?'

'No!' I exclaimed. 'Birds! Ask me anything you want to know about them. Go on.'

'I had a friend with a passion for trains,' she replied, disdaining my offer. 'He spent days taking down numbers. He knew the entire Berlin timetable by heart.'

'There's no comparison,' I said, more concerned to fight my corner even than to discover the nature of the friendship. 'Trains are inert. Mechanical. Birds are alive. They sing. They fly. They're intelligent.'

'What about birdbrains?'

'These ones are terns. I couldn't swear to the species – '

'You said I could ask you anything.'

'I'm not an expert on seabirds. At least not yet.' I trembled at my immodesty. 'If I'm right, these are Arctic Terns on their way home from the Antarctic. They go there every winter on a journey of nearly 20,000 kilometres. That's 40,000 there and back.'

'I can count!'

'What I mean,' I floundered, 'is when you think how much effort we make for a few days' holiday, let alone a voyage like this. And they fly all that way without the least fuss. We can learn a lot from birds.'

'What about thieving magpies or cuckoos that abandon their chicks? Or vultures?'

'What about them?'

'Should we learn from them too?'

'They're exceptions. Most birds are loving and loyal. You know, of course, about turtle doves?'

'All that billing and cooing. Yuck!'

'But have you heard of the huia bird, which died of grief when its mate was killed?'

'Says who? Have you ever seen one?'

'How could I? I've never been to New Zealand. In any case, it's extinct.'

'I'm not surprised.' She gazed at me triumphantly and I realised that I would be happy to admit defeat provided that I could see her smile. I studied her intently, to her alternate pleasure and annoyance. She was exactly my height. I was convinced that, if we stood back to back (or mouth to mouth, as my mutinous mind suggested), there would be nothing between us. She had frizzy auburn hair, pulled back in a band from which a few wisps strayed on to her forehead, and a patch of freckles around her eyes, which gave her a permanently summery look even when she scowled. She had a small turned-up nose, such bright red lips that I felt sure her teachers must have constantly asked her to wipe them, and a slight gap between her two front teeth. Shifting my attention lower, I could see that her figure was shapely – not a word much in vogue today but one which perfectly reflected my feelings, since I was impressed less by the nature of her shape than by the mere fact that she had one. Her amusement at my attentions made me blush and I quickly asked her name.

'Johanna,' she replied. 'Johanna Paulsen.'

'I'm Karl.' Then, suppressing a pang of disloyalty, I dropped the Frankel and all its baggage. 'Karl Hirsch.'

'I've seen you already. Yesterday. You were walking on the sports deck with a crippled Mongolian girl.' Her description of Luise made me shudder. Under normal circumstances, it would have put paid to both the conversation and our friendship, but my conviction that she spoke out of ignorance rather than malice prompted me to set her straight.

'She's my sister. She's neither Mongolian nor crippled but was born with a minor brain dysfunction, which impedes some of her faculties and enhances others.'

'What could it possibly enhance?'

'Her capacity for love,' I said, wishing that I could cite the piano-tuning skills of the blind rather than something so vague.

'I think it's wrong for a person like that to have a place on the ship when there are normal people stuck in Germany.'

'You sound like a Nazi,' I replied and, when she made no attempt to answer the charge, told her about Frau Herzen who had had a genuinely Mongolian son. Having been forced to put him in a home, she received a letter claiming that he had died of appendicitis, which was a medical impossibility since he had already had his appendix removed. It was then that, in the only act of protest left to her, she had come to work for Jews.

'I'm not a Jew,' she declared and I found myself transfixed by the medallion of the Virgin Mary dangling provocatively around her neck. When I urged her to explain, she replied: 'My father's Jewish, although I didn't have the least notion of it until I was thrown out of school. But I'm not anything. I'm not a German: the Germans don't want me; they treat me like a Jew. I'm not a Jew: the Jews don't want me since my mother isn't Jewish. She's taking me to Cuba to meet my father, but I won't be a Cuban. I'm nothing . . . no one. So leave me alone!'

She flung the final chunk of bread, uncrumbled, over the side, provoking a frenzy of flapping, and strode off, leaving me to spend the afternoon assailed by conflicting emotions: elation that we had met together with depression at what she had said. I felt the particular injustice of her position: suffering for being Jewish without ever having known the joys: the richness of the five thousand year history; the bonds that stretched beyond borders; the strength of a belief embedded not in books or prayers but in the blood. I wanted to share some of my own conviction, assuring her that, wherever she went in the world, even in Cuba, she would not be alone. I wanted to go still further, telling her she would never be alone again now that she had me. I was fired by a hope that the voyage might take me to an even more desired destination than Havana.

I took care to keep my feelings in check when we gathered in the dining room. News of my grandfather's condition had spread, and my mother responded to expressions of concern as though they were already condolences. I felt doubly guilty when my loss of appetite was attributed to worry and Mother, for once finding something in me to approve, squeezed my hand. All that changed, however, when I greeted her remark that there was a rabbi sitting with my grandfather by asking if he were a member of the crew. Shaking with incredulity, she demanded that I avoid the cabin for the next few hours. I went instead to the cinema with Sophie and Luise, who objected loudly to being separated from her friends. The room quickly filled with an audience that for too long had been starved of entertainment. My own anticipation was compromised by my search for Johanna. Disregarding her parting words, I planned to slip casually into a seat beside her and, when the moment was right, take hold of her hand. My nerves were so on edge that I jumped up at each new entrance, in spite of Sophie's strictures and the complaints of the man behind, who did not want to miss a fraction of even the empty screen.

Far from seeing Johanna, the only figure I recognised was Schiendick, who stood menacingly in front of the projection box, as if ready to cancel the film at the first sign of enjoyment. There was no chance of that during the newsreel, which was dominated by a face that we thought we had left behind us forever: his dank cowlick dangling and mean moustache bristling, as he inveighed against the worldwide conspiracy of Jews. There was a noisy shuffling in the seats and a widespread murmur of defiance. Luise, whose revulsion to the man had to derive from some instinctive sense of evil, emitted a low moan. Several passengers walked out, but I was determined to sit firm, even after spotting Schiendick grinning broadly in the light of the open door. My forbearance was rewarded by a romantic – and, according to Sophie, highly romanticised – account of the lives of Robert and Clara Schumann, which so perfectly fitted my mood that I found myself picturing Johanna in a crinoline. It must also have chimed with Sophie, who announced that, after putting Luise to bed, she was going to the nightclub, but, when I asked hesitantly if I might escort her, she laughed, explaining that, in the first place, her nursemaid duties were over for the day and, in the second, I had to be eighteen.

'I can pass for eighteen,' I said.

'In a total eclipse.'

'Ask Frau Singel!'

'The same Frau Singel who believes that the Garden of Eden was in Bavaria and the Tsar escaped the Bolsheviks dressed as her butcher?'

'How many Frau Singels do you know?'

'Exactly. Besides, it's eleven o'clock: time for all good little boys to be in bed.'

Neither her jibe nor her departure stung me as much as I might have expected. I returned to the cabin to find my grand-father propped on the pillows, looking far more animated than before. My mother instructed me to wake her if there were the least change in his condition, at which he told her not to 'worry the boy' and insisted that he would last the night. After she had gone, he beckoned me closer and extracted my promise to do something for him. Respect made me forego any proviso, so I felt perturbed when he asked me to fetch a cigar from his case. I was sure that it contravened doctor's orders, but even I could see that doctor's orders were little more than doctor's delaying tactics. I brought him the cigar, which he rolled lovingly under his nose, before sending me back for the cutter. 'One day,' he said, holding it up, 'one day very soon – now it's no use contradicting me – this will be yours. And it may well be the most precious thing I leave you since, by the time you reach my age, you'll know that there's no pleasure in the world to equal a good cigar.'

'None?' I asked, thinking of Johanna.

'None so pure, nor so purely indulgent. . . . Although it tastes better lit.' His addendum sent me scurrying for the matches. I watched as he inhaled deeply. 'How strange to think that this should be the closest I come to Havana!'

'You mustn't say that!'

'Oh I've no regrets, at least not about dying. I've far more about how I lived. But that's no longer for me to judge. In any case, I'm too old to start again or even to settle somewhere new.

I shall die happy to know that the people I love: the people I love more than I can say – although I'm sure I should have said so more often – are safe.'

You may suspect, in view of the horror that was soon to engulf the ship, that I have altered my grandfather's words to bring out the irony, but I must insist that, while I acknowledge the limitations of memory (although, in time-honoured fashion, the events of the voyage are clearer to me than those that took place last week), I refuse to resort to hindsight. How can I hope to inculcate you children with a regard for the truth if I ignore it myself?

As my grandfather lay back, I switched off the light and climbed into bed. I fell asleep almost at once and, when I woke in the night, my chest tight from the fumes but my lips clamped together to check any discouraging cough, I saw the faint glow of the cigar in the shadows and, every so often, a flicker of life.

The next morning, the thin rasp from his bed proved that Grandfather had been as good as his word and I was able to present a positive report to my mother. She led me up to the dining room, where I rushed through breakfast, confiding her warnings about indigestion to my file of phantom ailments, along with migraines from eating too much chocolate and baldness from not washing my hair. I ached to go out on deck to watch the ship anchor at Cherbourg, where it was to take on a final contingent of passengers, so I was doubly incensed when the Professor's wife asked Mother if I would be kind enough to fetch the novel which she had stupidly (itself said with a stupid giggle) left in her cabin, and Mother agreed, handing me over as casually as a tissue. Dismissing my protest, which by a super-human effort I had kept silent, she dispatched me with her most ingratiating smile.

I raced down the corridor, bumping into stewards at every turn. The fact that the wretched woman might easily have asked one of them for her book showed that her real aim was not to read but to demonstrate her power. The pathetic thing, as I acknowledged with perverse satisfaction, was that her victim was already the most put-upon person on board. I made a vow then and there that, when I grew up, I would never treat children as drudges (I trust you'll agree that I've kept it). I entered the Professor's wife's cabin, which smelt of mildew, and grabbed the book, Feuchtwanger's *False Nero*, which was so prominently placed that it could not have been left behind by accident. My haste to be out on deck allowed me no time to snoop around, and I hurried back to the dining room where, purring over the book, she underlined my servility by declaring that I would 'make some young lady very happy.' My current concern was to make one old lady thoroughly miserable, but I seized on the image of Johanna to boost my mood.

After promising my mother – for the third time – to meet her in the tourist lounge at noon, I went out on deck. The harbour was hazy, but I joined the crowds at the rail straining for a last glimpse of Europe, which was mercifully devoid of the Nazi flags that had marred our departure from Hamburg. Having witnessed the workings of a large department store, I failed to share the general fascination with the supply boats pulling up alongside us, so I strolled about the ship in search of Johanna. She proved to be as elusive as my father, whom I had mentally confined to his cabin in a drunken stupor. As I made my way to the rendezvous, I was filled with apprehension at the prospect of what my mother might have planned. Her refusal to explain the unlikely venue led me to suspect that she was in charitable mode and wanted me to welcome the new arrivals. I prepared myself for the same embarrassment as when she had forced me to man (a particularly inapposite word given the coercion) her soup kitchen. My greatest fear was that she would saddle me with a group of teenage boys. I wondered how old one had to be before age ceased to determine friendship and then amused myself by reversing our roles. 'Look, Mother, there's a middle-aged woman. Why don't you take her flower-arranging?'

As I walked into the lounge, not only was there no sign of any new passengers but the first person that I saw was Johanna, sitting with a woman whom I presumed to be her mother. Johanna looked lovely. She was wearing a green blouse which brought out the reddish tints of her hair (it was impossible to live with my mother and not learn about colour combination, even if the last thing to which she would apply it was clothes). Johanna's mother, who was dressed in self-effacing beige, looked kind, with round, rosy cheeks and fair hair packed on her head like a plaited loaf. I pictured her with a crotchet hook. Rubbing my palms on my trousers, I walked over to their table. Just as I was about to greet them, my mother stood up and summoned me in a voice that sounded far more piercing than it would have done in First Class. Desperate to avoid a reprise, I gave Johanna what I hoped was an endearingly nonchalant smile and, stifling my fury, made my way across the room to find my mother sitting with Luise and Sophie and, partially concealed by the wings of his chair, my father.

I swayed so violently that I forgot the ship was at anchor. I stared dumbstruck at the four figures grouped as casually as a family party and felt utterly betrayed. Time seemed to be frozen, until my father stood up with a grin that put me in mind of the lips that I used to paint on potatoes. He stretched out his arm, which shook. My horror at the thought that he might clasp my hand – or worse – made me recoil. I wondered why Orthodox Jews, who had such strict laws about the contact between men and women, had drawn up none to regulate that between a son and his errant father. As I gazed round the table in confusion, his arm fell to his side.

'You look extremely smart,' he said lamely.

'I'm wearing the same clothes as yesterday. I didn't want to disturb Grandfather. He's very ill.'

'Then it must come naturally.' He attempted another grin before sinking back into the chair.

'Do sit down, Karl,' my mother said. 'You're hovering like a steward.' I was appalled by her insensitivity. What would she have me do? Shake his hand? Hug him? She surely wouldn't ask me to kiss him? This was the man who had abandoned me without a word. This was the man who had assaulted her. Nevertheless, I pulled up a chair and, pointedly ignoring my father, fixed my eye on Luise and Sophie. Seeing them so calm, I wondered if I had been sucked into a parallel universe or else knocked out and lost my mind. The familiar timbre of my mother's voice cut off that line of escape and I turned to confront my father, partly out of defiance – I longed to see him wilt under my gaze – and partly out of curiosity, a desire to assess the many reports of our resemblance. I was relieved to find them wide of the mark. His face may have remained young, but it was far broader than mine and his features were thicker set. I looked no more like him than I did like Herman Göring: a thought that filled me with both comfort and shame.

'You've grown up so much. You're quite the young man,' he said, with woeful predictability.

'No, really? In case you've forgotten, I'm fifteen years old.'

'Karl . . .' My deep grievance made me deaf to the warning note in my mother's voice.

'I'm sorry but, if I'd shrunk, it might have been worthy of mention. "Oh, Karl, you're so much smaller than the last time I saw you. Pull up a flower-pot and sit down." But not "Oh Karl, you're one of the hundred million boys in the world to have grown up."' Luise clapped her hands and gurgled. . . . You never knew your great aunt, but, if you had, you would realise that she was responding to the tone of my words, to the rhetoric rather than the meaning.

'During the war,' my father replied, 'there were soldiers at the Front who didn't see their children for five years.'

'They were fighting for them. It was different.'

'And I was fighting for the children I hoped to have.'

'Then it's a pity you lost.'

'Karl dear,' my mother said, 'remember he's your father.'

'What do you mean? All I've ever done is remember. I haven't seen or heard from him for eight years.'

'Try to forgive me,' my father said. 'I know that the past is never past. But it doesn't have to be the only present. I've missed you so much.'

Then, to my horror, he began to cry. While my mother and Sophie vied to find him a handkerchief, I sat unmoved, since I was sure that, if they were analysed, his tears would be 30 per cent proof. Luise, however, who dwelt so close to tears herself that other peoples' were never a threat, gesticulated at him. 'She's crying,' she said. Then she slipped off her chair to plant a kiss on his cheek. He let out a loud howl, to the consternation of our neighbours, and clasped her to his chest. Neither my mother nor Sophie heeded my warnings that he was squeezing the life out of her. I, alone, seemed to be blessed with a memory . . . although it began to feel more like a curse, for, as I watched my father cradling Luise, my memory stretched beyond its regular eight-year span to flood me with sensations from early child-hood: the heady mixture of danger and security as my father threw me up in the air, and of wickedness and licence as he encouraged me to slide down the ballroom banisters; the wonder as he showed me a bird's nest; the pride as he told me stories of a mischievous Berlin boy called Karl. Then, just as I was in peril of warming to him, a very different set of sensations came back to me: the horror, greater even than that at the sight of a storm trooper, when my parents fought with each other; the longing for them to turn their anger on me since I was a boy and so couldn't help doing wrong; the fear of discovery when I hid behind doors and inside cupboards to make sense of a world that was fragmenting; the pain when, in the middle of one exchange, my mother screamed 'Keep quiet or my father will hear you!', yet made no mention of her son; the despair when, on one ever-to-be-repressed, never-to-be-forgotten occasion, an insult was followed by a slap and the cold, crystalline cry of 'I hate you,' after which they swiftly unravelled their marriage, making it clear that they had never been in love but had played a grown-up version of 'let's pretend'. As I shrugged off the memories and turned again to my father, it was clear why I would never be able to forgive him. I had no capacity for love. Luise may have been born of his drunkenness, but I was born of both my parents' hate.

My memories were interrupted by a waiter who came to take our order. While my father's request for lemonade failed to impress me, it delighted Luise, who poked her finger, first, at his chest and, then, at her own, repeating the word 'lemonade'. He asked her hesitantly if she knew who he was and, to my surprise, she replied, 'Daddy.' I presumed that either Mother or Sophie had coached her and comforted myself with the thought that the word meant no more to her than Chancellor or Gauleiter. Indeed, in view of their respective influence on her life, it probably meant far less. It nevertheless moved my father, who hugged her even tighter.

'Oh, my beauty,' he said, 'my beautiful, beautiful girl.' Luise became agitated and began to moan.

'She not beautiful.'

'But you are,' he said. 'You are to me.'

'No!' The intensity of the denial sent a shudder through her body, and Sophie, recognising the signs, stood up. 'She ugly. All ugly. All over her skin.' As her spasms grew more frequent, my father looked unsure whether to hold her tighter or to let her go. The decision was taken from him when Sophie eased her gently out of his arms. Luise, meanwhile, continued to mumble. 'Not beautiful. Ugly. Want to go to heaven and be beautiful inside.'

My father, who at least had the grace to look shocked, apologised. My mother assured him that it was not his fault, at which point I could no longer stay silent. 'Oh but it is,' I said, 'it's entirely his fault. He's the one who made her like this, just as if he'd been driving too fast and run her over or left a pan of hot fat on the stove which spat in her face.' They stared in horror, not so much at the speech itself as at my having made it. I was no longer a little boy scavenging for information but an equal possessor of the facts.

'You gave me your word you'd say nothing,' my father said to my mother. 'We agreed it was best that he didn't know.'

'And I've kept it,' she replied. 'To the letter. I don't understand.' Although I relished this sign of their dissension, quite different from the uncontrollable eruptions of the past, I felt obliged to defend her honour, adding that it was Grandfather who had told me: he, at least, didn't expect me to behave as an adult while treating me as a child. My mother, for whom her father could usually do no wrong, reacted with fury, claiming that he had gone behind her back, which, as I pointed out, was unfair since he had only told me the truth in order to reconcile me to her.

'Whatever do you mean?' she asked, amazed at the need for such intercession.

'It was a time when even Grandfather felt you'd been too harsh with me. To make me appreciate the pressures you were under, he told me how Luise was born: how he – ' I stared at my father with venom ' – poured kisses like whisky down your throat.'

I felt a strange surge of satisfaction beneath the pain that, for once, our roles were reversed and it was they who had to work out the implications of what I said. My mother looked unutterably sad, as if her whole world had been overturned and, this time, not by the Nazis. I was at a loss to know why since, although I was addressing her – and far too loudly for such a public place – the entire blame was directed at my father. He appeared to accept it, admitting, in a voice that slunk into my brain by stealth, that he had a great deal to make up for and asking how best he might start. 'The only thing you can do for me,' I said slowly, 'is to jump overboard and drown.' The words felt fragile even as I spoke them, but they shattered into a hundred pieces under the force of my mother's slap. The sting was intensified by the knowledge that two of the scores of eyes fixed on me were Johanna's. I turned to face my mother. 'That didn't hurt,' I said, choking back the sobs. 'What hurts is to see you being taken in by him.'

My exit from the lounge was as humiliating as my ejection from the school swimming pool. I reached the corridor moments before the tears streamed down my cheeks, and sought shelter in a nearby lavatory. As I locked the door, it struck me as fitting that my only refuge was the one closest to the dirt. I felt desolate and ill-used. I was unable to credit my mother's composure. It was clear that, for all my determination to shield her from pain, she had known of my father's presence on board all along. Far from my keeping the news from her, she had kept it from me, which led me to wonder how many other plots she might have hatched. Railing at the injustice, I offered a fervent prayer for the ship to sink, killing everyone on board, including myself. My reflections were interrupted by the twisting of the handle and the increasingly urgent knocking on the door. When they grew too intrusive, I ventured out to be greeted by a florid man who, after rushing inside and relieving himself, asked me in future to indulge my disgusting practices elsewhere, which struck me as unconscionably rude, not least when, to judge by both the noise and the smell, his practices were far more disgusting than mine.

The bell rang for lunch, which I resolved to shun, until I realised that, in my mother's current frame of mind, I would only be punishing myself. To my surprise, she appeared both subdued and apologetic, asking to talk to me after the meal and promising that, this time, there would be no mystery guests. We duly found ourselves a private spot on the sports deck, where I listened to her politely while paying close attention to a flock of gannets diving for fish.

'You're right to be angry with me, Karl,' she began.

'I'm not angry with you,' I replied. 'I'm angry with him.'

'You're right to be angry with us both. I should have done more to keep you in touch with your father but, at first – for quite some time actually – he was not in the best of states. And I was afraid of doing anything to upset you, especially with all that was happening in the outside world.'

'I didn't want him to keep in touch. I wanted him to keep away.'

'You're such a private boy. It's hard to know what's going on in your head. I thought you were happy.'

'Really?'

'You never asked about your father. I should have realised it was because you were afraid of the answers. Meanwhile, I was left being both father and mother to you, when to be even one successfully is hard enough.' For the first time, I saw how my father's defection had compromised my relationship with my mother as well as with him. 'Tell me, what do you know about how babies are born?'

'Everything,' I replied quickly, my horror at our sharing such intimacies overriding my hunger for knowledge. She looked relieved and explained that what Grandfather had told me about Luise was true but it wasn't the whole truth. My father had been drunk at her conception, but he had been drunk because he was unhappy and, for that, she must bear her share of responsibility.

'There are always reasons for everything,' she said, which confused me because it contradicted the Bible, which taught that people were responsible for their actions, right back to Adam and Eve. I wondered whether I were the only Jew left who believed in justice.

'If there are reasons for everything, then there must be reasons for the Nazis.'

'Yes, but the reasons aren't always good ones,' she said. 'I thought you thought that your father had left because he couldn't cope with Luise. I thought you thought him a coward.'

'Is that any better than a drunkard?'

'It does less damage.'

'Not to me.'

'I blamed everything on the drink. I clung to the hope that he'd come back once he gave it up.'

'But he didn't.'

'Oh he stopped drinking years ago. I think he was frightened that he'd start again.'

'He had no right to run away. We're his family!'

'His family was larger than he would have wished. It can be hard living in another man's shadow.' I presumed that she must mean Uncle Karl, but I had no opportunity to confirm it for she was already explaining how, although she had seen him only twice in the last eight years, they had kept in regular contact. I allowed myself a hope that he might have written for news but then, with Hitler's voice rasping in my head, I decided that the only news he would have wanted came in bank statements. She surprised me by saying that it was she who had suggested he sailed on the *St Louis*, overcoming his resistance by exaggerating the perils in store. Even so, he had insisted that she bought him the cheapest ticket since he did not want to cost her any more money, which, giving me an alarming initiation into the mysteries of adult language, she translated as not wanting to cause her any more pain.

'But why didn't you tell me he was coming? Why keep it a secret?'

'It never seemed to be the right moment. What with everything we had to do before we left.' I blotted out the image of her retreat into the studio. 'So I thought: why not wait until we're on the ship? It'll be a surprise.'

'A what?'

'You always used to like surprises.'

'Yes, "Guess what we're having for pudding," not "Come for a drink and meet your father."'

'I made a mistake, Karl. I'm sorry. Can you forgive me?'

'It's not fair to ask me like that. It leaves me no choice. You should let me decide on my own.'

'Though what matters more is that you forgive your father. We've a long voyage ahead of us. It's the perfect chance for you to get to know him. Don't squander it.'

'So, is he going to live with us in America?' I asked, not mincing my words.

'America's still a long way off.'

'Cuba then? That's only twelve days away.'

'It depends on so many things. Perhaps he'll live nearby. Like a cousin.'

'He's a father.'

'And a husband,' she said softly. 'But we'll have to wait and see. The important thing for now is that we're together on the ship. And we're safe.'

I felt far from safe as she ended the discussion, her pretence of treating me as an adult exposed by her kindergarten phrase about the healing powers of time. She went down to the cabin, leaving me to grapple with a mass of new information. There was no one to whom I could turn. Sophie had kept aloof ever since we came on board, choosing to spend her time in the night-club like a gangster's moll. Aunt Annette was preoccupied with my grandfather, towards whom I felt a wave of resentment, all the more bitter on account of its being irrational, for falling ill and leaving me to deal with the change of circumstances on my own. Wandering aimlessly from deck to deck, I would even have welcomed Luise's burr-like attentions, but she had attached herself to her friends, hobbling behind them like a reject in a three-legged race.

Filled with despair, I returned to the cabin, where further misery awaited me in the shape of my grandfather, stretched out like an effigy, his only sign of life the struggle for breath. My mother sat at his side, her face cupped in his inert hand. I longed to do the same, but I was repelled by the thought of the moribund flesh. As I berated myself for my callousness, the Doctor emerged from the bathroom. Collecting his bag, he promised to look in again during the evening. He then beckoned me to join him outside, which surprised me so much that I looked around to see if he was pointing to somebody else, at which he repeated the gesture more brusquely. Once in the corridor, he dropped all the cabin niceties and, with a gruff note of regret for my grand-father's condition and a pledge to ensure that his end was as comfortable as possible, asked if there were any deathbed customs in our faith of which he might be unaware. I was appalled, not just by his words but that he should have addressed them to me. All my anger at having to abide by adult decisions paled before the horror of having to make them myself. He ought to be talking to Mother or Aunt Annette. I was still a boy and should be protected from death.

'I'm afraid I can't say. I'm not bar mitzvah,' I replied, squeezing through the escape clause.

'I'm sorry?' he asked. 'Does that have any bearing on what we do.'

'Of course,' I said. 'It means I'm not a man in any religious sense. I have no authority. So I'm not the person to ask.' I strode off, anxious to put as much space as possible between myself and the cabin.

On board ship, that space was inevitably limited, but I made my way to the promenade deck and, in spite of myself, was caught up in the general excitement at the sight of a small boat arriving with the last thirty passengers. Their faces were darker than ours, but they had the same look of baffled resignation. I followed their progress up the accommodation ladder until I found, to my dismay, that I was sharing my vantage point with Schiendick.

'Ah,' he said, 'the Jew with two names. It's strange, wouldn't you say, that most ships try to rid themselves of rats, but we invite them on board?' I made to go, but he grabbed hold of my arm. 'The one thing that can be said in their favour is that they're not Jewish rats.'

'They're not?' I betrayed my surprise.

'They're Cubans, who've been fighting the war in Spain.' Having heard of no war in Spain, I suspected that this was more propaganda. 'Communist scum who tried to overthrow the government. So, of course, they lost.' My pleasure at their escape was tempered by the thought of the thirty Jews whose places they had taken. 'But the Generalissimo – the Spanish Führer – has shown mercy. He's sent them to rot in their own wretched country. As we have you.'

'But our country's Germany, not Cuba.'

'You don't have a country! You're parasites! A blight on every place you enter. Do you really think the Cubans want you, that they'll welcome you with open arms?'

'We have our landing permits.'

'Oh yes, they want your stolen money, but do they want *you*? Believe me, there are patriotic Cubans, admirers of the Reich, who are busy preparing for your arrival. I say this out of friend-ship – ' He flashed me a toothy grin as if to emphasise both the irony and the threat. 'Don't walk down any dark streets or drink from open bottles. Your two names won't save you then.' I fell back as, with a click of his heels, he saluted so sharply that he caught my ear and shouted two words, which stung me far more than the blow. . . . Perhaps now, Marcus, you'll understand why I objected so strongly to the youths with '88' embossed on their T-shirts. Far from being the blanket complaint of an old man forgotten by fashion, it was a considered protest at the venera-tion of the eighth letter of the alphabet, the double H of 'Heil Hitler!', which made it the most provocative number that they could have chosen, except perhaps for 666.

I sat in the lounge and ordered tea. In the absence of either a book or a companion, I was left to eavesdrop on the neigh-bouring table, where four old ladies indulged in their favourite pastime of grumbling about their daughters-in-law. I was distracted by a dark figure looming over me but, instead of the waiter, it was my father, who pulled up a chair as if I had ordered tea for two. I objected to the intrusion but, before I had a chance to say so, he launched into a long speech full of guilt and remorse, which ended with the fervent hope that we could make a fresh start in a country that was new to us all. Speaking as though he were an equal member of our group rather than one step up from a stowaway, he suggested that we regard the voyage as a period of probation. 'What?' I asked, taking my tone from Schiendick. 'Like seeing if we have sea-legs or enjoy playing deck quoits?' Then, to my disgust, he began to cry and repeated the plea that I might find it in my heart to forgive him.

'It's not up to me. I'm not the one you've wronged. It's Luise you should be asking.'

'But how would she know what I meant?'

'Exactly.'

At that moment, the waiter arrived with the tea and I seized my chance. 'This gentleman is confused. He isn't supposed to be here. Would you please show him to the tourist lounge.' My voice, an imitation of my mother's and grandfather's and, given its unpredictable crack, pitched halfway in-between, proved more effective than I had dared hope, since, whether in awe at my new-found authority or despair at my refusal to bend, my father allowed himself to be led away. My satisfaction turned sour, however, when I discovered that it was the old ladies who were now eavesdropping on me and shooting me looks of unconcealed disapproval. I concentrated on my cup and tried to suppress an uneasy feeling that they were right. It might be a single moment of rejection as against the constant rejection of the past eight years, but I had made his humiliation public. Moreover, I had appealed to an outside jurisdiction which, under the circumstances, was a betrayal not just of my father but of my fellow Jews. I was assailed by the image of the thousands of innocent men who had been led away by Nazi officials. . . . Pyrrhus surveyed his victory and wept.

Fleeing from the lounge to the dining room, I found that meals were taking on the character of a party game where, each time that we sat down, there was another empty chair. In addition to the persistent absentees – Mother, Grandfather and Aunt Annette – the Banker's wife had been confined to her cabin with what her husband delicately described as 'mal de mer'. This permitted the Professor to monopolise his attention, ignoring his own wife so pointedly that I wondered whether their private conversations amounted to anything more significant than requests to buy toothpaste and switch off the lights. She, meanwhile, having concluded that, due to their respective status, neither Luise nor Sophie merited her regard, directed the full blast of it on me. After demanding the latest bulletin on my grandfather, she could barely conceal her disappointment when I assured her that he was fine. She frowned as if she had caught me feigning illness in order to break the fast on Yom Kippur. Then, in a voice as sickly as the tart on which she was gorging, she expressed her sympathy for Mother and Aunt Annette: 'It's never easy, having two women in one household.'

'Is that so?' I replied slyly. 'Solomon had seven hundred wives – and three hundred concubines. And he was the wisest man in the Bible.' My retort had the desired effect as she choked on her pastry. I envied the Professor's licence to deliver three hefty thumps to her back.

After dinner I spent an hour at my grandfather's bedside, where I felt increasingly oppressed both by the sickroom atmosphere and my own lack of feeling. I suspected that my mother's assessment of my selfishness was correct and, at the risk of confirming it, I excused myself and escaped outside. I stood at the rail, marvelling at the stillness of the starlit sky and a sea that seemed to be teeming with squid. Wrapped in the darkness, I watched with a mixture of envy and distaste as three elderly couples strolled hand-in-hand like children in a crocodile. Walking up to the lifeboats, I distinguished shapes which, on close – and brief – inspection, turned out to be other, younger, couples, intimately entwined. I felt acutely aware of my isolation. Had I been a child, I would have been able to make friends as easily as Luise. Had I been an adult, I would have been able to invite Johanna to the nightclub. Instead, I was doomed to haunt the ship like the Flying Dutchman. Despair overwhelmed me and I decided to return inside, only to stop short when a ray of light fell on Sophie, who was clasped in the arms of a sailor as if she were posing for the cover of a cheap romance. Determined to intervene before she did anything dangerous, which I defined for myself as leaning back so far that she slipped over the rail and drowned, I tapped her on the shoulder.

'What the hell . . .!' She wheeled round in fury. 'Karl? What do you want? Have you been spying on me?'

'No, of course not. I've just come outside. How can you think that?' Mollified by an assertion of innocence which was for once genuine, she introduced me to her companion as casually as if we had met in a library. His name was Helmut Ritsch, and he was the ship's helmsman. It was hard to make out his features, let alone his expression, in the shadows, but I could see that he was tall with curly hair and, to judge by the glint of whiteness, a broad smile. I shook his hand and then, struck by a sudden fear that the ship might veer off-course, asked whether he shouldn't be on the bridge. He laughed and said that he had a deputy. 'I can't be expected to be on duty twenty-four hours a day.'

'Some of us are,' Sophie interposed.

Smarting under the implied rebuke, a far cry from her usual claim that she wouldn't change places with anyone, I explained that I had come to take her back to the cabin, where Luise needed her. Scared that, for the first time, she might decide to place her own needs above Luise's, I added that she was very disturbed – a much more powerful spur than *upset* – about Grandfather. Sophie turned to Helmut and, with a despondent shrug, apologised for having to leave him. He smiled – at least the glint grew wider – like someone who was saving his last square of chocolate in order to savour it all the more later. Even their words were as soft as caresses. I waited for them to slip into an embrace, exchanging kisses as if they were as precious as Grandfather's breaths, but Sophie shooed me away with the same affronted air as the couple at Lake Havel, who had supposed that I was training my binoculars on them rather than a pair of storks.

Even more painful signs of fraternisation awaited me on the lower deck, where I found Johanna deep in conversation with two sailors. I was torn between retreating to my cabin for the remainder of the voyage, never venturing further than the games room, where I would fetch spectacles and shawls for elderly ladies who heaped praise on the charming boy that they assumed me to be, and confronting Johanna like the angry and confused young man that I knew I had become. My dilemma was resolved when she beckoned me to join them, to the marked annoyance of her companions. Studiedly ignoring them, I asked Johanna if she needed help: a question which, for some reason, stuck her as hilarious. Nevertheless, she dispatched the sailors. 'I want to be alone with my friend', she declared, surprising me by her use of the word. Insisting that I had no wish to be censorious – and aware that it might not advance my cause – I warned her against any action, however inadvertent, that might lead the men on. Instead of deflecting the charge, she replied sadly that she had no choice. 'It's in my blood.' The phrase was particularly chilling to ears attuned to the Nazi slur that Jewish women were all Delilahs out to sap the strength of Aryan men. . . . And before any of you, although I suspect that it will be Marcus at his most punctilious, accuse me of forgetting that Delilah was a Philistine not a Jew, let me say that she features in the Jewish Bible and, for the Nazis, that was damning enough.

'What do you mean "in my blood"?' I asked. Instead of answering, she leant towards me and softly – miraculously – kissed my cheek.

'I wanted to kiss the spot where I'd seen you slapped.'

'I see,' I said, my joy in the kiss compromised by her pity.

'I'd never forgive my mother if she treated me like that,' she said, giving me the perfect opportunity to air my grievances. I explained how people had always envied me on account of my grandfather's store, which they pictured as my private store-house, whereas the reality was very different. She urged me to elaborate and, realising that for the first time I had someone in whom to confide, I provided edited – but authentic – highlights of my life-story. To my surprise, I found myself beginning with my father, a fact that I attributed to his recent return. I described how, in spite of all that my mother and grandfather had done for him, he had turned to drink and how it was his drunkenness at Luise's conception that had impaired her brain. Then, using a word I could make sense of only in the cinema, I whispered to her what I had barely dared articulate even to myself: Luise had been the child of rape. To my amazement, she was neither shocked nor outraged, but listened calmly to everything I said before kissing me on the other cheek.

'That's not the one that was slapped,' I said.

'I know,' she replied.

She reciprocated by telling me her life-story and, to my delight, I quickly discovered its affinities with my own. Johanna had never known her father. I bit my tongue before pronouncing it a blessing. Even her mother had barely known him, having met him in the restaurant where she worked and he ate occasional meals. Little by little, he became a regular customer, first of the restaurant and then of hers. I couldn't work out whether Johanna meant tips at the table or something more sinister. According to her mother, who made excuses for everyone (which Johanna ascribed to dullness rather than decency), her father had never lied about his marriage or his three children, let alone his intention of leaving them for her. She had, however, been so enchanted by this cultured, sophisticated man, who treated her with rare respect, that she had accepted the status quo. That is until she found herself pregnant.

'I was an accident. Those were her precise words. As if she'd been knocked down in the road.'

'There are people who believe that the entire human race is an accident.'

'Do you?'

'No.'

'Then why mention it?' To my relief, she did not dwell on my perversity but continued with her account. Her father paid all her expenses, both at birth and throughout childhood, but he never once visited her nor asked her mother for so much as a photograph. 'I was something that he brought into the world as casually as a burp.' Even so, she remained unperturbed until she went to kindergarten and found herself among children with the regular complement of parents. No longer satisfied with the simple fact of her father's death, she pressed her mother for details and was rewarded with the heart-rending story of his plunge from a roof while attempting to rescue a stranded cat. She returned to school fired with her father's heroism. Her classmates, however, were unconvinced and demanded evidence – medals, pictures, a grave – which she, in turn, required of her mother. The more she pressed, the more her mother prevaricated. Fear of what she might learn kept her from challenging her outright. Instead, she turned detective, sifting through cupboards and cases for clues. At every step, she drew a blank.

Matters grew worse when her beloved grandmother died. It seemed doubly unfair that she should have only one, along with one set of cousins and uncles and aunts (she was less concerned about the single grandfather on account of her aversion to beards). Even a dead father must have had a family. She failed to understand why her mother refused to let her meet them.

The truth became clear when the Nazis took power. Johanna's mother was a Catholic with a special devotion to Mary, whose intercession was as great a hope to her as her purity was a reproach. But, whatever effect her daily candle-burning may have had on divine judgement, it had none on Hitler's. Johanna's father was a Jew and, in a vain – now fatal – stab at respectability, her mother had entered his name on the birth certificate. When the race laws were passed, Johanna found herself classed as a half-and-half, an in-between, a *mischling* (a word for which, I am glad to say, there is no English equivalent). 'At first I thought my German half would save me,' she said. 'I pictured myself in a wheelchair, with all my Jewish blood drained into my legs but, since they didn't work, it wouldn't count. Then, I imagined them amputated, so that all that was left was German.'

'A pretty useless German.'

'But legitimate. But safe.'

She began to be picked on at school by both pupils and staff. Since all the full Jewish girls had been expelled, her history teacher made her stand in front of the class to illustrate the Semitic physique, key aspects of which were large breasts and wide hips (I forced myself to look horrified). In consequence, she starved herself. The constant talk of ignorant Jews eroded her confidence, so she quit school and worked occasional shifts in her mother's restaurant, where the incessant innuendoes of the male customers confirmed her opinion of her father's lust and her mother's shame.

Her father had meanwhile fled from Germany, along with his wife and two of his sons, the third having been killed in a clash with the SA. They were living in Havana until they reached their place on the American quota list. With his world in ruins, her father developed a conscience – or so Johanna believed; in her mother's view, he was finally able to reveal the love that for so long he had been compelled to hide. He expressed deep fears for Johanna's safety and offered to pay for her passage with the money he had been unable to take out of Germany. Her mother, using a phrase borrowed from one of her romantic magazines, reluctantly agreed to give her up. Johanna, however, had no intention of crossing the ocean to live with a man she had never met, a woman who was bound to hate her and two half-brothers who would regard her as fair game. 'One of them's married,' her mother assured her, prompting Johanna to laugh in her face. Despite her own misgivings, her parents were united in their insistence that she leave, their protracted correspondence making her departure the more pressing. They agreed that, if there were no alternative, her mother would accompany her. So, mollified by her mother's greater sacrifice, Johanna boarded the ship.

'That's my story then. Tawdry eh?'

'I'd call it tragic.'

'You're too romantic for your own good.' Then, despite the mockery, she kissed me again, full on the lips. I was so taken aback that I had no idea what to feel or to expect. It was a completely different order of kiss from any that I had known before: one that did not just say 'hello' or 'goodbye' or 'thank you', but changed the entire way that my body responded. I even understood the women who, having been kissed by Hitler, declared that they would never wash again. Not that I had any desire to follow suit. On the contrary, I resolved to wash more often. I wanted to be clean for Johanna: I wanted to be so clean that she would kiss me again and again and again . . . until she shattered my reverie by saying 'That's what I meant. I can kiss anyone. It means nothing. It's in my blood.'

Her words, which were as obvious a smokescreen as my own 'I didn't want to go anyway' when forbidden an outing, failed to dampen my spirits. That was left to Sophie, whose instinct for my whereabouts was as sharp on board ship as at home. Greeting Johanna with the curtest of nods and making no attempt at an introduction, she informed me that Luise was sleeping as soundly as she had been when she left her two hours before. Forced to improvise, which was never my forte, I suggested that she must have dropped off while waiting for us to return, but Sophie would not be placated. Instead, she launched into a wild denunciation of my selfishness, insisting that she was entitled to a private life and that I should be grateful for her consent to come with us – which was true, although my gratitude was lessened by the knowledge of the dangers she was leaving behind in Berlin. I told her that she was embarrassing me in front of my friend.

'The trouble with you, Karl,' she replied, 'is that you're always embarrassed, never ashamed.'

'I don't want you to be hurt.'

'I'm nearly twice your age. I think I can look after myself.'

'Men take advantage.'

'Oh Karl!' She laughed. 'You've got your first girlfriend, so you're suddenly an expert on relationships!'

'I'm not his girlfriend,' Johanna interjected crossly. I was terrified she might think that I had been discussing her behind her back.

'Very wise,' Sophie said.

'We're just friends,' I said, eager to retrieve the situation. 'We don't have to give each other labels. And at least Johanna's Jewish.'

'Half-Jewish. I've never met my father,' she explained to Sophie, who looked bemused.

'Whereas the sailor's Christian.'

'So? Not all Christians are hostile. To think that is to think like a Nazi. True, there are some Party members on board, but Helmut . . . my friend – ' she explained for the benefit of Johanna but with a glare at me – 'assured me that the Captain has taken a strong line against them. He's stopped them singing their marching songs in any of the public rooms and disciplined the steward responsible for showing the Hitler newsreel. He insisted that we should be treated the same as any other passengers, in spite of the steward's threats to complain to Berlin.' She concluded by saying that most of the crew were even less interested in politics than their counterparts on land. They had come to sea to experience different cultures, relishing the combination of a fluid world and a fixed order. So it was time for me to stop looking at life in black and white.

'And red?' I asked, thinking of the third Nazi colour.

'And red,' she replied, giving me a hug. 'Take no notice of me,' she said to Johanna. 'You'll find no better boy anywhere than Karl. I love every scrap of him.' She squeezed me so hard that there seemed to be several scraps fewer. 'It's just that sometimes he doesn't think.'

'You usually say I think too much.'

'You think about yourself and you think about the state of the world, but you tend to forget about anyone in-between.' Then, giving me a very different kiss to Johanna's, she strode back up the stairs.

No sooner were we alone than Johanna exclaimed how much she liked me, which gave me a giddy thrill, although I steadied myself by remembering that we had enjoyed no more than two brief meetings. I had read enough novels to be familiar with love at first sight but seen enough of life to be wary of second thoughts. Nevertheless, I was eager to respond to her declaration and edged my hand slowly along the rail; but, just as I was about to lunge, she turned to adjust her hair, leaving me to beat an impromptu tattoo on the wood. Trusting neither my words nor my body, I longed to give her a sure sign of affection and pictured the perfect gift concealed inside my shoe. I was certain that I could square it with my mother, since it wouldn't be the first time I had worn a hole in my heel. Then I recalled her fear that we would be denied access to our American accounts and, even at my most intoxicated (a word that had lost all its shades of my father), I refused to jeopardise the family's future. I resolved instead to build on our shared intimacies, remarking on the coincidence of our absent fathers. Johanna, however, regarded them as typical of their sex. As an alternative, I proposed my grandfather, for whom, despite our political differences, I felt total respect. She seized on the hint of dissension which, I explained, sprang from my growing despair at the lack of Jewish resistance to the Nazis. My rejection of a faith which favoured the scruples of age over the fire of youth was what lay behind my refusal to be bar mitzvah.

'What?'

'A ritual Jewish boys go through at thirteen.'

'In church, we have the first communion.'

'Girls too?'

'Of course, girls too,' she said sharply, as though I had cast a slur on both her piety and her sex.

'And is it a sign to the community that you've become a woman?'

'At the age of six? No, it's all to do with Jesus. You're old enough to share his body.' I grimaced at the thought of eating someone's flesh, which I knew was just a phrase, but that was bad enough. Moreover, I failed to see how Christians who put a cannibalistic act at the heart of their services could accuse us of a lust for blood. It seemed unfair, however, to lay that on Johanna, who straddled the two Testaments like the Apocrypha. So I simply explained that, for a Jew, being bar mitzvah was a sign that a boy had become a man and responsible for keeping the precepts of the Torah for himself.

'A man at thirteen?' Her incredulity diminished me and I felt like a character in an operetta who only came of age at forty-five. I described how my ban on being bar mitzvah had sparked the greatest family crisis since Luise's birth, with both my mother and grandfather accusing me of falling for Nazi propaganda and feeling ashamed to be Jewish. I told her what I had told them . . . and what I've told you children already, but then it can never be repeated too often: that I was proud of being Jewish, but ashamed of my fellow Jews. Unlike my family, Johanna neither questioned the distinction nor accused me of spite. Instead, she asked why anyone should be proud to be Jewish. For once I needed no time to prepare my reply, since it came from the heart: that we were a people who had survived; a people who had borne witness; a people who had entered into a special covenant with God and been tested on behalf of humanity: a people whose tradition was so rich that it had been the seedbed of other religions yet maintained its own integrity.

To my dismay, Johanna sounded unconvinced. She appropriated my words – methodically, not cruelly – to make a similar case for Christianity: that Jesus had instituted a new covenant; that he had been tested on behalf of humanity; that, through him, the old religion had been superseded. Then she said that, if God were testing the Jews, he must have found them wanting since their history was one of constant persecution. She refused to have any part of it, claiming that her Jewish blood was incidental. Her mother's customer might as easily have been Moslem or Chinese. She hated the Jews and, even if she lived for a hundred years, she wanted nothing to do with them.

'What about me?' I asked, more hurt than I could say. 'You're talking to a Jew now.'

'Given the passenger list, I don't have much choice. But don't expect us to stay friends once we reach Cuba. I intend to meet a plantation owner in a white suit. Or, better still, his son.'

'You sound like your mother,' I said, regretting the remark the moment it had passed my lips.

'That's the nastiest thing anyone's ever said to me.' I stammered an apology, which she cut short. 'And also the truest.' Then, changing tack with dizzying speed, she asked if I knew how to dance.

'No,' I replied, afraid that she would want to waltz round the deck, thereby exposing another side to my clumsiness.

'There's a dance in the social hall next week,' she said, leaving it unclear whether she were issuing me with an invitation or ruling out my attendance. 'Now I must go to bed.'

'May I see you again?' I asked tentatively.

'Since we'll be packed together on this ship for the next ten days, you can't very well avoid it.'

'I meant by arrangement, not chance.'

'Why not come to the lounge at tea-time tomorrow? I'll introduce you to my mother. She'll like you: you're rich.' Then, with an unexpected giggle, she kissed me on the mouth and vanished into the dark.

Her rapid shifts of mood had left me stunned. I felt as though I had been tortured and caressed by turn – and sometimes at the same time. I stood in the breeze, trying to make sense of my feelings, when a stray thought of my grandfather stabbed me with guilt and sent me rushing back to the cabin. As I opened the door, I caught sight of the Rabbi standing at the foot of the bed. He was silent, but the echo of his prayers filled the room as intensely as the odour of his sweat. I felt as uneasy in his presence as a pacifist, however principled, beside a soldier on leave from the Front. I followed his gaze to the bed-head, where the Doctor was preparing an injection. My faith in my grandfather's powers of recovery led me to suspect the Doctor's motives. He was a German first and a doctor second, and perhaps even a Nazi before both. For all I knew, he might be allied with Schiendick in a plot to kill off the passengers, one by one, during the course of the voyage. Even I had to admit, however, that his concern appeared to be genuine as he elicited a promise that I should call him if there were any change in my grandfather's condition during the night. He left, quickly followed by the Rabbi, whose blessing made me despair of my rusty Hebrew. I turned to Aunt Annette, who sat next to my grandfather, her face as crumpled as her clothes, slowly rubbing his hand. After struggling to register my presence, she roused herself to return to her cabin where my mother was already snatching some rest.

Part sentry, part night-nurse, I lay on my bed in my clothes. The heaviness of the air along with the headiness of my emotions sent me swiftly to sleep. An elusive dream in which I was sailing on a ship that was stranded in the desert was interrupted, first, by a buzzard's and, then, by my grandfather's cries of 'Karl!' Happy that of all the names at his disposal he had chosen mine, I hurried to his bed and clasped his hand. His eyes were closed and gummy, but his voice was clear, and I was amazed to find him begging me for forgiveness. He ignored – or, more accurately, seemed not to hear – my insistence that none was needed, addressing me with exam-room urgency: 'I know you were against it, but I believed it was for the best. We had to declare ourselves. We couldn't sit back while so many were dying.' Poised between sleeping and waking, it took me a moment to realise that he was talking about my bar mitzvah. I was overjoyed to learn that he had finally endorsed my stand. 'You were right. There is another way for us to live. Luise always said that I was too set in my ways.' I was still more confused, until I recalled that my sister had been named for my grandmother. 'Will you ever forgive me, Karl?'

I insisted once again that he had no need to ask, but my words were drowned in tears. I kissed his hands and his cheeks, which seemed to soothe him, and his speech dwindled first to an inchoate mumble and then to a stertorous rasp.

I must have drifted to sleep soon afterwards for, when my mother came in the next morning to wake me, I was still in the chair. She was clearly touched by my solicitude and planted a rare token of approval on my forehead. Mr Selfish, which she had deemed to be my middle name (not long before the Nazis changed it officially), had been replaced by Mr Vigilant. As we stared at the sleeping figure, I reported his outburst of the previous night and his anxiety that I should forgive him. She showed no surprise, either about the request itself or that I should be its recipient, describing both how much my grandfather loved me and the fresh hope I had brought him after my uncle's death. I wondered aloud whether it was me that he had loved or the idea of me: a new generation to inherit the store.

'You'd be wrong to think of the store as a business or even a way of life,' she said. 'For your grandfather, it was a reason for living. He felt as committed to it as a painter to his canvas – except that it was a canvas on which others had space to make their mark.'

'You mean like the Breughels or the Bellinis?' I asked, thinking of fathers and sons in the same studio. I knew that I had hit on the perfect analogy when she kissed me as tenderly as if I were six. Building on our newfound intimacy, she warned me that Grandfather might not live for much longer. Although she was speaking to me, I suspected that she was addressing herself and urged her not to worry. The doctor had diagnosed nothing more serious than exhaustion. We would soon reach the Azores, where he could regain his strength in the sun. But, in a phrase so unexpected that I felt sure Sophie must have told her about Johanna, she declared 'It's not only young men who die of broken hearts.'

She wanted some time alone with her father. So, grabbing my binoculars, I climbed to the upper deck in the hope of spotting a few birds before being harassed by talkative passengers. I was immediately disappointed. The sky was dull and overcast and there was not even a herring gull to be seen. Edging my way to the prow, up steps still slippery from overnight rain, I caught sight of Mark, the only other traveller willing to brave the billowing sea. He responded to my greeting with a grunt, which I considered an improvement on his previous rebuff. I asked if I might ask him a question: a formula designed to give it more weight than simply asking it outright.

'I hope you won't make the mistake of thinking I keep to myself because my mind's on higher things.'

'But I don't. Not at all. Anyway, it's not higher things I want to ask about – quite the opposite. Although you're travelling alone, in the past – in Berlin – you must have known lots of girls.'

'Must I?' He laughed. 'What girl would want to touch this face?'

'It's just a scar.'

'There's worse inside.'

'Besides, it wouldn't show in the dark. Last night, I was walking on deck and I saw men and women, some of them quite old, pawing each other like animals. Animals!'

'I grew up in a village in the Ukraine. One day, a gang of peasants marched in and slaughtered every Jew they could find. Hundreds of dead. Men, women and children. That night, the survivors lay together – and not just for warmth. It was an instinct beyond passion, beyond even personality. The most primal expression of life. It's the same on this ship.'

I thought that the most primal expression of life was to eat, sleep and give thanks to God for the right to do so, but I was too struck by his mention of the Ukraine to argue.

'Is the Ukraine like Lithuania?'

'Is Berlin like Paris?'

'Small villages with ancient communities of Jews?'

'Those villages are the same everywhere, as they have been for hundreds of years. Like a living death.'

I described how, during the War, my uncle had been in the German army which had liberated Lithuania from the Russians. He had been immensely moved by the chance to meet people who lived their faith, according to an age-old tradition, rather than trying to find a circuitous route around it. They had shown him new ways of being a Jew, which he recounted in long letters to my grandparents, while at the same time damning their quest for assimilation as a Faustian pact. I recalled my excitement when I first came across the letters – or rather, sneaked them from my grandfather's desk in a bid to discover the missing pages in our family history. I felt certain that, in spite of the names on the envelopes, my uncle had addressed himself specifically to me. It was as if he had somehow known that, twenty years on, he would receive a sympathetic hearing. I was therefore doubly offended by Mark's dismissal of his zeal as a rich man's romanticism. Having grown up among village shopkeepers, smallholders and farm labourers, he declared the reality to be very different. Theirs was a superstition as restrictive as a prison cell and an ignorance as crippling as leg-irons, from which only the horror of the massacre had enabled him to break free.

I asked if he had been happier in Berlin and he replied that he had merely exchanged the illusion of home for the illusion of freedom. Then the Nazis had come to power and destroyed both. In an attempt to discover whom, if anyone, he regarded as free, I suggested Hitler, at which he laughed and said 'No one looks over his shoulder more than the man who holds the gun.' Remembering the Captain's equation of sailing and flying, I made a second suggestion of seamen, to which he asked, with what seemed like a jibe at himself, what point there was in travelling if your mind stayed in one place. His gloom was as chilling as the weather and I determined not to be cast down. Despite our ignominious departure, my grandfather's sickness and even my father's reappearance, I felt full of hope, which I attributed to having met Johanna. In a burst of enthusiasm, I declared that my mind was travelling as fast as the ship, so fast that I would be happy to stay on board forever, visiting every corner of the globe.

'Like the Flying Dutchman?' he asked with a disturbing echo.

'Don't be silly.'

'First, you have to kill someone.'

'Oh sure, I'll just pull a name out of a hat!'

'Believe me, it's not hard. If you need any advice, I'm your man.' I looked at him with revulsion. 'Why do you think all the other passengers shy away from me? Thanks to you I've washed, so it can't be that they're put off by the smell. They see the mark on my forehead.'

'But that's absurd. My sister Luise is disfigured. Everyone talks to her.'

'Has she killed someone?'

'Of course not! You couldn't hope to find anyone more loving. Aunt Annette says she's been given a larger heart to make up for her smaller brain.'

'That must be a great comfort to her. I, however, have a smaller heart . . . or no heart at all.'

'I'm sure!'

'Why do you think I showed you my forehead?'

'To test me, like a riddle. To see if I could work out that your name was Mark.'

'In which case, you've failed dismally. The name on my passport is Sendel. But you know me better as Cain.'

'You are joking?' I asked with a shiver.

'Am I? I was doomed to walk the earth forever. Why shouldn't I walk near you?'

'When you said you'd killed someone, was it your brother?'

'I'd have thought a good Jewish boy like you would know that "Am I my brother's keeper?" has a wide application. Aren't we all brothers under the skin?'

My faith in a universal fraternity, which had received such blows in recent years from the viciousness of the Nazis and the disaffection of my schoolfellows, now received another from within my own community. He explained, in a tone more suited to a coroner's report than a murderer's confession, that he had killed many brothers down the ages, some of whom were blood relatives. His latest victim was a co-religionist, a toy-maker with whom he had shared lodgings in Berlin. 'As you so astutely detected, I'd been locked up in a concentration camp. I was let out in April on condition that I left Germany within two weeks. The joke was that leaving the country was even harder than living in it. There was no way I could come up with the money for my passport and landing-permit, let alone the 600 Reichsmarks it cost for my berth. Then it came to me. To celebrate my release, the toy-maker, with whom I'd barely exchanged five sentences, invited me to his room to share a bottle of schnapps. He couldn't hold his drink and began to boast that he wouldn't wait around for the Nazis to arrest him. He was planning to leave for Poland, thanks to the wad of notes concealed beneath the floor. Credulous fool! It wasn't hard to wheedle out its whereabouts nor – ' he added with almost artistic pride – 'to smash his skull with the floorboard I removed.' In a voice as pinched as a puppet's, I asked if the murder had been discovered. 'Yes,' he replied, 'although the murderer escaped scot-free. That is, unless you intend to report him to the Captain or set up a kangaroo court in the first-class lounge. But don't worry, no punishment can equal the one to which I've already been sentenced. Hang me from the chimney stacks or throw me overboard and I'm fated to return somewhere else, a stranger in my mother's womb.' With an anguished glance, he walked away as if to resume his wanderings, leaving me shaken and confused.

I promise you that this is not about to become a ghost story (although I know that, for Edward at least, that would be a welcome diversion), but I was at a loss as to how seriously to take him: whether he was playing an elaborate trick on me; whether he had lost his mind in the camp; or whether he was precisely who he claimed. After all, every Seder we laid a place for Elijah. What if I'd inadvertently conjured up Cain? I fear that, to you children, the question will appear academic. After all, you've grown up in a household where the Bible is, literally, a closed book. Why should the mark of Cain mean anything to you, when you have only the sketchiest notion of the man himself? For me, it was very different. Although my family was not religious, the Bible was central to our culture. My imagination had been steeped in the Scriptures ever since I was given a picture-book version as a child. Cain was the quintessential villain, the second man and first murderer. Suddenly he had materialised, whether from the pages of the Torah or his own imaginings. His identity may have been ambiguous, but it was mine that felt under threat.

Reeling from the encounter, I hurried down to the dining room, where my reticence at breakfast was attributed to worry about my grandfather. For once, the Professor's wife's half-chewed commiserations came as a pleasing distraction. Her expressions of concern remained curt because, in spite of her husband's strict injunction, she had news that she was 'simply bursting to tell', although it seemed to me that any imminent explosion was more likely to be induced by a fourth round of toast. She whispered conspiratorially that, having been told of some 'local difficulties' in Cuba regarding our arrival (a phrase she would come to regret), the Captain had appointed a passenger consultation committee, which the Professor was to head. It was clear that, however serious the difficulties – which in ordinary circumstances would have exercised me more – she was prepared to endure them for the sake of her newfound prestige, particularly in the eyes of the Banker's wife, who was outraged that the Professor's academic authority should be favoured over her husband's practical skills. Despite my preoccupation, I felt obliged to respond to the announcement and asked if the Professor were currently at a meeting. She replied, with amusement, that he was confined to the cabin on account of the swell. 'He lacks my stomach,' she said, drawing attention to her most prominent feature, which she then chose to fill with another chunk of cheese.

Although I suspected that the Professor's fragility was, in part, a ploy to escape his wife, it turned out that his caution was widely shared. I had the deck almost to myself as I grappled with the gale, revelling in the sharp spray on my face, the tang of salt on my lips and the elemental lash on my body. Not since the roller coaster ride at Luna-Park had I felt so secure in my flirtation with danger. My sole companions were children, for once justified in their claim that their parents' prohibitions had been swallowed in the wind. I was alarmed to catch sight of Luise lurching up the steps behind her two friends, but, like a freshly promoted youth leader, I remained too much the boyish ally for my decrees to have any effect. Instead, the sisters made me party to their pranks, explaining how they had locked various lavatory cubicles from the inside before sliding beneath the partitions to watch while increasingly queasy passengers were left hammering on the doors and then vomiting into basins and bins. 'She sick . . . she sick!' Luise exclaimed with pink-cheeked delight, as she was led away by her partners-in-crime like an elderly, much-loved bloodhound.

I returned indoors, strolling idly down to the games room where I found two teenage boys playing chess. They beckoned me to join them and I crossed the floor with what I hoped to be the correct degree of swagger. They held out their hands, intro-ducing themselves as if they were their fathers. The taller one with dark hair, a lazy eye and an enviable razor-rash on his chin was Joel Rathenau, a cousin of the one-time Foreign Secretary; the smaller one with reddish hair, freckles and eyebrows so faint that they might have been shaved was Viktor Ballin, the son of a violinist in the Gurzenich orchestra, which the Nazis had Aryanised by breaking the Jewish members' arms. They asked me my age, which I told them, only to regret my honesty when they both turned out to be seventeen. I resolved to make up for my youth with a display of intellectual vigour but, no sooner had I identified my favourite author as Sir Walter Scott, than Viktor topped him with Tolstoy. I felt so crushed that, when Joel offered me a cigarette, from an adult case rather than a schoolboy packet, I almost accepted, risking betraying myself by a novice's spluttering. 'My chest,' I said sadly, pointing to my scrawny frame and hinting at incurable lung disease.

We began to relax, swapping stories of our schools, our fami-lies and, above all, our girlfriends. I repaid their confidences by introducing them (and myself) to Annelise, a Berlin girl so perfect that she would never have given me a second glance. They chose, however, to ignore the implausibility, content simply to cap my claims of tongue-kissing with theirs of having gone 'all the way'. To complete my humiliation, Joel trounced me at chess which, since he insisted on commenting on every move, felt more like a lesson than a game. I made my escape, promising to meet them again soon, while determined to avoid them as assiduously as I did Schiendick.

After lunch, conditions on deck improved and the spray was replaced by prattle. I escaped indoors on hearing a silver-haired man inform a compliant crowd that the lavatories had been locked in a deliberate attempt to degrade the passengers. Finding no refuge in the cabin, which had been commandeered by Mother and Aunt Annette, I was left to wander the ship as aimlessly as Cain. On the stroke of four, I entered the tourist lounge, where Johanna's mother praised my punctuality: 'so much more admirable in leisured people'. I sat at her side and set about charming her, in the face of Johanna's pantomime grimaces. Her mother, who introduced herself by role rather than name, looked amazingly young, more like her sister, though I knew better than to say so in front of Johanna, whose sensitivity regarding parents was as finely tuned as mine. Christina, as I later found out she was called (a name that was far from neutral on the *St Louis*), was a woman of marshmallow pinkness, whose neck sank imperceptibly into her bosom and whose bosom swelled when she talked as though she were a singer practising scales. Fixing her with a grin which barely wavered in spite of Johanna's determined assault on my shins, I strove to prove that punctuality was merely one of my virtues. Then, asserting that a growing boy needed his tea (cue, smirk from the growing girl beside him), she summoned a waiter with the apologetic air of one more accustomed to taking orders. While waiting for him to return, she kept up a constant stream of chatter, which consisted largely of listing every item that she had ever bought at Frankel. After insisting that, despite the rival claims of Tietz and Schocken, it was the finest department store in Berlin, she reported how, on her last visit she had seen a sign in the window reading *Aryan store*, as if to reassure me that it was in safe hands.

Pausing briefly to pour the tea, she paid tribute to the kindness of our fellow passengers who had made her welcome, even when she had forgotten herself one morning and ordered ham. She declared that she had never known any Jews before. 'Except of course for Johanna's father', she added in response to her daughter's snort. 'I truly believe,' she said, radiant with righteous fervour, 'that all our problems would be solved by putting a group of Germans and a group of Jews together on a ship like this. After all, Jesus called all men his brothers. That includes the Jews.' When I pointed out that Jesus was himself a Jew, she corrected me, saying that he had been a *mischling* like Johanna. There had been a recent government edict that, since he was conceived by the Holy Ghost, he only had two Jewish grandparents, St Anne and St Joachim. I couldn't work out whether she were more pleased that her daughter's anomalous state had such an august precedent or that Jesus had been freed from taint. Finally, after helping herself to another cream cake which, she declared blithely, would prove to be her downfall, she insisted that we young people should go out on deck where we would find many more enjoyable things to do than to listen to her, a sentiment that I guiltily endorsed.

Johanna grabbed my hand and, eschewing the expected squeeze, virtually dragged me into the open air. I found it odd, given her ill-concealed contempt for her mother, that she had wanted me to meet her at all. Had it been me, I would have gone to the utmost lengths to keep us apart. My suspicion that it might have been a ploy to show me how much she suffered were borne out when, no sooner were we standing at the rail than she asked for my impression of tea, insisting that on no account should I try to spare her feelings. Wary of the pitfalls, I remarked on her mother's youthful looks (couched as the less contentious 'well-preserved') and asked her age. 'Old enough to know better,' she said sourly, before amending it to 'thirty-two'. Which meant that she must have given birth at eighteen: a mere four years older than Johanna was now. I grew sharply conscious of the promise – and danger – of her body and turned to face the sea. In a bid to anchor the conversation, I observed that my mother had had me when she was thirty, adding, in case she should suppose such tardiness to be a family trait, that it was due to the War.

'I won't ever have children,' she declared. 'I'll be like Marlene Dietrich with a string of lovers.' Although I had long looked to the cinema as a guide to adult emotions, there was an expression on her face, as there had been on Marlene Dietrich's, that frightened me. When I pointed it out, she laughed, saying that I would have to marry a quiet little mouse who wanted nothing more than to take care of me.

'I shall certainly marry someone,' I said, ignoring her tone. 'At his B'ris, a boy is sent into the world accompanied by three wishes: "May he enter a life of Torah, a life in marriage, and a life of good deeds." God himself commanded us to increase and multiply. That's one of the 613 precepts of the Torah a man is bound to obey.'

'And I'm supposed to lap it up just because it's in the Bible?' she asked. 'You're as bad as my mother hiding the dog's worming pill in his meat.' Terrified that she would walk away, I assured her that, until I did marry, I planned to be a joyboy. She looked so startled that I was forced to explain that I had read in *Der Stürmer* that Jews were natural joyboys. Shaking with laughter, she declared that she would never have imagined anyone could be so stupid. I was stung but, presuming that she meant my choice of reading, I let the matter drop. . . . I know, of course, even as I write this, that Marcus and Leila and Edward will have seen my mistake, and I expect that, by the time you read it, you too, Susan, will be laughing with them. I trust, however, that while you mock your grandfather's naivety, you will respect his nostalgia for a more innocent age.

A sudden cloudburst drove us indoors. Dismissing her claim that she looked 'a fright', I invited Johanna to the first-class lounge and, with a nod to my cinematic mentors, offered her a cocktail. She accepted on condition that I did not expect any favours in return. I feigned horror that she should consider me capable of such base calculation, while knowing full well that she had turned into Carole Lombard to match my Cary Grant. We continued the charade until the waiter blew the whistle with his assertion that we were too young to be served alcohol. His veto failed to dampen our spirits. We applauded the band, denigrated the other passengers and speculated on the dinner menu as assiduously as if our apple juice had been gin and vermouth. I was especially proud of my new-found taste for olives. My mood was shattered, however, by raised voices at the foot of the stairs, which, on investigation, I found belonged to my father and the waiter who had previously shown him the door. I sank down in my seat and fixed my glance so intently on Johanna that she asked if anything were wrong. Her question was answered by the waiter who, approaching the table, apologised for disturbing us and told me that the gentleman from yesterday had returned and was demanding to see me. He – the waiter – had thought it best to consult me before throwing him out. I thanked him and, while insisting that there was no need to call the Purser, agreed that he should send him away. He wove such an eager path through the tables that I wondered whether he found any incident, however ugly, a respite from his routine. Johanna was intrigued and, dropping her mask of languor, plied me with questions about the intruder, refusing to be fobbed off with either an equivocal smile or a proposal that I ask the band to play her favourite tune.

The waiter returned, although not to my rescue. His report of my father's claim to be my father made Johanna's eyes widen, to be joined by a dropped jaw at the subsequent appearance of the man himself.

'I don't *say* I'm his father; I *am* his father,' he declared. 'I'm sorry to interrupt you, Fräulein, but I have to drag Karl away. It's a matter of the utmost importance.'

'Please go,' I said, 'can't you see that I'm busy?'

The waiter, meanwhile, had summoned assistance with the same discreet nod with which he himself had so often been called to a table. In other circumstances, I would have admired the way in which they ushered my father out as coolly as if they were helping him on with his jacket, but, for now, my sole concern was that he should not compromise me with Johanna. To my relief, he put up no struggle, which I attributed to a history of forced exits from hotels and bars. He simply shouted that he could not shout but it was essential that I join him at once in my cabin. A moment later he was gone, plunging the company into apprehension and gloom at the sight of a fellow-passenger being led away by men in uniform, even one as innocuous as a waiter's jacket. In spite of the band's quickened tempo, the temperature fell sharply and two couples stood up and left. Johanna looked at me with suspicion.

'He said he was your father.'

'Well, he's not.'

'He knew your name.'

'It's no secret. You'll find it on your passenger list.'

'He looked like you.'

'Didn't they tell you at school? All Jews look the same. That's how they can pick us out.'

'Those are ugly Jews. You're good-looking.'

Before I had time to digest the compliment, the waiter returned and, with undisguised relish, suggested that I file an official complaint. I refused and, having sent him away, explained to Johanna that it was for a very good reason. The man had lost his mind after his son was murdered by the Gestapo. He had spotted me boarding the ship and, on the strength of a slight resemblance (I looked at her pointedly), had taken me for the boy, who he was now persuaded had not been killed but deported. His wife, to whom I was indebted for the account, had begged me to humour him for fear of driving him permanently insane. Despite grave misgivings I had agreed, even going so far as to call him Father – a neat precaution, I felt, should Johanna overhear us in future – but things had got out of hand, as he hounded my every step, humiliating me in front of family and friends. . . . I was unsure whether I had convinced Johanna, but I had totally convinced myself and, with a sad sigh, I concluded: 'I suppose that's what comes of trying to help people. It's hard enough having one father without having to play-act for someone else.'

Looking back from a distance of over sixty years, I see myself and shudder; however, I'm sitting at a sturdy desk in a book-lined study, not sailing precariously on the open seas (even Marcus at his most matter-of-fact must know that I'm not just speaking literally). I compare myself to Johanna who, for all her differences with her mother, had invited me to meet her, whereas I denied my father to his face. It would be easy – and less painful – for me to erase such moments from my account, but I'm deter-mined not to make the mistake with you that I did with Johanna and pretend to be someone I'm not. I may not always like the person that I was, but I acknowledge him. Which was one of the lessons that I learnt on the voyage.

Whether or not she were hoping for a fresh taste of drama, Johanna agreed to meet me by the lifeboats after dinner (I made a note to avoid spicy food). I returned to the cabin ready to plunge into a purifying bath but, as I turned into the corridor, I saw the Captain standing outside our door. My first thought was that he had been looking to swap notes with a fellow ornithologist. Then a wave of nausea swept over me and I stumbled towards him as though my brain and my legs were on different decks. Twisting his cap like the wheel in his hands, he expressed sympathy for my loss and pledged that he and his officers were at our service. I thanked him, and it now felt as if the dislocation were between my brain and my voice. He walked away, leaving me wavering on the threshold. I stepped inside and immediately wondered if I had misunderstood and the Captain, having read some secret file on our family history, had been offering his condolences on my parents' reunion, for standing in front of me was my father with my mother in his arms, while Aunt Annette sat weeping softly at the betrayal. Then, as I followed her eyes to the floor, my theory – and my world – collapsed at the sight of my grandfather laid out like a memorial brass.

My mind went blank. Elementary patterns of cause and effect eluded me. 'What's happened?' I shouted. 'Did he fall out of bed? Lift him! We must lift him up!'

My mother, alerted to my presence, broke away from my father and clasped me to her as though I were six. 'Your grandfather's dead, my dear.'

'Of course I know that! I can see that! I'm not a fool! But he's on the floor. We can't leave him there as if he'd been shot.'

'The Rabbi says it's the custom. But look, we've put a pillow under his head to make sure he'll be comfortable.' All my confusions about body and soul were exposed by the thought of making a dead man comfortable and I burst into tears, which prompted my mother to do the same, until maternal concern overrode filial grief and she composed herself enough to address me. 'We mustn't be sad – at least not for him. He was ready to go.' I looked down at the frail husk of the man I had always looked up to and felt full of despair that people were not more like trees, growing stronger with age. 'He was a good man. He had a rich and a happy life.' I pictured his eyes which, even when he smiled, had been flecked with sorrow and I supposed that she must have been talking of a time before I was born.

Incongruous, inconsequential thoughts raced through my head. 'Are you sure the carpet's clean?' I asked her. Then I was seized by the fear that I might trip – or even tread – on him. The next thing I knew, I was sitting dazed in a chair, my mother and Aunt Annette standing over me, the latter holding a glass of water to my lips. 'Drink,' she said, as if she were trying to replace the water lost in tears.

'Why?' I asked. 'Last week he was his usual self, taking charge of all the arrangements.'

'He was determined to see us safely on board,' my mother said. 'That done, his strength gave out.'

'He died for us.'

'He was seventy-six,' Aunt Annette said, 'you're fifteen. His fervent wish was that you should lead an honourable life.'

Their commonplace explanations failed to convince me. His strength should have returned as we escaped from danger. There had to be another reason and, as I looked up at my father, it became clear. 'Did Grandfather know about him?'

'What about me?' my father asked, butting in on our private conversation.

'That he was on the ship,' I said, sticking to the third person as resolutely as Luise.

'Of course,' my mother said, 'your grandfather bought his ticket.'

Deprived of my pet suspect, I tried a different approach. 'Will they perform an autopsy?'

'Heaven forbid!' Aunt Annette cried, shielding the body as if I were wielding a scalpel.

'Your grandfather's heart gave out,' my mother said. 'It had dealt with so much.'

'The doctor gave him injections! How do we know what they were?'

'Morphine! To ease the pain. You must give up these morbid suspicions. You make it hard for everyone. It's time to be a man.' I looked at my father, who had faded into the shadows, and said that I would do my best. 'Your grandfather loved you very much, Karl. He was so proud of you.' I conceded that that might have been true when I was twelve. 'He died calling your name.'

'Karl?'

'Karl.' For the first time I forgot my own grief and felt my mother's that the name had not been hers. 'I sent your father to fetch you.'

'I looked all over,' my father said, 'but you were nowhere to be found.'

I refused the solace of a lie that was clearly designed to compromise me in the future. 'Perhaps he had something to say to me,' I said. 'Something incredibly important that'll now be lost forever.'

'He could barely speak,' Aunt Annette said. 'The slightest sound was an immense effort. We heard "Karl", but it might equally well have been "Aarh!"'

I recalled myself in the lounge sending my father away and my guilt became as caustic as the grief that turned hair white overnight. 'I might have saved him, if only I'd got here in time.' My mother recovered some of her customary sharpness as she told me to stop talking nonsense. Nor did she demur when Aunt Annette suggested that he might have been calling for a different Karl, having clearly decided that the cost of asserting my unique place in my grandfather's affections was too high.

Further breast-baring was prevented by the arrival of the Rabbi, accompanied by the Purser and a steward. Our grief entered the public domain. My father slipped away in belated acknowledgement of his intrusion. The Rabbi placed his hands on my shoulders and, fixing me with his gaze, declared, 'Blessed be the true Judge.' The Purser offered more muted condolences, adding that he had come at the behest of the Captain to provide any assistance that we might need. The Rabbi took him at his word, asking first for a candlestick, for which the steward was dispatched to the dining-room, and then for extra towels to cover the mirrors in the bedroom and bathroom. He responded to my look of bewilderment by explaining that it was to prevent my grandfather's spirit being caught in the glass. The task complete, he stationed himself at my grandfather's head and, swaying back and forth in defiance of the ship's sideways roll, murmured incomprehensible prayers. Lowering his voice, either out of respect or embarrassment, the Purser asked about the funeral. I was appalled by his haste and insisted that we could leave such decisions until we reached Havana. He replied that there were insufficient facilities to preserve the body on board (my grandfather had been so dehumanised by the Nazis that this final instance scarcely stung me), so we had no choice but to bury him at sea. 'Flung overboard,' I asked, 'like refuse?' He assured me that he would instruct the ship's carpenter to make a coffin, complete with brass handles and a plate. My mother thanked him, but the Rabbi broke off his mumbling to point out that, since all men were equal in God's eyes, the plainest wood would suffice. He also vetoed the use of the ship's orchestra, on the grounds that nothing was required but our prayers. One point on which both Rabbi and Purser were agreed was that the ceremony should take place as soon as possible: the former because it was laid down by Law; the latter in order to limit any disquiet among the passengers. They set a time of eight o'clock the next morning, barely twelve hours away. As the Purser took his leave, I bridled at the hole-in-the-corner arrangements. My sole consolation was that, on balance, it was preferable to be eaten by fish than by worms.

The Steward returned with the candlestick and hurried away before he could be drafted into further service. As the Rabbi lit the candle, Aunt Annette muttered 'He was the light of our lives' so promptly that I was unsure whether it was her personal creed or a set phrase. The Rabbi placed the candlestick by my grandfather's head, lending it a disturbing illusion of animation. He announced that it was time to wash the body, adding that there were three members of a burial society on board, waiting in the corridor to perform the task. He asked my mother and aunt to leave but presumed on my staying. I wondered if I might be reprieved by confessing that I was not bar mitzvah, but I was reluctant to risk his scorn. On entering, the men all followed the Rabbi's lead and blessed the true Judge. I wedged myself into a corner, praying that I would not be called upon to do anything more than bear witness: my earlier horror of seeing my grandfather's nakedness compounded by the prospect of touching his flesh. The men shamed me by their lack of shame, paying no heed to the nappy-like stains on my grandfather's pyjamas. They washed every part of him (including the part which I was wary of handling even on my own body), treating him as tenderly as if we were in a hospital rather than a morgue. Finally, having used a sheet as a makeshift shroud, they bowed their heads in prayer, before shaking my hand and filing out.

The Rabbi asked me to fetch my mother and aunt from their cabin. On our return, he inquired tentatively, as though aware of my grandfather's lack of observance, whether we had a prayer shawl to place on his shoulders. I shared his surprise when my mother, whose reverence had long been reserved for the depiction of objects rather than the objects themselves, removed a small bag from a case and piously handed it to him. Her manner was partly explained by the shawl itself, whose white silk was shot with gold to form the most exquisite pattern, but more by her revelation that it had belonged to her brother. She turned to me and said that it would have been mine had I been . . . but, whether out of regard for the Rabbi or an unwillingness to resurrect painful memories, she broke off. The Rabbi, for whom the beauty of the shawl was secondary, announced that, before it was placed on the corpse, one of the tassels should be removed. I baulked at the desecration, which made my own rebellion seem so much more real. Not only was I losing my grandfather but this visible connection to his past. To add to my discomfort, my mother passed the shawl to me and said that I should be the one to pull off the tassel, which, in the event, proved to be so well stitched that it had to be cut. 'You're the man of the family now,' she said, triggering the thought that my grandfather's death was itself a kind of bar mitzvah and one that I could not escape.

We sat in silence while the Rabbi prayed. Straining my schoolboy Hebrew, I made out passages from the Psalms, but the words flowed so fast and so many were lost in his beard that I thought it best to view them as a background accompaniment like the cocktail music in the lounge. My mother and aunt gazed rapt at the body, with an occasional stifled sob to bear witness to the weight – and the discretion – of their grief. My own, meanwhile, was submerged in thoughts of base inconsequence. Instead of recalling my grandfather's life, I worried how to send word to Johanna cancelling our meeting. Instead of mourning his death, I wondered whether my closeness to it might lend me a tragic aura that made me more attractive in her eyes. The realisation of whose death it was that I was writing into my romantic scenario made my self-disgust swell to Göring-like proportions, and I bit my lip so hard that it bled, leading me to fear that she would be repulsed by the scar. Whereupon I bit it again.

Murmuring a few words that were as hard to decipher as the prayers, my mother left the cabin, returning a few minutes later with Luise and Sophie. Luise, whose aversion to black had led to several fraught incidents with rabbis in Berlin, clung closely to Sophie. Then, catching sight of the body on the floor and regarding it as the prelude to a new game, she let out a string of giggles. She knelt beside it and tickled the tummy. Unnerved by the lack of response, she prodded it, raising an arm, which she then let drop. I rose to grab her, but my mother warned me off with a sharp 'No!', insisting on Luise's need to register the truth for herself.

'Why she on the floor?' she asked, perplexed by the strange reversal. My mother crouched beside her and, with uncharacteristic patience (Luise's deficiency being as much of an affront to her as my defiance), explained that Grandfather was dead. Luise stared at her as if *grandfather* and *dead* had as little place in the same sentence as *Hitler* and *good*, before asking very slowly, 'Why she on the floor? Why not in Heaven?' My mother, even now refusing all easy consolation, told her that it was to give us a chance to say goodbye. Kneeling beside them, I determined to offer a balance. 'His body's on the floor,' I said, 'but his soul's in Heaven.' Far from taking comfort from my words, Luise emitted a plaintive moan and banged her head repeatedly against the bed. Sophie, as alert to the nuances of moans as a poet to those of language, sprang to the rescue, scooping her off the floor and out of the cabin. My mother adjusted the shroud.

'At least we tried,' she said, in a voice that spoke of a double bereavement.

The rest of the evening passed without incident. At midnight, the Rabbi left with a promise to return at seven the next morning. My mother proposed that I should snatch some sleep in her cabin, while she and Aunt Annette kept vigil. Exhaustion undermined my refusal, and I awoke at dawn in subtly unfamiliar surroundings to find my father sitting by my side. He told me with a hint of pride that he had carried me there himself. Aching with self-reproach, I jumped out of bed and ran back to my cabin, where my mother and aunt appeared not to have stirred all night. Dwarfed by their grief, I made for the bathroom, but my father, who had followed unbidden, informed me that family mourners were supposed neither to wash nor change their clothes for seven days. The injunction, which would once have offered enviable licence, now merely made me feel unclean. I pulled up a chair and contemplated my grandfather who, though barely twelve hours dead, seemed as remote as Bismarck. An hour later, the Rabbi arrived, filling the room with his guttural petitions, to be swiftly followed by two sailors carrying the coffin, which was as crudely constructed as a crate. They lifted the body off the floor and laid it inside, unnerving me with their routine efficiency. They were about to lower the lid when the Rabbi exclaimed that we must first place a bag of earth beneath my grandfather's head. Since earth was in short supply on the ship, I proposed using sand from the children's pit. My mother rebuked me for frivolity but, to both our surprise, the Rabbi overruled her and, handing me the bag from my uncle's prayer-shawl, dispatched me upstairs. Relieved to be of service, I knelt by the pit and pressed the damp grains into the bag as tenderly as if I were planting seeds. Then, alerted by the black trousers looming over me, I looked up at my least favourite face on the ship.

'It's the Jew with two names,' he said, with a smile like an open blade. 'What are you doing stealing Hapag company property?'

'It's only sand.'

'You Jews never miss a trick.'

'For my grandfather's coffin.'

'Oh yes? So, when he wakes up in hell, he can tell the Devil it's a bag of gold?'

Stung by his slur, I divulged far more than was wise. 'It's to represent Israel, so that, symbolically at least, he'll be buried in the Holy Land.'

'Germany is the Holy Land,' he replied. 'And you are defiling it. If I had my way, it's not just dead Jews we'd toss in the sea.' He strode away, leaving me to create a land of milk and honey from the empty sand.

As I returned to the cabin and put the sand inside my grandfather's coffin, I was tormented by the thought that he might have known the land itself if only he had taken my advice. I closed my eyes – in pain not prayer – while the sailors nailed down the lid, packing him up like an item from his own store. After leaden minutes in which we stared helplessly at the wood, the Captain arrived with a quartet of officers. With due ceremony they draped the Hapag flag over the coffin, a strangely apt touch given our outcast status, before forming a procession: first the Captain; next the Rabbi chanting prayers; then the officers carrying the coffin. As I stood with my mother, father and aunt, I realised that the order in which we followed would have implications far beyond the funeral. Only last night, my mother had named me the man of the family, a position now threatened by my father, whose morning shadow darkened his cheeks. As if to avoid the issue, she spurned us both, giving her arm to Aunt Annette. All thoughts of precedence were set aside, however, as I watched the coffin make its precarious ascent of the stairs to the sports deck, where a trestle-style bier had been erected next to the swimming pool. The officers lowered the coffin on to it and took up position by the rail, one section of which had been removed and a plank pushed through the gap like a makeshift slide.

The grey sky cast an appropriate pall over proceedings. The air was intensely still and I realised with a shock that the engines had been switched off. Surveying the assembled crowd, I spotted the Professor and his wife; the Banker and his wife; Helmut; Viktor and Joel; and, conspicuous by his isolation, Sendel. I wondered how they'd known to come: had a notice been pinned on the board next to that of our current position? Moreover, I wondered why they'd come: was it to pay their respects to my grandfather whom few of them had ever met; was it a rare distraction from the routine of the voyage; or had the Rabbi simply rounded them up to form a *minyan*? I blotted out the image of Johanna, who stood in the front row next to her mother. Any sympathy that she might feel for my bereavement would wither when she saw me with the man whom I had so recently, so publicly, disowned. I stared at my shoes while Sophie led out Luise, whose subdued demeanour revealed an instinctive sense of occasion. She tottered up to me and I gripped her rag-doll hand. Then, as the Rabbi recited the prayers, I followed the Captain's gaze to the chimney stack on which a solitary turtle dove was perched. My pleasure in its plumage was underscored by its biblical significance: not just in Genesis where it brought hope to Noah but in Leviticus where it was offered as an expiation for sin. I was roused by the Rabbi's announcement that it was time to perform *keriah*. Both my father and I were resolved to share the obligation with my mother, but, to my dismay, I found that, despite the Rabbi's incision, my shirt was too thick for me to rip. Fearful that Johanna would take me for a weakling as well as a liar, I redoubled my efforts, tearing it from neck to navel, far wider than the statutory hand's breadth. Any hope of its staying closed was dashed when I scattered sand on the coffin and found that even the smallest gesture exposed an expanse of pallid chest. To my relief, I was able to deflect attention on to Luise who, having been forbidden to tear her dress, made up for it by her relish of the sand game.

The Rabbi intoned Psalm 91, during which the officers moved forward and placed the coffin on the plank. Then, as the Captain gave a graciously neutral salute, the men raised the plank, sending the coffin sliding overboard. It bobbed in the water like driftwood and I had a vision of its following the ship like a friendly dolphin. Finally, to the accompaniment of Luise's frenzied clapping (so much more poignant than the prayers), it turned on end, twisted around and sank. As the Rabbi led the congregation in the *Kaddish*, I fell back from the rail and looked to the chimney-stack for reassurance, but the bird had flown.

Following my mother, I washed my hands from a jug held by the Professor. We stood in line while the congregation filed past. Christina's sympathy was clear from her watery eyes, but then, to her, every death was a portent of her own; Johanna's contempt was clear from her chilly handshake, although her capacity for warmth was apparent, as she had no doubt intended, in the kiss that she gave Luise. Feeling doubly bereft, I proceeded to breakfast. My one solace was to see family divisions restored when my father headed off to the second-class dining room, which my mother glossed over with the claim that he had no appetite. She evidently suffered no such lack herself. As she gorged on herring, tomato salad, corned beef, potatoes and finally, spaghetti, I remembered what Sendel (I refused to call him any other name) had said of his villagers' love-making after the massacre and wondered whether she might be equally crazed by grief. I would, nevertheless, have preferred her to exercise restraint and felt offended, not just for my grandfather, whom she had supposedly revered, but for myself as I pictured a similar response to my own demise. My speculations were interrupted by the Professor's wife, who was relishing her place among the mourners. She opined that my grandfather had died because of our setting sail on May 13th. 'Rubbish!' I said, stung by such trivialisation, adding gruffly that the jinx attached to *thirteen* derived from the Last Supper. It was absurd when cited by Christians but even more so when cited by Jews. Aunt Annette, who had hitherto kept silent, claimed – quite unnecessarily – that grief had made me forget my manners. The Professor's wife assured her that she understood, while informing me that she was perfectly justified in her belief, since Jesus' betrayal and crucifixion had been the gravest of all the misfortunes to hit the Jews. A warning glance from Sophie made me swallow my retort so, instead, I turned my attention to her.

'It was kind of Helmut to come,' I said, hoping to make amends for my earlier disapproval.

'Try *reckless*. One of the stewards is the Party representative . . .' As she spoke, I saw his features as clearly as the Führer's. 'Last night he called a meeting to remind the crew of the law against attending a Jewish funeral.'

'What about the Captain and the officers?'

'Official participants are exempt. Helmut could have volunteered to carry the coffin, but he wanted to make a point.' I wondered meanly if that point were aimed at Schiendick or Sophie. 'The steward didn't leave it at that. Apparently, he went to the Captain to remind him of company regulations that any coffin had to be covered with the swastika flag.'

'But that would be sacrilege!'

'Which is precisely what the Captain said. The steward then threatened to report him to Berlin.'

'Can you talk to a captain like that?'

'You can if you wear the right armband.'

'We're very lucky to have a captain who's a friend to the Jews.'

'The strange thing is that he isn't . . . not especially . . . at least not according to Helmut. He blames them for bringing a lot of their problems on themselves. But, while they're passengers on his ship, he's determined that they should be treated with respect.'

'You said *they*!'

'What?'

'Instead of *we*.'

'I was being Helmut . . . that is I was repeating his words.'

Her reply brought me little comfort and I returned to my cabin: the *my* being an even more painful pronoun. The stewardesses had cleaned the room. Only the water-stain on the floor gave a hint of any unusual activity and that was fading. I lay on my grandfather's bed, in a bid to avoid looking at it, and drank in the ferny scent of the freshly laundered sheets. A sense of despair enveloped me as I realised that, in focusing my anger on the Nazis, I had ignored a still greater injustice. I acknowledged the full horror of a world in which a man had no more control over his fate than a fly. Death flung open the door and he was wiped out like a roll of film in a darkroom. Old age was no compensation. Methuselah was a living, breathing being: he knew hope and fear; he made jokes and cried; he had children. Then, in a flash, he was gone. Whether the transition was expected or sudden made no difference; the fact was that it was absolute. Methuselah was no more, and all the rest, the memories and the monuments, was just wrapping on a broken gift. My grandfather was no more. A reunion in Heaven was a very remote prospect to one who could scarcely bear the wait until we reached Havana. Moreover, it would depend on my own obliteration. If God loved his people as much as the rabbis said, why must he prise them from a world which, however imperfect, was at least familiar? Why could he not visit us on earth as he did in the Torah? Death was less the gateway to God than the mockery of man. It was the ultimate expression of our helplessness and no amount of over-indulgence, in love-making or food, could conceal it. My grandfather's death might have raised my position in my family but it had diminished my sense of my own worth. I turned on to my stomach and buried my head in the pillow that would never again be his.

A gentle pressure on my shoulders made me start. I looked up to see Aunt Annette, her customary air of resignation having assumed an added significance. She asked if there were anything wrong, a question of such supreme superfluity that I neither ventured, nor did she wait for, a reply. She explained that she had come to pack away my grandfather's things in order to spare my mother.

'So she can spend more time eating?' I asked. She rubbed my forehead, as though trying to rub away the thought, and wished that I didn't feel everything so deeply. 'I thought it was good to feel,' I said. 'Don't we accuse Hitler of being unfeeling?'

'I expressed myself badly. What I meant was "take everything to heart".'

I was poised to say something cutting about *everything* being my grandfather's death when, to my surprise, I found that I was berating myself for not having treated him better. She held me tight and told me that everybody felt like that when a loved one died, which made me feel predictable as well as guilty. She reminded me of how much my grandfather had loved me. Although not a religious man, he had regularly quoted a verse from Proverbs: 'Grandchildren are the crown of the aged.'

'In his case, it must have been a crown of thorns,' I said, picturing the crucifixions in the Kaiser-Friedrich Museum. Then, to my horror, I began to howl. The suddenness of his death and the speed of the funeral, together with the advent of my father and Johanna, had left me no time to mourn. Now, alone with his closest friend – and my closest ally – I let myself go. 'He was so stubborn,' I sobbed. 'If only he'd left when I begged him, he need never have died. He wouldn't have been dragged off to the camp. He'd have been safe in Palestine.'

'Everything looks clearer looking back.'

'The Torah warns against making a god of gold.'

'Is that what you think he did?'

'Didn't he? He was afraid to give up his house, his store, his status.'

'His son. The one thing your grandfather couldn't leave behind was your uncle.'

'But he's dead! Isn't he?' I recoiled from the image of a shell-shocked uncle, more befuddled even than Luise, who was secretly locked in an asylum.

'Yes, of course. But your grandfather loved him more than your mother . . . more than your grandmother . . . more than anyone.' Her eyes filled with such tenderness that I failed to understand why she had no children. 'Your grandfather was prepared to abandon everything but the country his son had died for . . . the country for which he'd forced him to fight.' She went on to explain so much that might otherwise have died with my grandfather, things which showed my family – your family – in a new light, and so I set them out here for you. Uncle Karl had studied archaeology at Heidelberg and, although he had agreed to join my grandfather in the store, he was determined to devote his life and his fortune to the excavations at Troy. All that had changed with the War. My grandfather had insisted that it was his patriotic duty to enlist. When Christians were fighting for 'Kaiser, Fatherland and God', it was essential that Jews followed suit: the God might be different but the other two principles were the same. He regarded the War as a golden opportunity for

Jews to prove themselves as equal citizens of the Reich. My uncle was deeply sceptical. He believed that, win or lose, there was grave danger in Germany's militarisation. Nevertheless, his father put him under such pressure that he gave way.

'It's like Abraham sacrificing Isaac.'

'Except that, this time, there was no ram.' She described how my uncle had served, first, on the Western Front and, then, in the East, where he was killed. She declared that any guilt I was feeling at my grandfather's death was nothing compared to my grandfather's at the death of his son. All the Karl Frankel trusts and scholarships in the world could not begin to assuage it. Which was why he could not break faith with Germany. Even after he had been sent to the camp – even if he had been stripped of everything he owned – he would have stayed, had he not learnt that, at the express request of the Rector, all Jewish names had been expunged from the Heidelberg University war memorial. There was less trace of my uncle than of the heroes of Troy.

Her revelations moved me, although more on account of my uncle than of my grandfather. Given the weight of our family history, I had often wished that I had been called after someone else, but now I was proud to bear his name. I pondered the new set of relationships, while my aunt wrapped up my grandfather's hairbrush as lovingly as if she were brushing his hair. Her grief clogged the cabin and, when a steward brought me a summons to the Captain, I seized the chance to escape. The message was unexpected and I speculated that, sharing my disdain for all the hidebound old men, he wanted me to join the passenger committee. In anticipation, I took two of my grandfather's cigars and slipped them into my pocket.

My excitement increased when the steward led me through a door marked 'Restricted to Ship's Personnel', although the only visible distinction lay in the drabber décor. He asked me to wait in a small sitting room. I identified its owner at once by the prints that covered the walls: petrels; shearwaters; garnets; skuas . . . names that held far more romance for me than any capital city or mountain range. I was examining the pictures when the Captain walked in. I jumped back as though he had caught me rifling his desk, but he moved to reassure me, putting his hand on my shoulder and telling me of his own encounters with the different birds. In his thirty-seven years at sea, he had observed fifteen varieties of tern and fourteen of albatross, including the elusive Tristan. Unable to keep the note of envy from my voice, I confessed that it was my dream to see an albatross, although it would have to wait until I travelled further south.

'Don't be so sure,' he said. 'Birds, I'm pleased to report, don't read books of ornithology. I once came across an albatross as far north as the Azores.'

'I saw you staring at the dove during the service,' I said and then cringed, both at having revealed my own lack of concentration and in case he should suppose that I was condemning his.

'It must have blown off course on its flight back to Europe.'

'How will it find its way now?'

'It probably won't. You needn't look so sad. There are between one and two hundred million birds on the planet. We can bear the loss.' I wanted to explain that, right now, I couldn't bear the loss of a single ant but, fearing that he would misunderstand, I simply asked him who had counted them. 'Not me, I'm happy to say. Though, according to my wife, I might as well have done.' I was surprised to hear that he had a wife and wondered whether she were equally tiny. All such conjecture was set aside, however, when he moved to the desk and handed me a map neatly tied with a ribbon. He declared that it marked the exact spot where my grandfather was buried and hoped that it would be of some comfort to my family and myself. Having assured him that it would, I judged that the moment was right to offer him a cigar.

'Do you smoke them?' he asked in surprise.

'Of course,' I said, adding in case he should be in any doubt: 'I'm very grown-up for my age.' He thanked me and took one for after dinner. Suspecting that the interview was over, I realised that I would have to broach the subject of the passenger committee myself. I cited the rumours that the ship might be heading for trouble in Havana.

'Who told you that?' He frowned as though one of his officers had been indiscreet. I immediately identified the Professor's wife, whom I would have been happy to see clapped in irons and confined to the hold for the rest of the voyage.

'Her husband's on the advisory committee you've set up,' I said, giving him the perfect opportunity to increase its number.

'There'll be no trouble. None whatsoever. Everything's being handled by the Hapag officials on the ground. I'd be grateful if you'd reassure anyone who might be anxious.'

I refused to let the matter drop, as much to prevent his underestimating me as from genuine concern. 'People are saying it's to forestall further difficulties that we're sailing so fast.'

'We're making good speed because there are two other ships on our tail: one German; one French.'

'Both aiming for Havana?'

'Apparently.'

'And both with Jews on board?'

'So I understand. It makes sense to be the first to dock.' He appeared to lose his thread as he told me how distasteful he found the whole business, how he felt more like a warder than a sailor, and how he longed to go back to transporting normal passengers.

'Aren't we normal passengers?'

'Not any more.'

I spent the rest of the day attempting to dodge a stream of elderly passengers who seemed to believe that my grandfather's death gave them a licence to maul me. My cheeks were pinched, my arms squeezed and my hair was ruffled in dubious expressions of sympathy. The one person whom I wanted to see, not to say, maul me, was nowhere to be found, but I finally ran into her mother, who informed me that Johanna was feeling sick and resting in her cabin. I asked her to give her my best wishes (love was too precious to be entrusted to a third party), which she agreed to do, although, judging by the disparaging look she threw me, I felt sure that Johanna had told her about my lies and she was responding with one of her own. I walked away and straight into Sendel, whose contempt for social convention left me with no qualms about turning on my heels. To my dismay, he called me back. My grandfather's death was so raw that I had no wish to indulge a madman who held himself to be immortal. At least he offered no condolences on the demise of such a relative youngster, restricting his remarks to the dignity of the service.

'I expect you've been to hundreds of funerals,' I said.

'Thousands. But it's ages since I've been to a burial at sea.'

'Would that have been on the way between Ukraine and Germany?' This time he acknowledged my irony, although only with a laugh.

'Oh no. Long before. The Battle of Lepanto. Nearly four hundred years ago. I'm hopeless with dates.'

'You frighten me.'

'So I should. But don't worry, it's a fairground fright. I can't do you any harm.' I refrained from telling him that he had already done serious harm to my head. Instead, I asked if the reason he rarely washed was that he was in mourning. 'So many deaths,' he replied. 'So much mourning.'

Against my better judgement, I continued the conversation on his terms. 'What's always struck me about your murder of Abel is that you hit at the wrong man. He did nothing to hurt you. He prepared his sacrifice as required. It was God who favoured his at the expense of yours.'

'Bravo! I congratulate you. You're still very young but you've already learnt more than most men do in a lifetime: we fight one another but the real enemy is God. Let me tell you about my life . . . don't worry, only the most recent one. The entire cycle would take the rest of the voyage. As I've already mentioned, I was born in a little village in the Ukraine – the perfect place for a man at odds with history. My father was a rabbi: a scholarly man and in his way a holy man, but such a dull and blinkered man that it was in my blood, as well as my destiny, to rebel. I had three brothers and five sisters but I was the brains of the family.'

'Some might say that you had an advantage,' I said slyly.

'Very good. Yes, they might. . . . I was sent to the yeshiva in Kiev. But, far from immersing myself in the Talmud, I studied politics and economics. Revolution was in the air and I was determined to play a part. My father was appalled. He'd suffered grievously under the Tsar, but he respected one thing above all else: authority. Any attack on authority was an attack on God. We fought bitterly, until the advent of the War dwarfed our private quarrels. One of my brothers was killed and another lost his legs fighting the Austrians, but my father's grief at their fates was nothing to his shame when I refused to enlist. A certificate of exemption from the medical tribunal on account of my chest saved his face in the village, but he knew what was in my heart.'

'My grandfather forced my uncle to join up. He never forgave himself.'

'My father never forgave me. . . . Let's jump ahead to 1918. The Armistice was signed and the Great Powers were counting the cost, of which the dead were only a fraction, but, in the Ukraine, the war had barely begun. The country was plunged into chaos, with the Reds and the Whites and the Peasant Partisans all struggling for power. The only thing that united them was their loathing of the Jews. The Whites were the worst: they massacred as though they were on a mission. When they butchered a nearby village, a lone survivor managed to send us a message: "Tell your Jews to hide." But the postmaster failed to pass it on, leaving us helpless when the soldiers marched in. As the handful, and I do mean *handful*, of survivors bound their wounds and buried their dead – ' And made love, I remembered from his earlier account. – 'I tracked down the postmaster, who turned out to be a cousin of one of the partisan leaders and had taken refuge in his camp. All the hatred I'd felt for the Tsar, all the hatred I'd refused to direct against the Austrians, was now heaped on one man. On the pretext of selling them secrets, I sneaked into the camp and killed him. I fled back to my village, but the partisans followed me. They tortured my father, sister and brother in a bid to discover my whereabouts, but none of them gave me away. So they had to be satisfied with slaughtering them and defiling their corpses.'

'How did you escape? Where were you hiding?'

'In the cemetery. In a freshly dug grave.'

I pictured my grandfather crammed in his coffin and was afraid that I might be sick. 'It's not your fault that your family died. You didn't kill them.'

'As well as politics, I studied psychology. I could have run far away. I could have returned to the city. But I chose to go there. At the back of my mind I knew that the Partisans would come for me. . . . Different kinds of hatred. Different kinds of revenge.'

'Was that when you left for Berlin?'

'No, first, I went to the Reds. They were the least bad of the warring factions. That's not my clumsy German; it's the truth. I begged them to bring the killers to justice but they needed the peasants' support against the Whites. They ordered me to leave, which I did, ending up in Berlin, where I eked out a kind of existence. I could have done so much with my life but I chose to waste it – and make no mistake, it was a choice. What better revenge can anyone take on God than to squander the life he gave us? If we live well, he's won. If we kill ourselves, he's won too. But if we live badly, if we spit on our gifts and scorn our talents, then it's we who've defeated him. So I let myself go. I neglected to wash myself or my clothes. I made brutish love to miserable women – not rape: that would have required too much effort. I became an object of shame to my fellow-Jews and contempt to the Christians. But I felt free – do you understand that? – even in the camp I felt free. Because my quarrel isn't with the Nazis any more than it was with the Partisans; it's with the God who made them, and you and me, and looked at us all and saw that we were good. Can you credit such arrogance . . . such self-delusion? He looked at us all and saw that we were good! So you mustn't despair about your grandfather or being on this ship or anything else that happens to you. That plays straight into God's hands. Instead, you must use it – as I have – to bolster your cause against him.' He turned away, leaving me to stare blankly at his back until, summoning all my strength, I roused myself and bolted down the deck.

His words rang in my head until they were drowned out by the bell for dinner. I hurried to the dining room, where I found my mother presiding at our table, more elegantly dressed than at any time on the voyage. The rip in her blouse was covered by a diamond brooch, at which the Professor's wife cast covetous glances. Between them – in my grandfather's chair, which made his intrusion all the more glaring – sat my father. Aunt Annette, sensing my unease, patted the seat next to her, which was somewhat superfluous given that it was the only one left, although I was grateful for her concern. My mother was explaining my father's presence to our fellow-diners, a tortuous tale of how he had joined the ship at the last minute when all the first-class tickets had been sold, that was greeted with manifest scepticism by the Professor's wife, for whom the further we sailed from Germany, the more money reasserted its traditional power. Nevertheless my mother was undeterred, describing how she had requested, and the Purser granted, that my grandfather's ticket be transferred to my father, whom the Banker and his wife now welcomed as if he had been pulled out of the sea rather than merely jumped up a class. 'So you'll be sharing your cabin again tonight, Karl,' my mother said, staring at her soup as intently as a gypsy at tea-leaves.

'It'll give us a chance to get to know each other better, son,' my father said.

I was horrified by his use of a word that any other passenger might more legitimately apply to my age than he to our nominal relationship. I was disgusted by her issuing her decrees in public where I had no right of reply. So I said, as calmly as any twenty-one year old, that he could have the cabin to himself because I intended to sleep out on deck, the better to observe the birds at dawn. My words met with a chorus of objections, led by my mother, who managed to make 'ornithology' sound like a perversion. She announced that it was against shipboard regulations and a steward would undoubtedly order me inside. 'Very well,' I declared, 'I shall stand all night in the corridor as if I were being questioned by the Gestapo.' The table at once fell silent, causing Mother, who believed that embarrassment, like indigestion, was a condition unknown to the young, to tell me coldly that I had ruined everyone's meal. I followed her example and fixed my gaze on my bowl, deciding that the vermicelli at the bottom spelt Trouble.

At the end of the meal, I returned to my cabin and locked the door, a precaution that proved to be unnecessary since neither my father nor anyone else came near. In the event, I would have welcomed another presence, even his, since my dreams were a private *Walpurgisnacht*, crammed with witches and ghouls, which I knew that someone of my age should laugh off but which so infiltrated my consciousness that I had to sleep with the light on like Luise.

Anxious to avoid the dining-room, I breakfasted on chocolate from the shop and then joined the crowds at the rail craning to catch a glimpse of the Azores. I had been too absorbed in my own affairs to pay much heed to my fellow passengers, but I was deeply touched by their elation, the whoops of joy and weepy embraces, as they made out the windmills on the cliffs. Havana was still a week away, but there was no denying the promise of land. Unable to invest the craggy headland with suitable emotion, I strolled aimlessly about the deck until I stumbled on another crowd watching the swimming pool being filled. Far from obeying a Nazi edict forbidding Jews to enter, the crew had simply left it empty until the weather improved. A thump on my back alerted me to Joel, who challenged me to a race after lunch. I eagerly accepted, my love of the sport intensified by the chance to make up for my trouncing at chess. I asked, as casually as I could, if he had seen my friend Johanna and, when he made me describe her, found myself using language more appropriate to a lovelorn poet. Stung by his smirk and keen to escape any further ragging, I decided to look for her myself. After a morning of frustration, I wondered whether her sickness might have been serious, or even fatal, with the news of her death suppressed for fear of alarming the other passengers. No sooner had I conceived the theory than I acknowledged its absurdity. The plain fact was that Johanna was shunning me. Friendship depended on honesty and she knew me to be a liar. Bereft of hope, I punched the wall with such ferocity that a small boy who had lifted his younger brother on to a lifebelt ran off, leaving the victim to emit a terrified howl.

Lunch passed without incident, apart from the Professor's wife's fear that the pungent smell meant that the platter of cold fish was 'off'. I reassured her that the smell came from me and, directing my remarks less at her than at my mother, who had not only washed but thrown her ripped blouse in the bin, exclaimed that it was my sacred duty to my grandfather. She, in turn, accused me of ostentation, particularly when she alone was required to sit *shivah* and had decided, in view of my grandfather's own practice, that one day was enough.

'I expect it's a custom that makes more sense in Palestine,' the Professor's wife said, relishing our discord.

'Why?' I asked. 'It's hotter there. Mourners wouldn't just smell; they'd reek.'

'Don't try to be clever, Karl,' my mother said.

'I'm sorry,' I replied. 'I thought it was good to be clever. I thought that was why I went to school. I thought that was why I read books. I thought – '

'There's clever and there's snide,' my father interposed. When I realised that even he now had a right to criticise me, I vowed to myself that the moment the ship reached Havana, I would run away. I would work on a sugar plantation or in a cigar factory, condemned to a life of backbreaking drudgery, so long as I could be on my own.

After recovering for an hour in the company of *Ivanhoe*, I went up to the pool for my rendezvous with Joel. To my dismay, I found that it was packed, putting paid to any hopes of a serious swim, let alone of impressing him with my prowess. Nevertheless, as I watched men and women enjoying a pleasure that had been denied them for years and coaxing children whose only aquatic games had been in puddles, I began to relax. Then I saw that among their number were my father and Luise. The one thing that stood between my sister and drowning was a rubber ring. I rushed to the edge, where Sophie was dipping her feet dreamily, and asked what was going on. She replied that it was perfectly obvious, but I refused to be deterred by her tone.

'He might drown her. His hands aren't steady.'

'He doesn't drink any more, Karl.'

'Not in public, no. He's far too clever. I expect he has one of those hollow sticks like in the Alps.'

'You always claim to be grown up. Now's the time to prove it. Learn to live with your father.'

'That's rich, coming from someone who never speaks to hers.'

'It's not the same. I understand – believe me – how sore you feel at the way he neglected you, which is all the more reason to give him the chance to make up for it now.'

I explained, as simply as I could, that a person did not need a father at fifteen, when he could stand up for himself, but at eight, nine, ten and eleven, when he was abused and abandoned by his school-friends and living in a regime that had not only curtailed his childhood but crushed his very identity. At that moment, Luise caught sight of me and pounded the water so violently that my father and everyone in the vicinity were soaked. My father waved and Sophie responded furiously, to make up for my hands of stone.

'Luise is enjoying herself,' she said.

'Of course. Daddy's a new word to her, like Captain or Cuba. I expect she thinks he comes with the ship.'

'And you must have noticed the change in your mother.'

'And I'm supposed to be grateful? With my grandfather barely wet in his grave.'

'You make yourself ugly.'

'I'm not the one acting as if he'd been dead for five years.'

'I'm sure he'd want all of us, your mother especially, to be happy.'

'That's so easy to say. Well rest assured that, when I die, I want everyone to be miserable. I want you all to remember how cruelly you've treated me and be racked with guilt.'

'I give up,' she said, gazing back at the pool.

'No, I give up on you,' I replied, determined to maintain the advantage, and strode off.

Further disillusion awaited me on the sports deck where I found Johanna engaged in a game of shuffleboard with Viktor and Joel. Pain seared my flesh as though I'd stepped on a nail. My one hope – that she had been nursing her love for me alone in her cabin – was dashed at the sight of her flushed face and easy rapport with her friends. Left in no doubt that Joel had sent me to the pool as a diversion, I was doubly offended by the cordial wave with which he beckoned me to join them: a gesture that was repeated enthusiastically by Viktor, who appeared to have cast off his bookish ways along with his glasses, and, more stiffly by Johanna, who screwed up her eyes at the sight of me, although that might have been because I was standing in the sun. In a bid to punish them for their perfidy, I turned down the invitation, but, as I watched them return to the rough-and-tumble of the game, I was the one who suffered. Unable to bear a moment more, I walked away, resolved to spend the rest of the voyage in my cabin, when a cry of 'Wait!' changed my mood as emphatically as Willy Kirsei's scoring a last-minute goal. Johanna had made a choice which, to me, felt as momentous as any in a medieval woodcut. Too scared to express my relief, I asked if her companions wouldn't miss her. She replied cannily that she'd thought that I would miss her more.

'In which case, why have you been avoiding me?'

'You flatter yourself,' she replied (and the opposing team

came within an ace of equalising). 'I was stuck in my cabin with cramps.' I found it hard to reconcile such a long confinement with my own five-minute agonies, until she specified that they were stomach cramps. I knew somehow that these were peculiar to girls and felt strangely moved. As we strolled to the prow, I sensed her reluctance to come too close to me. Eager that she should not lump me together with Sendel, I explained that I had stopped washing out of respect for my grandfather. Thrown by her look of surprise, I added that it was an age-old custom, not a personal quirk. She asked if it were widespread, and all my resentment of my mother spilled out as I described how it was the rule in more devout families that, for a week after a parent's death, they would not leave the house, or wash or shave (the last injunction made me acutely self-conscious) but sit on a low stool and mourn. Twice a day, ten men would come to say prayers. There had to be ten to make up a *minyan*.

'But you don't have ten?'

'Not even one. Just smelly, inconsequential me.'

'People grieve in their own ways.'

'Yes. And, tucked up at night, Hitler reads the Torah.'

She urged me not to become bitter, claiming that, in the past, what she had most disliked about the Jews had been their negativity: the way that they were forever harking back to long-ago persecutions or harbouring grudges for some thousand-year-old slight. On the *St Louis*, however, she had formed a very different picture: one of kindness, resilience and laughter. She would hate me to convince her that her original view had been right.

I was conscious of a new responsibility: to my people as well as my cause. I realised, however, how much ground I'd already lost when she asked why I'd lied about my father. 'I didn't want you to connect us in any way,' I said lamely.

'He's a very handsome man,' she replied. For the first time, the connection seemed to work in my favour.

'People say I look like him.'

'Is he also a very vain man?' Even as I despaired, I knew her contempt to be justified. Then she laughed, and I realised that with girls, unlike boys, tone of voice mattered as much as words. I expressed my fear that he would cast a shadow over our friendship (a last-second substitute for *relationship*). She replied that I had encouraged her to make her peace with her mother and, while the change of surroundings might have played a part, she was already seeing her with fresh eyes. I insisted that the cases were very different. Her mother's offence had been youthful folly. My father's wilful crime was harder to forgive.

'But for how long?' she asked. 'It's years since your sister was born.'

'But only days since he came back. I can't just wipe out the whole of Luise's life – and half of mine.'

With nothing more to say but no wish to end our conversation, I led her towards the stern where, to my horror, I spotted my mother poised at her easel in a smock as splattered as her palette. She summoned me with a wave, which I had no choice but to acknowledge for fear that Johanna should accuse me of disowning both my parents. My mother radiated charm, complimenting Johanna on her hair, her clothes and her smile (all things that she purported to find trivial), while mortifying me with her request that I stand downwind. Johanna responded by quizzing her on the picture, whereupon my mother warned her that she ran the risk of alienating me. 'Karl,' she declared, 'feels threatened by my creativity. He lacks vision. He wants to circumscribe life.' She spoke as though I could appreciate nothing in a gallery but the frames. Johanna ignored the warning, lavishing praise that made my mother blush. She insisted that it was a mere sketch, adding that it was the first time she had picked up a brush in months. Johanna, whose attention to the canvas went way beyond the call of duty, expressed particular approval of the sea, claiming that she had never thought of its being yellow before but would no longer be able to see it any other way. If I had not known her better, I would have suspected her of sarcasm. As they discussed the finer points of Art, with an earnestness worthy of the capital, I grew increasingly disturbed by their complicity and feared that I might have identified the wrong parent as the potential threat. Anxious to reassert myself, I asked my mother whether painting were permitted in the first week of mourning. A cloud passed over her face.

'My pictures celebrate life. I know your grandfather would approve. He loved them.'

'He certainly *bought* them,' I replied and explained my emphasis by repeating what he had told me in strictest confidence, an injunction that had weighed heavily on me for years but which I felt sure had lapsed at his death. 'In an attempt to please you, he paid agents to buy up the paintings in all your exhibitions and kept them locked up at the store. There was no mystery about the mystery collector. It was him.' I felt a chill wind on my neck like the breath of ghostly displeasure. He had divulged the secret in order to make me more sensitive to her needs and I was using it to punish her for her insensitivity to mine. Nevertheless, I was determined to press my point. 'It wasn't your paintings he loved but you. Some parents try to protect their children.'

'And some children try to destroy their parents.'

Seeing her downcast face, I wondered if truth really were a higher virtue than compassion. Her refusal to challenge me owed less to a belief in my honesty than to a lack of faith in herself. 'Now you must leave me to work.' She flashed Johanna a brave smile. 'It's very good to meet you, my dear. I hope we'll have many more chances to talk. But I must press on before I lose the light.'

We left my mother picking up her brush in spite of the stacks of unsold canvases cluttering her view. Halfway down the deck, Johanna abandoned me, her studied silence a more eloquent comment on my conduct than the most vehement reproach. I returned to my cabin wondering why, when in the right, I so often felt as if I were in the wrong. My yearning to reach Havana was intense. I felt less like a passenger on a luxury liner than a prisoner in a rotting hulk. I tried to read but was mocked by the purity of Ivanhoe's love for Rowena. I buried myself in the bed, only to be roused by Aunt Annette, who entered with a knock as token as a steward's smile. She announced that she had spoken to my mother, to whom, confounding expectations, she had grown closer since my grandfather's death, and had come to see if she could mediate.

'Doesn't it ever get wearing,' I asked, 'always trying to keep the peace? You're not even one of the family.'

'Are you out to hurt me too?'

'I'm not out to hurt anyone.'

'You were very hard on your mother. She's suffered a great loss.' I sniffed. 'Yesterday, when I explained about your grandfather and your uncle, I didn't tell you everything.' I stared at her, both exhilarated and appalled by the prospect of further revelations. 'They were estranged even before the War. Karl despised what he called his father's "money-lined world". He longed for a simpler way of life.'

'Like me?'

'He was a lot older.'

'I'm not a child!'

'Then you shouldn't behave like one. . . . Your grandmother, of course, believed that her son could do no wrong – like all mothers.' The parenthesis was inaccurate but well-meant. 'She raged at your grandfather for forcing him to fight, vowing that she would hold him to blame should Karl suffer the least injury. In the event, she never forgave him for his death. A few months later, she killed herself . . . oh no!' she added in the face of my unconcealed horror. 'There was no gun or poison. She simply withdrew from life. She saw no one. She ate nothing. She refused to speak even when the hunger became intolerable. Indeed, she seemed to welcome the pain as her last link to her son before they were reunited.'

'So my grandfather had two deaths on his conscience?'

'And not only on his. Your mother loved your grandmother – let there be no mistake about that – but she didn't always show it. She was quick-tempered and headstrong. They clashed over many things.'

'Let me guess: would one of them be her art?'

'Your grandmother felt that your mother should paint the way that she herself worked on her crochet. There was never any question of her going to the academy where she might have to take . . .'

'Nude drawing?'

'Life classes. Amalia rebelled, not as effectively as her brother, who was hundreds of miles away in Heidelberg, but more persistently.' I said nothing, trying to absorb the new slant on a relationship that had been held up as exemplary. 'Even when your uncle died, she found it hard to console her mother. I suspect (I don't mean this as any kind of accusation) that, in among the tears, she felt an element of relief to be out of his shadow, which in turn increased her guilt. She told herself that she was not the one her mother wanted, until the smallest word of comfort felt like an intrusion on her grief. Then the chance to speak was lost forever, leaving your mother and grandfather doubly bereft, bound together by guilt. And guilt is a more powerful emotion even than love.'

A Sea Change

Her revelations did not stop there. My vision of my grand-parents as a latter-day Abraham and Sarah was shattered when she confessed that she had been far closer to my grandfather than to my grandmother even before the latter's death. She had not, as I had been led to believe, sacrificed her life with Gretchen-like devotion in order to care for her best friend's husband and daughter but had hoped to marry the husband herself. My mother, however, protested so strongly that any such hope was dashed. She was prepared to accept Aunt Annette as her father's companion but not as his wife. My grandfather, unable to contemplate the loss of a second child, bowed to her wishes. Aunt Annette had no choice but to accept the position or leave.

'It was easier than I thought . . . at least it became so in time. I established a strategy for coping. It was the little things that hurt: not being able to straighten his tie when we were out; never being the one to say "Bless you" when he sneezed; then, yesterday, not being required – or even allowed – to perform *keriah*.' I sensed the aching heart beneath the immaculately pressed blouse. 'It's so hard talking like this, but I know you're grown-up enough to understand.' I resented her blandishments and longed to retreat into a nursery-world full of cuddly shapes and primary colours. Yet, just as she felt that it was essential for me to know the truth in order to understand my life, so I feel that it is essential for you children to know it in order to under-stand my story . . . 'I hope you won't think any the worse of me,' she said. 'I hope you won't add me to your list of enemies.' I assured her that no one could make an enemy of her. 'No, I suppose that I'm no threat.'

She explained that my uncle's death had claimed a further victim, my father. He and my mother were distant cousins and their parents had pledged them to one another at an early age: the family tie making up in my grandfather's eyes for the finan-

cial imbalance. Whether out of affection for my father or obligation to her own, my mother astonished everyone by agreeing to
the match. My father, for his part, was expected to feel nothing
but gratitude. He had left university with a yearning to write,
which he would henceforth have the means to pursue. That all
changed, however, with my uncle's death and my grandfather's
need to groom a successor. My father's utter unfitness for the
role was evident to everyone except for my grandfather, who
believed that he could mould a man as easily as clay. Conscious
of his failure, my father took to drink, thereby giving his wife
and father-in-law fresh cause for complaint. So he drank more in
order to escape their censure, caught in both a vicious circle and
a downward spiral, which my grandfather, who abhorred any
form of confrontation, chose to ignore. Aunt Annette begged
him to buy my parents a house where they could set up on their
own, but he was desperate not to lose hold of my mother,
insisting on the need for families to stick together in such
troubled times. My father's drinking, meanwhile, took a turn for
the worse. He would disappear for days, only to return full of
remorse. Then, after one such bout, he came home spoiling for a
fight. My mother locked her bedroom door, but he broke it
down and forced himself on her. It was then that Luise was
conceived.

'*Forced*?' I interjected. 'I think the word you want is *raped*.'

'That I don't know.'

'You mean you won't say.'

'The next morning he disappeared. He lived . . . well, we
heard later that he'd been living in a doss-house.' For my fastid-
ious aunt, that seemed to be the most painful detail of all. 'He
came back once, about three years later.'

'Really? Are you sure? Why don't I remember?'

'I don't suppose he even knew that he had a daughter. He
must have done – but how . . .? We'd finally learnt the truth

about Luise's condition. Not even your mother could hide behind words like *placid* and *slow* forever, so she'd taken her to see the top specialist in Berlin. His diagnosis was unequivocal. Her brain had been damaged before she was born.'

'And Mother felt that my father should accept his responsibility?'

'Not so much your mother as your grandfather.'

'What?'

'I loved your grandfather very much, but there was a part of him – a small part, mind – that was grateful not to be the only one to have split his family. He told your father what the doctors had told us. Georg was completely distraught. We were afraid he might do some harm to himself, or even . . .'

'To Luise?'

'No! No, of course not . . . I don't know. But only out of pity. Because he couldn't bear to see her in pain.'

'She wasn't in pain. All the whirling and the head-beating came later. She just lay there, inert, barely focusing her eyes.'

'To your father that was pain. Not being able to express oneself was pain. Your grandfather made him a generous allowance – generous in size, that is, not in spirit – on condition that he had no further contact with any of us. And he didn't. Until your mother brought him back.'

'Why?'

'You'll have to ask her. Or rather . . . Perhaps she couldn't bear to think of him suffering in Germany. Or perhaps she felt that, in a new country, they might make a fresh start.'

'Don't you think she might have mentioned something – just an odd word – to the other interested parties?'

'Your mother was schooled by your grandfather. She believes, and I don't mean this as a criticism (at least not a serious one), that she knows what's best for her children. Just as he tried to safeguard her, so she's trying to safeguard you.'

'That isn't true! You just want to make me feel better.'

'Why should I lie and risk turning you against your grand-father?'

'Because he's dead, so you think it doesn't matter.'

'Oh it matters. But the truth matters more. I'm saying this not simply to fill you in on family history – '

'I have a right to know.'

'Maybe. But to bring home how complicated life really is. It can't be neatly set out in black and white like the two times table. There are hundreds of different shades.'

I shut myself in my cabin for three days. In answer to all inquiries, I said that I was sitting *shivah*, although I never uttered a single prayer. At a stroke the world had changed. In the past, it had been neatly circumscribed: at home; at school; in the streets. There was safety in boundaries, even when they were made up of Nazi *do-nots*. Now everything was as fluid as the view from my window. The only boundary left to me was my bed. I yearned to escape from the ship and pictured it striking a rock, with myself as the sole survivor, swept on a piece of driftwood to some deserted isle. Neither grief nor snakes nor an unbroken diet of pineapples could override the attractions of solitude. I yearned to withdraw and dreamt of a Jewish tradition of hermits who lived in caves or of rabbis who stood on pillars. In trying to free me from the weight of the past, my aunt had left me with a present as painful as a Gestapo torture. I was not naïve. I had known that grown-ups weren't perfect long before I went to kinder-garten, but I had presumed that their misjudgements were confined to children. I never realised that they could be as blind to one another as they were to me. The facts of the matter hadn't changed. My father was still a brute who had hit my mother (my own fists clenched instinctively), yet his motives turned out to be as complex as those of any king I had studied at school. The revelation of his desire to write brought back memories of childhood nights, when my room had been transformed into an enchanted forest or a sultan's palace or a great auk's nest. Recalling the stories he had told me made me ponder the ones that he might have told himself, especially of the War. Uncle Karl had died but he had survived, to be measured forever against a memory. To my surprise, I felt a rush of filial sympathy, although the sensation brought no relief. Life might no longer be black and white, but mine was an all-pervasive grey.

Aunt Annette and Sophie made repeated attempts to rouse me, offering such inducements as swimming and sunbathing by day and films and concerts by night. Once Sophie brought in Luise, who padded over to the bed and, with a sad cry of 'She sick!', laid her face on mine and gave me a dachshund kiss. The Professor's wife looked in briefly, although I suspected that her primary aim was to inspect the cabin. She brought me a life of Heinrich Heine, borrowed from the ship's library, with print so small that it might have been designed to inflame my headache. My mother punished me with a visit from the Doctor and then lingered while he made his examination. After plying me with endless questions about my health – plus the occasional one about my mood to show that he was modern – he assured her that there was no cause for alarm: I was simply suffering from 'growing pains'. He prescribed 'a good dose of sea air', as though it were a radical cure rather than an ubiquitous commodity.

In the event, I followed his advice, albeit incidentally, after opening the greetings card that had been pushed under my door. It was from Johanna, who had made it herself out of pictures she had cut from magazines. The result was an extraordinary mishmash, with Emil Jannings feeding a cream cake to the Sphinx, while Martin Luther sat at the wheel of a Bugatti. After laughing out loud at the incongruities, I found myself deeply moved that she should have taken such trouble. I was overwhelmed by the thought that, moments before, she had been standing . . . stooping outside my door. I pressed the card to my nose and, although the dominant scent was glue, I was sure that I could detect traces of something sweeter. I studied her words like a Talmudic scholar. No simple hope that 'we will soon be resuming our talks' can ever have been subjected to such scrutiny. Having exhausted the message, I focused on the script, which was exquisitely neat and rounded, the antithesis of my own spidery scrawl. I pondered on the differences in boys' and girls' writing and, unwittingly, found myself picturing the exquisite neatness and roundness of Johanna's breasts. I then turned my attention to Joel and Viktor and the whole company of sailors, all older and better-looking than me, who had no doubt exploited my absence to try to supplant me in her affections. At once, the atmosphere in the cabin became unbearable. I still felt the need to escape but now the prison was of my own making. After agonising over tactics, whether to trumpet my emergence or to take people by surprise, I opted for the latter, joining the crowd on its way to dinner. First, however, I scrubbed every pore. Then, basking in my restored cleanliness, I put on a fresh, unripped shirt. As I examined myself in the mirror, I noticed something different – older even – about my face, which I attributed to the hardened look in my eyes.

Luise greeted my reappearance by clapping so loudly that a passing waiter asked if it were my birthday. The rest of the table accorded me a welcome that was more muted but equally warm. Only my mother felt the need to inject a sour note, countermanding my order of roast beef, which she claimed would be too heavy on my stomach, and substituting steamed fish. The Professor's wife then leaned across the table and, in an ear-splitting whisper, commiserated with me on my diarrhoea. I was shocked, but not surprised, to find that my mother had stripped me of my mourning clothes and banished me to the lavatory. The Professor's wife, however, showed no qualms about recalling an evening when she had been in the throes of dysentery but, at Erwin's insistence (she flashed him a look of gentle reproach), had attended a formal dinner at the university. She had been seated at the top table next to the Dean (I wondered whether imparting that titbit might not be the point of her entire narrative) and, every time that she needed to go to the 'you know where' (a remark which, for some reason, she directed at Luise, the one person who had not the least idea where), the entire hall was obliged to stand. My father responded with the story of how he and some college friends had placed a laxative in their professor's food. Once again I was amazed at the double standards of the adult world. If I had told such a story, let alone perpetrated such a prank, I would have stood accused of puerility but, when my father did so, everybody laughed.

After dinner I made a tour of the ship. Although I hadn't dared to formulate a plan, even to myself, I found that I was heading for all the places where I had walked with Johanna. Her absence fuelled my most extravagant fears. In frustration, I ran down a corridor and straight into Schiendick, who was supervising the removal of the Führer's portrait from the social hall. His resentment at the transfer of the picture, which he treated as reverently as if it had been painted by Dürer, flared up at my clumsiness. I wondered whether, among the mass of anti-Jewish laws, contact with an Aryan image constituted a form of pollution. 'This is what happens when we take down the Führer's portrait,' Schiendick screamed. 'It is defiled.' I tried to retreat, but the picture was blocking my path. 'These people owe their lives to the Führer's generosity. And what do they do? Spit in his face.' One of his assistants reminded him that the portrait was being moved on the Purser's orders, so that the Jews could hold their service, at which Schiendick let out a stream of invective against 'that Jew-lover'. Then, yielding to the same impulse of which he had accused me, he aimed a ball of spittle at my feet.

I was confused by the reference to a service, given that it was Tuesday evening and the hall would be put to many other uses before the Sabbath. So I crept inside, to find some twenty or so passengers decorating the room under the direction of the Rabbi. Potted plants and palms had been brought from all over the ship and placed in the centre of the floor. Two elderly men were draping floral shawls over the balustrade under the critical eyes of their owners. The foliage looked more suitable to a party than to a service so, in an attempt to glean information without exposing my ignorance, I asked one of the men about the shawls. 'The synagogue is always filled with flowers on Shavuot,' he replied. 'These seemed like the next best thing . . .' I don't expect you children to know about Shavuot (I admit that I barely did myself), but, as a festival, it's second only to Passover, which precedes it in the calendar. In biblical times it was a celebration of the wheat harvest, hence the greenery. Later, it came to commemorate God's gift of the Torah on Mount Sinai, and the greenery became a symbol of the moment when the rock burst into bloom. As I write, I already hear you snort. We live in a world where *miracle* refers to nothing more remarkable than a racehorse or the effects of a ten-day diet. Meanwhile, the truly miraculous is downgraded. I recently read an article arguing that Moses' crossing of the Red Sea was a mistranslation of Reed Sea, making it less an expression of divine providence than an adroit piece of orientation. Whether or not the rock actually burst into blossom, it remains the perfect image for the flowering of faith following God's offering of his covenant.

Struck by the echo of our own exodus, I volunteered my services to the Rabbi, who immediately set me to work heaving pots. I found it a relief to exercise my muscles rather than my mind.

The transformation complete, he announced that he would lead the Shavuot vigil, at which I slipped off, determined to return the following day.

Shavuot is a joyous festival and I subscribed to its mood from the moment I awoke. Lapping up the sunlight that streamed through the window, I languidly stretched out, until a glimpse of the clock sent me leaping out of bed and into the bathroom. Examining my face in the mirror, I realised that the change I had previously identified was to be found not in my eyes but on my upper lip. I ran my fingers over the smattering of down that felt like one of my mother's softest brushes, and realised with a mixture of triumph and trepidation that I could finally shave. I was at a loss, however, how to proceed, missing my grandfather more than ever as I released the catch on his razor. I lathered my moustache and, in my enthusiasm, spread the foam to my cheeks, but I still could not bring myself to risk a blade which seemed more likely to draw blood than cut hair. I washed off the soap and replaced the razor, masking the reek of my failure in a liberal sprinkling of my grandfather's cologne. I made my way to the dining room, where my mother inexplicably chose to kiss me. She drew back with a start. 'Karl, what is that smell?'

'It's Grandfather's cologne,' I said defensively. 'I thought I might as well use it.'

'Yes, of course,' she replied. 'But you don't have to use it all at once.'

My father, intent on impressing my mother with his concern, inquired how everyone planned to spend the morning now that we had only three days left at sea. Swallowing a dismissive reply, I asked the Professor's wife to pass the toast. My mother, with an uneasy glance at me, announced that she planned to paint. I assured her that the light was perfect, at which Aunt Annette handed me the honey without being asked. My father added that he had promised to take Luise swimming, prompting her to slap the table so gleefully that the Banker spilt coffee down his sleeve. He accepted my mother's apology with a wan smile, which he failed to extend to Luise. Sophie offered to share pool duties until noon, when she had arranged to meet a friend. From the looks that were exchanged across the table, it was clear that this friendship had become common knowledge, and I wondered how far it had progressed during my absence. My father asked tentatively if I would care to join them. Resigned to my refusal, he seemed taken aback when I coupled it with thanks. I explained that I was going to the Shavuot service, trying hard not to let it sound like a reproach. I acquired two companions in Aunt Annette and the Professor's wife, the latter explaining that she always looked forward to Shavuot, partly because of the cakes (although I doubted that she needed any excuse for over-indulgence), and partly because it was when she had been confirmed. I was surprised to learn that she had been brought up in a Reform congregation, much to the horror of her Orthodox grandparents who had considered it tantamount to apostasy. I was even more surprised by her insistence that, in current circumstances, it was essential for Jews of all traditions to sink their differences: our adversaries were powerful enough without our quarrelling among ourselves.

One difference became apparent as soon as we entered the hall. The women were sent to sit at the side while I took my place at the centre among the men. Although loath to relinquish my masculine prerogative (not least when I was finally set to enjoy it), I felt such segregation to be more suited to a farmyard, a feeling that intensified when I found myself facing Johanna. I was amazed. Given her hostility to Judaism, she was the last person that I would have expected to see. At first I feared that she had come from a spirit of devilry, the mock-your-enemy principle I myself had adopted at the zoo, but the warmth of her smile reassured me, suggesting that she was driven by intellectual curiosity or even a flickering of faith. I tried to keep my mind on the service, but her presence was a constant distraction. I sneaked a second glance and received a further smile, before burying my head in the prayer-book in case she should think me insincere. I wondered whether she might even have come in the hope of meeting me, until I realised that there were far easier ways of making contact and, in any case, she could have had no idea of my plans. I tried to concentrate on the readings but, while salvaging enough Hebrew to catch the drift of Deuteronomy, I was totally perplexed by Jeremiah. I decided simply to sit back and enjoy the chanting. The Rabbi was a match for any professional singer. In another life he might have graced the stage of Bayreuth. Even so, I could have wished for a less Wagnerian length of service. Half the congregation drifted out, including the Professor's wife (I wondered wickedly whether it were a replay of the university meal). Johanna and I stayed put until the final hymn, after which I hurried to greet her.

We were at once easy and embarrassed in each other's company. She complimented me on the cologne, which I prayed had faded since breakfast. I thanked her for the card, claiming that it must have had healing powers. She blushed and said that she knew it was childish but she could think of no other way to reach me. Having looked for me everywhere, she had sought out my mother who had told her that I was sick and not to be disturbed (given the diarrhoea with which she had previously saddled me, I presumed that the delicacy was Johanna's own). I asked how she had spent the time, hoping desperately for a 'pining in the cabin' or else a 'sitting in the sun, grappling with Viktor's copy of *War and Peace*,' although I preferred to keep that connection to a minimum. She replied that she'd done nothing special, just wandered around, enjoying the general

mood of celebration. Even her mother was happy. Having made
friends with a group of widows who had taught her the rules of
canasta, she was playing for shipboard pfennigs every afternoon.
What's more, a middle-aged chemist from Augsburg had been
paying court to her. I asked what he was like and she offered the
single word 'clammy', which might have amused me had I not
dreaded an equally blunt description of me. Then, as casually as
if I were speaking of clouds on the horizon, I asked whether she
had seen anything of Viktor or Joel. Her reply delighted me: 'Joel
may be your friend, but he's dreadfully pompous. He thinks he
knows everything, but it's like he's made himself memorise a
page of the encyclopaedia every day since he was ten.' I could
barely stop myself kissing her. It was clear that she had no
interest in either of them but had simply been civil for my sake. I
declined to press the point, however, since I knew that girls hated
losing face. I asked, instead, what she was doing at the service.
She explained that, after hearing people talk about it at dinner,
she had wanted to see for herself.

'It's odd. I didn't understand a word. In church, at least
there's the occasional *Sancta Maria* to help you find your bearings. The men were shouting out different prayers like market-
traders. The women were pushed to one side like slave-girls in a
harem. The Rabbi's voice was so deep that it seemed to bubble
up from the engine room. Even so, I found it tremendously
moving. You may think I've been swayed by having found out
about my father, but it seemed to speak to something in my
innermost being, bringing out feelings I didn't know were there.'

'Jewish feelings?' I asked tentatively.

'Just feelings. I don't have to give them a name.'

'No, of course not.'

'I was too hasty before . . . no, not hasty, blind. I thought
Jews were sad, clinging to the past like my grandmother refusing

to put in electricity. But, here, everything seems different. Their faith – '

'Our faith.'

'Your faith defines your lives in a way that shames my own Church, which hasn't raised a finger against the Nazis. It seems to see them as a commercial opportunity rather than the enemies of Christ.'

'Who was after all a Jew.'

'He was everything.' Her voice grew serious and I anticipated a theological discussion but, to my delight, she took a different tack. 'Besides, if I've changed, it's because of you.'

'Me?'

'Is that so hard to believe?'

'No,' I lied. 'Just too much to hope.'

'I like you a lot. I didn't appreciate it till you weren't around. Even that way you have of clicking your fingers . . . No, don't stop! Well do, but not just on my account.'

'I only do it when I'm nervous.'

'You can't be as nervous as me.'

I have no idea whether I moved to her or vice versa (a confusion which was as real at the time as it is in memory), but we found ourselves kissing. Every sensation in my body had gathered in my tongue. For the first time I understood the place of kisses in films. They didn't hold up the action; they were the action. I wondered if my previous ignorance had been due to a lack of experience or of vocabulary. I marvelled that anyone could be so uninspired as to use the same word for Johanna's passionate embrace as for Aunt Annette's powdery peck. The Greeks had a range of synonyms for love; the Germans should have an equally wide one for kisses. Then Joanna rolled her tongue along the roof of my mouth and the need for words of any kind disappeared.

The Rabbi's cough thrust us back to the present. Marrying discretion ('you mustn't think I disapprove') with firmness ('this is a place of worship after all'), it sent us rushing out on deck. As we walked though the ship, Johanna claimed that, in spite of everything, we owed a debt of gratitude to Hitler, without whom we would never have met. I refused to accept that such a momentous occurrence could depend on chance of any kind, let alone the whim of a tyrant, so I declared that, in happier days, she would have come into Frankel and I would have shown her a tray of diamond rings.

'I could never have afforded one.'

'I would have sneaked it out when the other assistants had gone home. I'm the boss's grandson; they trust me.'

'Is that what you want to do for a job?'

'Be a thief?'

'No, stupid! Work in a shop?'

'If my grandfather hadn't died, he might have opened another store in New York and I'd have had to take it over. Or at least he'd have asked me to. Now there's no danger. I want to be an ornithologist.' Her blank look prompted me to a discreet elaboration. 'There are about two thousand species of bird on the North American continent, twice as many as in Europe. I shall make it my life's work to study every single one.'

'In swamps and deserts?'

'Or the ice-caps of Alaska, where it's too cold for snakes.'

'What?'

I deflected her question by asking what she wanted to be, at which she ran through as many options as in a guessing game: nurse; teacher; tennis instructress, before adding that she would be equally content as a farmer's wife with ten children and a herd of cows. I asked tentatively whether the cows might be replaced by birds, and she giggled.

'Do you think it's very feeble of me not to have more definite ambitions?'

'I think everything about you is perfect,' I replied, and she confirmed it with a heavenly kiss.

I grew aware that we were attracting attention, all of which was friendly, though I detected an air of condescension behind the desiccated smiles. Johanna was more sanguine. She held that people were simply feeling happy, for themselves as much as for us. The sun had lifted their spirits. I suggested that that was because it was the climate for which we had been created. All the coldness and cruelty in human nature arose when we migrated north. Pressed to elaborate, I cited our origins in the Garden of Eden. 'You mean you still believe that?' she asked, as astonished as if I had cited the Man in the Moon. I played for time. I knew, of course, that we had evolved from monkeys, just as I knew that matter was made up of atoms, but our animal past seemed as fanciful when I gazed into her eyes, as our molecular present did when I stood on the hardwood deck. The story of Adam and Eve might be a myth, but it was a far cry from Günther and Brunhild. Their fate made perfect sense of my own contradictions: how I felt at times that I could do anything to which I put my mind, and at others that nothing I did would ever work. Whereas the notion that we were monkeys who had lost our tails made sense only of my negative side; although I had to admit that it totally explained the Nazis. Since, however, I was more concerned to earn Johanna's good opinion than my own, I assured her that, when I had said the Garden of Eden, I had meant the Middle East.

We lay on two recently vacated deckchairs, pooling our revulsion at their residue of warmth. I ordered us both fruit cocktails, exotic concoctions as notable for their foliage as their flavour, and worried about my diminishing supply of shipboard marks. The obvious solution lay in my grandfather's wallet, which remained in the drawer by his bed, but I was less inclined to appropriate his cash than his cologne. Determined to banish the clouds from my mind, I pulled a protesting Johanna to her feet and led her to the rail. As our legs brushed, I felt a perverse nostalgia for short trousers. Powerful sensations surged through me, but they no longer seemed shameful now that I had found someone to share them. Rather than pressing my suit on an imaginary woman whom I had assembled like the collage on Johanna's card, I was standing beside a real person whose heart beat as fast as mine. She made even the most monkey-like part of myself feel pure. I longed for us to stay like this forever, and it was clear that she felt equally happy for she made me promise that, whatever else might occur, we would meet again in ten years' time.

'Won't I see you till then?' I asked, unable to conceal my horror at the prospect of such a wait.

'Of course. But just to be sure. So many things . . . unpredictable things, might happen.' The urgency with which she spoke made me wonder whether she had had a premonition.

'Where?' I asked. 'On a liner in the middle of the Atlantic ocean?'

'At this precise latitude?' She laughed. 'No!' Then, with a nod to her new homeland, she said: 'In New York, at the top of the Empire State Building.'

Looking at my watch, I said: 'It's a date: 3.47 p.m. on 25th May 1949.' She suggested that, for simplicity's sake, we made it 4 p.m. Then we sealed the promise with a kiss or, to be more accurate, we signed it, sealed it and tied it up with red ribbons. It was a far more lingering kiss than those that I had observed with such distaste earlier in the week. As we broke off, we found ourselves being gaped and giggled at by Luise's two playfellows, but I didn't care.

We met at nine the next morning for the second Shavuot service. Although we were once again forced apart, I felt as close to her as if we were sitting side by side. The focus of the prayers was on the dead (in the Rabbi's words, 'the departed') and, for the first time, I was reconciled to the loss of my grandfather. As we gave thanks for our forefathers and for all the blessed ones of Israel, I felt his passing to be a part of life rather than an affront to it. The chanting of the lamentations was intensely moving, imbuing the service with a beauty and a resonance that it might otherwise have lacked. The readings were unfamiliar and largely incomprehensible but, in his sermon (thankfully, in German), the Rabbi explained that, as was traditional at Shavuot, he had read from the Book of Ruth. Later, when I filled out the story for Johanna, who was as hungry for our history as our customs, she was captivated by the Moabite woman who left her home, threw in her lot with the Jews and went on to become the great-grandmother of King David. I was exhilarated by her suggestion that, of all the Bible passages that might have been chosen, it was one with a special application to her. My exhilaration grew even stronger with the announcement over lunch that all passengers should collect their landing cards from the Purser's office during the afternoon, in preparation for our arrival in Havana. Freedom was no longer a dream.

My happiness would have been complete had it not been for the fancy dress ball to be held that evening. By rights, I should not even have thought about going in the week of my grandfather's death, but the unique circumstances of the voyage supplied a dispensation. Moreover, I felt an obligation to Johanna, who had made her attendance contingent on mine. As well as guilt at abandoning my mourning, I felt at a grave disadvantage among people who had been designing their outfits for days. A ball was a frightening enough prospect without having to wear something witty. On top of which, Johanna's casual 'Don't forget to shave. It tickles,' had knocked me sideways. I was as mortified as if she had told me that I smelt. As I ran over and over her words in my mind, I longed for the salvo of *prickles* which, at least, suggested strength. *Tickles* was ineffective as well as unpleasant. What I wouldn't have given for a smooth skin! I thought back to the boy at school who'd had a disease that had made all his hair fall out. Baldness was a small price to pay for an uncompromised body. . . . Then I remembered the rumours that he'd paid a far higher price when he vanished abruptly in the middle of term, and even the boys who hadn't laughed at him never heard from him again. I swiftly resigned myself to my moustache.

My dining companions did not share my qualms about the ball. Even the Professor's wife took more interest in the costumes than in the food. Depending on their degree of preparation, people either pleaded secrecy or offered tantalising hints about their characters. My first suggestion was to drape myself in sheets like a Roman toga, but my mother, who anticipated a glut of indolent emperors, decreed it to be banal; my second was to borrow some chains from the engine room and go as a tortured prisoner, which would have the added benefit of restricting my dancing, but that was universally deemed to be in bad taste. Aunt Annette proposed that I wore Uncle Karl's uniform, which my grandfather had reverently preserved, and, to my horror, my mother concurred. Gripped by a vision of a tattered battledress, punctured by bullet holes, stinking of combat and, worst of all, stained with my uncle's blood, I insisted, with all the delicacy at my command, that it would swamp me. 'You're not a little boy any more, Karl,' Aunt Annette said proudly. 'You're almost as tall as your father.' The association intensified my gloom.

I was greatly relieved when, on our return to the cabin, Aunt Annette unwrapped the braided uniform and sash of a Heidelberg university drinking club. It struck me that my uncle might have joined any number of worthier groups, such as birdwatching or stamp-collecting or photography, but I was grateful for the pristine state – and smell – of the clothes. After my aunt's comment on my size, I was too embarrassed to take off my shirt in front of her and retreated to the bathroom, although, to spare her feelings, I left the door ajar. I hobbled back into the room, clutching a bunch of excess material at the waist, which made my spindly frame feel more freakish than ever, but Aunt Annette, recklessly applying pins to the trousers, told me not to worry: tailoring was in her blood.

Scarcely had she taken away the uniform for alteration than the fitting room was turned into a magic grotto by the arrival of Luise, sporting a wire-and-towelling tutu with a pair of cardboard wings and a crepe-paper crown. She waved a peacock-feather wand beatifically as she lurched around the room, transforming us into creatures from her unfathomable imagination. I complimented Sophie on the effect, but she immediately gave the credit to the other member of Luise's retinue. 'Your father made everything. I just put it on her.' For all my surprise, I thought it only right to repeat my praise. I watched Luise clinging to him and felt a pang of jealousy. I wondered whether, instead of my pitying her, it shouldn't be the other way round. Given the many problems that my intellect had brought me, her lack of it might even be a blessing. Then, just as I was succumbing to this sentimental vision, Luise waved her wand and toppled over. She let out the familiar moan and began banging her head. As always it was unclear whether she were punishing herself or the floor. My father looked so appalled that I was tempted to take his hand. He hovered ineffectually while

Sophie and I calmed Luise. My tapping her nose with the wand had the desired effect, and Sophie led her away to attend to the very unfairylike bruise on her forehead. My father and I were left alone for the first time in eight years. He asked about what he termed Luise's 'outbursts', which I explained were regular but unpredictable. The crucial thing was to ensure that she did herself no harm.

'You've no idea how much I long to turn back the clock,' he said, a doubly futile sentiment under the circumstances. The fairytale world had been exposed as an illusion. Time could not move backwards any more than cardboard wings could fly. 'But though we can't rewrite the past, let's at least put it behind us. I know that I've destroyed your sister's life. I couldn't bear to think that I've destroyed yours as well.' He looked as though he were about to cry, shocking me not just with his own vulnerability but that of his sex. I never knew that men could show grief. I thought that they had to be both controlled and in control like my grandfather, which was what prevented my joining their ranks. Before I had a chance to reconsider, I asked if he would show me how to shave. He looked as proud as if I had given him a medal. He moved towards me and I recoiled; I didn't need to be shown how to hug. Chastened, he led me into the bathroom where, strangely shy of my grandfather's shaving brush, he whipped up a lather and applied it to my upper lip. Then he passed me the razor and, placing his hand on mine, led me through the movements, only to tremble so violently that he had to let go. I attributed the trembling to anxiety, since there was no hint of anything untoward on his breath. His instruction became purely verbal and I succeeded in removing the hair without a nick. I washed off the excess foam and stared at myself in the mirror, transfixed by the new-found definition of my upper lip. It felt as though a shadow had been lifted from my face.

Aunt Annette returned with the altered uniform, which I put on while she sought out my sternest critic to judge the final effect. To my surprise, Mother endorsed both the fit and my fitness to wear it. I longed to know more about the drinking club, whether it had involved a skill such as wine-tasting or been sheer self-indulgence, but neither my mother nor my aunt wished to discuss it. I ascribed this reluctance to the presence of my father, whose edginess made me wonder whether membership of a similar club in Frankfurt might have been the origin of all his troubles. So I shifted the conversation to their own costumes, at which they became as irritatingly evasive as when they offered me a cup of wait-and-drink tea.

The Professor's wife's insistence on ploughing through every course had never been more insufferable than it was at dinner. While other tables had long since escaped to change, ours sat watching her guzzle the cheese. She announced that she would not be dressing up, since 'You probably think me peculiar enough already, don't you Karl?' Not even Aunt Annette's emphatic elbow could prompt me to deny it. The Professor remarked that he planned to go as an absent-minded Professor who had left his costume at home, which caused widespread mirth. His wife suggested that he would probably prefer to have left her at home, which fell flat. Her selfishness meant that, by the time I had re-emerged from my cabin, the party was in full swing. The social hall had been totally transformed since the morning service. Although most of the greenery remained, it had been supplemented by streamers and Chinese lanterns. The dais, which had held the makeshift ark, was now occupied by the ship's band, looking dapper in white dinner jackets. Hordes of children – or rather, princes and princesses, elves and fairies, and my own favourite, a goggle-and-flippered frog – frolicked, without any regard for either rank or role. Many of the adults wore simple evening clothes but, even as I deplored their lack of effort, I recalled that they had had so little occasion to wear them in recent years that it must feel like fancy dress.

The officers were all in uniform, which I presumed to be a company regulation. Seeing no sign of Schiendick, I decided that he must be the Devil, sporting a red silk-lined opera cloak and eye mask, with two papier-mâché horns on his head. I determined to keep him in my sights for fear that he should take the impersonation to heart, but my attention was diverted by Helmut, who had jettisoned Sophie in favour of a fellow sailor. I was appalled. I thought that it was only Orthodox Jews who danced with other men; although they would never have shown such passion. Praying that Sophie wouldn't notice, I scoured the hall in a bid to find and distract her. Then the music stopped and I realised that Sophie had not only noticed but that she was the sailor in question. Beating a hasty retreat, I bumped into Aunt Annette, who had been transformed by my mother's smock and palette, my own cap, worn back-to-front, and a cotton-wool moustache and beard, into a Parisian painter. Even that was less disturbing, however, than my mother's metamorphosis into a belly dancer. Dressed – albeit barely – in diaphanous veils, with a giant emerald stuck in her navel, she threw herself into her character, waving her arms and wiggling her hips at the surfeit of sheikhs, one of whom, having ignored her ban on bedspreads, was my father.

Mortified by the spectacle (and emboldened by my uniform), I ordered a beer from a sweating steward, who brought it with gratifying compliance. Sipping its sweet sourness, I resumed my scrutiny of the room, this time in search of Johanna. The closest I came was her mother, dressed as a schoolgirl in her daughter's gym-slip, with her hair tied in pig-tails and lipstick freckles dotted on her cheeks, although, given her youthful looks, it scarcely seemed like a disguise. She had attracted several admirers, among them the Professor, who addressed her with rare animation, while a vast gypsy woman, wearing curtain-ring earrings, a table-cloth skirt and size twelve slippers, whom I took to be the courting chemist, stood by and glowered. Fleeing the eccentricities of my elders, I ran into Viktor, with a sheepskin rug flung over his shoulders, his glistening face smeared with what appeared to be boot-polish and four pipe-cleaners hanging from his nose. When I asked him what he was supposed to be, he replied with an air of resignation, 'a wolf in sheep's clothing'. I contrived to look impressed. Joel, meanwhile, had managed with minimal fuss to come as an accident victim on crutches. I praised his skill at having seized on the telling detail whereas most of us had opted for the broad effect, only to find, to my embarrass-ment, that he was suffering from a genuinely sprained ankle as a result of racing round the pool: 'acting the goat', in the newly enfranchised Viktor's phrase.

Johanna's arrival was well worth the wait. Wearing a painted egg-box headdress, carrying an inverted plunger torch and draped in a red-and-white striped tablecloth pinned with forty-eight paper-napkin stars, she made a stunning Statue of Liberty. Her freshness and beauty combined with the simplicity of her materials to turn her costume into a universal symbol of hope. Although I was irked by the stream of people who came up to compliment her (and intrude on us), I was grateful that her determination to keep her torch aloft until the final judging relieved me of any need to ask her to dance. In the event, the Captain, dazzled by the tawdry charms of a mermaid who had simply sewn herself into a pillowcase and worn next to nothing on top, awarded Johanna the second prize, an injustice which I

felt more acutely than she did. I suggested that we should escape
out on deck and, with a knowing smile, she agreed. We stood at
the rail and gazed into the gathering darkness. There was no
sound other than the distant strains of the band. We spoke little
but, as I clung to my personal Statue of Liberty, I felt that I had
both Johanna and America within my grasp. Johanna, now
determined to see only the best in the very people of whom a few
days earlier she had thought the worst, was full of admiration
for the spirit of improvisation expressed at the ball.

'It's part of our heritage,' I said. 'We've always had to celebrate in adversity.'

'Not everything can be a celebration,' she replied.

'It can in America. Remember I told you that I wanted to be
an ornithologist? I might also become a gangster.'

'You?' Her laugh was affectionate but wounding.

'Like Bugsy Siegel. His real name was Benjamin Siegelbaum.
Then you can be my moll.'

'Your what?'

'That's a woman with blond hair and bright eyes, who
smokes cigarettes in a holder and speaks through the corners of
her mouth.'

'I can't wait.'

'She sits on his knee and then, when he has to meet an associate or shoot someone, he shrugs her off, giving her a slap on
the bottom.'

'A slap?'

'It's quite friendly and she usually wears a bead dress, so it
can't hurt.'

'You'd better not try slapping me.'

'Oh I won't. That wouldn't be till we're much older. This is
what I want to do now.'

I took her in my arms. She laid down her torch and nuzzled
my neck. Time dissolved into kisses. The air was alive with

movement. I felt grateful that we had met, not in Berlin, but here in the face of infinity. Love encompassed us at every point. We could redraw the map . . . remake the world. Finally she broke away and picked up the torch, which she brandished like a dagger.

'This moll is going to bed.'

Her delicate scent was wafted away on the breeze. I stared out to sea and thrilled to the boundless possibilities. Suddenly, I was struck by a surge of weariness, as violent as the water was calm. I headed back to the cabin, allowing my fingers to linger over every surface, whether rope or canvas or wood. I saw that other couples had also been touched by romance, although their connections were at once more immediate and less permanent than ours. I shrank from the sight of Joel, recognisable only by his crutches, pressed to the ample bosom of a lady whose grey hair had not been assumed for the night. I was as shocked by their difference in age as a Nazi by a difference in race. Doubly grateful for Johanna's youthful beauty, I sought to escape behind a lifeboat, but the undulating tarpaulin left me in little doubt as to the activity taking place underneath. I was sickened that people should be so in thrall to their baser natures. The sight of my recently sprouted hair had merely strengthened my resolve to exercise restraint. Besides, all that filthiness was quite unnecessary when there were such exquisite pleasures to be found in a kiss.

'You look mighty satisfied with yourself.'

I swivelled in surprise. I could just make out Sendel in the shadows, but I failed to see how he could make out the expression on my face. Determined not to let him lower my spirits, I addressed him as an ordinary passenger.

'You missed a wonderful ball.'

'Who'd dance with me?'

Refusing to lie, I said simply that the most unlikely people had taken to the floor. He replied, with infuriating portentousness, that they might as well enjoy it while they could for they would soon have to change their tune. He claimed to have been talking to two of the Gestapo firemen and, when I expressed incredulity, explained that, while strong men were secure in their power, weak men needed to be bolstered by fear. The particular fear which they were exploiting was that the boat would not be permitted to dock in Havana. The Cubans had passed a law restricting immigration shortly before the *St Louis* left Hamburg, and the Captain was worried that we would be forced to turn back.

The music that had provided such an apt accompaniment to my conversation with Johanna took on a mocking tone. I clung to the hope that Sendel, true to form, was playing on my anxieties. I insisted that the Captain would never have confided in the firemen, whom everyone knew had been imposed on the ship against his will.

'You stupid boy!' He spat out the words with a fury that betrayed his alter ego. 'They have spies in the radio room. They overhear every wire that the Captain receives.'

'But, if Hapag knew about this law before we sailed, why didn't they say?'

'They wanted money. The Cubans wanted money. And we were so desperate to escape that we closed our eyes. Meanwhile, Goebbels has been hard at work, ordering his agents in Cuba to stir up anti-Semitism and force the government's hand.'

'There are Nazi agents in Cuba?'

'No, of course not! The island's entirely peopled by brilliantined troubadours strumming mandolins and dusky maidens rolling cigars on their thighs. . . . There are Nazis everywhere. Everywhere!' His voice dissolved in pain.

'I may be stupid, but I always thought that Goebbels wanted us out of Germany.'

'So he does. But this way he shows why he wants us out: this way he shows that other countries don't want us in. He doesn't just punish the Jews, he embarrasses the world.'

Suddenly I felt like a stowaway. My ticket was valid for a different voyage. I asked whether we would have to go back to Germany.

'I shall never go back.'

'But if we can't dock – '

'I tell you, I'll never go back! I was only let out of the camp on condition that I left the country forever.' He rounded on me as though I were one of the guards. 'You think you've suffered because you were banned from cinemas and your parents weren't allowed to drive their cars.'

'We were made to give up our dogs.' The image of Winnetou and Shatterhand flooded my memory and tears welled in my eyes.

'Your dogs? Oh I'm sorry. Almost like members of the family, were they?'

'What's wrong with that?'

'I was treated like a dog! Worse. I was dragged off to Buchenwald to be blackmailed, starved and abused. I saw prisoners being given impossible tasks, only to be beaten for failing to carry them out. I saw them searching for puddles in which to clean themselves and forced to sleep in their own filth. I watched as row upon row of us had our heads shaved so that even our bodies became uniforms.' His rage was so intense and indiscriminate that I felt compelled to assert my own link to the suffering.

'Yes, row upon row. And my grandfather was one of them.'

'I know,' he replied with relish. 'That was the one thing that sustained me: that all the rich Jews, all the respectable Jews, all the Jews who believed that, by looking down on the likes of me, they would be safe from the Nazis; they were locked up there too and they were the ones who cracked, not me. So no, wherever else I go, it won't be Germany.' He burst out laughing as he walked away. 'Night night, little prince. Sleep well!'

The injunction lost its irony the moment that my head hit the pillow and Sendel's image was replaced by Johanna's. In my dreams, I displayed all the dexterity that had eluded me on deck, as I raced her to the top of a New York skyscraper without using the lift. At breakfast I discovered that our attachment had become a subject of gossip. My father even cracked a joke, asking if I were carrying a torch for Liberty. My mother laughed as though it were a line from Molnar, which jolted me out of my own concerns into a consideration of my parents' relationship. Her smiles and his solicitude were as eloquent as their carefully coordinated costumes at the ball. They put me in mind of a pair of amnesiacs who fell in love in hospital, unaware that they had known each other before. Try as I might, I was unable to decide how much it was simply a shipboard intimacy that would dissolve on disembarkation and how much a genuine threat.

I spent a magical morning with Johanna, poring over the attractions of the city where we were to dock the following day. The whole world seemed to be filled with a newfound sensuousness, right down to the pages of the guidebook. She giggled as I read out an extract – in suitably silky tones – that would never have passed the Nazi censor: *Havana is like a woman in love. Eager to give pleasure, she will be anything you want her to be – exciting or peaceful, gay or quiet, brilliant or tranquil. What is your fancy? She is only anxious to anticipate your desires, to charm you with her beauty. Go prepared to enjoy yourself and you will leave, loving her as deeply as any native son.* Johanna deemed the passage silly, claiming to admire writers who described what things were, not what they were like. So I slyly asked her to describe how it felt to be a woman in love. 'How should I know?' she replied, which she modified at the sight of my despondent face to 'That's for me to know and you to find out.' Curbing my attempts to do just that on the grounds that there were people watching, she lay back in her deckchair while I ran through the ship's repertoire of fruit cocktails and outlined the yet more exotic delights of *panal*, *pina fria*, *tamarindo* and *horchata*, that were promised as soon as we reached land. The guidebook was as helpful to the playful lover as to the thirsty traveller, and I informed her that, while *it is quite proper for a lady to go into the cafés of the better class adjoining Central Park after concerts or during theatre intermissions, under no circumstances should she appear by herself either in the streets or a public place after the early part of the evening.* I pronounced this to be proof that she would need me more than ever if she were not to spend her nights at home, making lace and small talk with her mother. Behind my levity, however, lurked the question that I had asked about my parents: how far would things change when we disembarked?

The prospect of an answer drew closer after lunch, when we stood together on deck and caught our first glimpse of America.

'So many trees,' she said, gazing at the verdant seaboard. 'In films, it's all mansions and skyscrapers. I never expected so many trees.'

'If we could just swim ashore!' I said. 'Jump overboard and forget about Cuba and quotas.'

'I will if you will,' she said and, for a moment, I was ready to accept the challenge. Gone was the timorous boy oppressed by a tyrannical world. With Johanna at my side, I was a match for anything. I could step out on the beach in nothing but my dripping clothes and, in a few years . . . months . . . weeks, I would have made my fortune. I would buy up woodlands and swamps to turn into bird sanctuaries. I would be a byword for philanthropy. I might even run for President. But, just as I was rehearsing my Inauguration speech (full of tributes to my beloved First Lady), reality intervened in the shape of my fellow passengers, cheering the sight of the promised land at the end of our latter-day exodus.

As we sailed down the Florida coast, people with stronger eyesight – and imaginations – than mine identified various landmarks. The greatest roars were reserved for Miami, whose skyline glistened in the sunlight like an Alpine range. Our euphoria spread to the crew, who dashed about clearing the decks in anticipation of our departure. The rows of chairs were soon replaced by suitcases, which passengers, as restless as a crowd outside the Hertha BSC stadium, dragged alongside the accommodation ladder. My own packing could no longer be delayed and I regretted the vehemence with which I had told my mother that I was old enough to see to it myself. I took my leave of Johanna and returned to the cabin, where I made desultory progress, unnerved by the constant reminder of my grandfather's absence in the cases neatly stacked behind the door.

Dinner was served early to allow for our dawn arrival. For all her insistence that she had had no time to work up an appetite, the Professor's wife made a valiant effort. She explained that she'd spent the afternoon cabling news of our approach to friends in Cuba. 'They'll find out soon enough,' her husband said, although relief at the chance to disband his committee tempered even his sharpest retort. The rescheduling of the meal enabled Luise to join us, yet, far from relishing the treat, she was jittery and badly behaved. My mother claimed that it was excitement, but I worried that she might possess some instinct for danger denied to the rest of us, like a sparrow chattering before rain. She turned on Aunt Annette when she tucked in her napkin, flicked crumbs at the Banker's wife, who gamely played dead, and clung to the sauceboat as if it were her favourite doll. Sophie, meanwhile, was so lost in thought that she might have been sitting at another table. I realised with a jolt that, whatever the effect of our landing on my relationship with Johanna, its effect on hers with Helmut was plain. Their choice would be between a few delirious days each year when his ship was in port and a lifetime of for-the-best forgetting.

The after-dinner sun was disconcerting and neither Johanna nor I chose to linger over our valedictory stroll. I returned to the cabin, changed into my pyjamas and prayed. Unlike my former school-friends, for whom the topic had become as taboo as circumcision, I found the concept of prayer more problematic than the practice. If God were omniscient, he knew what I had to say before I said it, so I was wasting both his time and my breath. On the other hand, I trusted that he would appreciate my effort. Struggling to keep my thoughts as lucid as possible, I ran over the key events of the voyage: my grandfather's death; my father's return; my love for Johanna; even, to my surprise, my clashes with Sendel; and asked for his help in resolving them all. The silence was huge but eloquent and I slipped into bed with a sense of reassurance, falling straight to sleep, to be woken before dawn by a blast on the ship's whistle.

Rushing to the window, I gazed out on a scene of unrelieved blackness. Gradually my eyes adjusted to the subtleties of tone: the thin blackness of the air and the dull blackness of the sea which gave way to the dense blackness of the cliffs (a conjecture which the beam of a lighthouse confirmed). Neglecting to wash, in celebration rather than mourning, I threw on my clothes and hurried outside, jostling the crowd to gain a place at the rail. I found myself squeezed between Joel and Viktor, who informed us with chalky pedantry that the castle on the cliff was known as

El Morro and had been hewn straight from the rock. A bid to secure a better vantage-point sent us scurrying to starboard (Joel propelling himself on his crutches like a cricket), to the fury of an elderly couple with a manifestly limited experience of delinquency. There we saw a longer, lower castle, identified by Viktor as La Pinta, which looked increasingly impressive in the breaking dawn. Eager to cause no further offence, we walked soberly to the prow, where we made out the narrow entrance of the harbour and, in the distance, illuminated only by the occasional headlight, the shadowy promise of Havana.

We gazed in silence at the town that would offer us refuge. I was seized with regret, firstly, that I had not spent more of my time on board learning Spanish and, secondly, that I was making such a furtive entrance in a boatload of exiles. I feared too that our welcome had been soured by Goebbels' agents, although I comforted myself that the source of that information was Sendel who, in the absence of any flesh-and-blood victim, had tried to murder my hopes. At the bell, both Joel and Viktor ostentatiously raised their wrists to reveal identical watches which, in order to use up their shipboard marks, they had bought from an enterprising steward. They urged me to do the same, but I insisted that a second watch would be of no more value to me than the money, which I had, in any case, decided to give to Helmut. Agreeing that it was time for breakfast, while disagreeing as to whether that time were 5.33 or 5.34, they raced me to the dining-room. Feeling far too excited to eat but aware that I needed to keep up my strength for the day ahead, I took my place among the bleary-eyed company and blithely informed the waiter that I would have everything. My mother started to object, but my father overruled her with a plea for tolerance (and a wink at me). The waiter returned, so laden with dishes that I felt like an entrant in a pie-eating contest at a fair. Honour-bound to eat, I took no part in the conversation, which was

brought to a halt by a resounding thud. I was at a loss to understand why we had dropped anchor outside the harbour and
yearned to join the passengers who had rushed unceremoniously
from the room but, this time, my mother's injunction held fast.
The Professor announced that the ship must be too big to navi-
gate the harbour entrance.

'Quite the opposite,' I declared, borrowing Viktor's statistics,
'the harbour has sea-room for a thousand ships.' The Professor
glowered at me as if I had elbowed my way into a lifeboat, trampling women and children underfoot.

'Perhaps the ship's papers aren't in order?' the Banker
suggested.

'Or maybe it's ours that are the problem?' my father said.

'How can that be, Georg?' my mother asked, with satisfying
sharpness. 'We have our vaccination certificates, together with
transit visas signed by the Director of Immigration himself.'

Even my mother, however, shared the general desire to be out
on deck to see what was happening. I was grateful for the chance
to abandon the meal with no loss of face, other than a sly gibe
about my eyes being bigger than my stomach from the person
least qualified to make it. Offering to take charge of Luise,
whom I had neglected for too long, I proceeded to the prow. The
early morning light gave definition to what had hitherto been a
blur: the two silver-grey fortresses on either side of the harbour,
the Cuban flag flying breezily from El Morro, and the city itself:
a dazzle of pink and white and yellow plastered walls; of red and
gold roofs; of the sheer trunks of coconut trees, crowned by
clown-like tufts of leaves; with the great dome of the Cathedral
rising at its heart.

By coincidence it was Saturday, and the Rabbi announced
that he would be holding a service in the nightclub (the choice of
room bore the signature of Schiendick) although, to judge by the
teeming deck, I feared that he would be hard-pushed to obtain a

minyan. The cynic in me, never far away when faced with my co-religionists, presumed that the need for prayer was less pressing now that we had reached land. The arrival of a launch sent a stampede to starboard, in time to witness a resplendently uniformed official climb to the top of the accommodation ladder, where he was greeted by the ship's doctor and nurse. Their presence was explained by a loudspeaker request for all passengers to assemble in the social hall for a medical inspection. Far from being a minister sent to welcome us on behalf of the government (my mother's suggestion betraying a naivety that was either charming or culpable according to taste), the man was the Port Authority doctor who, refusing to accept the Captain's assurance of our good health, was insisting on a general examination.

The ship was gripped by a sense of foreboding. As we filed docilely into the room, we were reminded not just of the conditions we had left behind in Germany but that we ourselves remained on German territory until we disembarked. My own fear was more specific. The Doctor's inclusion of 'the idiot or insane' in his list of those forbidden to enter the country made me tremble for Luise. A stranger might fail to grasp that her perceptions were not so much impaired as idiosyncratic. My fear appeared to be justified when, on approaching the Doctor's desk, she caught sight of his assistant. 'She burnt! She burnt!' she screamed and began to shake. I presented our vaccination certificates with my most winning smile, giving thanks for the language barrier that cut across the officials' comprehension. Meanwhile, my mother and Sophie tried desperately to reconcile Luise to her first black face. The Doctor wearily waved us through, with barely a second glance, even at Luise. My relief faded with the realisation that the entire exercise had been a sham: the Cubans were taking a leaf out of the Nazi handbook on humiliation.

The charade over, we went back outside and gazed across the still waters of the harbour. I cannot begin to convey the depths of our frustration. Think of longing to escape from a tedious lesson or lunch (or perhaps, by the time you read this, from a stifling job or relationship), multiply it by a hundred, and you may have some idea. . . . By mid-morning, the city was so distinct that I could make out toy-town cars and even figures on the esplanade. It was like staring at the window of a shop that remained closed – or rather, closed to Jews. Even the old were filled with a nursery impatience as they watched the growing bustle from which they were excluded. A group of Cuban policemen came aboard and lined the rail as impassively as an opera chorus. With their refusal to respond even to the Spanish speakers among us, we were left studying them as intently as the other landmarks. Meanwhile, several small craft had drawn up alongside the ship. The occupants' faces bore a reassuring resemblance to our own, as was confirmed by the shrieks and tears and airborne kisses with which people all around me greeted their relatives. I gave thanks that our family had no welcoming party to provoke such a spectacle. Although both the din and the distance contrived to conceal the visitors' words, the gist was far from encouraging. They insisted that everything would be resolved and we were not to worry, which of course made us worry all the more. Until then, we had supposed the delay to be purely administrative: a case of what we – who of all people should have known better – described as 'native mentality'. In fact, those natives showed remarkable presence of mind: within an hour a further flotilla appeared, turning the harbour into a makeshift market. Passengers tossed down coins (it appeared that even shipboard currency was acceptable) in exchange for bananas, pineapples and a range of exotic fruit, which were handed up to them by the policemen, who were happy to have found a role, however menial. My desire for a star fruit was vetoed by my mother who, finding the whole exchange undignified, promised me a plateful of them as soon as we reached the hotel.

Our visitors' fears looked to be misplaced when an official launch drew up, scattering several smaller boats in its wake and discharging a group of immigration officers. Oozing self-importance, they strode up the accommodation ladder to be met by the Purser, who ushered them out of sight. Our hopes of a speedy departure turned rapidly into resentment when we learnt that they had sat down to a meal but, as a sympathetic steward brought us word of the ever more lavish courses, Aunt Annette cannot have been alone in concluding that the delay was a small price to pay for securing their goodwill. The traditional German sausages and sauerkraut (we had devoured the menu as eagerly as they had the food) must have had the desired effect, for, after brandy and cigars (which struck me as taking owls to Athens), they moved to the social hall to process our documents. Shortly afterwards, the Purser broadcast a request for passengers whose names began with A or B to assemble outside. Meanwhile, a small crowd of the alphabetically less advantaged gathered nearby to gaze at the R stamped on their landing cards as reverently as if it had been inscribed by God. Once processed, the As and Bs proceeded to the accommodation ladder to wait for the launch. Among them was Viktor, who dashed over to shake my hand. His mother screamed at him to return, terrified of his taking the least step out of line. I managed to tell him the name of our hotel as he rushed back to his place. Banishing my horror of goodbyes, I waited to wave him off, but the opportunity never arose. Instead, as the launch returned, yet another official came aboard, pushing brusquely past the passengers and disappearing below deck. Moments later, the immigration officers emerged and, without a single word of explanation, descended into the waiting launch, leaving those of us from C to Z without even the regulation R.

The escalating tension was interrupted by lunch, although the Professor's wife's routine protest of lacking an appetite for once appeared to be genuine. Our premature goodbyes congealed like leftovers. Only Luise was cheerful, seizing the unexpected freedom to make a bread-roll doll. Even the waiters were surly, which Sophie, with her privileged information, explained by the crew's blaming the passengers for the Captain's cancelling all shore leave, a response that seemed as irrational as the Nazis blaming Grandfather for burning down his own store. On a happier note, she declared that the Captain was convinced that, if we were forbidden to land in Cuba, we would be welcomed in America, which would work to our advantage by enabling us to jump the queue. Everyone agreed, apart from the Professor's wife, who fretted about alerting the friends who were waiting for them in Havana.

'You can send them another telegram,' her husband said kindly.

'What with?' she asked. 'I've spent the last of our shipboard marks.'

'I can give you some,' I said, adding that they were really my grandfather's, in order to avoid any show of gratitude. The Banker, meanwhile, assured us that our fears were unwarranted. He had been able to elicit from the least impassive policeman that we would simply have to wait on board another two days until the end of Whitsun.

'It's understandable that they don't want us landing in the middle of such an important religious festival.'

'Why?' I asked. 'It isn't one they blame us for, like Easter.'

I shall skip over the endless rumour and speculation that gripped us for the rest of the day which, in time-honoured fashion, we filled with talk to give ourselves the illusion of control. . . . Nowhere have I felt the danger of losing your interest as acutely as here. Our progress, which I suspect has long been too slow for your spaceship tastes, now grinds to a halt. We lay at anchor, prey to every morbid anxiety, as I found for myself the following morning when I awoke to the sound of gunfire. Convinced that the Cubans were shooting at the ship, I ran next door to Luise and Sophie, cloaking my alarm in an offer of protection. While I was helping Sophie to lift Luise off the floor where she had curled up in a ball, my mother entered to assure us that there was nothing to fear. The harbour cannon were firing a salute to greet an American warship that had just sailed in. I was outraged by the difference in our welcomes.

I returned to my cabin, dressed and went down to breakfast, where I found my father deep in conversation with the Professor's wife. As I took my place, he explained that he had been up for hours to escape his roommate's snoring, a veiled reproach which I pretended not to grasp. She, meanwhile, informed us all that the Professor was currently meeting the director of the Jewish relief committee in Cuba, who had come aboard to help resolve the impasse. Although I joined in the general enthusiasm, I had little faith in the intervention of a fellow Jew. I was more encouraged by the seven passengers who had been allowed to disembark the previous afternoon, which showed that the process, however protracted, had begun. The Banker, bereft of his religious consolation, declared bluntly that four of them were Cubans and the other three held valid visas.

'We hold valid visas,' I said. 'I've seen them myself.'

'I think you'll find that they're landing permits,' he replied.

'What's the difference?' I asked.

'The right signature and about a thousand metres of sea.'

The explanation was all too plausible. I longed for someone to blame, but the only candidate lay buried at the bottom of the Atlantic Ocean. Nothing more clearly revealed the effects of his incarceration than that, having spent a lifetime poring over contracts, he should have committed such an oversight. The future had never looked so bleak. I hurried out on deck, to find that the original flotilla of small craft had doubled in size, their occupants desperately shouting up messages to their relatives on the *St Louis*. Two of the most enterprising had secured loudhailers, so intent on making themselves heard that they didn't care how widely their intimacies were shared. Meanwhile, Sendel sauntered up to me as if we were conspirators meeting in a city square. My customary unease in his presence was increased by the feeling that he relished the universal despair. While he likened the scene to prisoners talking through a fence, it put me in mind of a medieval Judgement Day although, out of consideration for his delusion, I kept the comparison to myself. We stepped aside to allow the woman who looked after Luise's two friends to bring them to the rail, where she pointed out their father holding up a placard scribbled with their names. When both girls declared themselves unable to see him, she lifted the younger one up, only to be shoved back by a policeman, who seemed to suspect her of planning to throw the child into the waiting arms below. A second attempt at identification, where she crouched at the girls' level and pointed out their father through the grille, met with no greater success, until the older one claimed to have spotted him, echoing my own childhood subterfuge when I had peered through my father's telescope and pretended to see Mars.

Escaping the crush, I ran into Johanna, standing with her mother who was scouring the boats for the familiar face. 'How can you hope to recognise him?' Johanna asked. 'You haven't seen him for fourteen years.' Instead of replying, Christina shot me a glance which revealed a long history of clandestine meetings, but it was not her betrayal that alarmed me so much as my own, since I knew that, in order to spare Johanna pain, I would be forced into a compromising complicity. I suggested that he might be holding up a placard, like the father of the two little girls, at which Johanna shuddered, making me realise how difficult she found the meeting, even without the attendant brouhaha. She insisted that, if her father were the distinguished figure of her mother's account (the accuracy of which she clearly doubted), he would never allow himself to be part of such a scrum nor, for that matter, would his wife. Christina, blushing at this public airing of her private life, reminded her of the wife's postscript to her husband's invitation in which she assured them that she bore no ill will. She then appealed to me for support.

'It's no use asking Karl,' Johanna said. 'You might as well ask Hitler to learn Hebrew. Karl's totally unforgiving. An eye for an eye and all that.' I wanted to tell her that I was no longer so doctrinaire, but I was afraid that she might think me fickle. In any case, her mother jumped in, reminding her of the Commandment to honour your father and mother.

'How can I honour him?' Johanna asked. 'I've never even met him.'

'Think of everything he's doing for you. He didn't have to send for us . . . you: it was you he wanted, not me. He could have turned his back on what was happening in Germany. He could have rebuilt his life with his family here in Havana. But no, he told them the truth. He risked appearing as guilty in their eyes as in yours.'

'Fine! I'm being unreasonable. He's the one who's suffered.'

'That's not what I – '

'If only we could leave the ship and get it over with. It's all this hanging about I can't stand.'

I was tormented by the thought that she was the one person on board who was more afraid of what would happen when we were allowed to land than if we were forced to set sail. As a distraction, I invited her for a cocktail, reluctantly extending the invitation to her mother, who shamed me by her effusion of gratitude. My indifference to using up my shipboard marks had at least ensured that the delay would not leave me destitute. The air of despondency that clung to the ship seeped into our every exchange. Johanna insisted that the drink, which I found indistinguishable from its predecessors, had been watered down as a sign of the crew's now open contempt. She pushed it away, at which Christina alternately chided her and apologised to me, thereby doubling my embarrassment.

Making an excuse that at once amused Johanna and appeased her mother, I returned to my cabin, to be confronted by chaos. Both my own and my grandfather's cases had been prised open, their contents strewn about the room. We had clearly been robbed, which, in line with the prevailing prejudice, I blamed on the Cuban policemen. After a desultory attempt to match up a pair of cuff-links, I made my way to my mother's cabin, where a similar sight awaited me, although the delicacy of the scattered garments made the violation seem even more cruel. The thieves, moreover, had ransacked my mother's paint-box and left a bestial pile of ochre in the centre of the floor. I scooped it up in a rag and, taking the symbol for the reality, flushed it down the lavatory. I returned to the bedroom to find Sophie, who informed me that we had not been robbed but subjected to a thorough search along with the rest of the ship. It was then that I noticed the Shirley Temple doll hanging limply in her hand. One of a batch that my grandfather had imported from America, it rapidly became Luise's prize possession, surviving even her most intemperate rages, only to have its neck broken by a clumsy – or callous – customs officer. Far more than all the human misery, it alerted me to the gravity of our plight.

I determined to right the wrong done to my sister, refusing to settle for clearing up the mess like the men and women forced to scrub the streets with their toothbrushes after *Kristallnacht*. I was a bona fide passenger and, for all that we remained on German soil, I felt sure that there must be some maritime law that afforded me protection. I resolved to put my case before the Captain and pushed my way defiantly past the No Entry sign into the crew area. Once there, I was plunged into confusion. On my previous visit, I had been guided by a steward; now, faced with the stark corridor and unmarked doors, I had no way of knowing if I were even on the correct deck. Trusting to chance, I descended a clanging stairway into an atmosphere so foetid that I could barely breathe. A sickly-sour smell, more elephant house than changing room, was a sign that I had moved from the officers' quarters to the men's. I made to retreat, only to be checked by a mocking cry of 'We have a visitor!' from one of the Gestapo firemen. True to form, they hunted in packs and, as I hovered uneasily on the steps, I was confronted by their leader, who ambled back and forth, snapping his fingers in my face. Feigning confidence, I elected to stand my ground.

'So what's a good little boy like you doing creeping around like a spy?' Schiendick asked.

'I'm not a little boy,' I said, praying that my voice would back me up.

'No, I can see that,' he replied with a grin, 'you've brought your dolly.' He grabbed it from my hand.

'Give me that,' I shouted and tried to pull it back, but he dangled it just out of my reach.

'Naughty, naughty!' he replied. 'Hasn't your mother ever told you that it's rude to snatch?'

'I'll report you,' I said, finding myself back in a classroom of Jew-baiting schoolboys.

'Oh, I'm so frightened,' he said, with pantomime shudders.

Assuming an air of authority, I explained that I was on my way to the Captain to complain about the ransacking of our rooms. Their derisive hoots revealed that they and not the customs officers were the culprits. Schiendick leapt up beside me on the precariously narrow step. He thrust his face into mine and I felt a gust of disconcertingly sugary breath. Laying an equal emphasis on every word, right down to the 'and's and 'or's, he informed me that he and his fellows had conducted a search for any firearms or explosives that might have been smuggled aboard. Given the current tension, they couldn't leave the crew exposed to an attack by anarchists and subversives.

His description of my fellow passengers was so patently absurd that I found it hard to conceal my contempt. Even so, I insisted that my objection was not to the search itself but to the manner in which it had been carried out. 'Do you really think that my mother hid bullets in her paint-tubes or my sister had sticks of dynamite sewn into her doll?'

'Why not? You Jews are masters of deceit.'

His logic was on a level with Luise's. So, making a last-minute switch of article, I asked him to give me back *the* doll and direct me to the Captain. His smile thinned, and he told me that I was much mistaken if I thought that that Jew-lover enjoyed the ultimate jurisdiction on the ship. It was he, Schiendick, who spoke for the Party. 'Schröder may have Hamburg behind him, but I have Berlin.'

I turned to go, but he jumped two steps to block my path. I

panicked as he also claimed the right to search suspicious passengers, a category in which he now placed me, flinging me down the stairs into the arms of his companions. Mocking my cries for help, they spun me around like a top. Then someone suggested upending me to see what was hidden in my clothes. Gagging my protests, they grabbed me, flipped me over and shook me by the legs. To my lasting discredit, I was concerned less about any damage they might inflict than that I would shame myself by being sick. They jiggled me up and down like a pestle, driving my head ever closer to the ground. Then, just when a collision appeared inevitable, a voice at the top of the stairs ordered them to stop. They dropped me unceremoniously to the floor, from where I looked up to see Helmut. Defying Schiendick's warning not to interfere, he denounced them all as bullies and cowards and threatened to have them sent off the ship in Havana. His righteous anger cowed them into submission, and he swept them aside to pick up the doll (now Marie Antoinette rather than Shirley Temple), as well as the wallet and penknife that had fallen from my pockets. He handed them all to me, along with instructions to return straight to the passenger decks. I scurried up the stairs in a welter of emotions. Gratitude for my rescue mixed with humiliation at my helplessness. I was mortified that, like some weakling in a Western, I had had to be saved by the sheriff.

Back on home ground, I gulped the air which, however humid, felt Alpine in contrast to that on the crew deck, before stepping outside to find a crowd of passengers lining the rail. Even those with no friends or relatives to greet them welcomed the distraction of the Cuban boats. I spotted Joel and Viktor talking to two unfamiliar men in their mid-twenties. As I moved towards them,

I saw that Joel had relinquished his crutches, only for Viktor to take his place on the injury list. One look at his bandaged face told me what must have happened; even so, I felt that I owed it to him to ask. He explained that he had been lying on his bed reading a favourite passage from *War and Peace* – something to do with a bear, which sounded unlikely – when the firemen burst in, ripping the book not just from his hands but from its binding. Furious, he lashed out, which gave them the perfect excuse to retaliate. His mother, horrified by Havana's affinity to Cologne, called the Doctor, who stitched his wounds and begged them to let the matter drop. He claimed that the Gestapo behaviour sickened the rest of the crew, but that there was nothing any of them – the Captain included – could do. The best hope for all concerned was that we should be allowed to disembark as soon as possible.

The Doctor's advice was scorned by Joel and his friends, who talked of forming an undercover resistance cell. Despite my disgust at the further instance of the firemen's cruelty and my reluctance to be considered a coward, I was too conscious of my recent failure to wish to play any part. Meanwhile, my thoughts were turning to Sendel. With his cropped hair and unsavoury appearance, he offered a constant provocation to Schiendick. Viktor's cuts would be mere scratches compared to the ones that had been inflicted on him. Knowing better than to expect thanks, I decided to seek him out. So, after locating the number on the passenger list, I went down to his cabin, half-fearing to find him unconscious on the floor. The response to my knock reassured me, and I entered to discover him lying on his bed in a room that was in even greater disarray than my own. He seemed neither worried about the mess nor surprised by my visit, making no attempt to stand up or to invite me to sit down. My fears about his injuries proved to be sound, but he dismissed my suggestion that he should see the Doctor. 'I'll survive,' he said. 'I've done so for thousands of years.' I was disturbed enough by the disorder in the room without dealing with that inside his head. I volunteered to help him tidy up, but he ignored me, declaring in familiar vein: 'It's God I blame. When he branded me like this, it was to prevent anyone taking revenge on me. And never let it be said that the God of our fathers doesn't keep his word. He stopped them killing me – oh yes – but he's allowed them to mock me and beat me and torture me ever since. No Grand Inquisitor, no Cossack commander, no Nazi guard is as pitiless as the Lord our God.'

The respite brought by the opening door proved to be temporary when, on turning towards it, I found myself facing my father. His entrance left me aghast. I realised that, as single passengers, both he and Sendel were obliged to share a cabin; what I hadn't expected was that it would be with each other. My father's immediate concern was practical and I stationed myself at the sink, washing out the flannel with which he cleaned Sendel's wounds. That done, he helped him off the bed and, having established that he could walk, insisted that we left him to rest. As we made our way up to the lounge, I tried to shrug off the image of Sendel's arm hanging around his neck. The thought of their proximity disturbed me. The worst I had gathered of his roommate was that he snored. For all his faults, my father deserved more than to be trapped with Sendel. So, in my most matter-of-fact voice, I asked if he would like my grandfather's bed. He stared at me in amazement. Embarrassed, I explained that it made sense since his cabin was so airless, with neither a bathroom nor a window. He pressed me so hard for another reason that I wondered whether he truly wanted to move. So I said that it would please Mother. She had been hit hard by my grandfather's death and it would mean so much to her to see us together.

'And what would it mean to you?' he asked.

'Probably a lot of inconvenience,' I replied crossly. 'I just don't like to think of you stuck in such a poky space.'

'Thank you,' he said, 'I accept.'

He promised to make it clear to Sendel that there was nothing personal behind the move, describing his roommate as a brilliant scholar who spent most of his time reading, which surprised me since he'd struck me as a man who was interested in nobody's ideas but his own. He barely looked up when I returned after tea to help my father with his bags. We declined to summon the stewards, who were already grumbling at having to bring in all the luggage that had been prematurely placed on deck. As I struggled up the stairs, I began to regret my generosity . . . a regret that grew substantially once we reached the cabin, where my father took up far more space than my grandfather, who had been unobtrusive even before falling ill. At least he unpacked only one case since he subscribed to the general view that, when the government offices reopened in the morning, the deadlock would be quickly resolved.

A few words from the Professor over dinner put paid to such hopes. He quoted the director of the Jewish relief agency on political allegiances in Cuba being less clear-cut than they were in Germany. For all the rumoured rivalries between Göring, Goebbels and von Ribbentrop, they pursued the same goal, as we knew to our cost. Their opposite numbers here were forever at each other's throats. Our landing permits had been signed by Manuel Benitez who, despite being Director General of Immigration, did not possess the necessary authority and was simply feathering his own nest. My affronted interjection that no bird would behave so despicably was dismissed as an irrelevance by my mother. Meanwhile, the Professor explained that Benitez was an associate of the most powerful man on the island, Fulgencio Batista, the army chief of staff. President Bru had imposed the strict restrictions on immigration both to expose Benitez's chicanery and to force a showdown with Batista. The *St Louis* had been caught in the crossfire.

While it came as a relief to realise that Goebbels' arm did not stretch across the Atlantic and that we were simply pawns in a Cuban power-struggle, it did nothing to alleviate our plight. The Professor's only advice was that people should give him, or other members of the Passenger Committee, the names of any influential friends in America to whom they might appeal for help (my mother reeled off a list as though she were suggesting sponsors for a charity gala). He proposed that, in the meantime, we enjoy the prospect of a few extra days aboard a luxury liner at no extra charge. His attempt at levity failed to convince his wife, who moaned about the sweltering heat, the sluggish service, the uninspired menu and, most bitterly, the news that, after complaints from the 'cheaper passengers', the Purser had decided to remove all demarcation between the classes. I was delighted by the thought that Johanna and I would at last be able to meet on equal footing. The Professor's wife, however, declared that it was unfair to those people who had paid more, directing her remarks at my father, whose upgrading she had never been able to accept. Her husband suggested that it was a valuable gesture of solidarity, but she refused to be appeased. 'In the past six years, we've been stripped of everything: position; home; job. We've become fourth-class citizens. We're finally given a scrap of status, and now even that's being taken away from us.'

'We know who we are,' her husband said, 'isn't that all that matters?'

'Maybe to Eskimos,' she replied, pushing away her plate.

Whitsun passed, removing any notion that our quarantine was religious, along with all hope of an early escape. But, while the

St Louis remained becalmed, more and more boats were sailing towards us, some filled with film crews and journalists, who yelled out their intimate questions as casually as if they were asking about the weather. Information was the ship's most precious currency and I was richly supplied, thanks to the Professor's reports from the passenger committee and Sophie's from Helmut. The former's optimism about the experienced Jewish negotiators flying down from New York contrasted with the latter's gloom about the ever more rigid line being taken by Havana. A constant concern was the welfare of the children, in whose ranks I was delighted to discover that I was no longer even nominally placed. Luise's two friends posed a particular problem. Their father arrived every morning, but their guardian, considering the experience too disturbing for them, refused to parade them at the rail. Moreover, she grew increasingly tense, regularly reminding people that she had no connection to the girls but had simply been approached at the Hamburg docks by a heavily perfumed woman 'dripping with diamonds and smoth-ered in furs' (a description to which she gave an increasingly sinister emphasis), who had begged her to look after them on the voyage. She had been happy to help, but that had been in the expectation that she would hand them over without trouble. She had never anticipated this. Sophie, who alone seemed to relish the delay for the added time it gave her with Helmut, offered to shoulder some of the burden and, to my astonishment, my mother followed suit.

'But you don't like children,' I blurted out. Her shocked expression showed that I had touched a nerve as sensitive as her art.

'Whatever do you mean? I love children!' While I pondered the distinction between *love* and *like*, she added: 'The only time I didn't like them was when I was one myself. Of course I like them. Why else do you think I had you?'

'For Grandfather's sake. To try and make up for his losing Uncle Karl. So that there would be someone to take over the store.' I confronted her with a mixture of my own deductions and Aunt Annette's disclosures.

'My dear Karl, do you really imagine that's how people behave? Would you do something so important – the most important thing in your life – just to please me?'

My first thought was that I would if I believed that it would make her value me, but I knew better than to say so.

'We forget,' she continued gently, 'with your seeming so grown-up, that you're still so young.' My own recollection was all too clear, as her words stung me like a nursery slap.

The strain was affecting the passengers in different ways. Some remained resolutely cheerful, displaying an almost Aryan contempt for 'the natives', insisting that the problem would be solved as soon as Hapag dispensed the requisite bribes. Others issued Jeremiads, declaring such exclusion to be the inevitable fate of the Jews. The Rabbi held a daily service in the social hall, for which the portrait of the Führer was no longer taken down but simply concealed behind a curtain like a cruel parody of the ark. I refused to join in the prayers, which to me smacked of defeatism, placing my trust in human diplomacy rather than divine intervention. In addition to which, there was a larger principle at stake. *Children* of Israel was not meant to be taken literally. We would never gain respect – our own or other people's – if we ran snivelling to God at the first sign of trouble. It was time that we learnt to stand up for ourselves.

Although the class distinctions had been removed, people tended to keep to the parts of the ship that they knew, and the Professor's wife's fear of being swamped by the hoi polloi was not realised. My own fear that my father would turn our cabin into a confessional proved to be equally groundless. When I returned from my late-night walks with Johanna, he was already asleep. Moreover, he never woke up in the morning until he heard me busy in the bathroom. On our first day together, he spotted me unpacking my binoculars. I explained their purpose.

'Still birds?' he asked, in a voice more suited to 'Still teddy bears?'

'Why not?' I replied, saddened by how little he knew of my life. He asked if I remembered how, at the age of four, I had climbed up to the attic of our country house and out through a skylight to the roof because I wanted to touch the birds. One of the maids spotted me crawling along a gutter and a frantic crowd gathered below. He, meanwhile, dashed up the stairs and scrambled out to save me. 'Did that really happen?' I asked. 'I've always thought it was a dream.'

'I rescued you,' he said.

'Well you needn't worry now,' I said in an effort to lighten the mood, 'I can take care of myself.'

'I rescued you,' he repeated and, to my dismay, his eyes once again filled with tears.

While I deplored such displays of mawkishness, I could well understand the desire to play the hero. My own consolation in our predicament was the chance to devise a spectacular plan to defy the authorities and save Johanna, which the many news crews present could then flash to an admiring public around the world. In company with Joel and Viktor, I weighed up the various options, from disguising ourselves as members of the crew, whose shore leave had been restored at Schiendick's insistence, to squeezing through a porthole. Joel worried that his ankle would be too weak to survive the fall and Viktor that the sea would be too shallow. My own fears concerned the floodlights that were switched on at night to deter any such attempt. They not only thwarted our escape but put paid to all other clandestine activities. With both of our cabins out of bounds, Johanna and I had relied on the darkness to provide us with moments of privacy. Those were now lost. Scared of attracting disapproval, she would barely allow me a goodnight kiss, let alone my hard-won blouse privileges. To crown my frustration, when I returned prematurely to my cabin, the light streaming through the curtains deprived me of sleep. 'It's just like being in the camp,' Sendel said cheerily, when I made my weary way back outside.

The next morning Johanna and I agreed to take charge of Luise and her friends, ostensibly to give Sophie a rest but, secretly, to experiment with the parental role. We were playing a game of whist (in Luise's case, I played while she held the cards), when a middle-aged man sped past, gibbering and gesticulating. Shocked by the blood dripping from his arms, I left Johanna with the children, a neglect of the parental role for which I had all too clear a precedent, and joined the crowd in hot pursuit. In spite of his bulk, the man outstripped us all, the pain in his wrists deadening him to the knocks and bruises that the rest of us strove to avoid. He reached the stern and, with a defiant glance back, leapt over the rail. The sequence was as predictable as a cartoon. A wild shriek from out of nowhere was followed by a garbled shout and a loud blast on the ship's whistle. I ran to the side and stared down at the sea, where the man was thrashing about in a murky pool of his own blood. A sailor, with a rare lack of deference, pushed me aside and threw down a rope, which the man resolutely ignored. Then, in a gesture I shall never forget, he raised his arms above his head and, with his right hand, plucked the severed veins from his left wrist, like a pathologist examining his own corpse. A nearby police launch swung round and headed towards him but, in the meantime, a sailor on the bridge had kicked off his shoes and dived to the rescue. The passengers lining the rail gave him a smattering of applause, but the man himself thrust him away so violently that (returning to the cartoon) it looked as though they were continuing a fight which had begun on board. The sailor's face and shirt were soaked in the man's blood, but he gradually pacified him, until even the cries of 'Murderers!' were reduced to a plaintive moan. Both men were then hauled into the launch, which spirited them away across the harbour, leaving a red stain on the water as if it were infested with sharks.

The incident laid bare the depth of misery on board. The *St Louis* held over nine hundred passengers, which meant over nine hundred reasons for leaving Germany, nine hundred hopes of starting a new life in America and nine hundred fears of returning to Europe. At a rough count, I was acquainted with about thirty of them. I now added one more. The would-be suicide's name was Loewe, and he was travelling with his wife and two daughters. According to Viktor, who sat at an adjoining table in the dining room, the family kept to itself, staying just on the right side of courtesy. Nevertheless, there was no shortage of people claiming friendship with them. Some maintained that Herr Loewe had been hounded by the Nazi firemen, whose patrol that afternoon was unusually restrained, others that he had been deranged by the expropriation of his business. Whatever his story, it galvanised the interest of the journalists, two of whom even managed to insinuate themselves on board. It struck me as doubly cruel that, while our friends and relatives were stuck gazing up at us as though we were the horses on the Brandenburg Gate, the journalists bribed their way on to a police launch and, by flashing bogus cards at the officials, convinced them that they had come to investigate the incident. In a sense, of course, they had, except that their investigation consisted of harassing Frau Loewe and her children. They were frustrated by a group of passengers, whose warning to the Captain prompted the immediate expulsion of the intruders. This in turn fuelled fears in some quarters that the Captain was trying to conceal our plight from the world.

Meanwhile, the hero of the hour, one Heinrich Meier, returned from hospital in Havana to receive the substantial sum that had been collected in his honour (evidence that ours had not been the only family to evade the currency restrictions). Meier brought the welcome news that Herr Loewe would pull through, but the Captain refused to be complacent, ordering that the lifeboats be lowered to anticipate any similar bid. Moreover, he asked the Passenger Committee to form a suicide watch to augment the crew's night patrols, as though we were facing a second Masada. I immediately volunteered my services, only for my mother to declare me too young. I considered appealing to my father and exploiting the dual authority that had been the salvation of so many of my friends, but decided that the price would be too high. So I sulked which, according to my mother, proved her point.

The next day, the fifth since our arrival in Havana, the temperature hit the hundreds even before breakfast. The air was humid and heavy. Well-wishers maintained their shipside vigil, but neither their messages of support nor their gifts, passed up to us by the policemen, brought comfort. The policemen's very amiability aroused our suspicions. With one hand poised over their holsters they prevented our leaving the ship while, with the other, they delivered presents and purchases and played games with the children. Luise came to lunch wearing a policeman's cap, which my mother's fiercest protests could not induce her to remove.

In spite of police concern, the children were bearing up well, even relishing the adventure, although the sight of captive Jewish boys throwing coins for their Cuban counterparts to retrieve from the seabed was deeply disturbing. It was the adults, among whom without qualm or qualification I now included myself, who were hit hardest by our confinement. With not even Frau Loewe permitted to enter Havana, we made our visits ashore vicariously. In our family's case, they were through Helmut, who returned from an afternoon's leave to relate how the esplanade had been turned into a vast fairground, where musicians, acrobats and animal trainers entertained the crowds who had come to gape at the ship. 'They'll make money out of us one way or another,' I said, holding the Cubans in a contempt which, to the dismay of my English friends, has persisted to this day. Helmut himself, who was less and less hopeful of our chances of docking in Havana (or, he implied, in any friendly port), was determined to rescue Sophie. To which end he devised a plan, more practical if less camera-worthy than mine, whereby two Cuban stevedores would hoist her off the ship in an empty crate. When she dismissed the idea out of hand, he enlisted my help to persuade her. I admired his ingenuity but was alert to potential disaster, with either the crate dropping and Sophie plunging to her death or else its being stacked at the bottom of a pile, leaving her to a fate of slow suffocation. Helmut swore that the men were a hundred percent reliable (and well-bribed), but Sophie overruled us both, insisting that her misgivings were not to do with the escape but with her future life in Havana.

'What am I supposed to do? Rent a room and wait for the *St Louis*' yearly visit like some local goodtime girl?' Pride at being treated as an equal partner in the discussion prevented my asking her to explain *goodtime girl*, a term as complex and confusing as *joyboy*. Although Helmut promised to join her in

Havana the moment that his current tour of duty came to an end, Sophie remained unconvinced. 'I've already turned my back on my real family. Must I do the same with my adopted one?'

'You can't spend your life taking care of everyone else,' Helmut said. 'It's time to put yourself first.'

'Oh believe me, I am.'

Infected by the prevailing gloom, I begged Sophie to accept Helmut's offer, since it was vital that one of us at least should be saved.

'You just want to get rid of me,' she said, but her eyes told a different story. Helmut became increasingly agitated, fearing that the stevedores would steal his plan and sell it to someone else. So, against Sophie's express wish, he appealed to my mother, who backed him up as vigorously as he had hoped.

'You mustn't make another mistake,' she urged Sophie.

'Is that what living with you has been?'

'If we're not allowed to disembark in Havana, we'll head straight for America. You can join us there.'

The flaw in my mother's argument, which must have been as obvious to Sophie as it was to me, was that, if she stressed how easy it would be for us to land in America, there seemed to be no reason for Sophie to go to such lengths to escape. On the other hand, if she stressed the danger of our returning to Europe, Sophie would refuse to abandon us. In the end, the argument proved to be academic, since the new surveillance methods in place on the ship, together with the random searches conducted on the quays, made the plan so risky that even Helmut was obliged to let it drop.

He protested that Sophie did not love him enough. Part of me – the old Berlin part – held her vacillation to be only natural, given the few weeks in which she had known him compared to the eight years in which she had known us. The other part – the part that had grown up on the *St Louis* – held that love made all such concerns irrelevant. When I was with Johanna, feelings which had been as fixed as points of the compass were subject to a new and more powerful magnetism. Sometimes its force was so strong that I seemed to have no being outside it, neither memory nor past, but I was happy since my one wish was to exist in the present, with her. The ruthlessness of my desire made me wonder what decision I would have made had I thought up an escape plan as effective as Helmut's. Would I have placed my love for Johanna above that for my family? Would I have deserted Luise at a time of peril? Far from relishing my newfound freedom, I shrank from the burden of the choice.

As we spent our sixth day at anchor, I felt as though my brain had also come to a standstill. The endless delay combined with the merciless heat to plunge the ship into a state of torpor. I was as listless as a lizard. Even when Johanna and I kissed, it was more to maintain contact than to make love. We whiled away the time studying the small craft clinging to the hull like tick birds to a hippopotamus. Several contained film crews, anxious to find a new angle for both their cameras and reports, and yet, as they yelled out questions to every passing passenger, they returned with dismal regularity to the subject of Herr Loewe. The nine hundred people incarcerated on the ship were deemed to be of less consequence to cinema audiences around the world than the one who had jumped off. Johanna and I shared a rare moment of animation as we fabricated a story, featuring an anarchist who had planted a bomb on board and issued the Captain with a thirty-minute warning, and a middle-aged woman who had given birth to twins, Johanna vetoing quads on grounds of cruelty. Our plans were overtaken, however, by the arrival of a launch, whose lone occupant (I have no idea if he was an official, a journalist or a sympathiser) called out the news through a megaphone that negotiations between Hapag and the government had failed, and the *St Louis* been ordered out of Cuban waters.

All at once the ship was plunged into a silence of biblical proportions, which was followed with equal abruptness by a cacophony of cries, shrieks and wails. Passengers, desperate to assert themselves, plied each other with questions to which they knew that there was no answer. The Cuban policemen took refuge behind the language barrier, while our own officers professed to be as bewildered as we were ourselves. I refused to believe that the Captain, who had always treated us so fairly, would give up without a fight. As if in confirmation, Johanna spotted him, looking even smaller without his uniform, hurrying down the accommodation ladder and into a launch that spirited him across the harbour. Rumour, filling in for fact, held that he had secured an audience with the President or his wife or even the elusive General Batista. While the popular consensus was that his mission would fail, I felt an unshakeable confidence in his powers of persuasion. I remembered his kindness towards me on our first day at sea and his interest in ornithology. That, in turn, served to remind me that I was leaving Cuba without so much as a glimpse of a bee hummingbird, as though the entire voyage had been nothing more than a field trip. On the other hand, I worried that the Captain's very decency might have put him in danger, leading him to jump ship rather than return to Hamburg to be branded a Jew-lover. Johanna, whose dismissal of my 'fantasies' was disturbingly close to my mother's, insisted that he was simply giving the ravening journalists the slip.

In the early afternoon, my worst fears seemed to be realised when, with the Captain still ashore, the *St Louis* began to shudder. Without warning, the crew had started up the engines. The sound tore through the ship like a knife through canvas. The deck filled with passengers howling that we were being sent home. Johanna and I dashed to the prow, eager to escape the panic. We were standing alongside the accommodation ladder when a dozen or so women made a concerted attempt to storm it. Raising their fists and shouting that they would not be transported like cattle, they marched on the startled policemen, who fled down the ladder. For a moment it seemed as though the assault would succeed and the policemen be forced into the sea or, at least, into their waiting launch, leaving the rest of us free to follow them into the many small boats moored nearby, but they regrouped with remarkable speed, pushing the women back up the ladder and stationing themselves at the top. Their hardened attitude became clear when one of the women tripped and they not only refused to help her up but aimed their guns at anyone who tried. As the women retreated screaming, the onlookers waited in horror for a massacre that we were powerless to prevent. The crack of a shot seemed to signal its onset, but Johanna quickly assured me that it had been fired in the air. The policemen's intention was merely to unnerve us and, judging by the ensuing pandemonium, it had worked. No longer the honorary uncles who gave piggybacks to Luise and lost races to her friends, they wielded deadly weapons and were willing to use them. Meanwhile our own men, humiliated by the attack on their wives and daughters, shook their naked fists at the guns. The First Officer and several of the crew intervened with an appeal for calm, finding themselves once again caught up in a conflict over which they had no control.

An uneasy truce prevailed, with neither side giving ground. The deadlock was ended by the arrival of the Captain, who stepped out of his launch and climbed wearily back on the ship. He gazed in consternation at the scene that awaited him. After a brief word with the First Officer, he ordered the policemen to lower their guns. They could not – or would not – understand him, but his subsequent mime left no room for doubt. Satisfied with their surly compliance, he turned his attention to the passengers, insisting that we would do no good by remaining on deck and urging us to return inside. When somebody asked if we were about to set sail, he replied that the proper forum for such questions was the Passenger Committee, which he would shortly convene. Then staring straight ahead, as though to betray any doubt of our assent was to impugn his own authority, he made his way to the bridge. His strategy succeeded; the tension was defused and the crowd dispersed.

I crossed off the minutes until dinner, when we could expect to receive an account of the Committee's deliberations. By the time we sat down, however, the Professor had yet to appear, and we were forced to endure his wife's report of the afternoon's events, which would have been more suited to a *Sturm und Drang* drama. I was particularly offended by her description of a woman 'in an interesting condition', as though I were a six year-old placing a sugar lump on the windowsill to greet the stork. So I asked her what was so interesting about throwing up in the morning and feeling hot and heavy for the rest of the day. I braced myself for a sharp rebuke from my mother but, instead, was rewarded by ill-concealed smiles from both her and my father and only the mildest tutting from Aunt Annette. The Professor's wife, on the other hand, pushed away her plate as though my coarseness might induce her to a similar bout of nausea. Her husband's arrival coincided with that of the fish. To my dismay, he was more intent on feeding his own hunger than ours, and I gave thanks, yet again, that I was not one of his students. Eventually, he put down his knife and fork long enough to inform us that the Captain had indeed gone to the presidential palace but had been refused admittance – I set aside my own concerns long enough to feel a surge of sympathy for a man whose status on the ship dwindled to nothing the moment he stepped ashore. Convinced that there was no further possibility of our disembarking in Cuba, he planned to sail at ten o'clock the next morning towards any port that would take us. Where that might be was unclear, but he remained confident of guidance from the Joint Distribution Committee in New York, which was working day and night on our behalf.

The Professor's speech was met by a silence so unsettling that I filled it with the clatter of cutlery which, for once, didn't seem to rattle peoples' nerves. My mother, having barely mentioned my grandfather all week ('out of respect for our feelings' – Aunt Annette; 'out of guilt about returning to Father' – Karl), assured us that he would have secured our release with a single telegram to his American associates. My father, shamed by his own lack of influence, doubted that it would have had any effect since he had heard whispers that several former concentration camp inmates on board had sworn to kill anyone who was given preferential treatment. The Professor's wife, more suspicious of my father than ever, accused him of talking nonsense. 'No Jew would murder one of his own.'

'A Jew committed the very first murder,' I said, only to realise with a pang that the same Jew must be the source of my father's information.

'Not so,' the Professor said. 'Since he lived before Abraham, Cain can't have been a Jew. In any case, he didn't live. The Genesis story is a myth.'

'A myth is even truer than history,' I replied, appropriating my German teacher's comment on *Siegfried*. 'A story is the truth about one man; a myth is the truth about every man.' Even as I spoke, I saw that I was blurring my own distinction between Sendel and Cain. My words cast a pall over the table and, in a bid to lift it, I offered to take bets that we would land in America by the end of the week, which only drew attention to the shortage of shipboard money. So I quickly asked the Banker how long it would take to travel from Florida to New York.

'A lifetime,' he replied, refusing to play the game.

After dinner, Johanna and I went out on deck to take our farewell of Havana, the ribbon of lights promising a warmth and a welcome that would never be ours. We barely spoke. I pondered the irony wherein a ship which had held out the promise of freedom had been turned into a prison, albeit one closer to the house arrest afforded some vanquished general than the forced labour endured by my grandfather and Sendel. My musings were interrupted by the arrival of a launch bringing a fresh contingent of Cuban officials. Johanna asked what I regretted most about their refusal to let us land, only to be taken aback by the bee hummingbird. In return, she cited the chance to visit the dance halls. I reminded her of the guide book's warning that no lady was safe to go to one alone. 'I didn't want to go alone,' she replied, 'I wanted to go with you.' Then to my amazement, not least in view of her reluctance to exchange so much as a kiss in public, she suggested that we dance together on deck. I thought with horror of my clog-like feet, which would be even more exposed without a musical accompaniment.

'What will people say?' I asked.

'That's the problem with being rich. You imagine people are talking about you all the time.'

'I think it's the problem with being Jewish,' I replied, more confused than ever by her change of attitude.

'I know! We'll pretend we're in a film. In films, lovers are always dancing to the music inside their heads. Is there no music inside your head?' Her voice was so plaintive that I could not bear to disappoint her. 'Now we just have to hope that we're hearing the same beat.' Fearful that she would view my clumsiness as a sign of a general ineptitude, I placed my right hand on her waist and my left hand in her right and, for the first time, felt more conscious of my own body than of hers. As we swayed to and fro (only the most cynical ballet teacher would call it a waltz), I was taken back to the children's game where I had to transfer an orange from under my partner's chin to my own. The memory relaxed me and I began to enjoy myself, even bowing to an elderly couple who might have been applauding their younger selves. The harmony, however, was shattered by the arrival of Christina who, without drawing breath, insisted that Johanna go straight down to the cabin since her father had come aboard.

'All my personal things are laid out on the bed,' Johanna replied, as if their exposure were the most threatening aspect of his presence. Grabbing her arm in a rare display of self-assertion, her mother insisted that there was no time to lose since the Purser had told her that he would only have half an hour on the ship.

'Please come too,' Joanna begged me. 'You must!' I was as reluctance to accede as Christina was to involve me. I was no longer her daughter's eligible friend but an intruder at a family reunion. I could not, however, ignore the appeal in Johanna's eyes. To abandon her now would be less like refusing to dance with her than leaving her to walk down a street lined with stick-wielding Nazis. So I clasped her moist hand and accompanied her to the cabin. Along the way, she bombarded her mother with questions: 'What does he look like? Does he look like me? Is he alone? What if I call the wrong man Father?' I realised that, for all the pain of my father's absence, I at least had had the balm of memory, whereas she had had only a wound. Christina did her best to reply, but Johanna paid little attention, showing that her greatest need was for the reassurance of her own voice.

The cabin door was ajar, which eased the transition. On entering, I drew back as befitted an outsider. I felt uneasy sharing Johanna's first glimpse of her father, a man to whom, by rights, she should have been introducing me. Subjecting him to the scrutiny which was also a father's prerogative, I saw a man of middle age and middle height, wearing a white suit (although his body was built for black), with a close-cropped beard, a pince-nez and a sinister gold-toothed smile.

'You must be Johanna,' he said to his daughter, who gazed hopelessly at her mother and me, as if to indicate the fatuity of the remark. 'I'm overwhelmed,' he added. 'You don't know how long I've waited to see you.'

'Fourteen years and five months. I know exactly,' she replied.

'Christina,' he said, in a belated acknowledgement of her mother. 'You defy the calendar.' His lips brushed her cheek. 'You put us all to shame.' I read the entire history of their relationship in their respective flattery and simpering. Johanna stared at them as fascinated as if she had unearthed a cache of wedding photographs. My presence could no longer be ignored and he threw me a questioning glance. Christina introduced us and he gave me a curt nod.

'We have no time,' he said to Johanna. 'We'll have to get to know one another in Havana.'

'We're not allowed to leave the ship,' she replied. 'We sail first thing in the morning.'

'Not necessarily,' he said, causing my heart to miss a beat.

'How did you manage to come on board?' Johanna asked, voicing the question on all our lips.

'Does it matter?' he replied and then, sensing that it did, explained. 'I've been here two years. I know – I make it my business to know – a lot of influential people. I'm not like the rest of them, marking time in cafés till their quota numbers come up. I oil wheels. I always have.'

'That must make you very greasy,' I said, insolence sneaking up on me unawares. He laughed coldly, before turning back to Johanna.

'You know, of course, that what's kept you out is your entry permits. They were issued by the Director of Immigration – an incompetent oaf called Benitez.' It came as no surprise that he objected to the man's inefficiency rather than to his corruption. 'Through my connections at the Foreign Ministry, I've managed to obtain two valid visas, one for you and one for your mother.' Christina's face flooded with relief and she kissed his hand, which might as well have been his foot given her effusion of servility. 'Now we have very little time. You must gather your things and come with me.'

I was stunned, both by Johanna's change of fortune and our imminent separation. My head rang with all the words I had left unsaid. My lips stung with all the kisses we had still to share. I began to understand why people killed themselves for love.

'What about everyone else?' Johanna's question surprised me since she had always regarded the other passengers as irritants. I presumed that she was playing for time while she adjusted to the idea of departure.

'They're not my concern,' her father replied. 'You are. You're my daughter.'

'How do you know?' she asked, retreating into melodrama. 'My mother might have been lying to extort money.'

'Oh Johanna,' Christina said, shame suffusing her cheeks.

'Don't do this to yourself,' her father said. 'Don't do this to me.'

'You want to make amends for the last fourteen years? Why now?'

'We only have a few minutes before the launch leaves.'

'Why now?'

'Two words: Adolf Hitler. Will they do?'

'I'm a part of this ship . . . these people.' I tried to look worthy of her declaration. 'I can't abandon them.'

'But they don't want you. They refuse to accept you. You're your mother's daughter.'

'It's in my blood.'

'You're young, so you think that persecution is romantic. But the truth is that it's vile and degrading. I'm giving you a chance to escape.'

'A month ago, I would have said "yes". I wouldn't have looked back if the ship had been sinking. But now I know who these people are. I've shared their lives. I've seen their courage . . . their decency.'

Her father looked suspicious, as though abstract virtues had no place in his world. 'Who is this young man?' he asked. 'Why is he here?'

'We're in love,' she replied, turning our secret vows into an established fact.

'Oh darling, how wonderful,' Christina said, the romance fleetingly overruling the danger.

'Don't be ridiculous! How old are you, my boy? Twelve? Thirteen?' I was determined to prove myself old enough to ignore the insult.

'Fifteen.'

'Fifteen, really?' He sounded as astonished as if I had declared myself eligible to serve as Chancellor rather than to love his daughter. 'If you multiply the years by seven to get a dog's age, then you should divide them by three to get an adolescent's. You're children! Still wet behind the ears.'

'We're in love,' I said, eager to speak the words in my turn.

'You think you're in love. There's a difference. You met on board. Am I right?'

'So what?' I said.

'Like sea-sickness, it'll vanish as soon as you're back on land.'

'You've no right to speak like that to Karl,' Johanna said. 'You of all people!'

'You say you love my daughter,' he challenged me. 'Very well then, prove it. Tell her to come with me. Help me to save her life.'

I hesitated. While the whole weight of my boyhood reading pushed me to make a romantic sacrifice, my need for her redressed the balance. Nobility was no longer as powerful as desire. 'I shall respect Johanna's decision,' I said, 'whatever it may be.'

Further discussion was prevented by the entrance of the Purser, too flustered to wait for an answer to his knock. 'The launch is preparing to leave, sir. You have exactly two minutes. Shall I send a steward for the cases?'

'Please, Officer,' he replied. 'Ten more minutes. Five!'

'The Cubans are starting to get jittery. If you're not careful, you'll find yourself stuck on board.'

'That's right, Pappi,' Johanna said. 'If you really want to make it up to me, sail back with us. You'll have plenty of time to get to know me then. I'm sure they can squeeze you in.'

'I'll try and stall them for a few minutes, but I can't promise,' the Purser said, hurrying out.

'Johanna, darling, we must go with your father. We've come all this way.' Christina spoke as though her greatest concern were the wasted journey.

'You've done so much for me, Mother.' She turned to her father. 'You've no idea how hard she's worked.' She took her mother's hand. 'You deserve a rest.' At that moment I knew that my fate was sealed. Johanna's obligation to her mother would offset both her hostility to her father and her love for me.

'That's right,' her father said. 'I've spent a fortune. You wouldn't believe how much these visas cost me! If my wife (may she rest in peace) had found out – '

'You mean your wife's dead?' Johanna asked.

'The heat. She was very delicate.'

'Did you know this?' Johanna asked her mother, whose crest-fallen face made an answer redundant. 'I see.' She turned to her father. 'So you only wrote to us once she was safely out of the way.'

'That had nothing to do with it.'

'What about her postscript to your letter?'

'A technicality.'

'You have sons too, don't you? My big brothers.' She spat out the words with chilling contempt.

'That's right. The eldest, Daniel (may he rest in peace), was murdered by the Brownshirts, but Otto and Johannes are both in America. It's easier for the young to slip through the net. They've done so well. A credit to their old father.'

'So they're not here either? How convenient! You lose one family and you bring in another . . . and not only a family but a cook-housekeeper to slave for you and a pretty girl to keep all those influential friends amused.'

'You're the only ones I'm thinking of. Don't you realise what'll happen if you're sent back home?'

'Who says we're going back home?'

The Purser gave him no time to answer, entering this time without even the pretence of a knock. 'You must come at once, sir, madam. The launch is about to leave.'

'Johanna please!' her mother beseeched.

'Johanna please!' her father ordered. 'Hate me if you will, but save yourself. I've done you a great injury, but I swear I'll make it up to you. If you go back to Germany, I'll never have the chance.'

'Sir, please. There's no time.'

'Christina . . . young man . . . you, Officer, you know what's in store for them, tell her! Make her see sense.'

'Goodbye Father,' Johanna said, holding out her hand. 'A pleasure to have made your acquaintance after all these years.'

Her father pushed away her hand and held her in an embrace so tight that I gasped. Then he dashed out, followed by the Purser, leaving the cabin as airless as a compression chamber. Christina slumped on the bed. Johanna gave her a hug. 'Don't worry, Mother. You've always said that the Jews were clever. They're bound to find a way out.'

Christina summoned a thin smile and asked us to leave her to rest. I found her quiet stoicism deeply affecting. As I accompanied Johanna down the corridor, I was struck by the reversal of roles. In the romances I read so avidly, it was the knight who made sacrifices for his lady, but she had renounced her chance to escape in order to stay with me. For all her horror at her father's duplicity and respect for her fellow passengers, I knew it was love that had governed her decision. Gratitude gave way to alarm that I would never live up to it. As though to reassure me, she evoked a biblical precedent. 'It was hearing how Ruth chose to remain with her Jewish mother-in-law rather than return to her own people, that inspired me. "Whither thou goest, I will go; and where thou lodgest, I will lodge: thy people shall be my people, and thy God my God."' She spoke with such sincerity that the familiar words sounded fresh. We went back out on deck, where we were barred from approaching within two metres of the rail by the suicide patrol, who responded to Johanna's challenge by threatening to escort her to her cabin. It was as though, in their misery, they believed that a show of officiousness would somehow secure their reprieve.

Despair stalked the ship, tightening its grip on everyone but me. I saw the pain etched on faces all around and I felt nothing, not even guilt at my own elation. It was as though I existed in two dimensions at once: real time and Johanna time. . . . I wonder if any of you can identify with that. Marcus, I realise with a pang, is as old now as I was then, but age may not be a valid criterion in a culture that equates maturity with cynicism. Even the love songs sound like amplified grunts. I, however, was blessed with a newfound eloquence. After years of supposing myself to be a misfit, I had discovered my place in the world. What's more, I understood my mother's clemency to my father. If my love were any measure of hers, it was worth braving everything – including her son's censure – to try to recapture it. I swore then and there that I would never betray Johanna and sealed it with a goodnight kiss so lingering that it looked set to become good morning, until she gently smiled and slipped away.

I awoke the next day to a faint vibration which threatened to lull me back to sleep, until I realised with a jolt that the ship's engines had been started up again. Throwing on my clothes, I ran out on to the desolate deck. Groups of passengers scrutinised each other as though searching for scapegoats, the bad Jews responsible for their exclusion. Making my way to the rail, now released from its night-time restrictions, I watched the flotilla of small craft drop away. Only a handful of boats remained, bearing our most stalwart supporters, no longer shouting encouragement but standing as still as the crowds at President Hindenburg's funeral. Among them was the father of Luise's two friends, his head bowed, too crushed even to look up at the ship. He failed to respond when Sophie, seizing the last chance for a family reunion, brought the girls to the rail and called out his name. Undeterred, she stooped at their sides and pointed him out. Her persistence – assisted by the lack of competition – paid off.

'Is it the man with the white hat?' the younger one asked.

'Yes, that's right. Well done!' Sophie hugged her.

'Why is he crying?'

'What? Don't be silly. He isn't crying. Not at all.'

'He is too,' the older one insisted.

'He's wiping the salt – that is the spray – from his eyes. Come on, time for breakfast.' Her own eyes were equally raw as she led the girls away. Meanwhile twenty metres below, their father finally looked up, too late to see his week-long vigil reap its meagre reward.

I followed them to the dining room where the Professor's absence held out hope of a last-minute amnesty, which was dashed an hour later by a loudspeaker announcement requesting us all to assemble in the social hall. As we filed in to learn our fate, I found myself alongside Viktor and Joel. Moments later, ten men walked in and sat down on the dais. Five were immediately recognisable as the Passenger Committee, two were Cubans in their now-loathsome uniforms, and the other three introduced themselves as Milton Goldsmith, the representative of the Joint Distribution Committee in Cuba, Lawrence Berenson, his colleague from New York, and Robert Hoffman, the Hapag agent in Havana. There was no sign of the Captain or any of his officers.

'Too busy,' I said to Joel.

'Too cowardly,' he replied with contempt.

Herr Goldsmith begged us not to lose heart, promising that people across the globe were working ceaselessly on our behalf, an assertion underlined by Herr Berenson's unshaven face and crumpled clothing. The Professor reported the Captain's intention of heading for Florida in the belief that the Americans would waive the quota restrictions and permit us to stay. The Cuban police chief, sweating profusely, apologised for his government's actions and trusted that we would soon dock at a more accommodating port. Hoffman expressed regrets on behalf of Hapag, although his sly smirk made it clear that he failed to share them. Then, without further ado, the five officials left the dais and walked straight off the ship. We trailed out transfixed, as if Havana were Hamelin. Their departure was followed by the last contingent of policemen, who descended the accommodation ladder into a waiting launch. To my surprise I found myself sorry to see them go.

Finally, at eleven o'clock, after a long blast on the whistle, the *St Louis* began to move. A low moan echoed across the deck in an expression of universal despondency. Clusters of passengers clung to one another in tears, irrespective of age or sex. As the shore receded, I was struck by the irony that it was Helmut at the helm: Helmut who, with a sudden twist, could drive the ship aground and, alone, achieve the result that had eluded a team of negotiators . . . but I knew his sense of duty to be as unswerving as his hand. I took a final look at Havana as at a stage set that was soon to be dismantled – the illusion permanently destroyed – before turning to the boats that had accompanied us from the harbour, sticking to us like burrs or, in the case of the journalists, like tick birds determined to suck the last drops of blood from our sores. One by one they fell away, leaving only the Hapag launch bobbing in our wake. When it too turned back, each of its three passengers took his leave in his own way: Goldsmith clasped his hands together as if in prayer; Berenson raised his fist in defiance; Hoffman thrust out his arm in a Nazi salute.

Our hopes receded along with Havana. People avoided each other's gaze for fear of seeing the reflection of their own pain. Wan smiles replaced conversation. I felt doubly downcast since Johanna was playing nursemaid to her mother who had taken to her bed, as distressed by her daughter's perversity as by the ship's departure. At least Joel and Viktor, whom I found playing a desultory game of deck quoits, spared me their usual quips about 'young love'. Declining to take part – thinking up ways to pass the time only made me more aware of how heavily it hung on me

– I returned to my cabin and an unsatisfactory encounter with
Rob Roy. The print wearied my eyes and, even after three or
four readings, the description of Frank Osbaldistone's quest
failed to engage me. I was perplexed by the fact that the closer I
drew to the hero in age, the harder I found it to identify with
him. Burying my head in the fusty pillow (a Hapag directive
having reduced the supply of fresh linen), I sought to banish all
thought, until an ill-suppressed cough announced the arrival of
my father, who perched on my bed and lowered his hand to my
shoulder, only to divert it at the last minute towards a nonexistent fly.

After eight years, his efforts at consolation were rusty. First
he informed me that he had been almost twenty before he went
abroad, as though to suggest that I should regard the voyage
itself as a privilege. Then he declared that the Americans were
bound to let us in since, in such a large country, 'nine hundred
Jews would be a drop in the ocean.' I gazed out of the window in
dismay. 'They could give us a piece of the Arizona desert and
we'd make it as green as a prairie.' Refusing to be cheered, I
voiced my overriding fear that we would be forced to return to
Germany, only to discover that we had nowhere to live. Our
house would have been expropriated by some Nazi grandee to
whom such theft was a patriotic duty, and we would be obliged
to take lodgings in the slums of the Alexanderplatz among
people like Sendel. My father insisted that my fears were groundless. 'Hitler may talk of a thousand-year Reich, but the man
himself is mortal. Remember Hirsch's first law of political
gravity: whatever rises must fall.'

'That's all very well, but what happens then? Hitler's bad
enough but he might be succeeded by a mass murderer like Ivan
the Terrible or Attila the Hun.'

'Impossible. This is the twentieth century. The world has
moved on.'

For all the lamentable ignorance of history among the young (and the not so young), you must have picked up enough to know that your great-grandfather's faith was seriously misplaced. I don't write this to bolster your sense of superiority (Leila's equation of human progress with the use of deodorants was disturbing enough) but to point out how different our perspective was then. What's more, although I remained unconvinced by his arguments, my father both surprised and moved me by declaring that, despite the many dreadful things that the Nazis had done, he couldn't hate them because they had brought us back together, giving him the chance to make amends.

'I've told you already,' I said, embarrassed by his intensity. 'It's Luise you have to make it up to. She's the one you've hurt.'

'No, she's the one I damaged. It's you I've hurt.'

I mulled over his words the next morning as I made my way to the social hall for Sabbath prayers. The room was packed although, as the Rabbi's grim smile acknowledged, despair was as prevalent as devotion. With my mother opting to paint (had she been Marie Antoinette, I felt sure that her last request would have been for crayons to sketch the scaffold) and my father asserting his agnosticism, Aunt Annette and I were the sole representatives of our family. Our motives, however, were very different. Whereas she came to beg God to deliver us from our enemies, I came to challenge him as to why he had delivered us to them. He thwarted me, however, by failing to reveal himself, and I sat through the service in growing frustration. Allowing my gaze to wander, I turned towards the women where, to my joy and surprise, I saw Johanna staring intently at the Rabbi. I tried to attract her attention but she refused to respond, as though a single stray glance would threaten her hard-won commitment. While my own ear gradually retuned to the language I had studied two years before, I feared that three hours of impenetrable Hebrew might send her running back to the

Latin mass. The sermon, once again, was in German, although, as the Rabbi expounded on his text, a dispiriting verse from the Prophet Amos: 'God said, You only have I known of all the families of the earth, therefore I will punish you for all your iniquities', I should have preferred Swahili.

'Privilege brings responsibilities,' my grandfather used to say when setting off to visit one of his charities. It seemed to me, however, that the privileges God had granted the Jews had brought us nothing but prejudice and pain. Christians managed things better. Their God suffered on their behalf rather than the other way round. I determined to consult Johanna, who had a unique vantage point, but, when we met after the service, she had no time to discuss anything, let alone the finer points of theology.

'Please try to understand,' she said. 'I have to go straight back to my mother. She needs me more than ever.' I tried to look sceptical but sympathetic. 'She's always felt guilty about my having had no father. Now she feels guilty that he's a Jew: that she's condemned me to a life of persecution.'

'That's the price of belonging to the chosen people.'

'You're not serious, are you? The chosen people chose themselves: they were the ones who wrote the story. Besides, isn't everyone chosen by God? That's why I like the idea of angels: each one of us with a guardian angel watching over us on God's behalf. Jews do believe in guardian angels?' she asked anxiously.

'Believe in them? We invented them. Then sometimes,' I said pointedly, 'they come down to earth in human form.' My words, which I was afraid would sound mawkish, moved her to tears, but she refused to give way. Mouthing 'I love you,' she scurried back to her cabin.

I went out on deck, averting my eyes from the Florida coast as resolutely as I had from the Michaelskirche as a child. My fellow passengers felt less constrained and gazed wretchedly at the glistening shore which, barely a week before, had held such promise. One man shook his fist at it and muttered a stream of imprecations, but the gesture served only to emphasise his impotence and was met with an embarrassed silence.

Climbing to the top deck, I found my mother at her easel, as indifferent to the public gaze as a student copying an old master in a museum. Although she was facing the sea, her picture was of life beneath its surface. The *St Louis*, identifiable only by the name on its stern, ploughed through an ocean filled with exotic fish and plants, above a seabed covered with coral-like bones or bone-like coral (I knew better than to question the ambiguity). While I was looking over her shoulder, desperate not to say the wrong thing, a sprightly old man approached from the other side and, after studying the canvas intently, showered her with compliments which made her blush as red as one of her fish. When he slipped away, expressing regret at having disturbed her work along with the hope that she would allow him to buy it, I was sure that he must be mocking her. So, following him down the steps, I asked what he knew about painting. Showing no offence at my tone, he replied that, until his dismissal, he had been professor of art history at the Akademie der Künste in Berlin.

'And you think the picture is good?' I asked, striving to conceal my amazement.

'I think it's excellent. You have a very talented mother.' I felt as flustered as if he'd praised her breasts. 'I've admired her work for years. I long hoped to acquire one for my collection.' He paused as if to wonder whether it still existed. 'But I was always too late. Whenever I went to an exhibition, the paintings had all been snapped up. Imagine my delight at learning that she was a fellow passenger. I feel inspired to start collecting again.'

As he tipped the brim of an invisible hat and sauntered off, I struggled to assimilate this new perspective on my mother's work. I thought of my grandfather's pre-emptive strikes and judged that he ought to have trusted his daughter a little more and protected her a little less.

The day dragged on interminably. The children had exhausted the possibilities of the sports deck and were forced to entertain one another with Chinese burns and hair-pulling. The adults had exhausted the possibilities of the cinema, with only the most devoted fans of Grethe Weiser able to sit through another showing of *The Divine Jette*. The rush to use up every shipboard pfennig before docking at Havana had left people with no money to buy drinks, let alone throw parties. The stewards became largely ornamental. Morning coffee and afternoon tea were the only diversions, although the band no longer requested our favourite songs but played doggedly through their repertoire. Even the library offered no escape since its shelves were packed with atlases and guidebooks. I longed for a respite from Sir Walter Scott and envied Viktor the compendious delights of *War and Peace* – or rather War or Peace, since the Gestapo firemen had ripped it in two almost exactly along the lines of its title. I went early to bed, hoping that dreams would provide some relief, but my mountain hike with Berlin school friends showed such disdain for our plight that I despaired of my unconscious.

I awoke the next morning to the sound of my father's snoring, but my irritation soon turned to alarm that it might be a further similarity between us and that my snores would disgust Johanna as much as his did me. I hurried up on deck where, turning my back on the mirage of Miami, I trained my binoculars on the sky, to be transfixed by the sight of a solitary bird trailing the ship. Its sweeping white wings and long hooked pink bill were unmistakable . . . but even the Wandering Albatross would not wander so far off course. Yet, despite the weakness of the lenses, the more I observed it, the more confident I grew of my identification. I decided to appeal to the one man on board who would give me a definitive judgement. I knew that, as a fellow ornithologist, he would never forgive me if I denied him the sighting. So without a second thought, I ran through the restricted area, this time easily locating his cabin. For all my haste, I remembered to wait for a reply to my knock. On entering, I was horrified to see Schiendick, who was now so cocksure that he pre-empted the Captain and asked how I dared intrude. The Captain cut him off with icy calm, as much to assert himself as to question me. At the mention of the albatross, he leapt from his desk and told me to lead the way. Schiendick looked nonplussed. 'I haven't finished yet,' he said.

'Oh but I have,' the Captain replied, heading for the door.

'I'm talking about the need, the absolute imperative, to head for home – our return is a matter of concern in the highest echelons of the Party – and you set off on a wild goose chase with this Jew!'

The Captain stared at him with contempt. He stood several centimetres shorter than Schiendick, but his inborn authority made the taller man cower. 'You can make as much mischief as you like in Berlin – and I've no doubt you will. But I am still the Captain of the *St Louis* and I warn you that, one more word, and I shall relieve you of your responsibilities. What's more, I shall see to it that you never work on another ship. Now leave my cabin.' Schiendick obeyed, flashing us both a look of pure venom. I rejoiced at having witnessed his upbraiding, although I feared that he would make me pay for it later. Pausing only to grab his binoculars, the Captain led the way outside. I regretted that none of my friends were at hand to see me in such august company, as we climbed to the observation deck where he quickly spotted the bird, wheeling and diving above the ship. His eye was so much more experienced than mine – and his lenses so much more powerful – that I was thrilled when he confirmed the identification. 'Its size means it could only be a Wandering or a Royal. It's not always easy to tell them apart, especially when they're young. So what decided it for you?'

'First, the bill. It's pink, while the Royal is more yellow.'

'Go on.'

'Then the shape of the head is sharper.'

'True, but still not conclusive.'

'But, most of all, the plumage. The Royal has the same black-tipped tail but a lot more black in the wings.'

'That's certainly the case for the Northern Royal, but not always for the Southern. Don't look so glum. You've done splendidly. But I'll let you into a secret. See the brown patch on its crown?' I studied the bird, which was now almost vertical in the sky. 'And the brown smudge on its chest?' I nodded, not wanting to miss a moment of its flight. 'Those are the giveaways. They're unique to the adult male Wanderer. And, to judge by the marking on the upper mandible and the almost entire lack of colouring on its wings, I'd say that this one was aged between ten and twenty. Well done! I'm most impressed.' His praise made up for all the swimming cups and essay prizes withheld from me at school. He spoke again of the albatross that he had sighted in the Azores, explaining that even non-migratory birds could sometimes be found thousands of miles from their natural habitat.

'So I might still find a bee hummingbird when we land in America?'

'You might,' he replied cautiously. His solicitude, together with his treatment of Schiendick, emboldened me and I asked about the danger of our returning to Germany. 'I shan't pretend that it doesn't exist,' he said, 'but you have my word that we'll explore every other avenue first.'

'There are an awful lot of Jews in America.'

'You must have realised by now that not everyone views that as a blessing. I'm as ignorant of how things are run in America as the Americans appear to be of events in Germany, but I do know that President Roosevelt is up for re-election, which means politics taking precedence over principles.'

'I hoped we'd left politics behind in Cuba.'

'They follow us like a trade wind. But you mustn't despair. I shouldn't really be telling you this. . . .' I knew from his smile that it was only a half-shouldn't, like a white lie or a 'cross my heart' with crossed fingers. 'But we may have found a haven in the Dominican Republic. Your representatives in New York are negotiating with them even as we speak. As I understand it, they require some sort of bond to be placed for every passenger.'

'If it's a question of money,' I said, 'my family has accounts in America. You need only speak to my mother . . .'

'I'm sure that won't be necessary. Though, once a figure is agreed, no doubt another will be thrown in for good measure. All this haggling over lives is quite sickening. I feel like the master of a slave trader.' He composed himself. 'No matter. It'll be over soon. Now I must go back to the bridge. By the way, I've informed your Passenger Committee of the offer but I've asked them to keep it to themselves – and the same goes for you.'

'Not a word, I swear.'

'Thank you. And thank you again for the albatross. It was a real pleasure. Here.' He held out his binoculars. 'Would you like to try these? I wouldn't even take that pair to the opera.' I wavered, acutely conscious of the trust he was placing in me and aching for stronger lenses, but the fear of damaging them made me decline.

We spent the morning cruising along the coast, once again attracting the attention of the local fishing fleet which followed us with, we suspected, a full complement of photographers on board. It was dispiriting to discover that the Americans were as ready as the Cubans to profit from our plight. Just before noon, a US naval cutter swept past, sending the passengers on deck into a flurry of waving. I, however, kept my hands deep in my pockets, entertaining no illusions as to what lurked beneath the breeziness of its flag. The only way that it would ever allow us to land would be if, having accidentally shot at us, it was forced to rescue us from the sea. With the chances of our being afforded a refuge in America receding by the hour, hope arose from an unexpected source. At lunch, the Professor told us not of the offer from the Dominican Republic, as I might have expected, but of a renewed offer from Cuba. He was convinced that, this time, the government was acting in good faith, even if that faith were dependent on the raising of a substantial bond. Provided that their negotiations with the Joint Distribution Committee were concluded satisfactorily, they were prepared to house us on the Isle of Pines, a few miles off the mainland. Since he had little information about the island, Aunt Annette suggested that I, as resident travel guide – a phrase that the Professor's wife purported to find hilarious – should consult my Baedeker. Needing no further encouragement, I hurried down to the cabin and leafed through the book, thankful that I had resisted the urge to drown it in Havana harbour. I was disappointed by the meagre description. The island seemed to be devoid of any notable or redeeming feature. I returned to report that it was fifty-seven kilometres wide, sparsely populated, and covered in rich vegetation, while keeping the fact that it was a former penal colony to myself.

No sea can ever have been as inconstant as the one on which we sailed. One moment we were being buffeted by disappointment and, the next, lapped by hope. Yet even those passengers who

remained suspicious of the Cuban offer couldn't fail to be heartened the following morning by the pod of dolphins frolicking in
our wake. As they showed off their acrobatic skills as brazenly as
schoolboys, it seemed that Nature herself were confirming our
change of fortune. For once we had a subject to photograph,
rather than the other way round. My own change of fortune was
confirmed when Johanna announced that her mother had abandoned her sickbed and was drinking coffee with the chemist,
leaving us free to stroll about the ship as happily as honey-
mooners or – not to tempt fate – a couple who were newly
engaged. Once again we had a chance to make plans, starting
with how to survive on the island. We agreed that we had
outgrown school and resolved to resist any attempt by the
teachers on board to persuade us otherwise. We determined,
instead, to find some secret cove, courtesy of Robert Louis
Stevenson, where we could spend our days, safe from prying
adults.

Our deliberations were lent urgency by the sight of an over-
dressed couple hauling their luggage up the steps. My initial
sense of déjà vu gave way to a newfound optimism, which must
have been widely shared for, by the end of the afternoon, the
deck resembled a dockside, prompting me to return to my cabin
to pack. While grateful that grubby clothes required no folding,
I trusted that the laundry facilities which had been reduced on
the ship (in theory, to save water; in practice, to compound our
humiliation) would be restored on the island. I decided to put on
my last clean shirt and gave thanks for my foresight when,
escorting Johanna to the social hall after dinner, I found that the
dance floor, which in recent nights had been deserted, was
teeming. Virtually every passenger of waltzing age was present
and Johanna refused to grant me an exemption. I was relieved,
at least, that the floor was too crowded to allow anything more

intricate than swaying. Besides, after a few moments, I lost my self-consciousness and became conscious only of her. From time to time, we bumped (in both the 'hello' and the 'ouch' senses) into family and friends: my parents who, to judge by their capers, were seeking at once to revive their youth and bury the intervening years in oblivion; Christina, bent on charming her chemist while protecting her toes; Joel, whose jokes about young love gained piquancy from his own grey-haired partner; Aunt Annette, whose unofficial widowhood offered scope for the Professor both to display his chivalry and to escape his wife. The one person not on the floor was Sophie who sat, eyes fixed on the door, waiting for Helmut. Twice during the evening Johanna dispatched me to ask her to dance and, to my surprise, she accepted. Each time, I could think of nothing but my feet.

At eleven o'clock, Johanna and I went out on deck where we yielded to the desire behind the dancing. I found that fingers, lips and tongues could move as harmoniously as toes. We climbed inside a lifeboat and I placed my hand casually on her knee. To my delight, rather than slapping it away, she gently opened her legs. Terrified of going too fast, or too far, I edged higher, brushing against the cotton of her pants. Although my knowledge of female anatomy was, to say the least, sketchy, having been gleaned either from the glazed statues in the Altes Museum or from childhood glimpses of Luise, my hand made instinctively for the moist cleft between her thighs. I had never realised that my fingertips could provide so much pleasure – and not just to myself since, far from indulging me, Johanna clearly responded to my touch. For the first time in the two years since my body had begun to betray me, I felt no shame at my arousal. On the contrary, as she rubbed it through the frustratingly thick trousers, my penis became a source of pride. I judged that my joy would be complete if she would only slip her hand beneath my waistband and, while I quite understood her reluctance and refused to destroy the evening by suggesting it myself, I longed for her to take hold of it: to legitimise it and make me whole.

Matters, however, had gathered their own momentum. My heart threatened to burst from my chest like a chick from an egg. My breath was as short as if I had swum the hundred metres freestyle. Scared of offending her, I made out that I was about to sneeze, but the power of her kiss tore through my pretences. My body felt as if it were exploding and waves of warmth surged over me. Johanna was so sensitive to my excitement that she broke into a sympathetic sweat. Then, all at once, the moment was over. We no longer fired each other but propped each other up. I removed my hand, which had become an intrusion. We smoothed our clothes, the thickness of my trousers now working in my favour, and climbed out of the boat. We walked to the rail and gazed at the sea, the prospect of a safe haven having removed the need for both floodlights and the suicide patrol. We did not speak but shared a perfect understanding. After a while – precision eludes me – she stroked my cheek and announced that she was going to bed. I offered to escort her but she urged me to stay and enjoy the stars. I then returned to my cabin where I was perturbed to find that my father was still awake. I felt shy and worried that he would see – or worse, smell – what I had been doing. Loath to risk undressing in front of him and yet refusing to retreat to the bathroom, I threw off my jacket, kicked off my shoes, and declared that I was so exhausted that I would sleep in my clothes. Far from reprimanding me, he smiled and said that I was taking him back thirty years. Then, to my surprise, he jumped out of bed, pulled the eiderdown on top of me and kissed the crown of my head.

I fear that I have let my memories run away with me. I can hear Edward spit out his trademark 'Gross!', turning the very word into a gobbet of disgust. I shall stand accused of conduct unbecoming to a grandfather. One of the many things, however, that I learnt on the *St Louis* – as you may too, depending on the age at which you read this account – is that no one is merely a grandfather. Besides, you need have no fears of a repetition. The mood the next day was far less conducive to romance. We awoke to find that the ship was travelling as slowly as if it were approaching port although we were still in the middle of the ocean. I felt an instinctive dread, which was confirmed at break-fast when the Professor reported on his early-morning meeting with the Captain. You know the English expression 'Don't count your chickens before they're hatched'? Well, all I can hear is the German 'One should not praise the day before the evening.' Suddenly a language for which I have no love – quite the oppo-site – is flooding my brain. It seemed that our negotiators in Cuba had been over-confident. There were considerable prob-lems in housing us on the Isle of Pines. The Captain was waiting for a telegram of clarification. Until then, he was marking time.

My stomach, which had survived all the turbulence of the voyage, rebelled, and I rushed from the table. Hope had been dangled before me, only to be snatched away like a coin on a schoolboy's string. I longed for the Captain to peel the photo-graphs from our passports and send them in a box to the Cuban president – not nine hundred names but nine hundred faces: Johanna's face; Luise's; Joel's; Aunt Annette's; even the Professor's wife's; young faces; old faces; strong faces; weak faces; faces lined with care and faces bright with courage; faces like those of the elderly couple who had set up camp on deck, perched on their cases. I watched while, first the Purser, and then a delegation of passengers, failed to move them. I applauded their intransigence and, to my surprise, even found myself wishing for a boatload of photographers to capture it, but the only witnesses were the passing gulls. I gazed out to sea and into a haze that seemed to extend across the horizon to cover our wider prospects. In normal circumstances I would have welcomed any distraction, but the sight of Sendel increased my unease. I assumed my sunniest smile as a defence against the cynicism with which I knew that he would engulf me. True to form, his first words rang with contempt for all the passengers who had fallen for the promise of the Isle of Pines.

'You never know,' I replied airily, 'there's still hope. Besides, if the Cubans won't have us, the Americans will.'

'The Americans hate us. Have you never heard of the Ku Klux Klan?'

'Are they Indians?'

'Hardly! Think of Hitler and Goebbels in cowls.'

'What about the Statue of Liberty?' I recited the familiar inscription, which I had endowed with talismanic power.

'The Statue of Liberty is on an island off the coast of New York. New York is an island off the coast of America. You might as well take what happens on Rugen as typical of Germany.'

My image of America was framed in the monochrome of Hollywood where, even in Chicago, the wickedest city in the world, the cause of good ultimately triumphed. I assured him that, for all their prevarication, the Americans would do what was right.

'What about the Church? In Germany, the priests reviled us from their pulpits to congregations of hundreds. In America, they revile us across the airwaves to audiences of millions. The wireless operators on the ship even picked up a broadcast, as a friendly fireman couldn't wait to tell me. The preacher was talking about the *St Louis* and how letting us in would destroy the nation's purity.' I was appalled by the notion of my body, to which I had finally become reconciled, as a source of infection. It was as though the *St Louis* were not a twentieth century cruise liner but a nineteenth century quarantine ship. I failed to under-stand how such a young country could bear such ancient grudges and asked Sendel if in America, as in Europe, they blamed us for the death of Jesus.

'Yes of course they do. And so they should.'

'What about the Romans? They were the ones who ordered it.'

'You coward!' he replied, startling me by his vehemence. 'Why refuse to take credit for the most glorious moment in our history – perhaps the only glorious moment in our history?' I had no great love for Jesus, nevertheless – and even without considering its consequences – I saw that the execution of one false Messiah paled beside the achievements of Moses and Joshua and Solomon. 'Take it from me: I was there.' I braced myself for another outburst of madness. 'When God condemned me to walk the earth forever, you don't suppose that he gave me a special dispensation for the thirty-odd years that his son was here or sent me to some far-flung city in Persia or Asia Minor? No, I was right there in Jerusalem when the Nazarene arrived on his final journey. I was then known as Ahasuerus.'

I felt sure that I had heard the name before and struggled to remember where.

'I was studying law at the Temple, where my father worked as a moneychanger. He was there on the day that the Nazarene and his followers burst in and sparked off a riot. I expect you can fill in the rest.'

I shook my head. I was familiar with only the broad outlines of the Christian story, having disregarded the details.

'You should know your enemies,' Sendel added emphatically. 'They certainly know you.' He went on to explain: 'The Nazarene showed up in the temple forecourt and complained that it had been turned into a bazaar. Then he went berserk, knocking over stalls, breaking scales, scattering money and freeing livestock. What he failed to acknowledge – and his apologists to mention – was that this wasn't some kind of sharp practice but a requirement of religious law. The Roman coin, that coin stamped with Caesar's head which he'd made the subject of one of his more asinine aphorisms, was held to be impure and couldn't be used in the Temple. So anyone wishing to pay his Passover tax or buy an animal or a bird for sacrifice –' (I shuddered) '– was obliged to go through my father and his friends. But the Nazarene chose to ignore this as he ran amok, smashing his abacus and table and flinging his entire reserve of cash into the drain, which was running with blood from the altar. My father came home that night, his hands and robe stained crimson, clasping the few coins he'd managed to salvage. He was a small trader: he worked to the narrowest of margins (and those too were strictly regulated). His livelihood lay in ruins, along with his self-respect. He, who had always believed that he was fulfilling an honourable, almost a sacred, function – yes, that in his own way, he stood as an intermediary between man and God, now heard himself condemned as a parasite. Even when, less than a week later, the Nazarene was tried and convicted, my father's spirits didn't lift. I begged him to join me when I set off at dawn to make sure of a decent place on the road to Calvary, but he was too crushed even to rejoice in the death of an adversary. So I stood there for both of us, pushing my way to the front of the crowd and, when the Nazarene staggered past, so crippled by his cross that even the hardest hearts were moved to pity, I jumped out and spat in his face: a revenge so sweet that it was worth the lash from the centurion's whip – which left this mark on my forehead.'

'I thought that God had given you that mark after you killed Abel,' I said, colluding in one delusion to escape the other.

'True, but it has to be renewed every generation.'

'Ahasuerus, of course. Now I remember who you were . . . are . . . were. The Wandering Jew. They made a film of the story a couple of years ago. It's the one time I was glad to be banned from the cinema.'

'Yes, condemned to wander the earth forever for spitting in the Nazarene's face. A pretty superfluous punishment in my case. Or was it an instance of poor communication between father and son? Never mind. If I can stand up to them, I can stand up to anyone. I won't be sent back to Germany. Some of us have come up with a plan.'

My interest was instantly aroused. For all my doubts about his identity, there could be none about the seriousness of our predicament. The mystery of whether he had lived for thousands of years or for forty was an irrelevance if he had devised a scheme that would save us. So I offered him my support, long before I knew what it might entail, countering his charge that I was a mere boy and thus incapable of either keeping his secret or assisting his cause, with a range of precedents from David and Daniel to Alexander the Great, although I was unsure how far he was won over by my arguments and how far by a desire to expose my naivety. I was under no illusions that, whatever his relationship to Cain, his threat to kill me should I breathe a word of what he said was not an idle one. He went on to explain that he and a group of passengers had resolved to take over the ship and force it to sail to a port in South America or Africa. With the advantage of surprise as well as weight of numbers, they would easily overpower the crew. When I asked whether any of the crew would be hurt, he flashed me a look of contempt, as though the question confirmed all his misgivings about my commitment. Then, telling me that I would be summoned when needed, he further underlined the need for secrecy with a throat-slitting gesture straight out of the world of Klaus Stortebeker.

I didn't so much break my word as stretch it when, in the cabin that night, during one of my increasingly cordial conversations with my father, I asked about both the ethics and efficacy of mutiny. I put forward Sendel's plan as though it were my own, but he refused to grant it a scrap of paternal indulgence, claiming that any such action would be futile, laying the perpetrators open to charges of piracy and so deterring even a friendly country from taking us in. He asked suspiciously if the plan existed. 'Of course not,' I replied. 'I just made it up to see if you'd have the guts to take action. And, surprise surprise, you don't.' With a savagery that came more easily in the dark, I unleashed my abiding resentment, claiming that it was because of men like him who let the world walk all over them, that I had refused to be bar mitzvah. 'You gave in to my grandfather. You gave in to the drink. And you're giving in again now. I thought you might have changed. I thought you might have turned into someone I could respect, but no! I'm ashamed to have you as my father.' His silence validated my indictment, and I covered my head with the pillow lest a half-stifled sob should make any claim on my sympathies.

I lay awake for hours and when sleep finally came, it brought no relief for, tunnelling into the Reichschancellery, I found myself bursting through the floor in the middle of a private meeting between Hitler, Himmler and Göring. Having caught the guards off duty and the politicians off guard, I raised my gun to shoot them, but my father crawled through the hole behind me and grabbed me by the legs. I managed to kick him off and shoot the three men in turn, but my triumph turned to horror when, as they fell, each one tore off a mask to reveal his true identity. Himmler was Helmut, Göring the Purser, and Hitler the Captain. I tried to force the masks back over their faces, only to be thwarted by the torrent of blood – far more than the regulation five litres. Blood pumped from their bodies and all over mine, until the room ran as crimson as the Temple drains. I looked up and there was Sendel, thickly bearded and robed like a biblical prophet, lifting up a limp old man whom I took to be his father. Meanwhile the blood had risen almost to the ceiling. I was floundering in it, gulping for air. I knew that unless someone came to the rescue, I would drown . . . and suddenly, I heard my father shouting. The blood seeped away and, although my legs were still flailing, they were flailing in my sheets. I awoke with a start to find that I had kicked most of my bedding to the floor. My father was shouting in his sleep. His speech was as fractured as the words on a Torah scroll. Nevertheless, he had saved me from myself.

My hope next morning that he might ascribe my attack to his own bad dream was confounded by the sadness in his eyes. There was little relief elsewhere. The Professor's grim face cast a pall over breakfast. When pressed, he disclosed that he had received information of grave importance which he had not yet divulged even to his wife, who gazed at him with a mixture of pride and reproach. He had therefore called a meeting of all the passengers for eleven o'clock. At the appointed hour the loud-speakers duly summoned us to the social hall, where we found the Professor and his committee already on the platform. I contrived to bump into Johanna at the door and her tender squeeze assured me that some things, at least, remained constant. We took our seats, only to hear the Professor announce that, negotiations with Cuba and the Dominican Republic having broken down and President Roosevelt remaining deaf to inter-national pleas, we were sailing back to Europe.

It was news that could have come as a surprise to no one, but its confirmation caused pandemonium. Moans, screams, shouts, calls on God and cries of 'Traitors!' broke out across the hall. Children, too young to know what was happening, exploited the general freedom to caterwaul. Christina burst into tears and I passed her my handkerchief. A row of young men backed up each other's demands that we should take control of the ship, declaring dramatically that a return to Germany would mean certain death. The Professor appealed for calm, insisting that the journey would last several days, leaving time for our friends around the world to make representations to sympathetic governments. He added that the Passenger Committee would pass on all helpful suggestions but it would not countenance anarchy. This, in turn, prompted cries of 'Stooges!', which might have carried more weight had they not come from some of the more assiduous members of the suicide watch.

We left the hall and made our way to the dining room, where the decline in our fortunes was immediately apparent. The elegantly embossed cards had been replaced by mimeographed menus and the rich variety of dishes been reduced to a blunt *either . . . or.* Our waiter informed us apologetically that there was a tight control on food since insufficient supplies had been taken on in Havana. Aunt Annette, with rare asperity, claimed that Hapag was simply cutting its losses on the extended voyage. After lunch, I took Luise to join Johanna on the boat deck where, the obdurate elderly couple having collapsed from exhaustion, their suitcases stood as forlornly as a jilted bride's trousseau. We had only walked a few paces before we came face to face with Schiendick and his firemen, who swept across the deck in close formation, laughing derisively at the passengers who scattered in their wake. They greeted everyone, whether rebellious young men or timid old ladies who had never so much as let their dogs loose in the park, with the same message: that by the end of the week, they would be locked up in a camp. Their warning to us was even more stark. Catching sight of Luise, Schiendick sneered that she would be sent to a special clinic where imbeciles were put out of their misery. A loud wail showed that she had caught his tone if not his meaning and so, leaving Johanna to comfort her, I squared up to Schiendick and threatened to report him to the Captain. He grabbed me by the scruff of the neck (had it not been so public, I felt sure that he would have snapped it) and repeated his claim that the Captain was now a spent force and that he – Schiendick – ran the ship.

Then he strode off with a parting blow that left me sprawling and humiliated at Johanna's feet.

Schiendick showed his strength again later in the day with an order forbidding any further fraternisation between passengers and crew. The signature on the notice was the Purser's, but the hand behind it was Schiendick's. According to Sophie, whom I found staring at the board as though at the date of her own execution, the Purser had raised objections but Schiendick insisted that such matters fell within his remit as Party Representative and that any complaints should be addressed to Berlin. The Purser who, like many of his fellow officers, was anxious to protect the Captain from any additional charge of being a Jew-lover, backed down. Sophie had learnt of the decision in a rapid meeting with Helmut, who was now one of its principal victims. She dismissed my suggestion that this must be why he had failed to turn up for the dance, explaining that he had been embarrassed by the black eye he'd sustained after tripping over a cable, an excuse that was even less convincing than when I'd employed it after being set on by the Hitler Youth at school. I asked how they were going to meet and she said that for the moment they wouldn't try since, following his 'accident' (the only consolation for which, according to one of Helmut's friends was that three Gestapo firemen had tripped over the same cable), Helmut was under constant surveillance. That same friend, one of the deck stewards, had offered to carry letters between them. Theirs would be a long-distance love affair conducted close at hand.

I gave Sophie a hug in which sympathy for her plight mingled with relief at my own good fortune. Before meeting Johanna, I might have assessed a romance by the obstacles that it had had to overcome. Now I knew better and gave thanks that we stood on the same side of the religious divide. When, however, I tried to express my gratitude by clasping her hand as we sat drinking coffee after dinner, Johanna tetchily shook me off. I had felt her to be on edge ever since our encounter with Schiendick and yet, when I urged her to ignore his threats, she replied that she was simply feeling ill ('Even prisoners are allowed to have headaches!'). Claiming that men (me) had no idea what women suffered, she jumped up and stalked out. I was nonplussed, both by the charge and her volatility. We were all facing the same dangers, although she was at an advantage since, should the *St Louis* sink and the passengers have to cram into lifeboats, it would be 'women and children first'. My bitterness was compounded by the coffee, which I had only ordered black in order to impress her. So, once I was sure that she wouldn't be returning to apologise, I abandoned it and made a desultory tour of the ship. In the social hall, the band played a quickstep for two lonely couples. On the sports deck, a portly man chased his stomach around the track. On the promenade deck, a family gazed at the night sky as if to identify which of the stars was to blame for our fate.

I made my way back inside where I was grabbed by Sendel, who announced that the assault on the bridge would take place the next day. 'Are you with us or against us?' he asked. 'Are you a man or a boy?' Whilst I knew that, for him, each question allowed for only one answer, I also knew that, for my father, it was quite the opposite. For all my brutal rebuttal of his arguments the previous night, I had taken them to heart and now repeated them to Sendel, who responded with characteristic scorn, which stung. It struck me as just recompense for the scorn that I had vented on my father and, as I walked down to the cabin, I wondered whether it might not be more grown-up to accept an unjust charge of cowardice than to seek to disprove it by an act of reckless bravado.

No sooner had I finished undressing than I was thrown into further turmoil when my father entered the cabin, his face bloody and bruised. He slumped heavily on the bed. My first thought – that he must have heard Sendel mocking me and taken up the cudgels on my behalf – vanished when I leant over him and smelt the brandy on his breath. I coldly asked what had happened and he told me that he had fallen down the stairs, an explanation confirmed by the fumes wafting my way. I could scarcely contain my revulsion.

'You're drunk!'

'What?'

'The ship's in mortal danger. We could all be behind bars in a week. Luise could be put in a . . . and you get drunk. Does nothing ever change?'

'Is that what you think?'

'Think? It doesn't take a genius!'

'I hoped we'd grown a little closer over the past few days, you and I.'

'You mean you hoped you'd pulled the wool over my eyes! I'm not as stupid as you seem to imagine.'

'I'm so proud of you, Karl. You've no idea.'

'Thank you! It's a pity I can't say the same.'

'No, I suppose not. I'm sorry, I've no right to expect anything different. I'm sorry, truly I am. I know I shouldn't ask, but please don't say a word to your mother. She'd only worry.'

'You flatter yourself! She wouldn't worry; she'd tell you how much she despises you . . . how much we all do. She'd order you to disappear and never bother any of us again. But never fear, I shan't give you away – though for her sake, not yours.'

'That's all right then,' he said and lay back on the pillow. I moved away, any thought of helping him lost in a welter of disgust and disappointment. 'Like this, you're safe,' he added, as though witnessing his shame were all that prevented my ending up the same way.

My fitful sleep at least enabled me to escape the cabin early, leaving my father stretched out on the bed where he had collapsed the night before. The sight of his stupor steeled my resolve and I made straight for Sendel's cabin. I entered to find it packed with conspirators, including Joel. My resentment at his failure to confide in me was offset by respect for his secrecy. Sendel appeared inordinately pleased to see me, given how little I could add to the strength already mustered. I was greeted less warmly by some of the others, who seemed to sense the hesitancy behind my late arrival. I stood next to Joel while Sendel, whose assumption of command was an accepted – if not universally welcomed – fact, announced that we would storm the bridge at 9 a.m. precisely and that no one would now be allowed to leave the room, an injunction that immediately drove me to practise the bladder-calming techniques I had perfected while watching *Tristan and Isolde*.

None of my fellows, not even Joel, had much to say to me and I spent an increasingly oppressive hour studying their faces, several of which I had never seen out on deck, where, to judge by their pallor, they rarely ventured. We were eleven in all: two thuggish types, whose expressions suggested that they had paid for their passage the same way as Sendel; a clean-cut trio, who would have been better suited to a university fencing club; a middle-aged man, whom I had observed by the pool playing with his children; two Hasidim, who seemed keen to emulate the Maccabees; Sendel, Joel and myself.

When Sendel announced that we would be going into action within ten minutes, one of the Hasidim proposed saying a prayer and, to my surprise, Sendel raised no objection. The man chanted a psalm, and I was now sufficiently well-versed in Hebrew to recognise the thanks offered to God for presenting us with the necks of our enemies (a gift which I trusted would remain symbolic). That done, we were sent from the cabin in twos and threes to rendezvous in the gymnasium, which was the nearest public room to the bridge. I had hoped to be paired with Joel, thereby maintaining a semblance of normality, but he went off with the middle-aged man while I was partnered with Sendel. My fears of running into someone I knew – not least, Johanna – were dispelled by the sounds emerging from the dining room. Never had the attraction of breakfast been stronger. Even the Professor's wife's twittering was preferable to what, with every step, seemed a more foolhardy mission. I trusted that it was simply my indecision that had left me feeling so ill-prepared and that the others were better briefed as to the plan of campaign. All I knew was that we were to take over the ship and either sail it to a friendly port or run it aground, but I had no idea of how we would put down any opposition or exercise day-to-day command.

We gathered in the gymnasium which, to my relief, was otherwise unoccupied. Then, on the dot of nine, Sendel gave the order and we burst into the bridge castle. Faced with the confusion of doors, even the hotheads faltered, until Sendel motioned towards the extreme right. I felt sick and longed to sneak out, but my only escape was a fantasy in which I as Frank Osbaldistone and Sendel as Rob Roy took up arms against the tyrannous English king. Reality returned as I found myself in the chart room, where the First Officer was poring over maps. His gasp of surprise was stifled by one of the students, while another tied his arms behind his back. Sendel instructed them to bundle him through another door on to the bridge where, to my horror, Helmut was standing at the helm. Though struck dumb by the sight of his trussed-up colleague, he had lost none of his other faculties and made a dash for the emergency bell, to be intercepted by Joel. Meanwhile, one of the two thugs (I prayed that it was simply my inexperience that made them seem so sinister) grabbed him by the neck. Sendel directed me to seize his left arm, but any hopes that the hold might be token were dashed by Helmut's desperate writhing together with my fellow guard's instruction to tighten my grip.

'Hands off, you bastards!' Helmut shouted.

'Keep still, Nazi!' the thug replied, an unconscionable slur that caused Helmut to freeze and me to squirm.

'Are you mad?'

'Keep still, I said, or you'll be sorry.'

'You'll pay for this, I'm telling you!'

'No, I'm telling you!' A sharp blow muffled Helmut's yells, which died completely when he turned to his left and came face to face with me. After advising both prisoners that further resistance was futile, Sendel briefly outlined our demands and, handing the First Officer a telephone, ordered him to summon the Captain.

My assumption that his words contained a coded warning was belied by the Captain's jaunty entrance. His mood instantly changed at the sight of his two captive officers. He turned to protest when, at a signal from Sendel, the remaining students leapt out from behind the door and pinned back his arms. In spite of the danger, I felt a momentary relief that, even when seized by men half his age and twice his size, his authority remained undiminished. He made no attempt to break free and, indeed, rebuked the First Officer for starting to struggle. He simply asked what we hoped to achieve by this charade (a word that brought home the hopelessness of our position). Sendel repeated our demands, which the Captain dismissed as casually as if they were complaints about the menu. 'You haven't the least chance of success,' he said. 'Firstly, you've neglected to secure the engine room. Secondly, you'll receive no support from your fellow passengers and will meet active resistance from the crew. All you're doing is laying yourselves open to charges of piracy.'

'That's our affair,' Sendel said.

'The ship can't change course without my express command,' the Captain said. 'And that I'll never give.'

'Then we'll hold you hostage until the crew obey us.'

'You can expect a long wait.'

'In which case, we'll kill you!'

'No!' I shouted, my heartbeat threatening to rival that of the bee hummingbird. 'If we did that, we'd be no better than Nazis.'

'What would you know of the Nazis?' Sendel countered. 'Ah, diddums! Did they stop you taking the waters at Wiesbaden?'

'They threw me out of school. They stole our store. They killed my grandfather.' I found myself making the connection that the intervening months had threatened to obscure.

'In which case you should have learnt. What happened before we left will be ten times worse if we go back. And I won't go back. Not ever.'

'Nor me,' echoed my fellow guard, tightening his grip on Helmut's arm.

'I give you my word,' the Captain said, 'that I'll do everything that lies within my power to stop you being returned to Germany.'

'Your word as a Nazi stooge?' Sendel sneered.

'My word as a naval officer. Like it or not. But one thing is sure: this madness won't assist your cause. On the contrary, it can only damage you.'

'So where will you go?' Sendel asked. 'Who'll take in the lepers?'

'I have high hopes that you'll find a haven in England.'

The mention of that country – now my country – had an immediate effect. I sensed my opposite number loosen his hold on Helmut, as though even he had faith in a nation that prided itself on playing by fairer rules than any other. Sendel made a final attempt to stoke up the rebellion, but it had already fizzled out. As one, we released our prisoners. The Captain and First Officer smoothed their uniforms as if our attack had barely creased their dignity, but Helmut swung round in fury, attempting to reassert himself with his fists. He was only kept from using them by the Captain who, placing his hand firmly on his shoulder, guided him to the wheel. Gripping it to stop himself shaking, he stared out to sea. I was transfixed by the ridges on his sweat-stained jacket like the lines on a freshly mown lawn.

The Captain turned to us, promising that, provided we gave him a pledge of good behaviour, he would forget the whole incident. From the sheepish murmur of assent, it was clear that I was not the only one to find myself back in the headmaster's study. He ordered us off the bridge and we filed out, with Sendel pushing angrily to the front. I was all set to escape when, in the outcome I most dreaded, the Captain called my name. I stood at the door, unable to look him in the eye. Before he could say anything, however, Helmut, who remained deeply distressed, interjected that we had been let off far too lightly: we should have been arrested and thrown in the hold. 'You, of all people,' he said to me. 'You, who she's devoted her life to. You who she chose over . . .' His speech petered out, making the Captain's call for silence a mere formality. I, meanwhile, would rather have been the object of Helmut's worst abuse than the cause of the Captain's disappointment. I felt that I had betrayed the man whom I admired above all others: the man whom, had it lain within my power, I would have chosen as my own father. I apologised for what had happened.

'What was that?' the Captain said. 'I thought we'd agreed that nothing did happen.'

'And nothing will happen?' I asked, years of broken promises having shaken my faith. 'Not even to the ringleader?'

'I trust that I'm an honourable man,' he replied. 'How can I punish a man for doing nothing?'

'Or even think badly of him?'

'Of him or of you?'

I was so desperate for him to think well of me that I took the opportunity to pour out all my woes, explaining how I had decided to join the attack at the last minute in despair at my father's drunkenness. He had attempted to drown his sorrows, whereas I was determined to transform them and the only means available were my fists.

'Rubbish!' Helmut said, grateful for another reason to despise me. 'Your father wasn't drunk. He'd been in a fight with a steward.'

'Which steward?' the Captain asked sharply.

'Schiendick,' Helmut replied. 'Who else? Or so I gathered from Herr Hirsch, who wasn't too coherent – although not from drink. He didn't touch a drop until I gave him some brandy.'

'You?' I asked.

'Yes, me. Why? Is there a problem? I found him flat out by a lifeboat. I wanted to call the doctor but he wouldn't let me.'

'Did he say what had happened?' the Captain asked.

'Something about Schiendick insulting his daughter.'

'You mean assaulting her?'

'I meant what I said.' Helmut forgot himself in his agitation. 'The girl's – ' he looked at me – 'a little simple.'

'That man again,' the Captain said. 'This time he's gone too far.'

'No sir,' the First Officer warned. 'Not according to his friends in Berlin.'

'One more such incident,' the Captain said, 'just one, and I'll send him packing. Friends or no friends!'

While the Captain fulminated against Schiendick, I thought

of my father and how my participation in the attack had been based on a false premise. I felt doubly ashamed when, after offering further apologies to the Captain and First Officer, who nodded brusquely, and Helmut, who turned his back, I walked off the bridge and onto the boat deck. Even without looking up, I could sense that the sky was as sombre as my mood. But a whisper in the air turned my attention heavenwards and I was rewarded with a view of the largest flock of swifts that I had ever seen: thousands upon thousands, as though the sky were scrawled with 'w's, flying north from their winter migration. And yet a sight that would normally have sent my heart soaring simply stung me with its irony, as I contemplated the very different circumstances of my own journey home.

Returning inside, I found to my surprise that I was trembling. I longed for a bath, but we had been asked to conserve water and I was reluctant to break the least regulation. So, finding the cabin mercifully free of my father, I lay down on my bed and began to review my life. I was both shaken and shamed by the morning's events. I had allowed myself to become another person or, rather, to assume a fake identity, one which suited me no better than a Hitler Youth uniform. I closed my eyes and attempted to dull my brain but was assailed by a succession of faces: my father's; my grandfather's; my uncle's; the Captain's; Helmut's; all offering clues as to the man that I was, the man that I wanted to be. Another face flashed in front of me, a scarred, sneering face, but I dismissed it and swore that I would never again pay it any heed. I felt sure that the attack on the bridge had been a turning-point and, for all the Captain's insistence that it had never happened, it was one that I was determined to mark. I had apologised to the officers, but the man I had most offended was my father. I yearned to make amends and, suddenly, the way became clear.

Eager for support, I sought out Johanna, whom I found on the promenade deck, quite recovered from the previous night's ill humour and talking to Viktor. Dispatching him to the games room in quest of Joel (and trusting that a last lie would not compromise my commitment), I flung myself down on his chair and told her what I had decided. I explained how moved I had been by her resolve to remain on the ship. I intended to make a similar gesture by becoming bar mitzvah. She was confused, presuming that I had lost my chance forever by renouncing the ceremony at thirteen. 'Not at all,' I said. 'In fact, in one sense it'll be superfluous. Bar mitzvah means Son of the Commandment, and every Jewish boy – even me – becomes it by virtue of turning thirteen or, to be pedantic, thirteen and a day. But two years ago, I felt very different, very disillusioned. There was no way I could celebrate growing up to be a Jewish man. Now things have changed. It's not just that I feel proud to stand alongside my forefathers (that bit's easy); I feel proud to stand alongside my father. What's more, I want to acknowledge it publicly. Here, on the *St Louis*.'

'On the ship?'

'Why not? Who knows where we may end up: in Africa, where there are no synagogues, or back in Germany, only to find they've all been burnt?'

'You said there was no chance we'd return there!'

'And there's not – but just in case. Besides, it's not only a question of doing what's practical but what's right. It's on this ship that I've truly come of age. So I shall go and see the Rabbi and ask if he can perform the ceremony on the Sabbath.'

'You mean Saturday?'

'That's right.'

'But it's two days away!'

She was astonished that it could be arranged so fast. I assured her that there was no fixed timescale: the only requirement was that I be able to read my portion. Besides, I was a quick study with an excellent memory (something, I might add for the benefit of Edward, whom I see as the most sceptical of my readers, that has stood me in good stead in preparing this account). Although the Haftorah, the reading from the Prophets, was the longer, it was the Maftir, the reading from the Torah, that would pose me the greater problems, since it was inscribed on a scroll without vowels. I knew instinctively that her next question would be 'why', and I had to admit to having no answer, unless it were to preserve the mystery should it fall into enemy hands.

'These days,' she said, 'you'd have thought the very fact of it being in Hebrew would be enough.'

'Ah ha,' I replied. 'You mustn't underestimate tradition. It's our lifeblood; our identity; our statute book; our flag.'

'So shouldn't you do the traditional thing and consult your parents?'

'Why? So they can throw a party? By Saturday the Purser may have rationed the food. I'll just have to brace myself to do without all the presents.'

'That's sad.'

'A hundred and fifty fountain pens? I'll try to bear it.'

'You deserve something.'

'When my Uncle Karl was bar mitzvah – let's see, he was born in 1897 so it would have been 1910, my grandparents entertained a thousand people.'

'At home?'

'Yes. We have . . . had our own synagogue.'

'That's amazing!'

'It's just another room, like the ballroom or the library. Except that it's used less.'

'It's a pity you can't hold the service there . . . tradition and so forth.'

'Who knows when we'll be able to go back? By then I might be the world's oldest bar mitzvah candidate, with one of my grandsons –' I toyed with *our* but dismissed it as precipitate – 'giving the father's blessing. No, all in all, I could find no better setting than this ship.'

The Rabbi applauded my impulse while mistrusting my impulsiveness. Assured that I was in earnest, he took out his prayer-book and looked up the portions for Saturday. The Maftir was the Shelach Lecha: the passage from Numbers in which God orders us to put fringes on our prayer shawls, a text of particular poignancy for me given that it was only three weeks since I had cut off my grandfather's. The Haftorah was the story of Joshua sending spies into Jericho, a timely reminder after the morning's fiasco of the need for an effective strategy. The Rabbi guided me through both sections, praising my command of Hebrew yet insisting on a review of my progress the next morning before he would grant the request.

Curbing my disappointment, I resolved to spend the rest of the day mastering the texts and retreated to my cabin, where I saw no one except Sophie, whose tears had an overriding claim on my attention. She poured out her heart about Helmut. Not only had he refused to see her but he had sent her a note to say that it was the last note he would send. Moreover his free-and-easy scrawl had been replaced by a laboured script in which words had been repeatedly inked over and, at several points, the nib had pierced the page. Touched that she should choose to confide in me, I suggested that he was trying to protect her, but she replied that they had already worked out a foolproof plan. To prove that there must be some other reason, she took out the note and, carefully concealing everything else, pointed to the cryptic phrase: 'Ask Karl.' I realised, to my regret, that she hadn't come to repair an intimacy that had grown frayed on the ship, but to gather information. I was uncertain what to say, knowing that I could reveal nothing of our assault on the bridge without compromising my fellow conspirators. Besides, I couldn't be sure whether Helmut was referring to that or to Schiendick's attack on my father and the fear that something similar might happen to her. So, feigning ignorance, I recommended that she write asking for an explanation. She told me that she had already done so, along with a pledge that, if she had heard nothing by morning, she would go up to the bridge to seek him out. She walked to the door and, as an afterthought, glanced back and asked what I was reading.

'*Ivanhoe*,' I replied secretively. She shook her head.

'When will you ever grow up? The ship is packed with people in various states of despair: we're sailing to God knows where; and you bury your head in a fantasy!' She walked out of the cabin, leaving me to my task.

Despite having promised the Rabbi that my father would read the final portion, I had no idea whether he would even consider it after my behaviour the previous night. In fairness to myself (a formula to which I was resorting with increasing frequency), he had made no attempt to set me straight. I was at a loss to understand why. Had it been me, I would have wanted my bravery acknowledged, particularly by the person who had most reason to doubt it, whereas he had not only hidden his best side but encouraged me to believe the worst. With other people he was more circumspect. Explaining away his bruises at dinner (like me, though for different reasons, he had missed both earlier meals), he stuck to his original story, prompting the Professor's wife to insist that he sue Hapag, since several of the stair-rods were lethal. He fixed her with an equivocal smile, wavering only when she asked whether they wanted us all to break our necks.

After dinner and a short stroll with Johanna, I returned to the cabin to continue my preparation. My father arrived soon afterwards, anxious not to disturb me and provoke another tirade. I longed to admit that I knew the truth, but that would mean revealing how I'd found it out, so I simply smiled sympathetically until I realised that it made him nervous. For all my eagerness to unveil my plan, I was loath to do so late at night for fear of obtaining an easy assent. So I studied my portion under the cover of Sir Walter Scott, and left the announcement until morning.

In spite of his own lack of faith, my father professed himself thrilled, not least by my request that he do the final reading. His excitement was quickly replaced by concern about his faltering Hebrew, so I assured him that he could take the time-honoured route of giving a blessing while someone else read on his behalf. Tears welled in his eyes and he hugged me tightly, but the moment was shattered by my mother, who rushed into the room in her dressing-gown. Her face conveyed her horror even before she spoke.

'Helmut's killed himself! They found him in the store room hanging from a pipe. The Purser's just asked me to break the news to Sophie.' Sweat broke out on my palms as I recalled restraining him the previous day.

'Did he give any reason?' I was afraid that she would dismiss the question as an irrelevance, but she replied with surprising softness.

'It could be one of many things: fear of losing Sophie if she settled abroad; fear of what might happen to her if she were sent home; or even fear of what might happen to him if their relationship were reported to Berlin. The Purser suspects that he was

being harassed by some of the crew.' From my father's grim
expression I could tell that we had identified the same culprits. 'If
only I'd been more persuasive. I begged her time and again to tell
him the truth.'

'What truth?'

'That she isn't Jewish.'

'Sophie?' I had read of a woman who lied to successive
doctors in order to undergo unnecessary operations but, at a
time of rampant anti-Semitism, Sophie's deception struck me as
more perverse, until my mother reminded me of the law that had
been passed four years earlier forbidding any Aryan woman
under forty-five from working for Jews. Following her estrange-
ment from her parents – whose Nazi sympathies suddenly made
sense – we were the only family that Sophie had. Refusing to
abandon us, she had taken on a Jewish identity, regardless of the
consequences. Now she was unable to go back. The authorities
would never believe her story and, even if they did, the mere fact
of her pretence would damn her irrevocably in their eyes.

Fearing that our attack had played a part in Helmut's death,
I waited for my mother to leave the room and then told the
entire story to my father. He listened quietly before responding,
not with some bland attempt at reassurance, which would have
had quite the opposite effect, but with the seemingly tangential
revelation that the most important lesson he had learnt in life
was to take responsibility for his own actions without taking on
guilt for other peoples'. 'We may never know what led Helmut
to kill himself, although I very much doubt that it was your
playing pirates. Instead, we must try to honour his memory by
living our own lives to the full.'

His words went some way towards easing my mind – in spite
of the courtesy 'we' – and I went to see the Rabbi, more intent
than ever on becoming bar mitzvah. To my immense relief he
agreed to conduct the ceremony, although I suspected that he

was prompted as much by a desire for a celebration as by confidence in my Hebrew.

The need to work on my portion gave me the perfect excuse to avoid seeing Sophie, but I couldn't hide behind it forever and, at my mother's insistence, I made the long journey to the adjoining cabin, where she sat very still, gazing out at the unruffled sea. I kissed her cheek, which was as impassive as if she were the one who had died. She turned towards me with dark-ringed eyes, as indifferent to my stuttered condolences as to a weather report on a day that she was confined to bed. When she finally spoke, she made no mention of Helmut. 'Your mother tells me you're going to be barmitzvahed.'

'Bar mitzvah,' I said, forgetting whom I was correcting, but she carried on as though she hadn't heard.

'Becoming a man? Wonderful! Someone who hates and bullies and kills and betrays. Is that what you want for yourself?'

I thought of the men on the ship: of my father, a man who changed; of the Captain, a man who forgave; of Helmut, a man who loved; and I realised that her view was as blinkered as Sendel's. There were ways to be the man I wanted to be and I felt confident that I'd find them. My first concern, however, was to avoid hurting her. 'I'm not expecting you to come,' I said. 'Not now.'

'Oh I shall come,' she replied. 'But first, I have another service to go to. A furtive affair that's being held at eleven o'clock at night to avoid distressing the passengers.' The allusion was clear and I assured her that I would be attending too. 'The hardest thing is to know that he died on account of my lie – an administrative convenience, no different from awarding myself a higher degree or adding a year or two to my age. After all, it's common enough the other way round. There are Jews kneeling at communion rails throughout Europe.'

'You make it sound as if you did something underhand. Far

from it! You wanted to stay with the people you love.'

'Do I?' she asked, as if she were genuinely trying to decide. 'I wish that I could be so sure. I'm afraid that right now, I hate you. I hate all Jews for having come between us. Illogical, I know. But then hatred is illogical – as illogical as love.' Having nothing to say that would not sound painfully obtuse, I simply listened. 'He wanted to take me home to meet his mother. He was her only child. Never mind about me, who's going to tell her? How will she survive never having her son home again, not even in a coffin?'

'Couldn't they keep him on board until . . .' I tried not to be specific.

'Think! You remember how it was for your grandfather. Besides, who knows when the ship will return to Germany? Who knows where it'll go? No, he'll be lost at the bottom of the ocean. His grave forever unmarked.'

'The Captain gave Mother a map.'

'Please go, Karl. I'm grateful to you for coming. Right now I need to be alone.'

Helmut was buried as quickly as if he had been a Jew. Barely fifteen hours after learning of his death, we joined a handful of passengers and an equally small contingent of crew on the sports deck. I feared that Schiendick might object to our presence, but neither he nor his cronies were anywhere to be seen. I wondered whether it were his threats of retribution – so much more potent now that we were approaching Europe – that had persuaded so many of his fellows to stay away. Passengers and crew stood apart, but I was confident that this sprang from sensitivity rather than mistrust. I took my place alongside Johanna in the row behind Sophie, whose black coat borrowed from my mother was the only sign of her special status. The band, whose services we had declined at my grandfather's funeral, played a discordant dead march on piano, saxophone, guitar and drums, as the

Captain led the swastika-draped coffin to the bier. He conducted a surprisingly perfunctory service, although I have to admit that my only point of reference was the psalm, before delivering a eulogy which sounded more like a plea for a reduction in Helmut's sentence than an offer of thanks for his life. After a hymn, which I hummed in order to swell the sound since I could not bring myself to sing the *Christs*, the four pallbearers moved forward and removed the flag, which they folded and handed to the First Officer, before lifting the coffin and carrying it to the rail. The Captain took a step forward and saluted while, to a particularly ragged drum roll, the coffin slid into the sea.

The congregation dispersed. My mother and Aunt Annette took Sophie back to her cabin, but I determined to stay on deck in order to clear my head and steer clear of her grief. Since Johanna was feeling cold (for which read *gloomy*), I strolled up to the boat deck alone. Spotting Sendel lurking in the shadows, I was at first tempted to sneak away, but the desire to assert my newfound independence made me stand firm. After a few inconsequential remarks about Helmut's suicide, for which he appeared to feel neither guilt nor compassion, he informed me that I smelt. I was grateful for the darkness which concealed both my rage and my blushes, as I reminded him that the laundry service had been suspended, while biting my tongue to stop myself asking what was his excuse. With a seigniorial flourish he told me not to worry, 'Alexanderplatz has come to Charlottenburg.' Then, with an abrupt change of tone, he asked if it were true that I was about to be bar mitzvah. While surprised to find that the news had spread, I was happy to confirm it. He demanded to know what pressures had been applied to make me change my mind and I assured him that the decision was entirely my own. I was proud of both my faith and my people, having recognised a latter-day heroism that was every bit the equal of the Biblical ideal.

'What Biblical ideal?' he sneered. 'All those poisonous old Patriarchs? Abraham, a man prepared to prostitute his wife, who as it happens was also his sister, and to murder his son?'

'Sacrifice,' I replied. 'He was instructed by God. Something very different.'

'Not to the victim! He could have squared up to God and told him that mankind had established a superior morality. But no, he went cravenly along with it.' I found it odd that a man who claimed to be Cain should cite morality, but I made no comment. 'Or what about his son, Isaac, and grandson, Jacob, both of whom were so prone to favouritism that it tore their families apart? Or his nephew Lot, who was ready to prostitute his own daughters to protect his simplistic view of the world? At least they took their revenge by sleeping with him.'

'That's not how the Torah puts it.'

'The Torah glosses over a great many things. For instance, that Lot's wife looked back at the devastated cities not out of disobedience but shame, and the salt into which she was transformed was that of her own bitter tears.'

'How do you know?' He took my hand and traced the scar on his forehead. I recoiled as if it were poker-hot.

'What about Cain?'

'What about him?'

'Won't you tell me the truth? Life's hard enough without any more uncertainties.'

'Why should you be the first person since Adam to live without uncertainty? I've told you who I am – as much a part of your heritage as all the other liars and lechers and hypocrites.'

'One of the teachers at the Jewish school suggested that you – he – might not even have been a man at all or rather, only half a one: that Cain was born of the liaison between the Serpent and Eve.'

'How long will they go on dragging up that tired old theory: a crude attempt to absolve Adam – and, by extension, God – of any responsibility for my nature? So I was conceived when the serpent gave my mother a foretaste of the forbidden fruit, was I? Rubbish! And what's worse, rubbish that insults the intelligence! I'm familiar with all the attempts to explain away what I did. Sophistry may be a Greek word but the practice was perfected in Hebrew. How about the claim that I couldn't really have been a murderer since no one had ever died, so I had no idea of the likely effects of my action? Forget the chicken and the egg, the real question is "which came first: the criminal or the crime?" Rest assured, when I picked up Abel's knife – that knife which he regularly used to slaughter his sheep – I had no doubt about what would ensue. If however, you're serious about wanting to resolve the enigma, what you should be asking is what I told him immediately before I killed him. That's where the Torah is at its most evasive. "And Cain talked with Abel, his brother." So what did I say? Did I reveal the secret meaning of the universe that men have been striving to discover ever since? Did I put forward such conclusive evidence of God's injustice that the old time-server Moses and his scribes couldn't bear to set it down? Or,' he asked with a cackle, 'did I simply warn him that some of his flock had escaped?'

I heard the pain in his voice and, for all my revulsion at his madness, I was moved to pity. 'How can you bear to live?' I asked.

'I can't, but then I can't die either, so I have no choice. People call me the first murderer, but that's to ignore God. He was the one who killed Abel by killing all that was good in me, by rejecting my heartfelt offering and setting me at odds with the person I loved most in the world. Ever since, he's done his utmost to ensure I survive. He's been profligate of his prophets but protective of me. And he'll go on punishing me till the end of time, not because of what I did but because of what I said: those words too terrible for the Torah, in which I exposed his intrinsic evil.' He walked away, leaving me more confused than ever. While I knew, of course, that the Torah accounts of the Creation and Expulsion from Eden were myths, I could reach no such clear conclusion about Cain.

I returned to the cabin, where the sight of my father practising his few lines of Hebrew threw me into a panic. I reached for my prayer-book but he intervened, insisting that what I needed most was sleep. No sooner had he switched off the light however, than he began to speak. In a tone better suited to the bedtime stories he'd told me as a child, he likened life to the *St Louis*, claiming that, on a ship whose destination was uncertain, it was all the more important to care for our fellow passengers. My suspicion that he was thinking of one passenger in particular was confirmed when he mentioned my mother and how, whatever else had happened – and might still happen – on the voyage, they had been given the chance to reaffirm their love. 'I refuse to say "revive" it because it never died. It didn't even lie dormant but, rather, was locked away in both our hearts.'

I was deeply moved, not least when he declared that his dearest wish was to resume his place as her husband and our father. 'Luise has already made me welcome, but I'm determined to do nothing that could hurt you.' Appalled by the perversity of a world in which a father asked his son's permission to love his wife, I immediately gave him my assent or rather, my blessing. I braced myself for him to leap out of bed and kiss me, but a simple 'Thank you' closed the conversation, enabling us both to sleep.

The next morning was four weeks to the day since we left Hamburg although, for me, it was imbued with a more personal significance. I woke early and shaved – for the sensation as much as the effect. I put on my best suit, which was greatly admired at breakfast, especially by the Banker's wife who asked why I couldn't look so smart every day. I was unnerved to find myself the centre of so much attention. The Professor and his wife both expressed their excitement about the ceremony, although her claim that it was the next best thing to a wedding made me wonder what she might have spotted after dark.

At the end of the meal I returned to the cabin and a final inspection from Aunt Annette, who appeared to regard my becoming a man as a further sign of her own obsolescence. In a vain attempt to prove otherwise, I allowed her to reknot my tie and wipe a nonexistent mark off my shirt. My mother's entrance provided a welcome diversion. She looked wonderful, with her hair freshly set in the ship's salon, wearing a dress fit for an elegant Berlin reception and a diamond necklace that, with open defiance, she'd unstitched from the lining of her coat. I was deeply moved not just by her beauty but by the knowledge that she'd made such an effort on my account. Clutching a white cloth, she declared that it had always been my grandfather's wish that I should inherit Uncle Karl's prayer shawl but, since that was no longer possible (I struggled to banish an image of its being ripped apart by sharks), she had taken a plain silk shawl and painted it herself. She handed it to me tentatively, apologising for the crudity of the design and the flimsiness of the tassels, which had been all that she could manage at such short notice. I gazed at the intricately decorated border and promised that I would treasure it more dearly than if it had been embroidered in gold. She flushed and showed me how to align it so that the radiant sun sat in the centre of my back. She was afraid that the cosmic imagery might rouse suspicions that I dabbled in Kabbalah, in which case she insisted that I blame it on her. Then, at the risk of cracking the paint, she hugged me and told me how proud she was of me. I felt a fraud and asked if she were proud of me simply because I was her son. 'Not at all,' she replied. 'I love you because you're my son. I'm proud of you because you're intelligent, sensitive, honourable and brave. Oh yes, and extremely good-looking.' Her compliments threatened to draw as many blushes to my cheeks as mine had to hers. 'I'm proud of you because, in the most inauspicious circumstances, you've grown into an admirable young man.' I found it hard to credit what I was hearing and, above all, whom I was hearing it from. I told her to stop or she would make my eyes so red that I would be unable to read my portion. 'Don't worry,' she replied. 'If my memory's correct, the service will be quite long enough for you to recover.'

We walked into the social hall, which was crammed. I felt humbled even though I realised that the majority of people had come for their own sake rather than for mine. I was led to a place of honour beside my father, savouring the surprised and, in some cases, critical glances that greeted my shawl – glances that, only a few weeks before, would have made me cringe. My mother and Aunt Annette took their seats in the front row of the women's section, which the Professor's wife had officiously reserved. For once I was grateful that Johanna was not in my direct line of vision since, even sitting at the side, her presence was a distraction. I had little chance, however, to concentrate on the service. While the Rabbi chanted psalms in unison – though rarely in harmony – with the congregation, men with whom I hadn't exchanged a word during the entire voyage came up and shook my hand. Joel, stopping to chat, joked that it must be shadenfreude, like a henpecked husband congratulating a bride-groom. I replied that, on the contrary, they were acknowledging the faith that had sustained us from the Exile down to the present day. Chastened, he resumed his place.

The Rabbi announced a period of silent prayer, during which my thoughts were more than usually clamorous. Scanning the hall under the guise of gazing heavenwards, I saw no trace of the passenger who, by his own account, had been present before both the Torah was written and the covenant between God and Abraham sealed. In relief, I turned back to the Rabbi, watching while he removed the scroll from the ark, in reality a battered suitcase, and carried it around the congregation. As I kissed it, I felt that I was doing reverence less to the words – Sendel's comments the previous night having convinced me that even in the Torah they were not the whole story – than to the Rabbi's own faith in transporting it halfway across the world.

The Rabbi then announced the readings. A young man, with a face as round as a figure in Luise's drawings, chanted all seven, each of which was preceded and followed by a blessing from a different member of the congregation; the last of whom was my father, in a voice both confident and clear. As soon as he sat down, I moved to the table. I suffered no nerves until a flurry of 'good luck's reminded me how much I needed. Staring into the hall, I was amazed to see the Captain and Purser standing at the back, which put me under even more pressure to distinguish myself and justify their defiance of the race laws. I gave the initial blessing and was starting to relax when Sophie crept in with Luise. A surge of annoyance at their late arrival turned to gratitude that Sophie had timed it so as not to tax Luise's limited concentration. Her throaty chuckle galvanised me and I chanted the Maftir without a single mishap. The Professor then elevated the scroll and the Banker dressed it, leaving me free to embark on the Haftorah, in which I paid for my over-confidence by stumbling over Rahab the harlot. I was briefly nonplussed by Luise's cry of 'She singing!' and the ensuing titter, but I swiftly regained my composure. Even the female pronoun, which had so horrified me when she used it in front of my school friends, had lost its sting now that I had been officially proclaimed a man.

After a warm – indeed, clammy – blessing from the Rabbi, who laid his hands on my head, I returned to my seat and a congratulatory hug from my father. My own concerns were soon subsumed in prayers for the ship's passengers and crew, along with Jews throughout the world and all people of good faith who were working to find us a safe haven. Looking round, I discovered that both Sophie and Luise and the man most occupied in securing that safe haven had slipped out. At the end of the prayers, the Rabbi took the scroll on a further tour of the hall before replacing it in the makeshift ark. He then preached a sermon in which, to my acute embarrassment, I found myself serving as both a beacon of hope and a symbol of persecution. Showing greater sensitivity to his surroundings than to our plight, he trusted that I would 'sail through life, with a firm hand on the wheel, charting a steady course in turbulent waters', before concluding with the claim that, just as God parted the Red Sea for Moses, so he would deliver us from the hands of our enemies and into the Promised Land.

At the end of the service, the Rabbi invited the congregation on behalf of my parents to the first-class lounge for the kiddush, where I was amazed to see at least a hundred bottles of wine laid out, along with countless plates of biscuits and cakes. Given her lack of shipboard marks, I was at a loss as to how my mother had paid for it and, for a thrilling moment, wondered if it had been ordered by the Captain. My mother explained, however, that she had sold my grandfather's watch and cigarette case to the Doctor, dismissing my objections by insisting that parties were more precious than things. The Rabbi called me to his side and asked me first to bless the wine and then to make a speech which, having fidgeted through my performances at various family celebrations, you children can vouch is a task that I rarely shirk. Sixty years ago, however, I was more bashful. I longed for a less toxic version of my father's Dutch courage. Then, as I surveyed the room, I experienced one of those rare moments when my words bypassed my brain and its amendments to come straight from the heart. I paid tribute to my family: to Aunt Annette and Sophie, my adopted grandmother and sister, who had indulged and scolded me as befitted their respective roles; to Luise, my real-life sister, who had taught me the power of unconditional love; to my grandfather, who would always remain my model of achievement; to my mother, who had shown me that being true to myself was the only way to be true to other people; to my father, who had shown me both the courage and humility required to become a man. My sentiments were greeted with loud applause, which delighted Luise who, in Aunt Annette's benign custody (Sophie having cried off the party), had built a tower of cakes, which she rapidly proceeded to demolish. I had others still to thank, however, including the Rabbi, my friends among both the passengers and crew and, indeed, the whole community. My gratitude grew so extensive that it was in danger of being devalued. So I narrowed my focus to one special friend, who had brought me so much happiness that I could wish that the voyage would continue not just for a month but for a hundred years. I sensed that I was losing my audience who, in view of the occasion, could no longer ascribe my remarks to boyish exuberance. So I added quickly that I would, of course, be far happier to continue our relationship on land.

My determination not to name and embarrass Johanna was thwarted by Joel's elaborate pantomime. I was struggling to think of a diversion when the Rabbi proposed a toast or, rather, several: to me; to my parents; to the Captain; to everyone on the ship. The atmosphere grew cloying and I longed to escape but, first, I had to unwrap a small pile of gifts. Far from lamenting the largesse, much of it no doubt courtesy of Frankel, that would have been heaped on me had the ceremony taken place in Berlin, I was deeply touched that virtual strangers should part with their precious possessions – a wallet, an edition of Lessing, a tiepin, a scarf – not from any sense of obligation but from a desire to mark the day. The Professor gave me a copy of his 'definitive study' of the Brothers Grimm, which he had intended for a colleague in Cuba. His wife pointed to the dedication praising her own 'forbearance and support' to show that it was from both of them. The Banker gave me a box of cigars, which he had bought from a hawker in Havana. His wife added that, if I should smoke one on board, I must be sure to save her the butt 'to use on my teeth'. Christina gave me a box of chocolates, apologising that all the hard centres had been eaten, whereupon the Chemist, stifling his pique at the recycling of his present, gave me a lavish bottle of eau-de-cologne. Joel gave me a Swiss army knife with a blade for every occasion, adding imprudently, but at least in a whisper, that it would come in useful were I to take part in another attack. Viktor gave me a well-thumbed copy of Turgenev's *Fathers and Sons*. Aunt Annette was the only member of my family to give me anything tangible: a framed photograph of my grandfather greeting the Kaiser 'as a sign of how things were and how they will be again.' After exhausting my expressions of gratitude, I finally secured a moment alone with Johanna, who judged that the focus of attention had shifted sufficiently to allow her to approach. She apologised for her mother's second-hand present, saying that she hoped that I liked soft centres.

'I like anything soft,' I replied shamelessly.

'I'm glad,' she said, with a blush, adding that, since the ship's shop had been closed and in any case she had no money, she hadn't bought me a present. Although I dismissed it as unimportant, I felt hurt that she hadn't applied the same inventiveness as she had to the greetings card and the fancy dress. She proposed, however, to make me a pledge to be redeemed later that night. And as she breathed it in my ear, I was certain it would prove to the best present that I had ever had.

She was as good as her word. While I spent the rest of the day surrounded by well-wishers, whose congratulations would, I suspected, have been rather less cordial had they known the real reason for my grin, Johanna was busy making plans. First, she persuaded the Purser to lend us a room – and no ordinary room but the state room reserved for Hapag directors. Next, she convinced her mother that, to relieve Sophie, whose grief was as affecting to Christina as our romance was to the Purser, she had offered to look after Luise. I envied her confidence as I hesitantly told my father that I intended to sleep under the stars with Viktor and Joel. Nevertheless, he raised none of the expected objections, neither citing shipboard regulations nor urging me to wear a coat. Indeed, he seemed so keen on the idea that I wondered whether he had been as disturbed by my snoring as I had by his. His one proviso was that I be certain not to change my mind ('even if it pours'), since he was such a heavy sleeper that, should I return to the cabin, he would be deaf to my knocks. I assured him of my resolve, after which he went off to meet my mother, leaving me to run a bath so hot that I leapt straight in and out, masking any lingering impurities in a cloud of cologne.

I met Johanna by the swimming pool as arranged, and we made our way to the state room which, in its overstuffed extravagance, gave the lie to my grandfather's belief that the public areas of an enterprise should be the most opulent. Suddenly shy of each other, we played for time by admiring the decor. While I praised the two French landscapes and the cabinet of Dresden china, my eye was drawn to the bed, with the sheets already turned back. Johanna was particularly taken with a mirrored wardrobe that was large enough to hide in, as I proved when she finally went into the bathroom to change. I had pictured her returning in a silk nightdress like Zarah Leander but, instead, she was wearing flannel pyjamas. My excuse to my father having precluded my bringing nightclothes, I had no escape from undressing in front of her. I kicked off my shoes far too fast and made up for it by the slowness with which I unbuttoned my shirt. By the time I shrugged it off, I was sweating so profusely that I yearned for more cologne. I forced myself to think of cold things (Eskimos, penguins, nuns) as I stood in nothing but my underpants, which I was as reluctant to remove as I had been in the school changing room, although my fear now was of revealing my excitement rather than my race.

Alert to my discomfort, she slipped into bed and patted the pillow invitingly. I accepted at once, only to wince at the fierce freshness of the sheets. Far from the anticipated kiss, we each stuck to our own side as discreetly as if we were waiting for room service. With only our fingertips touching, we might as well have been sitting in the lounge. I wondered why we were doing our best to avoid what we most longed for and compounded the problem by offering her a glass of water. 'I don't want one,' she replied miserably. Then, as though struck by the same impulse, we rolled into the middle of the mattress and fell into an embrace. While it eased the tension, it felt far less innocent now that it was a mere preliminary rather than an end in itself. I was desperate not to rush anything, but my desire was pressing me on – and, to my embarrassment, pressing on her. I tentatively undid her jacket and slid first my hands and then my lips over her breasts. I was glad that they were so unmaternal:

firm yet yielding, with rose-red nipples which were barely larger than mine but so much more enticing. Either in response to my tongue on her nipples or the arousal in my pants, she broke off to hand me a packet of sheaths, another gift from the Purser, whom I felt sure I would never be able to face again. Turning away, I peeled off my pants and tried to put one on. The process was complex and clinical and had such a dampening effect that, when I finally succeeded, I was afraid that the sheath would be obsolete. A single touch from her, however, revived me. Looking down at the rubber, so much coarser than my own skin, I felt clumsy and constrained, as though I were walking in flippers. She had no such qualms, stripping off her pyjama bottoms and eagerly guiding me inside her. I strove to be gentle yet, despite my best endeavours, she started to scream; but, when she checked my move to withdraw, I realised that these were helter-skelter screams ('No, no, no . . . yes!'). Her pleasure was tempered with pain, as mine was with responsibility, but for both of us it was paramount. I felt at once in control and out of it, invincible and helpless, as if I were being swept along by a cheering crowd. When I could no longer restrain the desire flooding out of me, the sensation was altogether different from when I had released myself into a void, since I knew that I was also releasing her. What's more, my climax no longer signalled the end of ecstasy, let alone the onset of guilt. I remained one with her, so full of passion that we continued to make love through the night. We didn't sleep, but nor were we fully awake: it was as if we had entered a new state of being where such sharp distinctions failed to apply.

We were, however, conscious of the dawn and the need to slip away before the decks began to fill. The Purser had promised Johanna that he would attend to the room but, even so, I was eager to leave no more trace of our activities than if we had been sharing a midnight feast. As we tidied the sheets, I was appalled by the sight of bloodstains and presumed that Johanna had suffered a nosebleed. She kissed me and said that I knew nothing; which was all to the good because, had I known what she went on to explain, I would never have made love to her at all. Feeling slightly unnerved in spite of her assurances, I returned to my cabin in time to see my mother creeping out, wearing the same dress as the night before. I ducked into a neighbouring doorway, but my reflexes had worked faster than my brain, since my first thought was that she had gone there to discuss some crisis and my second that it involved me, after either Joel or Viktor had blown my cover. It was not until I walked back down the corridor that it struck me that my parents must also have been making love. Far from horrifying me as I might have expected, the realisation filled me with hope, as though the new possibilities that we were all encountering were bound to extend to the wider ship. Nevertheless, my exhilaration did not preclude my teasing my father when I entered to find him awake at such an unusually early hour.

'You obviously missed me. I suppose you need the sound of another person's breathing to be able to sleep.'

'You're not indispensable, you know.'

'I never said that I was.'

The next three days were tense with negotiations. The Professor had little to report and it became increasingly hard to convince myself that his 'I'll tell you the moment anything changes' meant 'Don't raise your hopes too soon.' Meanwhile the Captain had run out of delaying tactics. He confided in the Passenger Committee that Hapag had ordered him to sail back to Hamburg with all haste, since the *St Louis* was booked for a pleasure cruise to New York. The strain began to take its toll.

We lived on our own nerves and got on one another's. Johanna and I had no privacy as the Purser failed to repeat his offer (I wondered whether he had been offended by the blood), leaving us reduced to furtive kisses. On Wednesday morning, after a night in which my father's snoring had been so heavy that even Hamburg began to have its charms, I went up to breakfast to find the Professor's face wreathed in smiles. This time he did say, 'Don't raise your hopes too soon,' or rather, 'We've been let down too often before,' but his expression contradicted his words. In the early hours he had received a telegram from Morris Troper, the chief negotiator on the Joint Distribution Committee, declaring that arrangements for our resettlement were almost complete. He was simply waiting for confirmation. I was so excited that I couldn't eat a mouthful and, for once, my mother made no attempt to force me. I rushed off to break the news to Johanna but arrived to find that the rest of the Passenger Committee had also elected to put faith before discretion, and a heady mood of anticipation had spread through the ship. At eleven o'clock an announcement summoned us to the social hall, where we found the Committee assembled on the platform, together with the Captain who, having witnessed our misfortunes for so long, evidently wanted to share in the good news.

The news could not have been better. After an initial offer by the Belgians to take in two hundred passengers, the British, French and Dutch had followed suit. Our ordeal was finally at an end. The Professor read out the telegram in a voice that banished forever any notion of academic dryness. He was met with an equally heartfelt response, as people cheered, sobbed, clung to each other and heaped praise on the Almighty. Some, such as Christina, did all four. The Professor recovered himself sufficiently to express his thanks to the Captain who, to my surprise, did not reply but simply waved in acknowledgement of the applause. Ignoring all our rules, I showered kisses on Johanna, before shaking hands with Viktor and Joel. Then, as one, we threw aside all adult reserve and fell into a Hydra-headed embrace. Weaving through a forest of hugs and hand-shakes, I made for my family group, where I twirled Aunt Annette, kissed my mother and father and lifted a bubblingly baffled Luise into the air. Only Sophie remained detached from the general euphoria, managing no more than a watery smile.

Unable to contain my excitement, I bounded up the stairs and tore around the deck as if it were an Olympic track. Sweat stung my eyes and a stitch pierced my side but I ran on in recognition of our freedom. It would be freedom to take exams and stand in queues and pay tolls and taxes, as much as to walk in woods and attend concerts and keep dogs, but I welcomed it all gladly since it was the freedom to be human: to enjoy an ordinary life. I would swap my *Seabirds of the World* for *Native Birds of Northern Europe*. I would finish school and go to university and marry Johanna and have children and grandchildren (so you see, you – or, rather, the idea of you – were already a part of my plan). I would sail through life in accordance with the Rabbi's bar mitzvah speech, as breezily as I circled the deck and, when the end came, I would lie down as happily as I was doing now, exhilarated by my exertion, with a broad grin on my face.

Carnival spirit enveloped the ship and, that night, an impromptu celebration took place in the hall at which a succession of passengers performed their party pieces. The chemist revealed unsuspected talents as a magician, while to Johanna's horror, her mother exposed generous amounts of flesh as his assistant. Luise's two friends were thrilled by the coins plucked from their ears, although Luise herself was ruffled by his request to pick a card from the pack. She grew fractious, refusing to hand it back, and Sophie, seizing the chance to escape, took her off to bed, thereby missing a man who played the flute, a boy who played the spoons, an elderly couple who sang a duet from *Madam Butterfly* and, most poignantly, a former Deutsches Theater actor who declaimed Hamlet's 'To be or not to be' soliloquy, which the Nazis had banned from any Jewish production of the play. An amateur comedian's quip that in the Third Reich, the quickest way from Hamburg to Antwerp was via Havana raised gusts of laughter, which reached gale force when his companion read out a claim from Hapag's promotional brochure that 'With our friendly staff and exceptional facilities, the *St Louis* has everything to ensure that you enjoy the voyage of a lifetime.' One member of staff clearly belied the epithet. Schiendick's face was flinty as he patrolled the back of the hall, eager to ensure that nothing might be said or done to dishonour the man whose portrait loured over proceedings. He could not have been encouraged by the sight of Sendel, a most unexpected participant, making his way on to the dais. He stood blinking in the spotlight, his scar more pronounced than ever, and without a word of preamble launched into a joke about an SS officer who, having arrested a Jew, offered to let him go if he could tell which of his eyes was the glass one.

'The left, sir,' the Jew instantly replied.

'How did you guess?' the Officer asked.

'It looks more human.'

At the punch-line, he glowered at the audience as though daring us to laugh and seemed gratified when we resisted. It was as if to *die* on stage fed some perversity in his nature or even, should the Cain story be true, as if it were the only death he would ever know. Either way he cast a pall over the evening which was lifted, first, by the Banker and his wife in an awesomely athletic demonstration of the tango and, then, by Aunt Annette, who built on her car journey recitals to give a heart-warming rendition of *The Merry Widow* waltz.

The following morning, as we woke to find ourselves moored off the coast of Belgium, our Atlantic detour seemed even more futile. At ten o'clock a launch pulled up alongside the ship and virtually the entire complement of passengers joined the Professor and his committee in welcoming Herr Troper aboard. At the forefront were Luise and her two friends, whom the Professor had appointed to do the honours. The sisters greeted Troper with a sing-song chant, thanking him for all his efforts on our behalf and regretting that they had no flowers to give him. They then led Luise forward with a substitute offering, a pineapple from Havana, which she wordlessly dropped into his hands. I was not alone in holding my breath as they drew back with a curtsey, but for once Luise's coordination proved to be perfect and her one lapse was the desire to lead her own applause. The ceremony was completed by the Captain, who stepped forward and officially welcomed Troper and his team to the *St Louis*. He assured them that all the ship's facilities were at their disposal, before returning to the bridge to pilot the ship up the Schelde estuary to Antwerp.

Troper and his team settled into the Social Hall, along with representatives of the four host nations. While accepting that there was no simpler way to arrange the dispersal of nine hundred refugees, I felt deeply uneasy to be once again standing in line and entrusting my future to bureaucrats. The process exposed the limits of the four governments' generosity, since each was anxious to secure passengers at the top of the American quota list and hence with the least likelihood of remaining in Europe. Troper's sole guarantee was to keep families together. I was tortured by the prospect of separation from Johanna, since Christina had applied to follow the chemist to Rotterdam, and I prayed that hers would be one of the requests to be refused. I begged my mother to consider the attractions of Holland, rhapsodising over Rembrandt and tulips and cheese, but she wouldn't be moved. I accused her of deliberately setting out to destroy my life although, in retrospect (a perspective that will become increasingly central to the narrative), she saved it. When we finally reached Troper, she insisted on our going to England, where she would obtain essential medical treatment for her daughter (whose corroborative fit might to some eyes have appeared calculated) and find a home with her sister and brother-in-law, whom she cited with such authority that I almost believed in them myself. Her request was granted, but there were doubts over Aunt Annette and Sophie, whose positions had never seemed so nebulous. Sophie professed indifference, but an expression of panic tore across Aunt Annette's face. It was as though her worst fears of dying alone and unloved were being realised. I was never so proud of my mother as when she declared that Aunt Annette was her father's common-law wife and Sophie her own adopted daughter: they were our family in all but name. She added that she would rather go to another country than allow us to be split up (a warning look made me bite back my suggestion of Holland). Her determination won through and we were allotted six visas. As we left the room, I shot a triumphant glance at the portrait of Hitler, confident that he would never again take control of my fate.

At five o'clock, Troper read out a list of the 214 passengers offered refuge in Belgium, among whom were Joel and Viktor and Sendel. His voice was so mournful that he seemed to be reciting a litany of the dead. No, I refuse to follow suit and will simply record that my envy of their leaving first turned out to be tragically misplaced. . . . The departing families were served an early dinner, which Joel and Viktor both raced through in order to spend their last hour aboard with Johanna and me. We occupied it in making plans for the future which, if we were to be believed, would consist entirely of reunions. In the absence of addresses, we agreed to send letters care of a local synagogue, Viktor's alternative suggestion of the German embassy meeting a barrage of 'no's. Then he and Joel were brusquely called away by their parents, who feared that the slightest delay might lead to the forfeit of their landing cards.

I attempted to comfort Johanna, whose grief at the departure of two people towards whom I had supposed her apathetic, set a disturbing precedent for our own separation. The sight of Sendel queuing at the accommodation ladder, carrying a suitcase so small and battered that it looked like a theatrical prop, distracted me and I ran up, eager to give him a final chance to admit that his life – or rather, lives – story had been a fiction: a tall tale to mock my gullibility. He, however, simply laughed and rubbed his forehead, an innocent gesture to anyone but me. Then, without a word of farewell or the slightest acknowledge-ment of what we had shared during the voyage, he walked off the ship. Despite the affront, I felt a pang of concern, picturing him in five years' time, tramping fields and sleeping under hedgerows or locked in an asylum along with the latter-day Napoleons and Jesus Christs. Then I wondered whether he might, after all, have been telling the truth and I should, instead, be picturing him in five hundred years' time. The thought was so alarming that I swept it aside. As he walked down the steps, I shouted a defiant 'God speed!', and I know that he must have heard since he visibly stiffened, although he refused to turn back.

Meanwhile, I steeled myself for a more painful departure. The next morning a steamer would take Johanna and a group of two hundred passengers to Rotterdam. We both knew that the evening would have to stand for the many we would miss until we were together again. In spite of our promises to meet at New

Year (the Jewish New Year in September since the Christian one was impossibly far away), neither of us knew whether our parents, whom we saw as the sole obstacles to our happiness, would allow us to make the trip. The most I could exact from my mother was an open invitation for Johanna and Christina to visit as soon as we found a house. We arranged a last after-dinner rendezvous on deck, but the bustle and lights of the port were less conducive to romance than the open sea and the stars. After a kiss had been greeted by wolf whistles from two stevedores on a passing tug, we went inside. This time I had secured the room, considering Joel's raillery a small price to pay for the key to his former cabin. The ribald note propped on the pillow, in place of the Purser's wrapped chocolates, set the tone for a night that was in every respect a shadow of the first. It may be that we were too weighed down by expectations or simply that, whatever the circumstances, we would have been doomed to disappointment. My feelings for her were as intense as ever yet, after making love, I was conscious not just of our impending separation but our intrinsic separateness, and I slept on my side rather than in her arms.

I was jolted awake by the Purser who, betraying no emotion, announced that it was seven o'clock and the passengers for Holland had already disembarked. 'Your mother's frantic,' he told Johanna, 'She's searched every nook and cranny, starting with this young gentleman's cabin.' He paused for effect. 'Your parents are afraid you might both have jumped ship. Fortunately, I remembered the one key that wasn't returned yesterday and put two and two together. If I were you, I'd hurry up and set their minds at rest.' Anxious to oblige while still preserving our modesty, we promised that we would be ready in five minutes. He left us to leap out of bed, throw on our clothes and splash water on our faces, before racing out on deck to find Christina in

MICHAEL ARDITTI

a huddle with my parents, Sophie, the Chemist and a group of concerned passengers. It was clear that the Purser was not alone in his calculations and, as I'd predicted, several of those who had greeted me so warmly on Saturday treated me coldly now that they saw the way in which my manhood was being expressed. There was no time for recriminations, however, as the steamer was waiting for Johanna. 'Why didn't you say you were slipping out early?' Christina asked her pointedly. 'I woke up to find you gone.' She didn't address a single word to me but gave me a haughty sniff as though to signify that her faith in my background and breeding had been sorely misplaced. Then she and the Chemist bundled Johanna down the accommodation ladder, leaving us no chance of a final wave, let alone a kiss.

I watched helplessly as the steamer pulled out of the harbour, its speed in stark contrast to the stately pace to which we had grown accustomed on the *St Louis*. I ran to the prow to prolong the view but, within minutes, all that remained was a plume of smoke. I walked back to the cabin aching with loneliness. This was my segregated swimming class times a thousand. Johanna was gone: three short words that opened up a compendium of despair. Six weeks before, I had been unaware of her existence; now her existence was indispensable to my own.

I tried to bury the pain in the routine of packing. To my relief, I had no visitors apart from my father, who announced that my mother had sent him to teach me the facts of life. Cringing, I assured him that there was no need, at which he grinned and said that he expected he would soon be taking lessons from me. Seeing my distress, however, he apologised and left me alone until lunch, when my torment increased. From the moment I reached the table, I was kept in no doubt of my disgrace. My mother addressed me in the hurt tones she adopted when convinced that leaving me to my conscience was a far more effective punishment than anything she might devise. The Professor made a studied reference to the lax behaviour of modern youth. Only Aunt Annette, who knew what it was to love without licence, showed any sympathy by giving me a surreptitious squeeze. Then, as the waiters served the pudding, the Captain's steward appeared and asked me to accompany him to the bridge. As I edged through the dining room, certain that every lowered eye was following me as intently as if I had been picked up by the Gestapo, I feared that the Purser must have informed the Captain of my conduct and, with Johanna being under age, I would be taken back to Germany and tried for immorality or, worse, with her being a *mischling*, for some breach of the race laws. So I was greatly relieved by the Captain's smiling announcement that he wanted to say goodbye. Having taken on fuel and supplies in Antwerp, the *St Louis* was to sail that evening for New York to pick up the passengers for a Caribbean cruise.

'I'd prefer a few days break but at least, like this, we don't have to return to Hamburg.'

'Where are you heading?' I asked.

'Bermuda.'

'Not Cuba?'

'No.'

'Are all the crew going with you?'

'Most. Not all the stewards. There's one in particular I shan't be sorry to leave behind. He says he has business in Berlin, which is no doubt true, although I shudder to think what it entails. Nor will we be taking the six firemen who were foisted on us. Apparently,' he added dryly, 'the risk of arson has receded.'

'It should make for a more agreeable voyage.'

'And, I trust, a less eventful one. In all my years at sea, I've never known a group of passengers to affect me so much.'

'I'm sorry for all the trouble we've caused you.'

'You shouldn't be. Quite the opposite. You've taught me so much as well. Now I'm almost forgetting. The reason I asked you up here wasn't for an inquest, but to give you a present. I'm afraid that I went to your bar mitzvah empty-handed.'

'I'm just so grateful you came. You've no idea how much it meant to me.'

'I hope that these will mean something too.' He handed me his binoculars. 'I'd like you to have them. That is if you still have room in your trunk.' I gazed at the robust and elegant binoculars, easily the equals of the ones that had been stolen in Hamburg. For all that I craved them, I knew that I had to refuse or else he would have no way to identify the birds that he saw in the Caribbean. He insisted, however, that I take them or risk causing him grave offence. His kindness only made the memory of our attack on the bridge the more painful, and I asked if he felt that I deserved them after such a betrayal. He replied that what I had done had been reckless and stupid but understandable. Honour did not always survive in a dishonourable world. 'Yours has,' I said. He then let me into a secret: he had been ready to act recklessly himself. Rather than sail the ship back to Germany, he had resolved to run it aground off Beachy Head and force the British to take us in. It went against all his training but, sometimes, humanity counted for more. I took the binoculars from their case, covering my tears by testing their strength. I felt that he was the most valiant man I would ever meet, and sixty years of an extensive and varied acquaintance have done nothing to persuade me otherwise. I wanted to hug him but knew that, if nothing else, his size precluded such presumption. So I held out my hand and he clasped it, man to man. Then after advising me to visit Lundy Island, a bird sanctuary off the southwest coast of England, he led me off the bridge.

I paced the deck examining a newly distinct Antwerp, until an announcement soon after two o'clock called on all remaining passengers to prepare to board the Rhakotis, an ancient freighter that was to transport us to France and England. Conditions on board were primitive with a mere fifty cabins for five hundred people, requiring the majority to sleep on bunks in the hold, women in the prow and men in the stern. The Professor's last official task was to allocate the cabins. Our family was given two, although the distribution differed from that on the *St Louis*. My parents, now an established couple, took one, and Aunt Annette and Luise the other, leaving Sophie and me to the bunks. My excitement at the makeshift dormitories, a relic of the school hiking trips from which I had been excluded, swiftly faded in face of the stale air and cramped conditions, and I joined in the general exodus to the deck. The night was so mild that it was no great discomfort and, moreover, it meant that I was on hand when, at twelve, the *St Louis* weighed anchor and put to sea. I saw that I was not alone in my emotion when, as the ship passed the Rhakotis, a large complement of the crew, the men and women who had witnessed, if not shared, our fate for the previous five weeks, raised their caps with a cry of 'Good luck to the Jews!' After waving back, I shifted my glance from the rail to the bridge where a solitary figure stood saluting.

The next morning, instead of heading for Boulogne, we docked at the quay, in the very berth that the *St Louis* had recently vacated. We were offered no explanation for the move and rumour ran rife, not to be quelled until Herr Troper came aboard to bid us goodbye. At three o'clock the ship set sail, hugging the Belgian coast. I spent the rest of the day on deck until a heavy shower sent me running below, where I passed a sleepless night in the foetid atmosphere, assailed by a cacophony of snores and grunts. To my relief the journey was short and we reached Boulogne before dawn, although we were once again forbidden to land and forced to anchor in the harbour. After breakfast a launch arrived to collect the 220 passengers bound for France, among them the Professor and his wife and Luise's two friends. Although the memory of my conduct was still raw, the Professor's wife displayed her magnanimity by clasping me to her bosom and kissing me on both cheeks. My discomfort was nothing to Luise's when the two little girls were led away. With no other guardian, they were being sent back to join their mother in Germany. Luise kicked and screamed as violently as if she had had a premonition of their fate.

No sooner had the Professor and his wife left the ship than I appropriated their cabin, but even the prospect of privacy failed to allay my desolation. The last few days had passed in a haze of goodbyes and, while my fractured sleep lacked the narrative of a nightmare, it was filled with a sense of dread.

Any doubts we might have entertained about opting for England were dispelled the following afternoon when we sailed into Southampton. Instead of the furtive acceptance of Antwerp and the quarantine of Boulogne, we were greeted with great fanfare. The docks were decked with bunting. Giant portraits of the King and Queen hung across two warehouses. A brass band played triumphal marches on the quay. In the harbour two fire-fighting boats sent jets of water soaring into the air. Reality only set in once we had stepped ashore to discover that the band was not performing but rehearsing; the portraits had not been put there to welcome us on behalf of the King and Queen but to welcome the monarchs themselves who were returning from New York the next day. It was as if fate were preparing us for the irony that was our adopted country's stock-in-trade.

After the mass of forms we had filled in on the *St Louis*, the bureaucracy on our arrival was remarkably relaxed. Barely two hours after landing, we were taking the train to London, reaching Waterloo station at five o'clock. A handful of aid workers were waiting on the platform, ready to direct us to temporary accommodation in private homes and boarding houses. It was then that my mother came into her own. Speaking far more fluent English than I had suspected, she announced that we had made alternative arrangements (which I prayed did not involve the sister and brother-in-law whom she had cited to Herr Troper). Then, although to my certain knowledge she didn't possess a single English coin, she hailed three taxis to take us, together with a mountain of luggage, to the Savoy, a hotel where she had regularly stayed with her father. Her claim that the manager would remember her did little to reassure me and I pictured our being deported for failure to pay the fares or, at the very least, being left to sleep on the streets. My fears, however, turned out to be groundless, the manager's memory being all the more remarkable given the seven years that had elapsed since her last visit. He immediately saw to all the arrangements: paying the taxis; finding us rooms; assisting my mother to telegraph my grandfather's bankers in America. Within days the necessary funds had been released and we settled into the hotel for the summer. I spent the time exploring London, in particular the Natural History Museum, while my parents searched the south coast for suitable houses, finally finding one near Bournemouth. It was large and secluded, with a landscaped park, and sufficiently close to Winchester where, in September, I was sent to school.

This is not the place to chart my school career. I prefer to end the story with our arrival in England: a convenient, if arbitrary, conclusion. The outbreak of war brought horror and devastation on a scale far too great for any single narrative to encompass. I simply wish to tie up a few loose ends, telling you what happened to my family and friends, and to Johanna, using information which, in some cases, I didn't glean until forty years later, and knowing that, in Leila at least, I have a reader who even at the age of five failed to find 'They lived happily ever after,' an acceptable answer to 'What came next?'

With the exception of the narrator, all of the principal characters are dead . . . although whether or not you consider that to be a happy ending will depend on your view of the afterlife, a subject which you are as loath to discuss with your grandfather as I was to discuss sex with mine.

The Captain was on the *St Louis* when war was declared. He managed to beat the British blockade of the Atlantic and made for Russia, from where he later sailed the ship back to Germany. He never went to sea again. Years later, when he was under investigation by a de-Nazification tribunal, I was pleased to put my signature to a letter exonerating him from any responsibility for our plight and, indeed, praising him for his efforts to relieve it. Schiendick, both the Captain's adversary and mine, found a post in the German secret service and was shot when the British captured Hamburg in 1945.

Sophie looked after Luise until her death and then became a language teacher, spending almost forty years at a girls' boarding school in Dorset. She never married and in later life became an ardent Theosophist. It was as if she found eccentricity the safest face to present to the world. She died two weeks before her ninetieth birthday. Marcus and Leila may remember visiting her although, outside the classroom, she took little interest in children. 'Bring them to me when they reach the age of reason,' she declared, in expectation of a lengthy wait.

Aunt Annette enjoyed even greater longevity. To my mother's and my amazement, she emigrated to Israel in 1952. Three years later, well into her seventies, she married a violinist with the Israel Philharmonic Orchestra and became such a rabid Zionist that, out of mutual respect, we agreed never to discuss politics. Until her ninety-first year she returned to England every summer, always bringing your mother and uncle certificates of the trees that had been planted on the Mount of Olives in their names, presents which they considered as inappropriate as you do clothes. Despite her advanced age, she was not destined to die peacefully but in a bomb attack on a bus station in Tel Aviv.

My mother continued to paint, and her growing reputation never ceases to delight me. It was consolidated by the retrospective held in Berlin in 1988 – two years after her death – which prompted my first and, to date, my only return to a city where little but the contradictions remain from my youth. Her legacy was enhanced by the scholarships she endowed to allow young artists from across the world to study and work in England. You yourselves have met several of the beneficiaries at our summer parties.

My father died in 1950, although in effect he never survived the war. Like many German nationals, he was interned on the Isle of Man at the outbreak of hostilities. The British authorities, who acknowledged no distinctions beyond friend and foe, little realised that, by mixing Nazi sympathisers and Jewish refugees, they were creating a microcosm of the Third Reich. By the time that my father was freed, he was a broken man, whom even I could no longer begrudge the solace of drink. In the event, it was not Johanna and I who confirmed her father's mistrust of ship-board romances but my parents, who never recovered the intimacy that they had enjoyed on the *St Louis*, although my mother took care of my father until his death.

Of the final member of the family I shall say little. Luise died of kidney failure in 1944. Her loss, more than any other, still tugs at my heart. I wish that you could have known her and at an age when you were young enough to see her through your own eyes rather than the world's. Perhaps it was because her body was so impaired that her spirit soared so far beyond it. She had an extraordinary talent for inspiring love and I for one remain forever in her debt.

As for me, I left school in 1942 and joined the Pioneer Corps, transferring to the Intelligence Corps immediately it became possible the following year. You may think it strange, given my detailed dispatches from the bedroom, that I have no wish to dwell on my military career, but I subscribe to the unfashionable view that it is more important for children to learn about love than war. In 1946, I took up my scholarship to Balliol. The incongruities of Oxford – its youthful zest and hidebound traditions, its intellectual freedom and petty feuding – must have struck a chord for I have lived here ever since. Perhaps it was because I travelled so far in my youth that I needed to stay in one place, or perhaps because, after the revelations of Auschwitz, I needed to stay in the one place which, at least in spirit, seemed to be furthest from the camps. Or perhaps it was simply because Oxford, more than anywhere else, enabled me to make a virtue of detachment. Like every survivor since Noah, whose drunken-ness, I remember Sendel saying, was no mere indulgence but an attempt to blot out the image of his drowning friends, I have been wracked with guilt. From the first newsreel pictures of skeletal figures squashed into catacomb-like bunks, I have sought to purge myself of emotion. One of your grandmother's main attractions for me is that she's so English, as pragmatic as the Prayer Book. She, in turn, knows not to push me too hard. Her one sorrow – at least the only one that she has voiced to me – is that we didn't have more children. She longed to recreate the benign chaos of her own childhood and presumed that, if nothing else, the genocide would have left me with an atavistic urge to replenish the stock. The only urge I felt, however, was to obey the Torah obligation to have two children. Any more seemed to be tempting fate. Besides, fewer domestic ties allowed her to spend more time in her studio. She balanced her commitments so skilfully that, unlike my own resentment of my mother's paintings, your mother and uncle both treasured her pots.

I am proud of my wife and children and – although who knows how much more you may have achieved by the time you read this – I am proud of you. Nevertheless, I always carry a shame inside myself. Sometimes that shame has a number – a number of devastating roundness – and sometimes it has a face.

I kept my promise to Johanna, writing care of several Dutch synagogues. I continued until the letters would have put her in danger, although I never received a reply. Three months after the War I took the ferry to Holland. I searched for her in Rotterdam, Amsterdam and the Hague, moving on to smaller towns and villages where disguise would have been harder, but I found nothing. Anyone with any knowledge was anxious to hide it, especially from an Anglicised German Jew. I left my name with various relief agencies; I pored over the 'P's on countless casualty lists: all to no avail. Then in 1949, I made a second trip across the Atlantic, this time aboard the Queen Mary. My mother was overjoyed that I was finally taking a holiday, until I explained that I was keeping my ten year-old tryst with Johanna in New York. Realising that she could not dissuade me, she tried to prepare me for disappointment. I was adamant however that, despite all the horrors of the past decade, Johanna would have kept faith and the only reason for her failure to contact me was that she was planning an incomparable romantic reunion (you can imagine my dismay when, sitting in my local Odeon eight years later, I saw it copied by Cary Grant and Deborah Kerr!). I spent an exceptionally windy day on the observation deck of the Empire State Building, to the alarm of the guards who suspected a would-be suicide, and the delight of Melanie, a student from Sarah Lawrence, who was soaking up the atmosphere for a short story. When the building closed, she invited herself back to my hotel and I discovered how easily pleasure could coexist with pain.

I never saw Melanie again. The excitement was too heady to survive at ground level. The week that remained to me in New York – a week that, against all odds, I had planned to fill with treats for Johanna – was filled with despair. However absurd it may sound, I grew convinced that it was my readiness to leap into bed with a total stranger that had kept her away. Oh, I don't mean that she had seen it all from some hidey-hole behind the postcard stand, but rather that God, Fate, the Universe, call it what you will, had anticipated my weakness and acted accordingly. The guilt that was never far away when I thought of her – the conviction that, had our paths not crossed, she would have accepted her father's offer, married her plantation owner and now be happily bouncing little Josés and Marías on her knee – multiplied a hundredfold when I pictured how I had repaid her sacrifice with my betrayal.

Writing this account has been an attempt to make amends. When I began, my aim was to give you a clearer idea of where I – and, dare I say it, you – came from. More and more, however, I've found that I want to tell you about Johanna. She was no Anne Frank: I may be the last man alive who remembers her. She deserves a more substantial memorial. Let there be no mistake, I love your grandmother very much. She has been my life and I could have asked for no better. But Johanna was my youth. She taught me what love was and what life could be. We shared something on the *St Louis* – an intensity, a promise – that I have never been able to recapture. Of course there have been compensations (I'm addressing four of them now) but, when Johanna walked down the accommodation ladder, something inside me died. You may recall Aunt Annette declaring that my grandfather's greatest wish was for me to lead an honourable life. It's one that I echo in respect of all of you. Even more, however, I wish you love – love in all its tenderness, its danger, its fulfilment; in short, its humanity – and once you've found it, may you treasure it for the rest of your days.

There is a postscript to the story. Some three decades after that trip to New York, when *The Great Philosophers* had brought me a measure of celebrity, among the sack-loads of letters I received was one from Christina, who had watched the series when it aired on Dutch TV. In a few lines she broke the news, much amplified on our subsequent meeting, that she had married a Flemish farmer, both Johanna and her stepfather, the Chemist, having been gassed in Sobibor in 1943. For years I'd been reconciled to the inevitability of Johanna's death, as well as to its probable manner, but the confirmation peeled open the wound. I knew that Stalin was wrong: no human life was ever a statistic. Meanwhile the sight of Christina, still plumply beautiful in her seventies, the hint of sadness in her gaze offsetting her delicate smile, made the loss of her daughter even more acute. I saw then that in order to stay sane, I had to put the Holocaust behind me and live as determinedly in the present as an advertising executive: a resolve I maintained until I received an invitation to the *St Louis* survivors' fiftieth anniversary cruise off the Florida coast. I accepted by return of post. It helped that it coincided with my retirement from my Oxford chair: not as momentous as the rite of passage I had celebrated on the *St Louis*, but nonetheless worthy of note. I took along your grandmother in the hope of making it as much of a holiday as possible. In that respect I failed. Most of my friends among the passengers were dead, some even from natural causes, and those who remained were indistinguishable from their grandparents. I found myself tongue-tied, not so much because of what we had lost – I was no stranger to death – as because of what we had shared. I couldn't bear to confront my fellow witnesses.

I was standing in the cocktail lounge, attempting to rescue your grandmother, whose attention to a spry octogenarian's fanciful account of my violin recital at the final concert did credit to her training, when I found myself hugged, or rather stifled, by Viktor, now fleshy, bearded and bald, but still my one remaining soul-mate from the ship: a fact that we both acknowledged by bursting into tears. We introduced our wives and swapped details of our families and careers. He was a retired town clerk in Limoges with five daughters (I saw your grandmother's eyes glisten). Yet for all my delight at finding that he had not only survived the War, hidden in a monastery, but prospered after it, I felt first uncomfortable, then treacherous, and finally desolate at seeing him in the absence of Johanna and Joel.

Confident that nothing I told him would be binding, I explained the plan that I had been hatching ever since receiving the invitation: to write a memoir of the voyage for my grandson. His response was unequivocal. 'I think it's a brilliant idea. All boys love adventure stories.' The description surprised me since I had perceived it as a story of discovery: self-discovery, to be sure, but as revelatory in its way as the voyages of Captain Cook. He questioned me on my approach but I had little to add except that I doubted I would aim it specifically at boys . . . which is just as well since, in the intervening fifteen years, not only has Marcus grown up but my readership has expanded to include two granddaughters. Gazing at the heap of typescript, I wonder how much it represents an attempt to relive my youth and how much to escape it. I trust that, having reached thus far (always provided that Leila has avoided her usual trick of turning straight to the final page), you will find it easier to understand – and perhaps even to forgive – your grandfather. If nothing else, you will appreciate why a man who has boarded only four ships in his life should have stipulated that his ashes be scattered at sea.

Acknowledgement

For the facts of the *St Louis* sailing, I am indebted to *Voyage of the Damned* by Gordon Thomas and Max Morgan-Witts, published by Dalton Watson Fine Books, 1974.

UNITY   ISBN 1 904559 12 3, £8.99

A groundbreaking novel that examines the personalities and politics involved in the making of a film about the relationship between Unity Mitford and Hitler, set against the background of the Red Army Faction terror campaign in 1970s Germany.

Almost thirty years after the film had to be abandoned following its leading actress's participation in a terrorist attack, the narrator sets out to uncover her true motives by exploring her relationships with her aristocratic English family, the German *wunderkind* director, a charismatic Palestinian activist, her university boyfriend, a former Hollywood child star and an Auschwitz survivor turned high-powered pornographer.

Unity paints a deeply disturbing picture of corruption and fanaticism in both Britain and Germany from the 1930s to the present day. Startlingly original in concept and treatment, this remarkable novel is a profound and provocative exploration of the nature of evil.

'The most intriguing and thought-provoking novel I have read this year' *Daily Express*
'Highly intelligent . . . well worth reading' *Sunday Times*
'Deftly written, deeply intelligent and wholly admirable' *Literary Review*
'Farce and intensity blend in a deftly layered version of Hitler's legacy' *Guardian*
'Strikingly original in form . . . a remarkable, unsettling book . . . compelling' *The Times*
'Uncompromising drama of ideas' *Independent*
'Chilling in the extremity of its import . . . hugely ambitious in its scope' *Financial Times*

GOOD CLEAN FUN   ISBN 1 904559 08 5, £8.99

A young boy discovers the ambiguity of adult affection. A camp comedian cracks up on stage. A picture-restorer learns to accept her husband's true nature. A travel agent tastes the mysterious power of the Internet. A honeymoon couple take an unconventional route to love . . . This dazzling collection of stories employs a host of remarkable characters and a range of original voices to provide a witty, compassionate yet uncompromising look at love and loss, desire and defiance, in the twenty-first century.

'Funny, beautiful and chilling' *Independent on Sunday*
'Witheringly funny, painfully acute . . . these stories simply and elegantly break your heart' *Literary Review*
'Arditti imbues his stories of loneliness, confusion and the uncertainties of sexual neophytes with genuine pathos and an appealing line in dry humour' *The Times*
'His characters seduce us with nothing more than the ordinariness of their lives' *TLS*
'A simply outstanding collection . . . Elegant, tender, full of wit and insight' *City Life*
'By turns humorous, moving and profound, Arditti has the ability to paint vivid and engaging pictures' *Tribune*

Merete Morken Andersen OCEANS OF TIME £8.99 ISBN 1 904559 11 5
A divorced couple confront a family tragedy in the white night of a Norwegian summer.
International book of the year (*TLS*) and nominated for the IMPAC Award 2006.

Booktrust London Short Story Competition
UNDERWORDS: THE HIDDEN CITY £9.99 ISBN 1 904559 14 X
Prize-winning new writing on the theme of Hidden London, along with stories from
Diran Adebayo, Nicola Barker, Romesh Gunesekera, Sarah Hall, Hanif Kureishi,
Andrea Levy, Patrick Neate and Alex Wheatle

Hélène du Coudray ANOTHER COUNTRY £7.99 ISBN 1 904559 04 2
A prize-winning novel, first published in 1928, about a passionate affair between a British
ship's officer and a Russian emigrée governess which promises to end in disaster.

Lewis DeSoto A BLADE OF GRASS £8.99 ISBN 1 904559 07 7
A lyrical and profound novel set in South Africa during the era of apartheid, in which the
recently widowed Märit struggles to run her farm with the help of her black maid, Tembi.
Longlisted for the Man Booker Prize 2004 and shortlisted for the Ondaatje Prize 2005.

Olivia Fane THE GLORIOUS FLIGHT OF PERDITA TREE
£8.99 ISBN 1 904559 13 1
Beautiful Perdita Tree is kidnapped in Albania. Freedom is coming to the country where
flared trousers landed you in prison, but are the Albanians ready for it or, indeed, Perdita?

Olivia Fane GOD'S APOLOGY £8.99 ISBN 1 904559 20 7
Patrick German abandons his wife and child, and in his newfound role as a teacher
encounters the mesmerising 10-year-old Joanna. Is she really an angel sent to save him?

Maggie Hamand, ed. UNCUT DIAMONDS £7.99 ISBN 1 904559 03 4
Unusual and challenging, these vibrant, original stories showcase the huge diversity of new
writing talent coming out of contemporary London.

Helen Humphreys WILD DOGS £8.99 ISBN 1 904559 15 8
A pack of lost dogs runs wild, and each evening their bereft former owners gather to call
them home – a remarkable book about the power of human strength, trust and love.

Linda Leatherbarrow ESSENTIAL KIT £8.99 ISBN 1 904559 10 7
The first collection from a short-story prizewinner – lyrical, uplifting, funny and moving,
always pertinent – 'joyously surreal . . . gnomically funny, and touching' (Shena Mackay).